IN SPITE OF THUNDER

THOMAS MARK MCKINNON

Published by Bittaman Books

The story, all names, characters, and incidents portrayed in this production are fictitious. No identification with actual persons (living or deceased), places, buildings, and products are intended or should be inferred.

Cover art by Cherie Foxley

1st edition 2025

Library and Archives Canada Cataloguing in Publication
Title: In Spite of Thunder / Thomas Mark McKinnon
Names: McKinnon, Thomas Mark, author.
Description: First Canada Edition 1083899 B.C. LTD.
Identifiers: ISBN 9781069647405 (softcover)
Subjects: LCGFT: Novels. / LCGFT: Thrillers (Fiction) / LCGFT: Crime (Fiction) / LCGFT: Detective and Mystery (Fiction)

ISBN 978-1-0696474-0-5 (softcover)
ISBN 978-1-0696474-2-9 (hardcover)
ISBN 978-1-0696474-1-2 (ebook)

For Charlotte and Maverick,

live a life you will be proud to remember.

CHAPTER one

The bullet pierced Frank's left shoulder, traveling through a faded tattoo that some forgotten artist had inked twenty-three years ago. He hadn't felt the searing heat of a foreign projectile since his days in the Marines as a much younger man. A cascade of syrupy blood coated his muscular arm, penetrated the fabric of his sleeve, and began to drip miniature Rorschachs onto the ivory-colored tiles next to his tactical boots. By the time Frank collapsed to the floor, the shooter had already disappeared out the door of the warehouse bathroom.

"Shots fired! Shots fired!" Mike's voice suddenly reverberated inside Frank's earpiece, which had dislodged itself and come to rest in the pool of slowly expanding blood. Frank felt his vision begin to tunnel, and darkness crept inside his headspace as he heard Mike's footsteps pounding heavily on the carpeted hallway, closing in on his location.

Upon arrival, Mike kicked open the door and found his partner splayed out on the floor. He maneuvered himself inside the ferrous-scented room, confirmed the space was free from additional threats, then knelt next to him.

"I'm here, Frankie," he said, attempting to assess the seriousness of the wound. *"Agent down!"* Mike shouted into his radio. *"I repeat—Agent Adler has been hit!"*

* * * * *

The siren song of a beckoning New York paramedic began to penetrate Frank's mind as he blinked his way back into consciousness.

"Agent Adler?" coaxed the brunette, sitting across from him inside the stationary ambulance in her freshly pressed blue uniform. "Can you hear me?"

Before Frank could respond, Mike suddenly chimed in. "You got blood on my favorite shoes, asshole..."

Frank looked down the cot, beyond his boots, and saw his forty-six-year-old, sable-haired partner standing at the foot of his stretcher. The joke, along with the crooked smirk on Mike's face, was an obvious attempt to veil his relief.

Frank cracked a grin of his own, finding his mouth severely parched.

"How you feeling, big guy?" Mike asked, causing the medic to turn her attention back to the monitor in front of her, allowing the two FBI agents a moment to speak.

"I'm fine," Frank reported with his usual stoicism. He rubbed his palm against the back of his nearly shaved head and swung his powerful legs over the side of the stretcher, setting the soles of his boots on the sterile, rubberized floor. Turning his attention to his shoulder, he found that the wound had already been dressed and bandaged, and his arm was cradled inside a triangular cotton sling. "Everybody else, okay?"

"Yeah, all good," Mike nodded. "We found three perps inside the bay who have connections to the Mexican cartels, along with a couple of their low-level associates."

The neutral expression on Frank's face remained unchanged as he tested his ability to turn his head.

"We think Victor Ramirez may have taken off in that van we saw flee the scene earlier," Mike continued, "but everyone else has been detained. And considering one of those bastards shot an agent, we've got some pretty good leverage to work our way up the ladder now." A sly grin suddenly appeared on Mike's face. "I've just been doing my best to keep it under wraps how shitty you are at your job. That way, it might seem like a bigger deal than it actually is." He winked at Frank, who chuckled, causing the fresh sutures in his shoulder to protest in pain.

Mike leaned in, and the smirk fell from his face. "What happened out there, Frankie?" he wondered. "I was trying to reach you on your radio..."

"I think my unit must be busted," Frank suggested. "Or maybe the battery was dead."

"I guess we didn't exactly have time to test our equipment properly before we made entry, did we?" Mike recounted the rushed moments before they had converged on the warehouse. "Did you at least get a look at who shot you?"

Frank shook his head.

"Shit," said Mike, studying his partner's face for a moment before a thought popped into his head. "Oh, hey, you know who we found inside?"

"Who?"

"Adrian Jackson," Mike revealed. "He was involved in that big arms deal that went sideways up in the Bronx a few years back. You remember that guy?"

"Yeah, I think so," Frank replied flatly, seemingly uninterested. "What kind of merchandise did we confiscate off these guys today anyway?"

"A few keys of coke, a bunch of pills, a couple crates of knock-off designer bags..." Mike ran down the list. "To be honest, there wasn't all that much left in the bay. They must have moved most of it in that van by the time we arrived."

"And that thing will be ghost by now," Frank figured.

"Agent Adler..." the medic spoke up, having been waiting for a pause in the conversation.

Frank turned his attention to her.

"The bullet passed through your deltoid cleanly," she explained. "Structurally, the damage was fairly minimal, but you did lose a sizable amount of blood rather quickly. Fortunately, your partner was there to apply pressure to stop the bleeding."

"Holy shit," Mike piped up. "Did you hear that, Frankie? She said I saved your life. I'm a goddamn hero!" he joked.

The ambulance attendant flashed a toothy smile. "I'd like to suggest that you come to the hospital overnight to be monitored, but having just reviewed your medical history with us," she tapped the tip of her ballpoint pen on the screen in front of her, "I doubt I have any chance of convincing you of that, do I?"

Frank confirmed her hypothesis with a nod.

She retrieved two bottles of prescription pills from inside a sliding glass cabinet next to her elbow. "I'm giving you some antibiotics," she told Frank. "And something for the pain. Take the antibiotics twice a day until they're gone. As for the pain meds, you can—"

"*Those*, you can keep," Frank said, referencing the analgesics. He removed the other bottle from her freshly manicured fingers. "Twice a day..." he parroted back. "And I'll be sure to keep an eye out for any signs of infection in the meantime."

"Feel free to remain in the ambulance for as long as you like. I'm just needed out there for another patient assessment."

"One of our guys?" asked Mike.

The attendant shook her head as she shuffled past the agents, heading toward the rear of the ambulance.

"Let him suffer," Mike joked before she pushed open the doors, stepped onto the pavement, and quickly disappeared from view.

"Do Donna and Sara know I—" Frank had just begun to ask Mike when his eighteen-year-old daughter, Sara, suddenly appeared at the back of the ambulance, nearly out of breath.

"Daddy!" she called out, worry plaguing her voice. She climbed inside the back of the vehicle and rushed to her father's side. "Are you okay? What happened?"

"Mike shot me." Frank pointed an accusatory finger at his partner, attempting to keep a straight face.

"Sure, someone gets shot and everybody starts blaming the Latino guy," Mike joked. "Trust me, Frankie, if I had shot you, I would have aimed a little higher and gotten you some plastic surgery for that ugly mug of yours."

Sara took a moment to leave her father's side to give 'Uncle' Mike a hug.

"It's not a big deal." Frank downplayed the event. "I'm not sure why they had you come all the way down here for this. In fact, I've just been released."

"You're certain you're alright?"

"Positive." Frank nodded.

"Should we cancel our breakfast plans for Sunday at the cabin?"

"Of course not."

"Okay, well, see how you feel tomorrow, and if you're not feeling up to it, we can always reschedule." She hugged her father, doing her best to avoid his injured appendage.

"I'll see you Sunday," Frank doubled down.

Sara exchanged farewells with Mike and then exited the ambulance.

Frank spotted his black tactical pack next to Mike's at the end of the stretcher. "Did you grab that?"

"Yeah, you left it on the other side of the building when you took off for the gate," Mike reminded him.

Frank stood up, unzipped the bag, and removed his navy-blue FBI windbreaker. He slipped his uninjured arm into one of the sleeves, allowing the other to drape over his slinged shoulder.

"Here, I can carry the packs back to our vehicles," Mike said, quickly grabbing Frank's bag before he could refuse the assistance. "And you don't even have to give me a tip for the service," he grinned.

The two agents abandoned the back of the ambulance and found themselves standing in front of the warehouse. Frank took a moment to survey the still-hectic scene and saw a slew of other federal agents and forensic scene specialists coming and going in all directions. He turned to Mike, and his expression became markedly more serious.

"Where are the guys they detained?"

Mike shrugged, slinging a pack over each shoulder. He glanced lazily around the parking lot. "I think they were being cuffed somewhere over *there*," he pointed his chin towards the street, "but I—"

Before Mike had even finished his sentence, Frank took off, ducking under a strand of neon-yellow caution tape and weaving his way between evidence collection tables. He beelined for a row of parked NYPD cruisers, while Mike followed at a distance.

Inside the back of an idling police car, Frank spotted two shadowy figures and wasted no time yanking open the door. The man seated nearest Frank was Caucasian, with pale, acne-pocked skin and greasy, shoulder-length, brown hair. He looked to be in his twenties and was someone Frank didn't recognize. Next to him sat Adrian Jackson, the African American gangster Mike had mentioned in the ambulance. He had an athletic build, closely cropped black hair, and a jagged, three-inch scar behind his left ear. Jackson had been a Brooklynite his entire life and was believed to have connections with one of the Mexican cartels.

"Well, look who it is!" Frank hollered at him across the back of the cruiser. The nearer detainee's eyes grew large when he caught sight of the six-foot-two, two-hundred-and-fifty-pound federal agent now leaning inside the back of the vehicle. The shouting caught the attention of the police officer leaning against the hood of his cruiser, chatting idly with a heavyset colleague.

"Easy, Frankie!" Mike called out, closing the gap. Once he arrived, he placed a hand on Frank's uninjured shoulder and attempted to coax him back out of the vehicle. Frank shook off his grip with ease and climbed further inside.

"Which one of you pricks shot me?!" Frank demanded, driving his elbow into the nearer gangster's face, nearly knocking him unconscious. Frank continued across the backseat and grabbed a fistful of Jackson's shirt in a violent rage.

"Fuck you, Adler!" Adrian shouted, struggling fervently against the tight metal cuffs restraining his wrists behind his back.

"Enjoy another stretch in prison, you piece of shit!" Frank taunted the hoodlum, finally releasing his grip and allowing himself to be removed from the back of the vehicle. Mike turned Frank away quickly and offered the NYPD officer an apologetic shrug for the sudden outburst.

* * * * *

Frank and Mike had made the five-minute walk back to the McDonald's parking lot where they had parked their vehicles, mostly in silence. When they reached the door of Mike's black SUV, he finally spoke up.

"You still doing alright, Frankie?" Mike inquired with a hint of concern in his voice. "Still back on track?"

"What, *that?"* he downplayed the outburst. "Sometimes you just gotta put on a bit of a show..."

"Fair enough." Mike shrugged. "Hey, just so you know, I submitted a preliminary report with the arriving supervisor while you were being packaged into the ambulance. I told her we would both write down our accounts of tonight's events while they are still fresh in our minds, but I asked that an official debriefing be delayed until Monday, on account of you being shot and all."

"And she agreed?" Frank raised an eyebrow.

"Hey, I didn't score the sixteenth-best mark in my negotiations class at Quantico for nothing," Mike smirked.

"Sixteenth, huh?"

"Actually, I can't be entirely certain of that figure. I may have been last in math."

"Well, either way, thanks for getting us out of that debriefing," said Frank. "But I think the real magic trick was how you kept the ambulance free from agents coming to check in on me. How in the hell did you pull *that* off?"

"Oh, *that*? That was easy," Mike replied, opening the door of his immaculately detailed vehicle. He climbed inside, started the engine, and lowered his window. "Once that paramedic lady said you were going to be fine, I announced over the radio that you were in stable condition but had shit your pants when you got shot and were too embarrassed to have any visitors." Mike was barely able to control his laughter by the end of the story.

Frank shook his head with a smile. "You cunt."

"Good luck trying to squash that rumor on Monday morning, buddy." Mike put his vehicle in drive and crept away slowly, ensuring to keep eye contact with his partner for as long as humanly possible.

Frank walked over to his decade-old gray half-ton pick-up and unlocked the doors. Once inside, he twisted the rearview mirror towards himself and took a long, hard look at his reflection.

CHAPTER two

The melodic sound of morning birds discovering first light penetrated the single-pane window inside the bedroom of the tiny cabin, waking Frank. He and his wife, Donna, had originally built the DIY shack on the ten-acre plot of land as temporary living quarters for when construction was supposed to have begun on their new house in the countryside. However, since everything had gone to shit, all plans had been put on hold, and Donna and Sara continued to live at the old house in the city that had been taken off the market. Today's breakfast date with his daughter marked only the second time Frank had attempted to regain some normalcy in their relationship since his self-imposed isolation had begun.

Frank was sitting on the edge of the bed, pulling on a pair of socks, when he heard Sara's rusted Honda Civic crunching down the long gravel driveway. He rose from the cheap mattress and donned a flannel, high-collared shirt, attempting to conceal some of the ripe, rainbow bruising now displayed across his shoulder, chest, and neck from the shooting two days prior. Frank exited the bedroom, made his way across the cabin, and pulled open the front door. Sara had already parked her car and was approaching with a green grocery bag hanging from her right hand.

"Just woke up?" she questioned her father as she neared.

"Are you kidding? I've been awake for hours," Frank responded, leaning against the doorframe.

"That's not what those pillow creases on your cheek are telling me," Sara smiled, gently touching her father's stubbled chin with her free hand as she stepped past him into the cabin.

Frank smiled.

"How's your shoulder, Daddy?" Sara asked, making her way over to a small countertop and removing a carton of brown, free-range eggs from the sack.

"Actually, now that you mention it..." Frank said, following her into the kitchen space. "I think it might be even stronger than before," he teased, rubbing his bicep as if it contained mystical powers now.

"Oh God, here we go!" Sara rolled her eyes.

"Honestly, it's fine, sweetheart. How's school going?" Frank inquired, removing an induction cooktop from one of the cupboards.

"Pretty hectic, actually," Sara admitted. "I think some of my professors give assignments just to see the look of utter confusion on their students' faces," she suggested, locating an orange-handled paring knife in one of the drawers and using it to cut into the waxy red skin of a sweet bell pepper.

Frank plugged in the appliance.

"Have you talked to Mom yet?" Sara's voice gained a degree of seriousness.

Not offering an immediate response, Frank removed a small bottle of olive oil from a neighboring cupboard, poured some into a stainless-steel frying pan, and set it on the burner.

"When are you coming home?" Sara pressed him. "It seems like you're doing a lot better now. And I miss you. *We* miss you."

The words cut through Frank like the bullet in the warehouse.

"I know you do, sweetheart," he finally responded, recalling the mistakes he believed he had made in his dogged pursuit of answers. "It's just..." he searched for a way to tell her something that could not yet be revealed. Just then, he felt her gentle hand on the middle of his back.

"It's okay, Daddy. You'll come home when you're ready." She attempted a smile, but Frank could see the undercurrent of disappointment in her eyes.

*****

Once the cooking assignments were completed, Frank and Sara took their places on the cabin's beige, two-seater sofa. Frank's laptop was on the coffee table, still open from the night before. Sara set down her plate and logged on to a streaming site, quickly searching for an old, corny sitcom she and her mother used to watch religiously while Frank was working nights.

"Nice!" Sara cheered when the title appeared on the search screen. "Do you remember this show?"

Frank took a sip of his water and glanced at the image on the laptop. Two middle-aged women, wearing goofy expressions, were attempting to flip pancakes inside a purple-walled kitchen where it looked like a bomb had gone off inside a bag of flour.

"Don't think so."

"Oh, you're going to love it!"

Frank smiled. "I'm sure," he said, not convinced in the least that he would.

*****

Having finished eating, Frank noticed Sara beginning to nod off on the couch next to him, having spent another late night studying at the library on campus. She tucked herself beneath his uninjured arm, and her tiny ribcage began to rhythmically expand and contract next to his as she sank into a deeper slumber. Frank glanced down at her arm, which had come to rest next to his thigh, and suddenly his mind conjured up the hideous needle marks that had been there when he found her inside that Mexican warehouse nearly three months ago.

A cascade of memories sent him back to when everything had first begun...

CHAPTER three

Donna, Frank's wife, a tall, picturesque auburn-streaked brunette with the lean build of a seasoned triathlete, was helping Sara pack the plethora of outfits she would be bringing on her month-long trip to the West Coast. Sara and her best friend, Marla, had both recently been accepted into Columbia University and had decided to embark on a summer of exploration and surfing with the money they had saved from their part-time jobs during their senior year of high school.

The journey was set to begin in San Diego and proceed north until the girls reached their final destination of Tofino, British Columbia, a quaint surfing town located on Vancouver Island in Canada. Along the way, they were planning to spend anywhere from three to ten days in each location.

Initially, Donna had not been thrilled by the idea of her eighteen-year-old daughter leaving for such an extended period, but the combination of the girls' maturity and Frank's reassurances had convinced her that a healthy dose of independence would help transition them into the nearing responsibilities of college life and adulthood.

Donna folded the last of Sara's brightly colored bikinis, certain that if Frank had been involved in the selection process, the garment's inability to provide ample body coverage would have been called into question immediately. Donna placed the swimsuit inside the suitcase and took a moment to observe the beautiful young woman rummaging through the closet on the other side of the room. It felt like only yesterday that Donna had dropped her daughter off for her first day of elementary school.

Frank's voice arrived from somewhere down the hallway.

"What time are you wanting to leave for the airport?"

"Ummm, I was thinking 5:30 or 5:45 should give us enough time," Sara replied, regarding her flight departing from JFK later that evening. With the time change, the girls were set to arrive in San Diego just before midnight.

"17:30 it is," Frank decided. "Because if you miss your flight and I don't get to start on that cabin in the morning, I might just have to disown you," he teased.

"Oh wow! I'll miss you too, Daddy!" Sara replied, smiling at her mother.

* * * * *

Frank stood at the front door, glancing down at his watch. It was 5:34, and he had just finished loading both of Sara's overstuffed suitcases into the box of his pickup truck.

"Ladies! The Frank Adler Express is leaving the station in exactly one minute!" he announced in his best train conductor's voice. "If anyone is still interested in a ride to the airport, please report to the front door immediately! If we have no takers, I will be diverting the locomotive to Mike's house for beer instead!"

A distant commotion could now be heard down the hall. A few moments later, Sara and Donna appeared at the top of the stairs, each carrying a collection of colorful handbags that Sara could undoubtedly explain as a dire necessity for the trip. They descended the steps, exiting the house past Frank, with the reddened cheeks of a mother and daughter who had already exchanged their first round of tearful farewells. Frank was seasoned enough to know that there would be at least one more good cry before the two officially parted ways.

* * * * *

Impossibly, JFK seemed even busier than usual, as soon-to-be travelers—and those tasked with seeing them off—moved hurriedly from one location to another inside the chaotic terminal. Most of them were deeply immersed in their cellphone screens, while others attempted to guzzle last-minute, nine-dollar caffeine fixes before the monotoned TSA agents herded them like cattle, lulling them into a false sense of security. Frank's counter-terrorism experience with the FBI had dashed such nonsensical beliefs long ago.

"There's Marla!" Sara exclaimed, having spotted her traveling companion and her mother, Carol, arriving through Entrance 16 amidst the frenzy.

Frank had always been extremely fond of Marla, a petite blonde who stood just over five feet tall, with a fun-loving personality big enough to seize control of any room she entered. Her mother, who had once been the spitting image of her daughter, had gained a substantial amount of weight over the years, likely due to the stress and loneliness of losing her husband, Jack, a NYFD firefighter, in a car accident just shy of ten years ago. The tragedy had left her a widow with two school-age children at the time.

"Hellllllllllooooooo, Adlers!" Marla called out over the raucous crowd once she had spotted them. Janice tried to keep up with her daughter, dodging opposing foot traffic with a fully loaded luggage buggy.

"Oh my God! I love your outfit!" Donna complimented Marla as she approached in a forest green romper. The two embraced in a heartfelt hug.

"Do you think the handsome guys up in Canada will like it too, Mr. Adler?" Marla teased Frank, flashing him a smile.

"Don't even start!" Frank chuckled. "I'll turn this vacation into a backyard camp-out."

"Hi, Carol!" Donna welcomed Marla's mother as she arrived.

"Hello, everyone!" Carol replied with a smile of her own, nearly out of breath.

The three parents had known each other nearly as long as their daughters had, and Donna and Carol had gained a particularly strong bond after Jack's sudden passing. The group made their way toward the check-in counters, and Frank decided to use the time to review a couple of ground rules for the girls.

"Try to move in groups as much as possible," he suggested. "And if your hotel room has a safe, make sure to use it for your valuables and passports. If it doesn't, you can always ask the front desk clerk to hold onto something for you while you're out. And always keep an eye on your drinks."

"Hey, Mr. Adler?" Marla cocked her head to one side slightly as they walked along. "Once we've locked ourselves securely in the hotel closet, what should I do if I need to take a pee? Do you think the hotel will provide me with a police escort to get to the bathroom?" she teased him, causing the others to burst into a fit of laughter.

"He's going to kill you," Sara warned Marla with a smile, then turned her attention to her father. "Don't worry, Daddy. We'll be smart."

Just then, a gray-haired, middle-aged ticketing agent summoned the girls to her station with a wave of her hand. Frank, Donna, and Carol removed themselves from the line-up and made their way toward a pair of conveyor belts used to check luggage. While the mothers caught up on recent life events, Frank directed his attention back to the girls, who were now fully engaged in an excited conversation with the primly dressed airline attendant, gesturing enthusiastically in a friendly, makeshift social sign language. At that moment, Frank felt pleased that Sara and Marla had decided to reward themselves with this trip, as they would soon be embarking on the next chapter of their promising young lives.

CHAPTER four

"Has Sara texted you yet this morning?" Donna asked Frank as she leaned inside the passenger-side door of her electric sedan, where she had left her cell phone to charge.

"Negative," Frank replied. He was twenty feet away, scratching a pencil mark onto a 2x6 piece of lumber that would act as a support beam in the tiny cabin's foundation. "Didn't she send you a message when they arrived in California last night?" He glanced at his watch. "I can see the helicopter parenting is already in full swing."

"Never mind you," Donna stuck out her tongue. She set her phone back down on the seat and walked over to Frank, who stood up from his crouch and wrapped an arm around her shoulders. The pair gazed off towards the distant mountains and felt that their future was as bright as ever. The euphoria was only disrupted when Donna's phone began to ring, and she made her way back to the car.

"Hello?" Donna answered after the fourth or fifth ring, unplugging the device so that she could move around freely. "Hi, honey! It's great to hear your voice!"

Frank grinned, resuming his carpentry.

"What are you two up to today?" Donna asked, making her way back to the worksite. "Yes, your father is right here. We just finished setting all the concrete blocks for the foundation." She gestured with an open hand, as if Sara could see the progress. "Yes. I'll be sure to tell him. Okay. Send me a text later if you have time. Talk soon. Love you, too. Bye for now."

*****

In California, Sara had only just disconnected the call and removed the phone from her ear when a young man with jet-black hair approached her from behind. By the time she placed her device into the front pocket of her cut-off jean shorts, he had closed the distance and wrapped an arm around her neck. Immediately, she felt his grip tighten.

"Hey!" Sara let out a light-hearted giggle. "My mom almost heard you!" she said with just a hint of unease in her voice.

"Oh, sorry, I didn't know you were talking to your mother," the attractive twenty-four-year-old Californian with emerald-green eyes apologized, his cheek next to hers.

"No problem, I don't think she *actually* heard you," Sara replied, turning her attention to Marla, who was sitting closely with a young man named James on a comfortable-looking chocolate-brown sofa. "We just have to make sure that our parents don't find out we're staying at your place, is all. They would seriously lose their shit."

The two young men nodded in compliance.

Marla had been corresponding with James on social media for six weeks prior to the trip. He was two years younger than Steve and possessed a slightly slimmer build, flowing shoulder-length blonde surfer's hair, and a tan to match. He had first communicated with Marla after she had posted a question in an online forum, asking for tips regarding local excursions and social events that she and Sara might attend while in the San Diego area. Mixed in with the random replies arrived a message from James, in which he explained that he lived sixty miles from the city and provided her with an exhaustive list of outings that she and her friend might enjoy. Over time, that simple act of helpfulness had blossomed into something more, and the two ended up hitting it off.

As the girls' vacation approached, James explained to Marla that his roommate, Steve, had recently broken up with his girlfriend. He wondered if Sara, whom Marla had described in great detail, might be interested in being introduced. At first, Sara had expressed reservations regarding the acquaintanceship. However, as Marla became more infatuated with her new fling, Sara felt an in-person meeting with Steve in California was inevitable. So, she decided it might be better to vet the potential weirdo from a distance electronically first.

To Sara's surprise, Steve admitted that he also had reservations about being introduced to a stranger, which helped put her mind at ease. Fortunately, over the next couple of weeks, they found themselves sufficiently attracted to each other and continued exchanging texts, pictures, and stories as the trip approached.

Just days before the girls' flight, the two young men offered to host the girls at their house in Temecula during the first leg of their trip to save them money on pricey California accommodations. Sara and Marla quickly agreed but decided against revealing these new lodging plans to their parents, wanting to avoid an awkward conversation and inevitable backlash that would surely arise. Besides, the girls thought, if things happened to work out romantically going forward, there was a chance they might all meet one day in the future, anyway.

"Phone call time with your parents is sacred," James said from his seat on the couch next to Marla, kissing the top of her hand.

Steve nodded in agreement.

CHAPTER five

The doorbell chimed inside a two-story brownstone, just east of Prospect Park in Brooklyn. Janice, Mike's wife, set her book of crossword puzzles on the glass coffee table and rose from the cream-colored couch she had been warming for the last twenty minutes. She and Mike were high school sweethearts, and despite her being a year his junior, they had graduated in the same year due to her skipping a grade in elementary school. Nearly every aspect of their personalities seemed to be in direct opposition. Mike was loud and boisterous. Janice was reserved and calm. Mike's parents had arrived from Mexico shortly before he was born, whereas Janice's had been first-generation immigrants from Sweden. Despite many of these superficial differences, they were still as in love as the day they had tied the knot twenty-six years ago.

For many years, they had attempted to conceive a child but were unsuccessful. However, their saving grace was that each of them came from a large family with many nieces and nephews nearby to share their endless love with. They took tremendous pride in their roles as aunt and uncle, a relationship that extended fully to Sara.

"Come on, babe," Janice touched Mike's shoulder gently as she passed behind where he was sitting on his well-worn gray recliner that he refused to retire. "Come greet our guests."

"Greet them?" Mike questioned, his eyes glued to the television's pre-season football report. "What do you think this is? Buckingham Palace?"

"Why, yes, it is. So, you better get your royal butt in gear," she replied with a smile.

Mike closed the leg rest of the noisy recliner and sprang up to his feet in one fluid motion. "You know, hun, I'm feeling *pretty* good these days," he told his wife, wearing a crooked smirk. "I'm thinking I should probably swing down to MetLife Stadium for a tryout next spring," he said, pretending to tuck an imaginary pigskin under his arm. He head-faked the coffee table as he made his way to the door.

"I'm sure they'd be lucky to have you," Janice played along, always willing to keep her husband's high school *'glory days'* football memories alive—no matter how mediocre his athletic performances had been all those years ago.

Janice pulled open the door to reveal Donna and Frank standing outside on the small concrete porch. Donna was holding a bottle of Chilean red wine, while Frank had a cardboard bakery box, wrapped with a decorative silver ribbon, in his hands.

"Welcome! Welcome! Welcome!" Janice greeted the couple, embracing Donna with a hug. "Hi, Frank! Come on in!" Janice stepped back to make room for their guests.

"Frankie!" Mike called out to his partner in his usual, one notch above appropriate, volume setting. "Janice and I were just discussing my football comeback!"

"Oh yeah? Which team is looking for a new water boy?" Frank wondered. "Or are you finally going to live out your dream of becoming a professional cheerleader?"

"Congratulations, Frank, you just shit-talked yourself out of my entourage," Mike broke the news. "Donna, you're still in, but only if you divorce Frank."

"Hmmm, it *has* always been a dream of mine to be a part of a real-life entourage." She smiled.

"So, whose turn is it to cook tonight?" Mike asked the group, knowing full well that he and Frank had taken on those duties during their last get-together.

"Well, we did it last time," Janice was the first to respond. "Right, Donna?"

"Yeah, we made those fish tacos."

Mike and Frank exchanged a glance, now questioning the certainty of their pre-meal football watching.

"Wait, I thought—" said Mike.

"We're kidding, you goofs!" Donna gave up the ruse.

"Oh my God!" Janice laughed, taking the dessert container from Frank's hand. "I bet we could have *actually* gotten them to cook again tonight."

"Go watch your silly game, boys. We've got this one," Donna said as she and Janice headed toward the recently renovated kitchen.

"That was close," Mike grinned at Frank. "You want a beer?"

"Sure." Frank nodded, and they made their way down a hallway toward the den.

"You can change the channel in there if you want," Mike told Frank. "It's probably still another ten minutes 'til kickoff. I'll go grab us a couple of cold ones."

Frank entered the freshly vacuumed den and took a seat on one end of the U-shaped beige sectional. Locating the remote control, he began flipping through the channels, searching for something to pass the time before the game started. He paused briefly on a popular sitcom with a grievously overused laugh track, then on a nature special featuring Australian marsupials, and eventually came across a dull-looking congressional hearing on one of the 24-hour news channels. Bored with his options, Frank returned the television to the pre-game show.

"Can you believe that fucking guy?" Mike's voice suddenly arrived from behind Frank, having re-entered the room with the beers he had promised.

Frank searched the screen for the source of Mike's ire. "Who? The coach?"

"No, that business guy they were questioning on the other channel," Mike clarified. "Did you catch any of his testimony from the other day? What a fucking creep. Turn it back and check it out."

Frank complied and then traded the remote control for his beverage. "So, who is this guy?"

"Some bigwig CEO of a massive pharmaceutical company," Mike explained, taking a sip of his lager. "Some of the guys at work were watching it in the lunchroom a couple of days ago. His name is Ken, something-or-other, and his company has been jacking up the prices on prescription drugs by like ten thousand percent or something insane. I guess Congress finally called him in for one of these public hearing things."

*****

The chamber in Washington, D.C. was stale and stuffy as Ken Collins sat wedged between two of Zinex Pharmaceuticals' high-paid lawyers. At only thirty-seven years old, Collins had already become the CEO of one of the largest drug companies in the world. His slicked-back obsidian hair, dark as a raven's wing, sprouted from deeply tanned skin that could only be maintained through the continual use of a high-powered tanning bed, or perhaps by living on the surface of the sun.

This was not the first time Collins had been summoned to testify in front of the House Oversight and Reform Committee. Four years ago, he—along with a short list of other grossly overpaid business executives—had been summoned to shed light on their excessive salaries, as well as the monopolistic practices that had seemingly become mainstream in the industry. Due to the broad scope of those original hearings, most of the money-hungry figureheads leaned heavily on their Fifth Amendment rights, frustrating and infuriating the Congressional panel to no end.

The O&R Committee was hopeful that things might be different today. For one, they had summoned Collins individually, attempting to shine a spotlight directly on Zinex's questionable business practices for the American public to see. Perhaps the concentration of pressure might cause the businessman to falter this time around.

Even though the CEO's lawyers were confident that their Ivy League-educated client possessed the intellectual capacity to portray himself as any of the various phony personas powerful men like him had created for themselves over the years, they knew that he wouldn't have to do so. His Fifth Amendment rights were just as intact today as they had been four years ago, so the high-priced suits advised him to simply adhere to their tried-and-true playbook: give vague, looping responses, disclose nothing of significance, and if you happen to find yourself in trouble, immediately fall back on those beautiful self-incrimination rights.

However, unbeknownst to his attorneys, Collins had already decided against comporting himself in such a manner today. Instead, he would present himself just as he was—a brash, self-assured, unapologetic capitalist, forced to live in a society that apparently craved the American dream but couldn't handle it when the spoils of success went to someone more capable and deserving than themselves.

Douglas Simpson, an overweight African American Congressman from Pennsylvania, was recently appointed head of the O&R committee and would oversee the proceedings today. He sat squarely in the middle of the polished, mahogany rostrum on the far side of the room. Surrounding him was an allotment of governmental representatives, each engaged in the usual paper shuffling and small talk that preceded such hearings.

The jowly Simpson leaned forward into his microphone.

"I'd like to start by saying a good morning to everyone in attendance today," he began in a baritone voice that bore the last remnants of a childhood spent in a north Chicago neighborhood.

The room came to order.

"Today, we have Mr. Collins joining us," Simpson announced, directing his gaze at the CEO sitting across the room in his black square-shouldered blazer, crimson tie, and patternless white dress shirt. "If none of my colleagues have any objections, I'd prefer to get straight into the matter at hand."

Everyone in the room seemed to agree with their silence.

"Mr. Collins, I only have a few questions for you today, but I want to make you aware that many members of this committee have been waiting patiently for this day to arrive."

The CEO's expression remained neutral.

"In recent years, Mr. Collins, Zinex Pharmaceutics has been heavily involved in acquiring a substantial number of its competitors, which includes gaining access to hundreds of patented medications. Would you say that is correct?"

The gray-haired, fifty-something lawyer on Collins's left leaned into his client's microphone. "Mr. Collins would like to plead his Fifth Amendment rights and respectfully declines to answer the question," the Harvard Law graduate stated in a pleasant yet monotone manner.

"Now hold on just a second here!" Simpson responded immediately. "*You, sir,*" he pointed his finger directly at the offending lawyer, "are not the one who was summoned here today. And although I respect your right to be seated next to your client and to guide him in an advisory capacity, I also expect, *at a bare minimum,* that Mr. Collins speaks for himself today."

The handsome, cleft-chinned attorney returned to the microphone. "My apologies, I'm just so used to speaking for clients in these types of settings."

The chairman accepted the rationale before focusing his attention back on the CEO. He decided to change gears. "Mr. Collins, please allow me to be frank with you. My colleagues and I are well aware of the previous hearing you attended, the one in which you and the others repeatedly declined to answer our questions. Though I cannot speak for anyone else up here this morning, I feel it is our duty to pose each and every question we have for you today, even if it means enduring the endless invocation of your Fifth Amendment rights. I believe, at the very least, this will show the American people exactly how you chose to comport yourself."

Collins stared directly at Simpson, wearing a relaxed smirk that oozed a palpable smugness.

"I see you grinning, Mr. Collins, but let me assure you that the public doesn't think your presence here is any laughing matter."

The CEO held his unflinching pose for a few seconds longer. Finally, he leaned forward and spoke.

"That won't be necessary," he said matter-of-factly.

"Excuse me? What *exactly* do you think is unnecessary?" the Chairman responded quickly, obviously incensed by the cryptic comment. "I assure you that we will be asking our questions whether you feel them *necessary* or not!" he lectured.

"You misunderstand me," Collins asserted flatly, drawing additional looks of contempt from the officials on the other side of the room. Murmurs began to sound in the crowd of spectators behind him. "I was referring to your previous statement," the CEO clarified. "I am stating that it *won't be necessary* for me to continually invoke my Fifth Amendment rights *because* I intend to answer many of your questions today, quite candidly," he declared with supreme confidence.

It took a moment for the revelatory statement to register with Zinex's attorneys, but when it did, the Korean American lawyer on Collins' right immediately reached out for the thin black microphone, attempting to shield it from any further lunacy. He requested a short recess to speak privately with his client.

"It sounds to me as though Mr. Collins is more than ready to proceed," Simpson denied the request, sensing a rare opportunity in the making. The lawyer shoved the microphone away, and the three men huddled into a hushed, face-to-face meeting.

"What are you doing?" the gray-haired lawyer questioned Collins immediately. "The board decided on a complete invocation of your constitutional right to silence. You are not to provide *any* statements that could potentially harm this company's reputation or your own. I need to make myself perfectly clear here. I see *absolutely* no benefit to answering any of these questions candidly."

"*Mr. Collins*?" Simpson tried to wrangle the CEO's attention back from the lawyers.

Collins held up a finger to the Congressman across the room, then returned his concentration to the privacy of the huddle.

"Listen here," he confronted the two suits in a stern whisper. "Zinex, and its board, do whatever the *fuck* I tell them," he hissed. "Ken Collins is sick of seeing the names of this country's best and brightest being dragged through the mud," he stated in an obnoxious third person. "Tired of listening to grown-ass men acting like a bunch of fear-stricken pussies! I'm a fucking genius! An innovator! And *those* assholes over there," he referenced the panel across the room, "are a collection of ignorant simpletons that can't understand the first thing about industry, economics, or capitalism! The *only* reason any of those dinosaurs are here today is to placate their hordes of dim-witted constituents before they all die of old age."

The two lawyers sat in wide-eyed speechlessness.

Collins leaned forward, breaking the huddle, and adjusted his microphone towards himself. "Be aware that I have just informed my council of my decision to speak openly with you today, and they have agreed to sit silently for the remainder of the session," he lied. "*If* they are unable to do so, I will remove them from the proceedings myself."

The two attorneys melted into the backs of their chairs, staring straight ahead, contemplating their future employment prospects after experiencing such a public embarrassment.

"I want to be very clear with all of you today," Collins addressed the entire committee. "If, at any time, I feel that a particular line of questioning is not deserving of an answer—whether that be due to its irrelevancy or unintelligible nature—I will instruct the inquirer to move on. If you are unable to follow that simple guideline, I can assure all of you that I can and will transition back to my Fifth Amendment rights *extremely* quickly. Do you understand?"

A deafening silence plagued the room as the spectators waited with bated breath for an official response. Collins sat back in his chair, confident and relishing in the tension he had created. Across the room, Simpson looked like a boxer trying to compose himself after being pummeled with a flurry of unexpected punches.

"Although I cannot say I am fond of the manner in which you have just spoken to the members of this committee, if you are, in fact, sincere in your willingness to answer our questions openly and candidly today, I am willing to overlook the *unorthodoxy* of your statements, so we can continue."

The self-assured smirk returned to Collins' face.

"Well then, Mr. Collins," Simpson picked up where he had left off, "do you agree with my earlier statement? Does your company acquire competitors with the intent to absorb their portfolios of patented medications?"

"I agree that is *one* of the ways in which Zinex obtains patents. However, as a corporation, we also strive to continually produce novel medications by way of research and development."

"And you would say that research and development is considered a *major* expense in your company, Mr. Collins?"

"I would."

"I see..." Simpson lifted a thin stack of papers, flipped through the first few pages, and located the one he had earmarked earlier. "Well, if these figures I have in front of me are correct, Mr. Collins, they suggest that in the last twenty-four months, you and two other top Zinex executives have received combined compensation packages totaling one hundred and ninety million dollars. Is this also accurate, Mr. Collins?"

"I am not interested in discussing the compensation packages of individuals who are not present today," the CEO replied bluntly.

"The only reason I ask, Mr. Collins, is because you just stated that research and development is a *major* expense in your company. However," he removed a singular spreadsheet from the pile and held it in the air for the cameras to see, "over that same two-year period, research and development expenditures were *less* than those compensation figures, weren't they?

Collins stared at the politician, the smirk never leaving his face.

"I don't have the exact figures in front of me, but I imagine for that very *specific* period you are referring to, that could very well be the case. Sure," the CEO shrugged.

"So, just to connect your two statements, Mr. Collins, it seems that you are trying to suggest that a pharmaceutical company spending *less* on research and development than it does on the compensation for only three employees still qualifies it as a major expense."

"No," Collins rejected the statement. "That's not what I was suggesting *at all*, actually."

The chairman feigned befuddlement. "But Mr. Collins, you yourself just agreed—"

Collins cut him off. "All I agreed to is that when someone like *you* cherry-picks random data within limited timeframes—which is obviously what you have done here today—then yes, Zinex's R&D contributions *might* possibly be less than the executive compensation for that *very* specific moment in time. That is all to which I agree, sir."

"Wh—"

Collins interrupted him again. "Companies like Zinex must consistently shift their focus between research and development and competitor acquisition. It's fluid. And it's dictated by market conditions and a multitude of other factors that someone like you could not possibly begin to understand," he lectured. "You people like to throw around attention-grabbing words like *monopoly, limited competition,* and *buy-outs,* but you know what I never hear any of you asking about? Why do promising medications—*life-saving* medications—get stuck in limbo for years, imprisoned by companies without the financial means to make these drugs available to the public in a timely manner? I don't see any of *those* companies sitting here today being questioned about why they lock up some of our country's most promising scientists under contract, hamstringing their novel pursuits toward promising research due to a corporation's monetary constraints. Do you know what solves those problems, Mr. Simpson?" He refocused his attention on the Chairman again. "An acquisition by *my company* solves ALL those problems simultaneously," Collins stated with conviction. "Now, like you, I can't speak for the other members of your committee, but I believe that your voters deserve to have *more* life-saving medications on the market in a *timelier* fashion, not less. Wouldn't you agree with *that*, Mr. Simpson?"

Collins leaned back from the microphone, fully aware that the majority of what had just come out of his mouth was utter bullshit, but it didn't matter. Politically, he knew it was irrefutable.

Simpson seemed to be at a loss for words.

"Well, yes, of course, of course, I think the public deserves to have medications, uh, expediently," he sputtered.

One down, the CEO thought to himself.

Simpson straightened in his seat, attempting to regain his composure. "I believe at this time it may be prudent for me to yield my remaining minutes to Ms. Jennings," he suggested. "I know she has been waiting patiently for this hearing to arrive."

Collins was acutely aware of the Democratic Senator representing the State of Washington. And he knew she wasn't going to be a pushover like Simpson. In fact, Sandra Jennings had run entire political campaigns focused on pharmaceutical reforms, and there were even rumors that she had ambitions for the White House down the road. However, none of this could dampen the CEO's unwavering self-confidence.

"Thank you, Chairman Simpson," said Jennings, seated three places to his left. "Mr. Collins," she wasted no time taking aim at the man in the hot seat, “may I ask why you have agreed to speak to us openly today, as opposed to your previous appearance?”

Collins leaned into his microphone, holding eye contact with the forty-one-year-old, red-headed politician in her stylish cobalt blue pantsuit. “I came here to give you all a lesson.”

“Oh, is that so?” Jennings raised an eyebrow. “And what type of lesson should we be expecting, exactly?”

“Economics, capitalism, deficiencies in governmental procedure,” Collins began to list. “We’ll just have to see what we have time for.”

The Senator seemed to consider the statement for a moment, unwilling to fall prey to the bait. “Well, I’m certainly looking forward to it,” she flashed a smile that read as confidence to the cameras but conveyed the direct message of *Fuck You* to the smug CEO across the room.

“Mr. Collins,” Jennings continued, “do you believe that the United States Government has a duty to monitor and intervene in industries such as your own?”

“You’d have to be more specific.”

“Do you believe that if illegal activities are becoming rampant within an industry in our society, the American government has an obligation to intervene?”

“Certainly.”

“And you understand that we have laws that exist *solely* to limit a corporation’s ability to engage in monopolistic activities?”

“From a personal standpoint, I believe in a free market, but yes, I agree that there are other people who believe that this country should operate in that manner.”

“Are you suggesting that laws can be interpreted in the manner by which they best suit you, Mr. Collins?” she attempted to goad him.

Collins grinned. “Quite the opposite, actually...” he replied evenly. “I am merely *suggesting* that the only reason I am sitting here today is because you and your colleagues are doing such a thing.”

"Oh, is that so? Would you care to enlighten us, Mr. Collins?" She attempted to hand the CEO the metaphorical rope to publicly hang himself with.

The lawyers on each side of Collins tensed at the mere thought of their client fielding such an inquiry, but Collins was smarter than that.

"Ms. Jennings, what I know for certain is that Zinex has done nothing illegal and continues to follow the laws and mandates laid out by politicians like *you*," he suggested. "Which leads me to believe that I can only be here for one of two reasons. Either you people simply enjoy wasting my valuable time, or—and for the sake of our political system, I dearly hope this is not the case–you have misinterpreted your own legislation."

The Senator felt herself struggling to maintain her previously calm demeanor, but she had promised herself that she wouldn't bite, no matter how much of a gigantic, arrogant asshole Ken Collins truly was. Instead, she took a silent breath, located a piece of paper in front of her, and held it up in the same manner Simpson had. "I see here that Zinex purchased two corporations last year, Mr. Collins."

"We certainly acquired more than two," Collins nearly laughed.

"Yes, but the two *specific* corporations I am referring to had rival patents for a pair of life-saving medications," she explained, scanning the paper in her hand to the spot where she had written the drug names phonetically. "Diladrodin and Nycadoraphin," she announced. "Did I pronounce those correctly?"

"Close enough."

"Although Zinex now has both medications on its books, it only manufactures one. Is that correct?"

"I believe so."

"Why is that, Mr. Collins?"

"I imagine my team compared the two medications more extensively once they were acquired and felt the benefits of the first outweighed the negative side effects of the second."

"Is the negative side effect you are referring to the fact that it costs your company five times more to produce Nycadoraphin than its counterpart?"

"No," Collins denied the claim.

"I'll tell you what I think, Mr. Collins—and trust me, I'm not a high-profile, jet-setting CEO like yourself, *or* a scientist—but if I were going to spend millions of dollars acquiring a company, I'd probably conduct my due diligence *before* making a major purchase."

Collins stared at her with disdain.

"What you don't seem to be taking into account, Ms. Jennings, is that these companies we acquire hold hundreds, perhaps even thousands of patents, and it would be impossible to put every single medication under such a rigorous examination before acquisition. Certainly, we don't expect every product we acquire to be a home run."

Sandra sidestepped the bullshit response and continued forward. "After shifting to the sole production of Diladrodin, can you tell us what happened to its price?"

Collins hesitated. "It increased, I believe," he replied, knowing full well it had.

"Increased, you say?" Jennings grinned cagily. "Why don't you *educate* us on how much you increased the price, Mr. Collins?"

"Off the top of my head," the CEO continued to feign uncertainty, "I'd say about $100."

"Wow! $100! That seems like quite a substantial increase for a bottle of pills, don't you think?" the Senator responded, setting the stage perfectly. "Especially for the hardworking people out there who depend on that medication for their very lives. Wouldn't you agree?"

"I—"

"Oh, I'm sorry, excuse me," Jennings interrupted him with a flawless tone of passive aggression. "It wasn't $100 for an entire bottle of pills, was it?"

Collins didn't bother responding. He knew exactly where this was headed.

"Just to make sure I'm being accurate, Mr. Collins—as I'd like to avoid any further accusations of *misinterpretation*—it was, in fact, a $104 increase, *per pill*, wasn't it?" She tapped her finger sharply on the paper she had laid on the desk.

Collins cleared his throat. "That sounds accurate," he said, sounding wholly undisturbed by the gargantuan price hike.

"Can you tell us how much the company you acquired the patent from was charging for the same pill before the acquisition?"

"I can't recall off the top of my head."

"How does $9.25 sound to you, Mr. Collins? That's more than a 1000% increase," Jennings calculated for everyone in attendance. "How might you explain that to a single mother, or a retired veteran on a fixed income?"

Ken Collins straightened himself in his chair and scanned the faces of the committee members momentarily before returning his sharklike eyes to Jennings. "I suppose I would begin by asking that single mother if she knows just how little the United States government subsidizes her life-saving medication," Collins replied. "I bet you don't have *that* figure in front of you, do you?" Collins volleyed back the passive aggression. "How does zero dollars sound?!" he stated dramatically. "What exactly do *you* tell the single mother or the veteran? What do *you* tell people who have paid their taxes their entire lives, and yet—"

The television suddenly changed channels, and two middle-aged football commentators were announcing tonight's rosters as both teams took the field for kick-off.

"Can you believe that arrogant prick?" Mike asked Frank, holding the remote control. He took a swig of his beer as if he were trying to wash a bad taste out of his mouth from what he'd just witnessed. "That guy is so full of shit. He doesn't give a fuck about anything but money."

"He didn't seem too worried about being in the hot seat," Frank remarked.

“Yeah, the guys at work were saying that his company hasn’t technically broken any laws in terms of like monopoly, or price gouging, or whatever,” Mike explained. “So, I guess that’s why he could be so brazen.”

Frank nodded, placing his beer atop a circular coaster on the side table.

“That Senator from Washington started grilling him on his company’s role in the opioid epidemic, but she ran out of time. He didn’t seem as willing to trade punches with her on that topic, though.” Mike explained, settling himself on the far side of the sofa. “Oh well, forget that clown. Game’s on!” he shouted as the ball left the kicker’s foot and soared towards the endzone.

CHAPTER six

The cool, briny waters of the Pacific Ocean five miles off the Californian coast looked inviting, but Sara and Marla had elected to bask in the radiating warmth of the unobstructed sun instead. They were lounging on the shimmering bow of a twenty-six-foot boat that Steve and James had rented for the day. It had been a surprise that the girls very much appreciated.

"Hey, I meant to ask you," Marla spoke to Sara quietly enough not to be heard by their male companions, who were swimming somewhere off the stern. "Did you ever tell Steve that your dad is an FBI agent?"

"No. Why?" Sara's face tensed a little." Did he say something?"

"No, no," Marla quickly reassured her. "I was just curious."

"Oh my God, can you even imagine? '*Hey Steve, just so you know, my dad—who doesn't know I'm staying with you—happens to be an FBI agent and a former Marine.*' Yeah, I'm sure that would go over *really* well," Sara laughed. "I think I just told him he works for the government or something."

Just then, a hand reached up and took hold of the boarding ladder at the rear of the boat. A lean, bare-chested James, sporting a pair of powder-blue board shorts, ascended its rungs. He stepped his foot down onto the sunbaked deck and looked over at the two girls lying at the other end of the vessel.

"I'm just heading below deck to shower off the salt water," he called out over the sound of waves slapping against the boat's carbon fiber hull. "Can I get either of you another drink while I'm down there?"

"No thanks," Sara replied, holding up what was left of the slushy purple concoction she and Marla had created before posting up for their tanning session. "We're still working on these!"

James nodded and flashed a smile before disappearing down a set of narrow steps.

Marla sat up and slipped her feet into a pair of pink flip-flops.

"Where are you going?" Sara wondered, blocking the sun from her eyes with an outstretched hand.

"I could use a shower myself."

"There are two showers down there?"

"Nope..." Marla replied with a devilish smile, wrapping the lower half of her body in a soft, white beach towel.

Sara giggled, then flipped over onto her back. Soon, the combination of the sun's warmth and the rhythmic rocking of the boat put her to sleep.

* * * * *

A high-pitched screech from an overhead seagull roused Sara from her catnap. She craned her head back to where James and Marla had disappeared down the stairs earlier and found Steve leaning up against the boat's gunwale, staring at her intensely. The moment their eyes met, he averted his gaze, making her question whether he had only been enjoying the distant horizon behind her.

PING!

A text message suddenly arrived on Sara's cell phone, redirecting her attention. She sat up and reached her hand beneath a towel that was protecting the device from the sun's powerful UV rays.

'Just finished laundry and lunch,' a text from her mother read. Before Sara had the chance to reply, her phone chimed again. *'Heading to finish some work on the cabin.'* Then once more. *'What are u girls up to today?'*

This was her mother's usual texting style—a flurry of messages sent back-to-back-to-back. In fact, Frank had once suggested that Donna may be *'a pioneer in the field of stream-of-consciousness text messaging'*.

Sara typed a reply, *'Been at the beach all morning...beautiful weather...miss you guys!'*, electing to keep the message short and sweet, without any mention of the boat. As she sent the text, Marla and James suddenly reappeared from below deck, each carrying a round party platter full of snacks. Marla's tray held a pyramid of triangular sandwiches, while James' contained brightly colored tropical fruit.

"Who's hungry?!" Marla called out with her usual infectious enthusiasm. Steve pressed himself off the silver railing and selected a turkey on rye, thanking his server in the process. The trio made their way over to Sara, who set down her phone and chose a slice of juicy-looking pineapple and a few fresh strawberries before the group re-engaged in a conversation they'd been having earlier.

CHAPTER seven

Winston Percival, a *Technology and Engineering Logistics Specialist* for the FBI, emerged from a bank of silver elevators and began to make his way toward Frank and Mike, whose desks were located near the middle of the open-concept fourth floor of the Manhattan FBI building. Winston possessed a thin build, hair the color of freshly fallen snow, and the graceful gait of a man who had been raised in an upper-class English school system. He had been working on one of the underground levels of the building for many years before Frank and Mike were hired, and though he didn't look it, rumor had it that the Brit was well past his eightieth birthday. Spry, deeply loyal, and brilliantly intelligent, Frank and Mike had developed a tremendous amount of respect for their colleague. Although Mike seemed to have developed a predilection for incessantly trying to cause the older man as much grief as humanly possible.

Winston arrived at their desks.

"Do you have any idea how much these cost?" he questioned the pair, holding up a bird's nest of frayed black wiring connecting a pair of rectangular mechanical components, one of which contained a bullet hole.

Mike looked up from the report he was engaged with and studied the contraption. "Hmmm, not sure. Are we talking dollars or pounds, Jeeves?" He instantly attempted to push Winston's buttons.

"It took us two months to develop a microphone that would fit inside without disrupting the signal."

"You got the wrong guys, Winny," Mike continued to feign ignorance. He stood from his chair, inspecting the contents of his coworker's hands more carefully. "Nope. I don't remember any microphones or modems—"

"You being unable to *remember* something is hardly surprising," Winston replied. "In fact, if I'm being completely honest, I find it absolutely astonishing that you can even remember to unzip your fly before urinating."

Frank grinned. "I'll make sure we're more careful in the future," he assured Winston.

"That would be much appreciated," Winston nodded at Frank before dumping the pile of useless debris into the garbage bin next to Mike's desk. "Now, if you two have a spare moment, there's something I'd like to show you."

*****

The *Science, Engineering, and Technology* floor never failed to amaze Frank and Mike whenever they had the opportunity to visit. The division housed twenty of the FBI's finest scientific minds and always seemed to contain the sweet scent of freshly polished stainless steel combined with a hint of burning solder.

Frank and Mike exited the elevator and followed their host across the smooth concrete floor. Pairs of bespectacled eyeballs stared curiously at the two special agents from all directions, like a herd of deer gazing at a pair of hikers who suddenly appeared on a secluded back-country trail in the middle of a densely thicketed forest.

"This way, gentlemen..." Winston led them into a room containing a large, sterile stainless-steel table with a treasure trove of electronic contraptions on top. "I recently began working on something after you mentioned the trouble you've been having during your motel room stakeouts."

Frank nodded, recalling a particular bust.

"We have another one lined up next week," Mike informed Winston. "It sounds like a shipment of firearms is arriving from Montreal."

Winston cleared his throat. "Well, in that case, I may be willing to *lend* you this particular piece of equipment," he said with a touch of hesitation in his voice. "If you give me your word that you will do your best to bring it back in one piece."

"Oh boy, Frankie! A new toy!" Mike said with excitement. "What is it, Winny?"

Winston remained steadfast, waiting for his condition to be met.

"Okay, fine, fine, fine," Mike said with the exasperated tone of a child wanting to open his first gift on Christmas morning. "I promise I won't shoot it, or smash it, or blow it to pieces."

Winston turned to Frank. "You know I'm going to hold you responsible for his actions..."

"That's a tall order." Frank grinned. "But I'll try to keep an eye on him."

"Very well then. As you know, criminals are becoming more sophisticated, constantly adjusting their tactics and learning our surveillance patterns. In the past, during a standard motel operation, you'd simply be able to listen from a neighboring room."

Frank nodded. "Yeah, but they've learned to rent out the neighboring units and conduct their business in the centralized space."

"And it seems like everybody has access to advanced bug detection equipment nowadays, too. It's completely taken away our ability to put anything directly inside the meeting room before they arrive," Mike added.

"Precisely," said Winston, opening a drawer and removing a sleek black telescope-shaped device that was ten inches long. "If you'll follow me, please," he directed the pair, making his way back towards the door.

The trio arrived at an elevator on the opposite side of the floor from where they had arrived. Winston entered first, selecting an unmarked button near the bottom of the panel. Once Frank and Mike had filed inside, the doors closed, and the elevator descended deeper into the ancient bowels of the building. A few moments later, the doors reopened.

The ceiling on this level was as high as a gymnasium, and the space looked like a film set from an old-time Western. The three men exited the elevator and began walking down *Main Street* between towering plywood structures. On the left was a bank. Next to it, a rough-and-tumble saloon complete with brass rails and spittoons. On the other side of the street stood an apothecary, next to a general store, whose windows and doors had been shuttered. Each structure was riddled with hundreds of bullet holes. Agents had once used this level for marksmanship practice, but it had been decommissioned long ago. The group arrived at a two-story, six-room structure at the end of the street. A chalkboard sign was affixed to the front, identifying it as *The Ritz Motel.*

"Michael, if you would be so kind as to place yourself in the central room on the ground floor," Winston directed.

"Wait a second..." Mike looked suspicious. "You're not going to fill it up with water, or try to electrocute me, or some other crazy bullshit, are you? I know exactly how you weirdos like to get your kicks down here in the nerd dungeon."

"Not this time..." A sly grin spread across Winston's face as he remembered a few of the glorious instances when he had tricked Mike into being an unsuspecting guinea pig. "Frank, please follow me."

The two men made their way up a set of rickety wooden steps to the upper level of *The Ritz.*

*****

Frank and Winston found themselves inside the central room on the second floor directly above the space Mike now occupied. The room was dark and mostly empty, except for a four-rung aluminum step ladder in the center. Winston instructed Frank to remain at the entrance while he extracted a thin braid of copper-colored wire from one end of the telescopic device. He walked over to the ladder, ascended its rungs, and attached the tubular object to a chrome hook embedded in the ceiling. The device was now suspended six or seven feet from the floor. Winston climbed down, folded the ladder, and leaned it against the wall. He reconvened with Frank near the entrance and produced a small remote control from his pocket.

"Each of these numbered buttons corresponds to a surrounding wall," Winston explained to Frank. "And this one *here* is for the floor itself." Winston pressed an additional button, causing a tiny glass bead to silently protrude from the bottom of the suspended device. He took a small step back towards the wall. Frank did the same.

Suddenly, the glass sphere began to radiate an iridescent blue light that was cast onto the surrounding walls, reminding Frank of the nebular projections he had seen in the back of a movie theater during his childhood. The azure illumination quickly transformed into a laser-sharp grid of white squares that changed dimensions as they rotated around the walls in a technological waltz.

"It's reading its surroundings..." Winston whispered to Frank.

Frank turned and looked at the wall directly behind him, noticing that the pattern was completely unbroken where his shadow ought to be. "This thing isn't frying our balls or anything, is it?" Frank inquired, half-jokingly.

"You aren't planning on having any more children, are you?" Winston replied evenly, still focused on his dangling device.

"Uhhh, no..."

"I'm only kidding," Winston reassured him with a smile. "The device is completely harmless."

Just then, the rotating grid blinked three times and disappeared.

"What happened?" Frank looked around the walls. "Did we break it?"

Winston shook his head. "The device has completed its initial measurements and transitioned into a wavelength outside the visible spectrum."

Winston handed the remote to Frank. *E1, C2, E3, C4, and C5* were flashing on the tiny screen.

"What's all that mean?" Frank wondered.

"Those are alphanumeric indicators that explain to the user that the device has successfully scanned two of the four surrounding walls, hence the C2 and the C4 you see there," he explained, pointing at the wall directly across the room and then wrapping a knuckle on the plywood behind them. "And the C5 indicates that the room below our feet has also been successfully scanned."

"And what do the two E's stand for? Error?"

Winston nodded.

"What's the problem with those two walls?"

"To complete a scan, there must be defined parameters behind each of the walls so that the device is able to reflect data back to itself.

Frank paused for a moment, contemplating. "So, it needs an enclosed space on the other side."

"Exactly."

"Does it have any other limitations?"

"We attempted to penetrate the walls on that bank safe mock-up on the second floor," Winston recalled. "The density and thickness resulted in error codes, but for the building materials you'll commonly find out in the field, it won't be an issue."

"So now, what? We can listen in on the three rooms without error codes at the same time now, or something?" There was a touch of disappointment in Frank's voice.

A smile appeared on Winston's face. "Oh, it can do *much* more than that," he assured him. "Try selecting C5 on the remote."

"That's the one for the floor, right?" Frank recalled, scrolling through his options until the C5 was highlighted. Just before he pressed the *ACTIVATE* button, Frank heard what sounded to be Mike's muffled voice coming up from the room below.

"Am I supposed to just stand in here all day?" Mike shouted impatiently at the ceiling. *"There's not even any food in this fridge!"* he complained, shutting the door of the non-operational appliance.

Frank pressed the button, and instantaneously, the floor vanished beneath his feet. The visual shock was enough to cause his knees to bend, and he placed a hand on the wall behind himself for balance. *"Holy shit..."* he whispered as he attempted to regain his bearings. He and Winston were now looking down at Mike as if the floor didn't exist. Mike hollered up at the ceiling above his head again, only now his previously muffled voice was clear as day.

"You jokers invite me down here and then ditch me," Mike complained, moving around the room, childishly touching every surface and object he could get his hands on. Just then, his elbow contacted an empty flower vase that had been resting on a table, sending it crashing onto the floor. Mike froze and looked around the empty room. Satisfied with his solidarity, he lifted the corner of a brown area rug and gently kicked the shattered earthenware beneath it.

Frank looked over at Winston, who was already shaking his head.

"Hey, Mike!" Frank hollered down to his partner. "When you're done breaking shit down there, you have got to come check this out!"

Mike's head snapped up toward the ceiling, and a look of surprise and guilt spread across his face.

* * * * *

Winston removed the telescopic device from the hook and descended the step ladder, having just finished demonstrating the object's full range of abilities to both Frank and Mike.

"That thing is wild," Mike said for the third time since he had joined the two men on the upper floor of the mock motel.

"How is it that there was no disturbance in any of the images when we were moving around the room between the device and the wall?" Frank inquired.

"This technology uses a simultaneous collection of data, both reflected as well as through line of sight," Winston attempted to explain. "Therefore, each projection you see might have hundreds, perhaps even thousands, of triangulations that are being broadcast back to home base at any given moment. I modeled it after the visual cortex of the human brain."

Mike looked as if he had understood a grand total of three words in Winston's statement.

"In what way?" Frank asked.

"As you may be aware," Winston said to Frank, "*or not...*" he looked at Mike, "our vision evolved to search for patterns in our surroundings. We have blind spots—due to the position of our optic nerves—however, we are essentially unimpeded by them because our brains have the ability to fill them in unconsciously.

"Yes, yes, indubitably..." Mike mocked him in a high-brow English accent.

Winston ignored the jest and continued.

"In a similar way, this device harnesses previously collected data to *fill in* any discrepancies caused by our movements or signal blockages. In fact, *motion* actually forces MARTIN to collect additional images, thereby further stabilizing the—"

"Whoa, whoa, whoa. Hold on a second," Mike suddenly cut him off, a smile forming on his face. "Who's Martin?"

"Well, the device, of course," Winston responded evenly. "It's an acrony—"

"Holy shit, Frank! Did you hear that?" Mike turned to his partner, mouth agape. "Winston named his robot!" Mike began to laugh hysterically. "Winston needed a friend down here, so he named his fucking robot! Hahahaha!"

Frank decided to step in before the inevitable back-and-forth escalated. "Very impressive, Winston."

"Thank you, Frank. Once I get it fully calibrated, I'll drop it off at your desk." Winston said, checking his watch. "Oh, you'll have to excuse me. I'm running late for another meeting. Frank, would you be so kind as to escort your dim-witted troglodyte of a partner back to the elevator, please? I wouldn't want him to get lost."

"Will do." Frank grinned.

Winston slipped the telescopic device into the hip pocket of his lab coat and then quickly disappeared out of the room.

"Hey, Frank..." Mike said, looking around the empty walls.

"Yeah, buddy?"

"What in the hell is a troglodyte?" he asked with the goofiest of grins on his face.

CHAPTER eight

"Explain to me again exactly why I'm down here in Mexico wasting my fucking time, Derek?" Ken Collins demanded into his cell phone, causing the young attorney seated next to him in the back of the moving town car to flinch.

"Because the acquisition contract specifically stated that an in-person meeting must occur before the deal was finalized," Zinex's CFO, Derek Crenshaw, explained.

"And why couldn't you go? Or Barbara? Or literally *anyone* else?"

"They specifically indicated that you be the one to attend," Crenshaw reported, attempting to calm his boss like a fussy toddler in need of a nap.

Collins rolled his eyes.

"Considering the price we got," the CFO continued, *"I think it's well worth it. In fact, Zinex is the only company that has ever even gotten a sniff at purchasing those laboratories down there, so please, just sign the papers this afternoon, make your way back to the hotel, and get yourself some room service. You'll be back in New York by tomorrow af—"*

Collins ended the call abruptly and turned his attention to the blonde, baby-faced lawyer next to him. Scott Tremblay had recently graduated at the top of his class from Yale Law School, resulting in multiple job offers from numerous corporate giants, including Zinex. However, at this moment, he was simply trying to appear busy by perusing legal documents in the hopes of avoiding any unnecessary conversation with the aggressively unpleasant man sitting to his left. Prior to the trip, Scott had only heard rumors about the CEO's distasteful behavior, but he was now beginning to fully grasp why none of his colleagues had volunteered to make the cross-border trek.

"Don't drag this fucking meeting on any longer than it needs to be," Collins barked at him. "We get in. We get out. You got it?"

"Yes, sir." Scott nodded sheepishly, his eyes never leaving the papers.

The driver banked left, and the car descended a gray concrete ramp into the underground parking garage of a modern, glass-faced, ten-story high-rise, eventually coming to a stop in front of a pair of elevators. Collins waited impatiently for the valet to open his door, then stepped out, straightened his tie, and proceeded forward with Tremblay in tow.

"What floor?" the CEO demanded once they were inside the elevator.

"Ten."

Collins selected the appropriate button and then immediately wiped his finger on the arm of Tremblay's suit jacket, as if the mere thought of touching a public surface in Mexico repulsed him. The young attorney pretended not to notice, and the doors slid shut. A bronze placard with Spanish writing was mounted on the wall, listing the businesses housed inside the building. They included a dentist, a consulting firm, two accountants, an advertising agency, and a medical supply distributor. The top floor—where the two Americans were headed—was simply labeled *OCUPADO*.

"Remember what I told you: in and out," Collins reiterated his demand as the elevator slowed to a halt. The doors opened, revealing a cordoned-off reception area with a pristine white marble floor in front of a frosted glass wall. Everything looked bright, fresh, and clean. An expansive walnut-colored desk was occupied by two olive-skinned twin brunettes with tight ponytails. The woman on the right was typing on her keyboard, while her sister was finishing a phone call.

Collins stepped off the elevator and aimed himself toward the desk. Tremblay followed. The secretary on the left, wearing a fitted black sleeveless dress, set down the phone and greeted the Americans with a bright smile framed by vibrant raspberry lipstick.

"Good afternoon," she greeted them in perfect English. "How may I help you today?"

"Why, *hello* there," Collins responded jovially, returning the smile.

Tremblay stared, shocked by his boss' near sociopathic ability to transform his demeanor from one minute to the next to suit his needs. It was like observing a chameleon.

"Ken Collins," he introduced himself with bravado. "I'm here to see, uh, Mr. Garcia, I believe it is." He wrapped his knuckles playfully on the desk.

The young woman nodded, then shifted her attention to the calendar on her monitor. This gave the CEO a moment to glance over at the pair of white leather sofas on the other side of the reception area. There, a serious-looking Mexican man with mocha skin and a razor-shaved head was seated on the right couch. He was dressed in a well-tailored charcoal suit and reading a *La Prensa* newspaper. Collins observed as the man flipped from one page to the next, exposing intricate sleeve tattoos that ended just above his wrists.

"Mr. Davidson is ready for you," the receptionist announced to the pair. "Please follow me."

"With pleasure," Collins replied, turning his attention away from the man across the room, relishing the opportunity to ogle the young woman's curvaceous backside as the group made their way to a securitized door that would lead them further into the tenth floor. After entering a six-digit code, the receptionist pushed the frosted glass door inward and led the Americans down a tightly carpeted hallway. Every office that flanked their path seemed to be unoccupied.

"Not exactly a beehive of activity in here today, is it?" Collins commented, continuing to leer at the receptionist.

Not offering a response, she opened the last door on the left and made her way inside. Collins and Tremblay followed, entering a medium-sized conference room with a large table surrounded by half a dozen high-backed leather office chairs. Beyond the table were floor-to-ceiling windows that offered an unobstructed view of the majestic mountains in the distance. Two men wearing nearly matching navy-blue suits stood at the glass, appearing to be enjoying the panorama.

"Mr. Collins and Mr. Tremblay have arrived..." the receptionist announced to the pair, who turned and offered welcoming smiles to their north-of-the-border visitors. "There is coffee, tea, and water on the table in the corner over there, along with some pastries," the receptionist explained to the Americans. "And if you require anything else, please let me know," she added, before disappearing out the door.

"I'm so happy we have the chance to meet in person," greeted the now-approaching Marcus Garcia, the balding fifty-year-old head of HTB Industrials—the company from which Zinex was purchasing the labs. He reached out and shook his guests' hands with vigor. "This sure is exciting, isn't it? After all those phone calls and emails. To finally be here all together in one room," he beamed. "Oh, my goodness! Where *are* my manners?" he apologized. "This, of course, is Henry Alvarez, one of HTB's attorneys." The overweight lawyer behind Garcia stepped forward, resulting in another round of introductory handshakes.

"Please, please, why don't we all have a seat?" Garcia suggested.

Collins and Tremblay took their places across the table from their counterparts. The Mexican lawyer spoke first, with a more pronounced accent than his colleague. "As you are aware, we were able to sign the majority of the paperwork digitally."

"Yeah, it almost makes the need for a face-to-face meeting like this *pointless,"* Collins responded, unable to help himself.

Picking up on the passive-aggressiveness, Garcia stepped in. "Yes, you'll have to excuse the insistence," he apologized, "but the *powers that be* were adamant that I get you down here."

"Sounds like I'm not the only one with a pain-in-the-ass executive board," Collins mused.

Garcia seemed to hesitate. "Something like that..." he said with a grin.

Just then, Tremblay felt his boss stomp on his shoe beneath the table, jolting him into action. "Oh, uh, yes, I have the final documentation here," he said, referencing his briefcase, "so if we are ready to complete a final read-through and collect the outstanding signatures, we can get everything buttoned up quickly."

* * * * *

Thirty minutes later, the door next to the reception desk opened.

"I'd like to thank you gentlemen once more for making the trip down here to see us," Garcia said with a smile as he led the Americans toward the same elevator they had arrived in. The receptionist rose from her desk and joined the moving formation.

"Your town car is waiting for you in the parking garage," she announced from the back of the pack.

Collins looked back and flashed her another greasy smile. "Perfect," he replied, taking a final opportunity to look her up and down.

"And you're certain you can't join us for dinner tonight?" Garcia pressed the CEO a second time.

Collins noticed that the man in the charcoal suit was still sitting on the couch, engaged with his newspaper. "As I already said," he redirected his focus back to Garcia, "I haven't been feeling well since I arrived this morning. It's probably best I just head back to my hotel room and get some rest."

"I completely understand," Garcia replied, as the two Americans stepped inside the elevator. "Have a safe flight tomorrow, gentlemen."

"Thank you," Tremblay replied graciously, while Collins offered only a bland nod. The elevator doors closed.

"I think I might have some Advil and Vitamin C back at the hotel in my toiletry kit," the young attorney said as the elevator descended toward the parking garage.

"Huh?"

"For your illness, sir?"

"I'm not sick, you idiot. I don't get sick," the narcissistic businessman claimed. "I just don't want to eat with *those* people."

"Oh," Tremblay responded quietly, "I see."

The doors opened to the parking garage, and they climbed inside the idling town car.

"The less time I have to spend awake in this shithole country, the better," Collins doubled down as the vehicle crept forward.

Tremblay opened the manila envelope containing the documents from the meeting and removed the freshly signed pages, causing Collins to look over.

"And you can stop pretending to read all that shit, too," he said, pulling out his cell phone and beginning to scroll through emails. "I have absolutely no desire to talk to you either."

Tremblay's face turned red with embarrassment.

* * * * *

Collins sat on the edge of his hotel suite's king-sized bed and loosened his Stefano Ricci paisley-patterned tie with one hand. With the other, he scrolled through the channel guide on the television while a half-eaten tray of room service sat idle on the table across the room. Finding nothing of interest to watch, he turned the television off, stood, and elected to take a shower instead. As he approached the bathroom, a knock suddenly sounded at the door.

"Jesus Christ. Can't I get a fucking moment's peace?" Collins whined, redirecting himself to the front of the upscale suite. He opened the door and discovered an intense-looking Mexican in his thirties, dressed in a charcoal-colored suit, with a shaved head and dark, unflinching eyes.

"Yeah?" Collins questioned the stranger curtly.

"Are you alone?" the man responded in a gruff, heavily-accented voice.

"Huh?" The CEO's eyes squinted, and his face scowled.

"Tremblay with you?" the Mexican specified in a slow, unnatural cadence. "Or are you alone?"

"Who the f—" Collins' memory suddenly caught up. "Wait a minute... you're that guy from the office building earlier today. You were reading the newspaper on the couch."

The serious-looking visitor didn't offer a response; instead, he elected to stick with his stone-cold stare, causing the CEO to default back to his usual abrasive demeanor.

"What do you care if I'm alone? You work for Garcia or something?"

Still no response.

Collins finally lost what little patience he possessed. "Listen, asshole, unless Garcia sent you here with a bunch of hookers and blow, I'm not interested. So fucking beat it." Collins slammed the door in his face. *"Fucking idiot,"* he muttered under his breath, spying on the stranger through the peephole.

The menacing man stood in place for a few more seconds, then finally disappeared. Collins shook his head and abandoned the door, making his way back to the bathroom. He had barely gotten inside and removed his dress shoes when a knock sounded at the door again.

"For fuck's sake!" Collins hollered, now fully aggravated. He stomped across the carpeted hotel room floor in socked feet and set his eye to the peephole once more. To his surprise, he found a much older, much shorter Mexican on the other side of the door. He was wearing a beige fedora that matched his vintage three-piece suit. Collins hadn't planned on reopening the door, but the sudden body swap piqued his interest enough for him to do so.

"Well, you've aged terribly," Collins said to the stranger, smirking at his own joke.

"Good evening, Mr. Collins," the aging Mexican greeted him in a gravelly voice, with a calm cadence that flowed like maple syrup. "I hope Rico didn't startle you, but I needed to make sure that our conversation tonight would be, how do you say, confidential."

The visitor looked familiar to Collins, but he couldn't quite place him.

"Please allow me to introduce myself," the man continued. "My name is Ernesto Diaz, and I was hoping you might be so kind as to invite me inside."

The second half of the man's dialogue hadn't even registered with Collins because as soon as he had revealed his name, a mental reel of newspaper articles and internet videos began to cycle through the CEO's mind. Each story contained the bloody exploits of cartel turf wars, images rife with murderous decapitations, and news anchors speaking of the endless supply of drugs, guns, and money flowing back and forth across the border. Collins realized that the stranger standing in the hall was the most dangerous and powerful cartel boss in Mexico's history.

"Mr. Collins?" the gangster prompted, helping to bring the CEO back to the present. The henchman with the charcoal suit was now standing behind Diaz. "I assume by the look on your face that you know who I am?"

Collins nodded slowly.

"If you'd be so kind to invite us in..."

"Uh, yeah, sure," Collins finally agreed, attempting to pull himself together as best as he could. He opened the door fully and stepped back to make room.

"Gracias," Ernesto tipped the brim of his stiff fedora with a finger as he entered the suite, with the muscle following closely behind.

"Would you like to have a seat?" Collins offered.

Diaz parked himself at the table with the room service tray, while his compatriot began checking around the room to ensure the privacy of the conversation. Once satisfied, he returned to the door and stood guard.

Collins settled into the seat across from Diaz, who had already removed his hat and placed it on his lap. The old man ran his fingers through his thinning gray hair and stared intently at the American, studying him.

"Can I offer you guys something to drink?" Collins elected to break the silence, unsure of the proper etiquette for entertaining the head of a massive criminal empire. He turned and looked at the unblinking statue at the door.

"No, no, that is quite alright," Diaz answered for both of them. "I apologize for my unexpected intrusion this evening, Mr. Collins. But I found it necessary to come speak with you, considering it was I who brought you down here in the first place."

Collins couldn't wrap his head around the statement.

"You see, Mr. Collins, I am, how you might say, *associated* with the company you acquired the labs from today."

The CEO's heart skipped a beat.

"Six months ago," the kingpin continued, "I became aware that an American corporation was using pressure tactics in an attempt to force negotiations with HTB. As you might imagine, I was not very impressed."

"I had no idea that someone of your, uh, *stature* was involved," Collins said, swallowing despite his parched throat. "Frankly, I would have hoped that my due diligence team would have been adept enough to discover such a connection." The vengeful businessman was already thinking about who he would fire when he returned home.

"Now, Mr. Collins..." Diaz leaned back in his chair and crossed a leg. "Do you really think I would have gotten to where I am today if my business connections could be easily identified?" He raised a suggestive eyebrow.

The naïveté of his statement dawned on Collins.

"I'm going to be completely honest with you," the cartel boss continued. "When I caught wind of your tactics, I had originally planned on sending a few of my American associates to your penthouse at 1895 Mariana Drive, to express just how displeased I was with you."

The sound of his personal address coming from the aging gangster's mouth nearly buckled Collins' usually iron-clad resolve. "Listen, we only just signed the papers today," he began to backpedal immediately. "I can have the agreement dissolved. It's no problem. In fact, I'll get Tremblay in here right now. I'll get him on the phone and—"

"Someone showed me a video of you from the internet, Mr. Collins," Diaz continued, ignoring his offer. "In it, you were being questioned by a governmental committee. Do you know the video to which I am referring?"

Collins slowly nodded, thinking back to that day in the muggy chamber.

"Those politicians sat behind their fancy desks, questioned you publicly, attempting to pick apart your actions and destroy your character," Diaz recounted. "Do you know what I saw that day, Mr. Collins?"

Collins glanced over his shoulder at the henchman behind him and then back across the table. He shook his head.

"I saw a man who wasn't afraid to stand his ground."

The statement seemed to alleviate some of the tension squeezing Collins' chest.

"Do you know what else I saw? I saw a man I believed I could work with..."

Collins' eyebrows raised involuntarily. "*Work with*? What do you mean? So, you *don't* want to kill this deal?"

"Quite the opposite." Diaz flashed a cigar-stained smile. "Of course, my closest associates believe that any interest in a man like you is completely *loco*, but the way I see it, you've already had the spotlight on you twice now, and both times, you came out unscathed. I highly doubt your government is keen on being publicly embarrassed for a third time."

The statement reinvigorated the CEO's self-assuredness. "Yeah, they had no idea who they were dealing with," he suggested. "But what could you possibly want with me? With Zinex?"

"The man you met with today..."

"Garcia?"

Diaz nodded. "He and I had a standing agreement in place. I won't go into specifics, but when he needed something—a building permit, a rezoning application, to pass an inspection—I would ensure these things were *taken care of*, if you understand my meaning, Mr. Collins?"

He did.

"Competition in his industry was also reduced substantially," the cartel boss explained as he reached out a crooked finger, touching the rim of the half-consumed can of Coca-Cola near the edge of the table. "And in exchange for these *privileges,* Mr. Garcia used the vendors and suppliers that were suggested to him. He and I built, what you might call, a symbiosis relationship."

"Symbiotic," the CEO corrected out of habit.

"Yes, of course." Diaz grinned.

Collins still didn't understand how any of this could pertain to him. "The thing is, Mr. Diaz... Zinex is a massive corporation and has long-standing contracts with our suppliers. Transitioning to a group of unknown vendors would be extremely dif—"

"You misunderstand me," Diaz cut him off politely. "I am not interested in the same arrangement I had with Mr. Garcia. If that were the case, I would have kept the situation as it was and not allowed the acquisition to proceed. What I am suggesting moving forward is something...*different.*"

"Different, how?"

"I assume Zinex is planning to use these newly acquired labs to manufacture pharmaceuticals, yes?"

"Of course."

"And you will be conducting scientific research as well, I imagine?"

"That's how all these multifunctional labs operate nowadays." Collins nodded.

"And when your chemists perform testing trials, what exactly happens to the waste products?"

"Well—"

"For example," Diaz continued. "If a batch happened to become *tainted,* or it didn't meet the exact specifications for the final product. What happens to those types of waste products?"

Collins thought for a second. "You mean, like if the chemical composition was off?"

The kingpin nodded.

"Well, it all depends, I guess. In some instances, we can separate individual compounds to reuse them for subsequent experiments. But if I'm being honest, nowadays, it's rarely worth the effort. So, generally speaking, the waste products are just taken away by our disposal company."

The Mexican nodded as if it were the exact answer he had been looking for. "From what I understand, these waste products can be quite substantial in quantity, yes?"

"For sure," the CEO confirmed with a nod. "But that's just what we call a *built-in* cost of development. In the end, we just pass those extra expenses on to the consumer."

"What would you say if I told you there was a disposal company here in Mexico that I think you should seriously consider using, Mr. Collins?"

"Well, I—"

"First, let me assure you that this particular corporation has an exemplary track record that spans back many years and can withstand the most rigorous scrutiny and due diligence that your people could apply."

Collins leaned forward and pressed the tip of his finger against his lips.

"In fact," Diaz continued, "when the time comes for you to choose a disposal vendor down here, I would even go so far as to encourage you to hold an open competition, and I will *guarantee* that this company will outshine the others and beat the best bid by at least twenty percent."

The CEO's head tilted ever so slightly.

"I'm sure savings like that would be greatly appreciated by your shareholders."

Collins was impressed. The cartel boss had obviously done his homework on the pharmaceutical industry. "And how exactly would this disposal company operate?"

"A majority of the waste products would be disposed of in typical fashion."

"And the rest?"

"Perhaps it may be best we avoid specifics at this time." Diaz grinned.

"I only ask because if some of the substances haven't even passed trials, there's a good chance they wouldn't be standardized from one disposal batch to the next."

"That won't be a problem, Mr. Collins."

The wheels began to turn inside the CEO's head. "Oh, I see what you're looking to do—"

"I'm not *looking to do* anything," Diaz stopped him, still wearing the grin, "I am simply *suggesting* that you consider a very reputable disposal company when the time comes." The kingpin uncrossed his leg and removed a sleek black fountain pen from his coat pocket. Leaning forward, he scribbled on the back of an unused napkin, turned it over, and slid it across the table. Collins lifted the square, examining the figure scrawled on its backside.

“If we proceed, *that* is the amount of money you can expect to be deposited into an untraceable offshore account with your name at the end of every month.”

Collins’ eyes darted up from the napkin.

“And all I have to do is hire a company with a legitimate track record, who can underbid its competitors, and will take responsibility for the waste products once they leave our facilities.” He looked down at the napkin once more. “Am I understanding that correctly?”

Diaz nodded, knowing the hook had been set.

“I’m in,” announced the greedy businessman. “Let’s do this fucking thing.”

CHAPTER nine

Sara was on the phone with her mother when she entered a large bathroom on the second floor of James and Steve's two-story house in Temecula. She closed the door behind her.

"Hi, Mrs. Adler!" Marla called out from her place in front of a rectangular mirror that sat above a pair of twin porcelain vessel sinks, where she was brushing her teeth. James was downstairs somewhere, and Steve had left the house early that morning, planning on meeting the others at the nightclub after they ate dinner.

"Yes, the hotel has been great..." Sara lied, casting a guilt-ridden glance at Marla's reflection. She felt relieved that this phone call had taken place at a time when her father was not home, as he seemed to be particularly attuned to detecting her fabrications, no matter how thoroughly she prepared herself. "How's the cabin coming along?" she changed the subject.

"Nearly done," Donna reported. "These DIY kits go up so fast. It's just like building a giant jigsaw puzzle. I'll be sure to send you some pictures once it's complete."

"Sounds good! And make sure that Daddy takes a break once in a while," she said, knowing her father's dogged tenacity for completing a task once it had begun.

Just then, there was a soft tapping on the bathroom door. Marla, who had just plugged in her curling iron, set it down and made her way over. Pulling open the door, she found James standing in the hall. His long blonde hair was tied up into a temporary man-bun, and he wore trendy blue jeans and a black, button-up dress shirt. A thin silver chain hung around his neck. Marla held a finger up to her lips.

"Well, Mom, Mar and I are just about to head out for something to eat," Sara said, attempting to bring the conversation to a speedy conclusion.

"Oh, so soon?" Donna replied. "I'm just kidding, sweetie," Sara could hear her mother's smile through the phone. "Send me a text in the morning if you can, okay? And be safe tonight. Love you guys!"

"Love you too, Mom. Tell Daddy I miss him! Bye!"

"I didn't mean to rush your call," James apologized once Sara had hung up. "I just wanted to let you know that our reservation is for seven, and it's probably going to take at least an hour to get there with the traffic."

"Let's get a move on, girl!" Sara prompted Marla, scooping a bag of colorful cosmetics into her hands.

"We'll be down in ten minutes," Marla assured James, giving him a quick kiss on the cheek.

CHAPTER ten

Frank and Mike entered one of the countless beige conference rooms inside the FBI building in Manhattan. There were a dozen or so other special agents and analysts already seated in a space that could hold fifty. The two partners climbed the first few steps of the auditorium-style seating and found their usual places near the middle of the room.

"Any idea who won the football pool this week?" Mike asked Frank as he surveyed the growing crowd for familiar faces.

"Not sure," Frank shook his head. "I think it was between Rawlings and Dougie C. going into the final game, but I was out of the running long before that."

"Rawly!" Mike hollered across the room, having spotted the curly-haired forty-three-year-old data analyst who was currently working for the National Cyber Investigative Task Force.

"I *fuckin'* lost," Tim Rawlings broke the news to Mike in a downtrodden Brooklyn accent, perfectly anticipating his question.

"You took the Giants?" Mike winced.

"I figured you gotta support the hometown boys, *right?"* the analyst attempted to explain himself with a dejected shrug of his shoulders.

"I guess that depends on whether you like winning money or not," Mike chuckled, causing Rawly to drop his head in mock shame.

Just then, Jack Morrison, a newly promoted Assistant Director, entered the room. He was chatting with a short, bob-headed female agent, whom Frank and Mike didn't recognize.

"Good morning, ladies and gentlemen!" Morrison greeted the group with his usual upbeat energy, eliciting a half-hearted echo back from the crowd. He had been leading these briefings for the past few months, ever since his predecessor's retirement.

Jack was over six feet tall, lean, with a military-style haircut similar to Frank's. Approaching sixty, he could pass for forty-five, thanks in part to his strict diet and extreme physical training regimen. In fact, during his tenure as an agent, Mike had started a tradition of sending the newly hired Quantico graduates down to the gym to join Jack for his morning workouts. Without fail, the shellshocked youngsters would be seen limping back to their desks after one of the AD's gladiator-style training sessions, inevitably sending Mike into stitches across the bullpen.

"I've asked a few different divisions to be here today," Jack explained. "That way, we should be able to collect a varied perspective moving forward."

The lights dimmed, and an overhead projector attached to the ceiling flashed to life, causing the crowd to collectively straighten in their seats. An image of half a dozen eighteenth and nineteenth-century oil paintings appeared on the screen at the front of the room. The artwork was propped up against a white wall of what seemed to be a customs checkpoint.

"As I mentioned in the briefing email," the AD continued, "there seems to be a significant increase in the number of high-value artworks being transported across our southern border recently. Intelligence indicates that one of the cartels is involved."

"They're stealing them?" inquired a stocky-looking agent on the left side of the room, sporting a thick black beard and rimless eyeglasses.

"That's a negative," Morrison shook his head. "And that's what makes all this particularly interesting."

"What, are they opening a fucking museum down there?" Mike chimed in, garnering laughs from his peers.

Jack smiled and pressed a button on the remote control in his hand. The image on the screen was swapped for a decades-old mugshot of Ernesto Diaz.

"I'm sure most of you are familiar with this man..." Morrison said, allowing the image to be displayed for a few seconds before proceeding to a much more recent surveillance photo that had been taken by the CIA during a stakeout in Mexico City. In this image, Ernesto and his brother, Dennis, were exiting a pair of oversized wooden doors at the front of an upscale restaurant in the Polanco neighborhood. "And for anybody who has been living under a rock, let me introduce you to the Diaz brothers, the most powerful and brutal kingpins in cartel history." Jack changed the image once more. Ernesto now stood proudly between two Renaissance-era paintings balanced on easels, wearing an ominous look on his face. "What you may not know about our little friend here is that for the last couple of decades, he has amassed one of the largest private art collections in the entire world."

"For what purpose?" asked a handsome, green-eyed Indian American agent three rows behind Frank and Mike.

"Well, for starters, he seems to have a genuine interest in it," the AD reported. "But recently, we believe that he may be using his art collection as a means of wealth diversification. Massive piles of cash have become a headache since the cartels began to consolidate themselves."

"I could use a headache..." Mike whispered to Frank, poking him in the arm with his elbow.

"What's our play on this, then?" asked a serious-looking female with short strawberry-blonde hair in the front row.

"At this time, we don't have one," Jack admitted. "For now, I want to continue collecting information. Our cyber division is going to be monitoring online chatter. Intelligence will be working on the chains of custody. As for our agents in the field, I want you to start leaning on some of our informants with cartel connections to see if we can generate some leads without tipping our hand. With all that, I think we should be able to start *painting a picture* of how this network is operating by our next briefing." Morrison grinned. "Dismissed."

The lights came on, and the crowd stood from their seats. They slowly began to file toward the dual exits.

As Frank and Mike approached Morrison on their way out, Mike couldn't help himself. "I bet it took you all night to come up with that stupid play on words, didn't it, Jack?" he ribbed his old friend.

"Yeah. In fact, it took me so long that I had to tell your wife not to come over for the first time in years," Morrison countered without missing a beat.

Frank fist-bumped the AD on his way by for the snap comeback.

"You guys are dicks," Mike, defeated at his own game, said with a smile.

CHAPTER eleven

Sara savored the last bite of the decadent chocolate cake that she and Marla had been sharing, then set down her fork inside the trendy San Diego restaurant. Across the table, James was pouring the final remnants of a third bottle of Pinot Noir into Marla's wine glass. The two girls had obtained fake IDs before leaving New York, but hadn't been required to use them so far.

"Is there anything else I can get for you?" a boyish-looking waiter with dark Beatle-esque hair asked, arriving at the table.

"That was *amazing,* Mateo!" Marla complimented, having managed to extract the Peruvian-born waiter's name—along with half his life story—throughout the evening. This was nothing new for Marla; she had an innate ability to make even complete strangers feel comfortable and included.

"I'll second that!" James raised his glass and downed his drink. "Unless the ladies would like anything else, you can just bring the bill whenever you have a moment."

"Oof, I couldn't eat another bite if I tried," Sara admitted.

"Me neither," Marla agreed, pushing out her belly and tapping it humorously with her hand.

"Excellent." Mateo flashed a smile and began expertly stacking the dinnerware into an impressive tower on his serving tray. "I'll be back momentarily."

James turned to the girls. "If you don't mind, I think I'll just leave my car here in the parking lot, and we can take a cab to the nightclub. I'll come pick it up in the morning."

"Good call," Marla said with a nod. "None of us are in any condition to drive."

Sara felt her phone vibrate inside the handbag that was resting on her lap under the table. She and Steve had only texted twice since he had left the house that morning, and both messages had been short and to the point. At nearly the same time, James' phone chimed as well. He picked it up and looked at the screen.

"Perfect timing!" he announced to the girls. "Steve has arrived at the club and says that our table will be ready when we get there."

"Awesome!" cheered Marla.

Moments later, the waiter returned with the bill. James quickly checked it over and handed him some cash. Sara stood from her seat and removed her phone from her purse.

'I'm here,' was all that Steve had texted.

*****

After a forty-minute drive through the darkness of the night, the taxi finally arrived at a foreboding, industrial, steel-sided building located on a seemingly never-ending gravel road. It was a considerable distance off the main highway on the outskirts of San Diego. During the ride, James had explained that in recent years, some of the city's nightclub owners had opted to relocate their businesses to more remote locations to take advantage of lower lease rates.

Sara and Marla stepped out of the back of the cab and into the moonlight.

"Keep the change, bro," James instructed the Iranian driver before shutting the door.

"We could have at least paid for the taxi," Sara told James.

"No way," James politely refused the offer. "You two already had to pay for your flights out here from New York. It's the least I could do!"

James took Marla by the hand, and the trio made their way across the front of the building as the taxi's taillights disappeared over a ridge.

"It's not exactly the Vegas Strip out here, is it?" Marla mused as they rounded the front corner of the structure. The nighttime air was still and hushed, carrying the spearmint-like smell of the surrounding Torrey pines. Just then, Sara spotted a refrigerator-shaped bouncer standing next to a steel door near the back corner of the building. A lonely yellow lightbulb cast a weak spotlight down onto the doorman's cinderblock head.

"You must be Memphis?" James asked the fair-skinned, baby-faced hulk dressed in black, who was somehow even more imposing up close. "I was told you'd be expecting us."

The broad-knuckled beast only offered an unenthusiastic nod before turning to pull open the door, revealing a dank, dimly lit interior. The girls peeked inside the inky space and discovered a fifteen-foot grated steel platform leading to a second door. To the left were a set of descending stairs. The hulk motioned with one of his massive paws for the group to proceed inside.

"Down below," James explained to the girls.

Sara and Marla exchanged uneasy glances before cautiously stepping onto the shadowy platform. As instructed, they turned left and began to make their way down the unforgiving steps, with James following closely behind. A dull vibration seemed to permeate the walls around them as the bouncer stepped onto the platform above and pulled the door shut with force, sending a pressurized blast of air down the stairs, causing the girls to flinch and then break out into nervous giggles. The steepness of the steps, combined with the effects of the earlier wine, required them to keep a steady hand on the railing as they descended.

Sara, Marla and James reached a concrete landing at the bottom of the stairs and arrived at a door with a camera mounted above flashing a tiny red light. The bouncer arrived next and reached a hand between the girls, pressing a button on a square intercom box next to the door, producing a high-pitched squeal. A few seconds later, a security bar being released on the other side of the door sounded, and James placed his hands on the girls' shoulders. He leaned his face between them. "Sorry, ladies..." he said just before the door was pulled inward.

Suddenly, a blinding deluge of neon lights, chest-pounding music, and humid air came rushing into the stairwell. Sara and Marla looked inside and discovered a massive crowd of inebriated partygoers bouncing and gyrating to ear-piercing music inside the subterranean playground.

"I forgot to mention earlier," James continued his statement, attempting to top the music, "we have to check our phones in with the big guy here," he gestured with a thumb towards the bouncer. "I'm not sure this place is fully licensed yet, and they don't want people posting pictures and videos on social media or whatever. Feel free to check your purses in, too, if you want. Our drinks are already paid for," he explained, handing his phone to the hulk and receiving a little red ticket in return. He began moving his body in synchronicity with the heart-pounding electronic music, as the girls surrendered their belongings to the bouncer next.

"Woooooooooo!" Marla shouted with excitement as the group moved away from the door, stepping deeper into the dopamine-spiking psychedelic chaos. James took her hand, and she grabbed Sara's, creating a human chain that began to snake its way through the densely packed crowd. Sara looked back towards the door and, for a fleeting second, she locked eyes with the towering doorman before he resealed the party inside.

"This is AWESOME!" Sara called out to Marla as they were dragged further into the pandemonium by James.

Marla looked back. "What?!"

With no chance at rivaling the music, Sara simply flashed a thumbs up with her free hand, and Marla responded with an enthusiastic smile and nod.

*****

After fifteen minutes of non-stop dancing, Sara could taste sodium-rich sweat forming on her upper lip as the crowd on the dance floor pulsated as one massive ball of uncontainable energy.

"Hey! Want to get a drink?!" James shouted to the girls over the noise.

"Yes! I'm dying!" Marla replied, pretending to pant like an overheated dog.

Sara agreed.

"This way!" James said, leading them between a group of five gyrating females wearing heavy make-up and little more than lingerie.

The trio exited the dance floor and navigated themselves through an open passageway that was guarded by another stoic bouncer. They entered a semi-enclosed area, one-fifth the size of the last, where the walls helped to dampen the chest-thumping music to a somewhat more reasonable level. Sara scanned the room, discovering small groups of partygoers dancing, talking, and lounging around circular tables, sipping high-end alcohol. James led them to the freshly polished bar and flashed three fingers at the male bartender with a gravity-defying ruby red mohawk and uncomfortably tight V-neck shirt. The mixologist withdrew a sapphire bottle from beneath his bar and expertly filled three shot glasses to the brim without spilling a drop. The black lighting installed overhead illuminated the booze into a mesmerizing neon yellow.

"Cheers!" said James, handing the girls their shots.

"Cheers!" they parroted back in perfect unison, before downing the acrid liquid. Marla's face winced due to the strength of the high-octane alcohol, and she let out a few tiny coughs. "Smoooooooth," she joked to Sara, who was wearing the same pucker-lipped look on her face. Marla suddenly stepped forward and wrapped her arms around James, and the two began to make out. Sara smiled and turned away, using the opportunity to further study her chaotic surroundings as the alcohol worked its way through her system. Everyone in the back room seemed to be having a great time, and Sara decided there was something refreshing about people not being glued to the phones they had been forced to check in. It was allowing them to truly experience a night out.

Just then, she spotted Steve standing at a table near the back of the room. Across from him was a middle-aged man with a dark complexion. He was short, slightly overweight, and had a large, bulbous nose with heavy bags under his eyes. His unkempt salt-and-pepper hair peeked out from the bottom of a brown Borsalino hat.

As Sara continued to observe the pair, it became obvious that the older man was berating Steve, his hands gesturing wildly as he did so. Suddenly, he poked Steve in the chest. When he finally finished his animated tirade, the browbeaten Steve looked away, and his eyes met Sara's across the room. Confused, she attempted a smile and lifted her hand to wave, but his muted expression remained in place. Sara slowly lowered her hand and watched Steve turn back to the stranger. He said something quickly and then stepped away from the table, making his way in her direction.

"Steve-o!" James shouted out when he noticed his approaching comrade. He released Marla from his grip and darted out to meet his incoming pal, throwing an arm around his shoulders and turning to face the girls again. As they closed in on the bar, Sara looked back across the room and found the older man had disappeared. Marla intercepted Steve with an inebriated hug when he arrived.

"This place is amazing!" she professed to him enthusiastically.

Steve attempted a smile but failed to match Marla's energy. Once they had separated, Steve moved in and wrapped a flaccid arm around Sara.

"Is everything okay?" she asked, her face next to his.

"We need to talk," he responded flatly.

"Soooooooo? Are we all set?" James asked Steve, who released Sara from his grip and turned to his roommate.

"Yeah, but for some reason, they set up our bottle service near the entrance." He pointed back to where the group had just come from. "Do you mind going to the front and asking them to bring it to the VIP section in the back?"

"Did you hear that, Sara!?" Marla said. "We're *very* important!" She puffed out her chest and pretended to be a huge deal, causing Sara to laugh.

"Uh, yeah...alright," James said, looking a bit confused by Steve's request. "I'll go let them know."

Sara watched James disappear through the passageway. As soon as he was out of sight, Steve turned to the girls.

"Come with me," he instructed, then headed toward the back of the room.

"Is there a bathroom back here?" Marla asked once they had caught up to him.

"Yeah," Steve said quickly, sidestepping a couple of tipsy patrons and eventually moving past the table he had been arguing at moments before. The trio ducked through a door and into a red-carpeted hallway. Steve took a quick left. Marla followed. Sara glanced to her right and discovered three doors with cameras above them.

"It's like a giant maze back here!" a wide-eyed Marla commented once Sara had caught up again.

"This way!" Steve ordered, slipping through a door with an emergency exit sign posted above it.

"Are we even supposed to be back here?" Sara questioned from the back of the pack, feeling increasingly uneasy about being in the shadowy labyrinth. Steve didn't respond. Soon, they found themselves at the base of a set of metal stairs that looked identical to those they had descended on the other side of the building.

Sara had finally had enough.

"Steve!" she shouted, as he began to climb the steps. "What the fuck is going on? What are we doing back here?"

He stopped, looking up at the illuminated exit sign at the top of the steep stairs. He turned back to face the girls, and there was a look of panic in his eyes that they had never seen before.

"You need to listen to me," he said a bit more softly now. "I have to get you out of here. I can't do this. You're not safe. Once I get you guys out of here, I'll explain everything. But for now, you're just going to have to trust me."

Marla turned to Sara. Her eyes were frantic. "What's going on?"

"I have no idea." Sara placed a hand on Marla's shoulder, helping to encourage her up the stairs. "But we need to leave. Now!"

The group clambered up the steps as quickly as possible, with their footsteps echoing chaotically off the surrounding walls. When Steve finally reached the upper platform, he turned back and faced the girls. They stopped a half dozen steps below.

"Once we get outside, no matter what happens, just try to act as naturally as possible," he instructed, sounding like he was attempting to convince himself as much as them. "Don't worry. I'll get everything figured out."

Steve took hold of the silver doorknob, inhaled deeply, and then slowly pulled the door inward. A cool breeze entered the corridor, and the girls dropped their heads to commence their climb.

BANG!

A deafening blast rang out, rocking their eardrums and sending reverberations deep inside their skulls, stopping them in their tracks. Sara's eyes shot up to Steve, who stood motionless, staring blankly out the door.

"Steve...?" escaped her mouth in something less than a whisper.

He took a slow step back and then pivoted to face the girls. His eyes were distant and vacant now, like a deer caught in headlights. Sara suddenly noticed the hole in the chest of his white dress shirt. It suddenly turned red and rapidly expanded in diameter. He dropped heavily onto his knees.

"I'm sorry..." he murmured as blood began to fill his lungs.

BANG!

Steve's head jolted sideways, ejecting a geyser of coagulated blood and brain matter across the platform. The impact sent him crashing into the handrail before his lifeless body began to tumble down the steps. Sara and Marla pressed their backs tightly against the wall to avoid being struck by the descending corpse, which eventually came to rest at the base of the stairs.

The terror-stricken girls stared up at the vacant platform above, holding their breath, as an ominous shadow began to grow on the wall. Suddenly, James stepped onto the grated metal, holding a silver gun in his left hand. He stared menacingly at the two paralytic females below, causing Marla to let out a high-pitched scream. Without hesitation, James closed the distance between them and pressed the barrel of his gun forcefully into the center of her forehead.

"One more *fucking* peep out of you and you'll be at the bottom of the stairs with him!" he threatened her in a voice that was now completely devoid of humanity. "There's a car waiting outside. Now get moving! Both of you!"

Marla collected herself just enough to begin climbing the remaining steps, while Sara continued to look down at Steve's lifeless body.

"I said MOVE!" James hissed at her.

Outside, a black limousine with tinted windows and a running engine was parked ten feet from the door. Sara looked to her right and saw an open gate leading back to the gravel road they had arrived on. She scanned her darkened surroundings and found nothing but black, silent emptiness.

Marla climbed into the back of the limo first, followed closely by Sara. They took seats next to each other, facing the rear of the vehicle. James entered next, gun in hand, and sat opposite them. He pulled the door closed, and the locks engaged with a loud *thunk!* that was nearly as terrifying as the gunshots.

"How 'bout one last drink tonight, ladies?" James motioned the tip of his weapon toward two shot glasses sitting on the console next to Marla's left thigh.

Neither girl budged as they felt the limousine begin to slowly crawl forward.

"It's NOT optional!" James raised his voice.

Startled, Marla reached out and took the two glasses into her trembling hands, as tears began to stream down her cheeks. She passed one to Sara, and they looked at each other helplessly before consuming the bitter-tasting liquid.

"Why are you doing this?" Marla sobbed, setting the empty glass back on the console next to her. Sara dropped hers onto the floor.

"It's just business," James replied without remorse.

"Where are you taking uuuussssss?" Sara demanded, noticing her voice trailing off into an unexpected slur. "Our parents will come looooooookkkkkkiiingggg fooooooorrr—"

"Oh, don't you worry about that, sweetheart," James smirked. "By the time they even realize anything is wrong, you'll be loooooonnnnggggg gooooooonnnnnneeeeee."

Sara felt a tingling sensation creeping down her extremities. She gave her head a shake, trying valiantly to fight off the effects of whatever she had just consumed. Her vision began to wax and wane, and she noticed her and Marla's phones and purses on the seat next to James. Turning her head slowly, she discovered that Marla had already succumbed to the potion and was now leaning unconsciously against the console. Sara looked back at James and found that his voice sounded distant and incomprehensible. Glancing out the tinted window to her right, she caught a fleeting glimpse of the gigantic bouncer as the limo drove past him and disappeared into the darkness of the night.

CHAPTER twelve

Turbulent puffs of white smoke escaped from the barbecue near the back of Frank and Donna's nearly completed cabin, catching Mike's attention. *"Oh, shit..."* He took off towards the grill in hopes of rescuing the hamburger patties that he had been put in charge of. Upon reaching the barbecue, he jerked open the lid and quickly deactivated all four burners. Inspecting the beef, he discovered that not only was it still edible, but it was perfectly cooked.

"Ha!" Mike called back to Frank, who had witnessed the entire ordeal. "Got 'em in the nick of time!"

"You only had one job," Frank reminded him.

Just then, Donna and Janice reappeared from around the front of the cabin, back from a short walking tour of the new acreage.

"How's dinner coming along, boys?" Donna wondered, oblivious to the events that had just transpired.

"I guess that all depends on how *well-done* you like y—" Frank began to answer.

"Great!" Mike cut him off. "Burgers are ready."

"Perfect!" said Janice. "We'll go inside and grab the condiments and sides."

Frank retrieved a serving platter from atop the plastic folding table that Mike and Janice had brought from their house in the city, and met Mike at the grill.

"Oh, hey, I forgot to mention," Mike said as he transferred the protein onto the tray. "Janice and I have an announcement to make tonight."

"For the last time. Donna and I are *not* interested in swinging with you guys," Frank joked. "Although, maybe if she found herself a different husband..."

"Is this your way of telling me I'm losing my sex appeal, Frankie?" Mike grinned.

"If it makes you feel any better, I'm not sure you ever had any."

*****

"So, how's Sara enjoying California?" Janice asked Frank, spearing a forkful of lettuce in her salad bowl.

"Seems to be liking it alright." Frank nodded.

"Have you heard from her today?" Donna asked him.

Frank shook his head. "No, you?"

"I'm expecting a text at any time now," she replied, retrieving a pack of gum from her purse and setting it down on the table for the group. "I imagine they'll probably be heading out for the evening pretty soon."

Frank turned his attention back to Janice across the table. "So, your husband tells me you have some news?"

"Oh yeah!" Janice replied excitedly. "So, there's this older couple who own a restaurant down in Long Beach."

"It's right near the water," Mike specified. "It's really nice."

"Recently, I heard they were looking to sell," Janice continued, "because they want to retire down in Florida."

"And they offered to adopt Mike and take him with them?" Frank said, before taking a sip of his beer.

"No," Janice smiled. "I've made the decision to sell my catering company and buy their restaurant."

"Oh wow!" Donna cheered enthusiastically. "You've always wanted to do something like that! That's incredible! Congratulations!"

"That's great, Janice," Frank agreed. "Good for you."

"Yes, I'm very excited. I know it's going to be a huge transition, but I think I'm ready."

"Of course you are," Donna encouraged.

Frank looked across the table and found Mike staring directly at him, smiling. Frank glanced at the two women for a clue, then returned his gaze to his partner. "Can I help you?" he grinned.

"So, here's the thing, Frankie. Connected to the backside of the restaurant is an old run-down sports bar, and I was thinking, maybe, you'd be interested in helping me fix it up? You know, return it to its former glory."

Frank looked at Janice. "Let me get this straight..." he spoke to her directly. "I'm already forced to put up with this guy at work five days a week, and now you want me to spend my weekends making sure he doesn't burn your place to the ground?"

Mike spoke up again. "I figured it would be a nice place for you to loiter around when you retire down the road. We all know Donna isn't going to want you shuffling around the house in your slippers all day, bothering her. So, it's either *this*, or you'll have to become a Walmart greeter, you old fuck," Mike teased.

"Old?" Frank chuckled. "I'm only two years older than you."

"Yeah, *biologically,* maybe. But I've got some kind of Benjamin Button thing going on here..." Mike claimed, causing Donna to nearly spit out her drink.

"Wow! *Really,* Donna?" Mike turned to her, smiling. "I hope you're not suggesting that Brad Pitt is better looking than me? Don't let all that Hollywood magic fool you. That's just makeup and camera angles. But *this* right here," he drew a circle around his face with his finger. "This is all-natural, baby!"

"You've got some mustard on your chin there, Fabio," Frank pointed out, sending the women into a fit of laughter.

Mike picked up a napkin and wiped the canary yellow streak off his face, grinning. "So, what do you think, big guy? I might even consider letting you hang up some of your shitty Mets' memorabilia in a dark corner somewhere." This was a massive deal for a diehard Yankees fan like Mike.

"Please... with all the pennants they're going to be winning in the coming years, you'll need a second venue just to fit it all inside."

"Oh Christ, here we go again!" An exasperated Mike turned to his wife. "You know what, on second thought, I'm not sure we should be associating ourselves with this level of delusion."

Frank smiled. "I'd be happy to help you guys out. And again, congratulations on fulfilling your dreams, Janice," He raised his beer, and everyone brought their drinks together in celebration. A moment later, a text message arrived on Donna's phone.

"It's Sara," she told the others and began to read the text aloud. "She and Marla are going to bed early tonight because they leave tomorrow for their five-day snorkeling excursion off the coast."

"Oh wow! That's exciting!" said Janice.

A crooked smirk appeared on Mike's face. "Tell her that Uncle Mike says that nobody has been eaten by a shark for a long time, so they're bound to be *really* hungry by now."

Donna shot him the look of a protective mother as another message from Sara arrived.

"Oh, and Frank, she says that the tour guides mentioned that they won't have any cell service out there, so she'll just text us when they get back on the mainland Thursday."

Frank nodded, then removed his phone from his pocket and sent Sara a quick message to enjoy the experience.

"God, I wish *we* were snorkeling out in California!" Janice said to Mike, who agreed with a nod.

Frank's phone vibrated, and he looked at the screen. *'Thanks Dad. We will!'*

Frank smiled.

"What's so funny?" Donna wondered.

"Well, after eighteen years of being called *Daddy*, it only took a few days of solo vacationing for me to become... plain old *Dad.*"

CHAPTER thirteen

A freshly waxed black limousine came rumbling down a long cobblestone driveway, passing between a pair of imposing wrought iron gates leading to the front of Ernesto Diaz's massive Mexican compound twenty-five miles outside the city of Guadalajara. Ken Collins was the sole passenger in the rear of the vehicle, having just landed at a nearby airstrip in a private jet provided by his host. The CEO had already grown accustomed to this type of treatment since Diaz had shown up at the door of his hotel room three months prior. Although this marked Collins' third cross-border trip since then, it was the first occasion in which he had been invited directly to the kingpin's primary residence.

Jose, a lanky, sharp-featured chauffeur, sat quietly in the driver's seat, separated by a thick layer of bulletproof glass. As the vehicle approached the front of the house, a muscular, heavily-tattooed gangster with a nickel-plated handgun holstered against his ribcage approached. The moment the limo came to a stop, he pulled open the door. Collins stepped out and looked up at the massive, fifteen-thousand-square-foot, baroque-style mansion, where hordes of pink and purple bougainvillea snaked up the walls, giving it an old-world charm.

Collins followed the guard through an oversized solid oak door and into the foyer, where the soles of their shoes echoed rhythmically off the ceiling. The interior architecture was ornate, with every wall and surface tastefully adorned with paintings and other beautiful works of art. Collins began to notice some of the signatures scrawled on the bottom corners of the canvases he passed by: *Rembrandt...Caravaggio...Picasso.*

As they approached the back of the house, the CEO began to hear what sounded like music. His guide arrived at a set of white-curtained French doors and shoved them open, introducing a wave of bass-heavy music into the house. Collins stepped into the blazing sun, discovering a Las Vegas-style party happening around a sprawling, crystal-clear swimming pool. The pool was surrounded by elaborate stone fountains, cabanas, tiki bars, chairs, tables, and at least thirty beautiful women wearing sundresses, bikinis, or in some cases, even less. The women were socializing with an equal number of serious-looking Mexican gangsters, some decked out in shorts and tank tops, while others wore full business attire.

"Let's go!" the impatient guard shouted back at Collins, having ducked behind a row of four-foot-tall, landscaped hedges that created a walking path parallel to the back of the mansion. The CEO quickly caught up, and the path eventually terminated into a set of torch-blown white marble stairs that led up to a glass-walled eagle's nest gazebo overlooking the pool. Collins followed him up the sunbaked steps and entered the air-conditioned structure above. Through the glass, the back of the property seemed to stretch endlessly to the south. Across the room, four middle-aged men were smoking cigars and holding tumblers filled with rich, amber-colored liquor. The guard set himself into a militaristic stance, interlocking his hands behind his back and lifting his chin high into the air.

"Your guest has arrived, Mr. Diaz," the henchman announced, sounding wholly unimpressed with the American.

The conversation across the room stopped, and each of the four men turned to face the door.

"Ah, yes!" Ernesto said in a welcoming voice. He stood up and approached while the others remained in place.

"Thank you, Miguel," the kingpin nodded at the morose guard, who immediately took his leave.

"I'm glad you were finally able to come to my home, Mr. Collins," Diaz greeted.

"Thanks for having me."

The kingpin placed his hand on the American's shoulder and led him over to the others. "I'd like to introduce you to a couple of my associates."

Upon their arrival, two of the three seated men rose to their feet.

"This here," Ernesto referenced the shorter of the pair, "is Hector Velazquez."

Collins shook hands with the forty-six-year-old Mexican gangster, with thinning salt-and-pepper hair, brown eyes and a nose that had obviously been broken a time or two.

"He oversees our gambling operations," Diaz explained.

The man said nothing and simply nodded graciously.

"And *this* is Vinny Cambodi," Diaz pointed to the fifty-something dark-haired Italian with green eyes, and a dense rug of black chest hair peeking out from the top of his blue dress shirt.

Collins shook his hand next.

"Vinny was an Italian immigrant in the US in the 1990s, working for one of the *families*. But after the RICO trials in '04, we were able to recruit him down here, and he quickly became one of our most valuable import and export specialists."

"If you need something moved over a border—and I'm talking fuckin' *anything,* pal—I'm your guy," he boasted in an overemphasized Italian-American accent.

Collins nodded.

"And of course, you've met my brother Dennis," Ernesto said, referring to the only man who had failed to stand. Dennis was more solidly built than his brother, with shark-like eyes set prominently above an aquiline nose and snow-white goatee. He glared menacingly at Collins from his seat. "He, of course, is still in charge of everything related to production, manufacturing, and distribution," Ernesto continued, referring to the copious amounts of narcotics they had made their fortunes in. Dennis was universally known to be a loose cannon, far too impulsive and reckless to be the face of the cartel. But that didn't bother him; he preferred spending his time in the trenches, where it was dark and dirty.

"Nice to see you again, Dennis," Collins lied.

Just then, the doors on the other side of the room were shoved open, and in strolled an American with sandy-colored hair. He was dabbing at a water stain on the sleeve of his white dress shirt with a hand towel he had obtained from one of the seven bathrooms in the house. He looked up, and a giant smile spread across his face.

"Sorry about that, gents!" he apologized loudly in a thick Texas accent, tossing the rag on a nearby surface and continuing toward them. "But nature called, if ya know what I mean?!" he shouted, followed by an infectious laugh that seemed to spread to the men surrounding Collins. "Now, *who* in the hell is this handsome son-of-a-bitch!?" the stranger asked, arriving directly in front of the CEO. Before anyone could answer, he reached out and grabbed Collins' palm and shook it vigorously. "Don't worry, partner, I washed my hands! Honest!"

More laughs.

"Let me introduce you to Hank Phillips," Ernesto said to Collins. "Like you, he has a very keen business mind and has been working with us for, oh, how long has it been now?"

"Hmm, let me think for a minute now, will ya..." The Texan squinted his eyes for full effect. "Musta been almost ten years now."

"Pleased to meet you," Collins said with a bit of reservation. "I'm—"

"Ah, hell, no introduction necessary!" Hank cut him off. "I was only kidding. I know *exactly* who you are! Ernie here has told me *all* about you. And by the sounds of it, you two have got some big things going on down here!" The Texan's smile grew even larger, and he leaned in. "And let me tell you something, Kenny, these four hombres right here, well, I reckon they're just about the best group of guys you and me could be working with on the whole damn planet!" He slapped his thigh with excitement.

"You are too kind!" said Ernesto, before looking at his watch. "You'll have to excuse the four of us, but we are needed for a pressing matter in the city. I can't imagine we'll be too long. In the meantime, perhaps the two of you can get acquainted and enjoy yourselves down at the pool?"

"That sounds like one helluva good idea to me," Hank agreed heartily. "What's your poison, Kenny boy?"

"Uh—"

"The second I laid eyes on you, I said that there's a Johnny Walker man if I ever saw one." Hank wrapped his arm around his fellow American. "Am I right, or am I right?"

By this point, even a self-centered cynic like Collins was finding it difficult to resist Hank's upbeat, sociable personality. "Well, I suppose I've been known to have one or two of those in the past." The CEO finally cracked a little smile.

"See! What did I tell ya, Ernie? I knew I was going to like this guy!"

The four cartel men made their way toward the exit.

"We'll be back in a couple of hours," Dennis said to Hank from the back of the pack. "Keep your eye on him." He glared at Collins.

"You got it, boss!" Hank offered him a playful salute.

Once the others had disappeared down the stairs, Hank turned to Collins. "Alright, buddy, let's fucking party!"

* * * * *

Down at the pool, there had been an influx of guests who had spread themselves between the deck tables and sun-shielding cabanas. The two Americans located a pair of vacant, red-cushioned couches, separated by a rectangular glass table and an oversized white umbrella. They sat facing each other, and Hank immediately flashed a series of hand signals across the pool, catching the attention of a tall, black-haired server who was standing next to three gangsters chatting idly with a group of scantily clad women.

"How's everything going at the new labs?" Hank asked, adjusting himself on his cushion.

"Pretty good..." Collins responded reservedly, unsure how receptive Ernesto would be to him openly discussing any of their *arrangements*. "Sure is hot out today," he attempted to steer the conversation in a different direction.

For the first time, Collins saw a look on Hank's face that wasn't jubilant.

"Oh, it's like *that*, is it?" Hank replied, splaying out his arms over the back of the couch. He looked off across the pool, clearly unimpressed with the CEO's response.

Collins hesitated.

"Ahhhhh! I'm just *fucking* with you, Kenny!" Hank broke the awkwardness with his usual booming laughter. "You keep your cards close to your chest! I like that! It tells me you're loyal *and* smart! That's the kinda thing that will get you far around here, my friend."

Collins grinned, always appreciative of praise.

"But truth be told, I'm fully aware of the situation you've got going on down here."

"Really?"

"Hell yeah! In fact, that disposal company Ernie hooked you up with. That's actually one of my little *creations* from a few years back."

Collins leaned forward, intrigued. "What exactly do you do for these guys?"

"Well, that's as good a question as any, now ain't it?" Hank leaned forward as well, resting his elbows on his knees. "I guess you could say I try to anticipate the future needs of the Diaz brothers by creating legitimate businesses that might be useful for them down the road."

"Like a disposal business..."

"Bingo!" Hank nodded. "I make sure all these entities operate above board and make a profit regardless of whether the cartel ever needs to use them."

"That way, you develop clean track records."

"Precisely," the Texan smiled. "I've provided our boys with transportation companies, security firms, crematoriums, accountants, insurance agencies..."

Collins was impressed. Behind Hank's affable facade of Southern charm, there was a shrewd, calculating businessman.

"Hot damn, Kenny! Check *that* out!"

Collins turned and spotted the sable-haired server approaching with a bottle of brown liquor and a pair of glasses. Flanking her were four attractive, bikini-clad females between the ages of eighteen and twenty-five.

Collins looked back at Hank, eyebrows raised.

"Order's up!" The Texan winked.

The server arrived and set the glassware on the table between the two men and began to pour their drinks.

"Good afternoon, gentlemen," she greeted with a Sofia Vergara-esque accent. "Nice for me to see you again, Mister Hank."

"Oh, heck, you better knock off that *mister* stuff! How's them boys of yours doing?"

"Very good! Thank you much for asking."

"Kristina here has a couple of the best little soccer players in all of Mexico, I'm told," Hank explained to Collins.

She flashed a flawless smile.

"And a HELLO to all you ladies as well!" Hank greeted the surgically enhanced foursome, clinking his glass into the one now sitting in front of Collins.

"Don't be shy now, girls! Come join the party!" Hank invited.

Without hesitation, the harem stepped forward and began tucking themselves in on the couch, flanking the two Americans.

A young woman with piercing aquamarine eyes, platinum blonde hair, overdone lip injections, and well-defined tan lines placed her freshly manicured hand high up on Hank's thigh, while an athletically built Asian with pink streaks in her ebony, shoulder-length hair took his other hip. "Hi there, I'm Je—" the blonde attempted to introduce herself.

"Whoa, now," Hank cut her off immediately. "Let's not play the name game, honey," he said, his eyes squarely focused on the curvaceous Mexican with heavy eye makeup and a zebra-print bikini who had taken a seat next to Collins. On his other hip was a wafer-thin redhead in a revealing pink floral-patterned sundress with spherical breast implants, wearing oversized black Versace sunglasses. "Unless you're into that sorta thing, Kenny?"

"Fuck, no," Collins shook his head at the mere notion of humanizing any of them.

Just then, the music on the poolside speakers increased in volume, causing the bikini-clad blonde beside Hank to stand up and begin moving her body in perfect harmony with the music. Collins watched from the other side of the table as she turned sideways and made her heart-shaped glutes bounce up and down just inches from Hank's face. The Texan suddenly pretended to bury his face into her backside, causing Collins to crack a smile. The Asian and Mexican girls joined in on the dancing, and Collins turned to look up at the Latina's stunning, yet vacant eyes. Just then, he heard Hank laughing across the table. He looked over and discovered him pointing a finger at the redhead behind him. Collins turned and discovered that she had passed out and was now slumped against the armrest. He reached out a hand to rouse her, but before his fingers made contact—

SLAP!

An open palm had arrived over the back of the couch and struck the girl violently across the face, knocking her sunglasses down to the concrete, startling Collins. He turned around and found Kristina hovering over the now fully conscious girl, who sprang to her feet with a red mark already forming on her cheek, looking terrified, confused and embarrassed. The server grabbed her by the upper arm, yanked her around the back of the couch, and berated her with

Spanish expletives. She proceeded to shove her in the back, sending her down to the concrete. The girl clumsily regained her footing and stumbled off toward the house.

"I'm so sorry, gentlemen." Kristina returned to the table and apologized.

Collins looked around at the remaining females, expecting to find horrified expressions on their faces. Instead, he discovered they had continued dancing through the entire ordeal as if nothing had happened to their companion.

"I find you another?" Kristina asked Hank.

"No thanks, darling," he declined. "Kenny, my boy, which one of these two do you like better?" he asked of the women on his side of the table.

Collins leaned back and took a good, long look at the pair. Eventually, he pointed a finger at the Asian girl, as if he were selecting a pastry from a bakery display case.

"She's yours!" Hank hooted. "Sweetheart," he tapped her on the thigh with the back of his hand, "join my friend over there, would ya?"

Without missing a beat, the black-haired beauty complied, moving seductively around the table.

"What about you?" Collins asked, noting the imbalance of numbers.

"Kenny, I've been at this goddamn party for a week now," he explained. "I just don't have the energy for two today. Trust me, you're doing me a favor!" He stood up from his couch and slung his arm around the waist of his remaining companion. "What do you say we all head inside?"

Collins quickly downed his drink, and the group abandoned the table.

*****

Collins watched as the alluring naked bodies of the two young women abandoned the bed after a session of sexual debauchery. Each one slipped into a bleach white bathrobe that had been strategically hung on a hook next to the door. Without so much as a word, the two dark-haired beauties exited the bedroom and closed the door gently behind them.

Collins had just laid his head back down on the pillow when a faint knock sounded at the door, interrupting his moment of bliss. He assumed one of the girls must have forgotten something.

"What?" Collins barked at the door, having absolutely no desire to see either of them again so soon. The door slowly crept open, and Hank's face suddenly materialized in the void. He was wearing the same grandiose smile he had on when he left Collins in the hallway earlier to go partake in his own hedonistic adventure.

"How was that, partner?!" Hank asked loudly, inviting himself into the bedroom.

"Pretty good," Collins undersold the experience, from beneath the silky red bedsheet.

"That a boy!" Hank hooted. "I just came to let you know that Ernie and the others are on their way back." His voice grew more serious. "And if he finds out you fucked his granddaughter, we're both dead men."

"What?!" Collins' heart skipped a beat.

"That brunette that was in here. The Mexican one," Hank specified. "She's a Diaz. You didn't know?"

Before Hank could say another word, Collins jumped off the mattress and was pulling on his pants, scrambling to dress himself as quickly as possible.

"What the fuck, Hank!" he hollered, yanking back the bed sheets, searching for his shirt. "How the fuck would I know she was his granddaughter?! What the fuck is she even doing here? Why wouldn't you tell me th—"

Hank suddenly burst into a fit of laughter. "I'm joking!" he admitted between wheezes. "I'm joking!"

Collins paused his search and looked at the Texan. "You cocksucker," he said, half-pissed but fully relieved. He located his shirt, slipped it on, and began to button it up.

"I gotta tell you," said Hank, still smiling, "it's good to know that even *Mr. CEO* himself is not immune to getting a little shaken up."

Collins shook his head.

"Quite the set-up these boys have going on down here though, huh?" Hank commented, looking around the room.

"Yeah. Not bad at all. Where do they find these whores anyway? They certainly are well-trained."

"You ain't kidding! I think—"

"But don't they have any American broads?" Collins interrupted him as he pulled on his socks.

Instead of answering right away, Hank walked to the door and peeked out into the hallway in both directions, ensuring they were alone. This allowed Collins time to slip on his shoes and make his way over.

"Between you and me, Kenny, these boys cherry-pick the best females from the shipments they send down to Panama."

"Panama? What's in Panama?"

"That's the launch point for all the merchandise heading over to Europe and the Middle East."

"You mean like sex trafficking?"

"Yeah," Hank nodded, "but they're pretty careful not to call it that."

"What does that have to do with me not getting any American tail down here?"

"From what I heard, American girls have been off limits for a good while now," Hank explained. "I think it's less of a hassle if a shipment gets pinched and it's full of women from Central or South American countries. The authorities just think it's a load of illegal immigrants. And that way, Uncle Sam doesn't get involved."

"Some of the broads out by the pool looked to be Eastern European or something, no?"

"Could be. I heard they make exchanges with some of those countries." Hank shrugged. "But that's probably about as close as your pecker is going to get to anything American around these parts."

"Were those girls we had all fucked up on drugs or something?" Collins wondered. "Don't get me wrong, they knew *exactly* what they were doing, but it was like the lights were on, but nobody was home."

"For sure, partner!" Hank grinned. "They're all fucking addicts."

"They must get pretty haggard after a while?"

"Ab-so-fucking-lutely! Those girls we had today; they're only in the infancy of the game. The cartel will keep them around for a short while until they've slipped a few rungs down the skank ladder, and then *BOOM*, they'll be sent off overseas. I mean, by that point, they're basically just zombies anyway."

"Well, I still think it's a shame I can't get any American pussy around here," Collins whined some more.

"You're not the only one. I've heard there are sultans and oligarchs across the pond willing to pay ten, hell, even twenty times as much to get their hands on Americans. But I guess if it gets your entire operation shut down, it just ain't worth it."

CHAPTER fourteen

"Fifty million dollars in cash might weigh half a ton," AD Jack Morrison explained to the same group of agents, nearing the end of a second briefing regarding the artwork being shipped into Mexico. "Getting that kind of heft over a border, whether by plane or in a vehicle, obviously has its challenges. Now, imagine being able to replace that entire load with a single, legally purchased item that might only weigh five or ten pounds," he paused, to let it sink in. "Now, I can't speak for any of you sophisticated socialites, but I can't tell the difference between a Picasso and something my four-year-old granddaughter drew at pre-school last week."

A chuckle spread throughout the room.

"And unless customs has recently hired a team of museum curators that I don't know about, I can't imagine that many of these shipments are being stopped."

"What more do we know about how they've been implementing their new system?" a well-built African American agent with a hi-top fade seated by himself in the sixth row inquired.

"I'm going to have James Caulder field that question, Tim. He's been working point on this thing for the last few weeks here," the AD explained.

A heavy-set man of fifty with a silver-speckled walrus mustache stood up and traded places with Morrison at the front of the room.

"Good morning, everyone," he greeted, scanning the crowd for familiar faces. "As previously mentioned, it seems that the Diaz brothers are attempting to evolve their business model." He shuffled over to the giant whiteboard on the front wall, removed a red dry-erase marker from the ledge, and drew a rudimentary map of the North American continent on the melamine. "In the past, the cartels have always moved narcotics and cash across our borders using standardized methods—land, air, sea," he explained, drawing three arrows advancing from Mexico into the southern states. "Once the drugs were sold here, the money would work its way from street dealers to middlemen, middlemen to collectors, and then be stored inside a stash house. At that point, two things would generally occur." He inked two bullet points in the Atlantic Ocean. "*First*, they would attempt to send smaller amounts of cash back to Mexico, which were deemed non-detrimental if seized. *Second*, they would launder the remainder of the money through American businesses, like casinos, exchanging it for clean cash. The Achilles heel of this system has always been the cartel's desire to get as much money back to Mexico as quickly as possible because the longer it sat here in no-man's-land," he drew a lopsided circle in middle America, "the greater the chances of something going wrong—whether that be a raid by us, or someone on the inside ripping them off."

"What's changed?" Mike asked, sitting next to Frank, three rows up in the center of the room, seeking information that the crowd wasn't already familiar with.

"We believe they have now implemented a complex system for purchasing high-value artwork, in which all acquisitions are being made legally between legitimate art dealers and collectors in a wide variety of countries. None of these participants has any obvious ties to Mexico. Additionally, the cartels are showing the patience to allow the paintings to remain in place for extended periods after purchase, causing the trail to run cold. *This*, ladies and gentlemen, is about to make our jobs exponentially more difficult."

CHAPTER fifteen

A splitting headache throbbed deep inside Sara's skull as her eyes slowly began to open. The horrific events of the nightclub suddenly materialized inside her fog-filled brain, causing her to jolt upright. She found herself beneath a set of dull, yellow bedsheets on a cheap twin-sized bed in the corner of an unfamiliar, white-walled bedroom. Instinctively, she attempted to draw her legs up towards her chest. The right complied, but something was restraining her left. Removing the sheets from her body, she discovered a metallic cuff securing her leg to the bed's cast iron frame. Sara looked to her left and found Marla—equally restrained—lying unconscious on an identical bed on the other side of the room.

Sara looked toward the door and discovered that it was partially open. Through the gap, she could see a hallway. A cheap plastic clock hanging on the wall displayed the time as 12:19, and the sunlight filtering through the blinds of the barred window between the two beds suggested it was daytime rather than night.

"Marla!" Sara whispered as loudly as she could without allowing her voice to be carried out into the hall. "Marla!"

She didn't budge.

Sara maneuvered herself to the edge of her mattress and began to contort herself over her shackled appendage, angling herself down onto the gray carpet below. The sharp metal cuff dug into the tender skin of her ankle as she reached out towards Marla's bed, but came up short.

"Wake up!" Sara demanded, attempting to drag the heavy bed across the room, quickly discovering that it was bolted to the floor.

"Mar!" she whispered a bit louder, twisting and torquing her body in every imaginable position to gain a few extra inches of reach. Finally, the pressure became too much, and she felt a *POP* in her knee, and a lightning bolt of pain registered deep inside her brain. Her face winced as the connective tissue burned like fire beneath the skin. Despite the ferocity of the pain, Sara knew she didn't have time to dwell on it. She flipped onto her back and swiped a hand blindly above her head until she felt her fingertips contact the edge of the bed frame. Bridging herself onto the back of her head and shoulders, she was able to gain a slightly better grip on the underside of the bed.

"Wake up!" Sara grunted, shaking the rail as hard as she could, quickly sapping her limited energy.

Just then, Sara felt a tiny movement through the frame. She craned her head back and discovered that one of Marla's arms had fallen over the edge of the mattress and was now dangling in the air. Suddenly, she noticed the unsightly purple and yellow bruises in the crook of Marla's elbow, causing her to inspect her own arms, which were pocked with the same ugly blemishes. Immediately, she realized they were track marks, which explained Marla's current level of incapacitation, as well as the persistent waves of nausea she had been experiencing since waking up inside this terrifying ordeal. However, as with the damage to her knee, Sara knew she couldn't dwell on this discovery either; instead, she needed to rouse her friend and determine a way out of this nightmare.

Sara grabbed onto Marla's dangling fingers, walked her grip up to her wrist, and shook her arm as violently as possible, given her outstretched position.

"Wake up!"

"Mmrruugghh," a groggy groan finally sounded from atop the mattress.

Sara continued to jostle her arm. “Yes! That’s it! Wake up!”

“Saaaarrrrr?” Marla slurred, pulling her arm onto the bed, away from Sara’s grip.

“It’s me, Mar! It’s Sara! We need to get out of here!”

“Wheeerrreee arrreee yooouuuuu?”

“I’m down here.” Sara grabbed onto the bed frame again and gave it another shake.

Marla’s face crept sluggishly over the edge of the mattress until the sight of Sara sprawled out on the carpet caused her eyes to open fully. A spike of adrenaline shot through her body, countering the tranquilizing effects of the narcotics, and she too jolted upright on her mattress.

“Oh my God!” she exclaimed too loudly. “Where are we? How—” Sara watched Marla’s face drop as the horrific events of the nightclub began to flood back into her disjointed mind. Tears welled in her eyes, and she fell silent.

“We have to be quiet,” Sara urged her. “I have no idea where we are, or if we’re alone. I just woke up, too.”

“What do we do?” Marla lowered her voice. “It feels like the whole room is spinning.” Just then, she discovered the cuff encircling her bruised and swollen ankle. She stared at it in disbelief.

Sara climbed back onto her mattress.

“Look, I know it’s hard, but we both need to stay calm,” Sara instructed from across the room. “I think they’ve been injecting us with something—to keep us sedated.”

Marla looked down at her forearms, discovering the needle marks. She covered her mouth. “How long do you think we’ve been here?” she whispered into her palm.

“I shaved my legs before we went out that night, and they’re still pretty smooth. So, it can’t have been more than a few days,” Sara explained.

“Are they going to kill—”

"We can't think like that." Sara cut her off immediately. "We just need to concentrate on getting out of here before they come back to give us more drugs."

As Marla looked around the bedroom, Sara noticed the wild wisps of her unruly blonde hair bobbing back and forth on her head.

"Hey, do you have any pins left?" Sara inquired.

"Huh?"

"In your hair?

Marla searched her scalp. "No, they must have all fallen—" Just then, her finger contacted a single strip of wavy metal. She removed it, sending another strand of yellow down in front of her face. "I found one!"

"Toss it over," Sara instructed. "Maybe I can use it on these cuffs. My dad showed me once when I was little."

Marla attempted to lob the fastener to Sara, but her energy-sapped arms under-delivered on the throw. It hit the edge of Sara's mattress and somersaulted spastically towards a hungry-looking air register between the beds. Marla watched in horror as it landed across the grates, teetering above the blackness. Sara scrambled off her mattress and rescued the hairpin before it disappeared, but in the process, she had placed additional strain on her injured knee. She slowly pulled herself back up onto her mattress and cradled her throbbing joint.

"What's wrong?"

"I hurt my knee before you woke up," she explained, touching it gingerly.

"Oh my God. How bad is it?"

"It doesn't matter." Sara downplayed the extent of the injury, forcing the pain out of her mind once more. She inserted the bobby pin into the keyhole of her ankle cuff. "I'll work on mine first and then—"

Just then, two male voices arrived from somewhere down the hall. Sara and Marla both froze in place, staring at the door. The men seemed to be speaking Spanish, and the girls looked at one another in terror as the voices began to increase in volume.

"Quick," Sara whispered to Marla, "pretend to be sleeping."

The girls adjusted themselves and pulled the sheets over their bodies. Sara turned her head and mashed the side of her face deeply into her pillow, allowing herself a single squinting eye to monitor the door and Marla's bed simultaneously. A moment later, a pair of unfamiliar men appeared in the hallway

"¿Necesitan más drogas?" the taller of the two men asked his companion as he pushed open the door and evaluated the captives inside. He was wearing blue jeans, an orange t-shirt, and sported closely-cropped black hair that matched the five o'clock shadow on his face.

"No estoy seguro," the stockier man, wearing tapered black sweatpants, a wrinkled gray tank top, and white Converse high-top sneakers, responded with a lazy shrug of uncertainty. He entered the room and moved towards Marla's bed, while his companion remained at the door. As he entered her view, Sara spotted a large, intricate tattoo of a fire-breathing dragon inked on the left side of his neck.

Across the room, Marla had positioned herself face down on the mattress and, to her credit, looked every bit as unconscious as before. Sara observed the olive-skinned stranger approach the foot of her bed and place a hand on Marla's lowered leg, caressing her calf softly. He moved his way up the back of her thigh until he reached her backside. Every ounce of Sara's being wanted to scream from across the room, objecting to the disgusting act that was taking place, but she knew that if she did, it would destroy any chance they had to escape. The predator's hand slithered up onto Marla's back. Just before it reached her neck, he finally removed it from her body.

Thank God, it's over, Sara thought to herself.

CRACK!

The man suddenly slapped Marla in the back of the head, causing Sara's nausea to intensify and igniting a burning rage throughout her body. Unbelievably, Marla had managed to keep her composure, refusing to flinch. The creep looked back at his partner by the door and smiled, apparently satisfied with his victim's level of incapacitation.

Sara knew she'd be next.

As much as she wanted to keep an eye on the predator, Sara shut her eyes and relaxed her facial muscles. When the man approached, she could smell his vile, sour stench, and her mind screamed when she felt him remove a single strand of auburn hair from her cheek with his fingers. She waited anxiously in the darkness of her mind, readying herself for the same violent cuff to the back of the head. Instead, the man took hold of her shoulder and a belt loop on her pants and began to shake her forcefully. The pain in her knee grew exponentially as she bounced up and down on the mattress. But somehow, just like Marla, Sara remained strong. After a few more torturous seconds, it was over.

"¿Americanas?" the man standing at the door asked his partner, seemingly confused by the ethnicity of the two females.

The other man didn't respond, only offering another shrug.

"¿Sabe el jefe que tenemos Americanos?" the taller man asked him something else.

The tattooed captor finally left Sara's bedside and made his way back to the door, mumbling something to his partner before they disappeared out the door.

Sara opened her eyes and focused on Marla across the room. A single tear rolled down Marla's cheek.

"We're going to get out of here, Mar," Sara said, trying her best to comfort her traumatized friend. "I promise."

Sara returned her attention to the cuff. "What was that guy at the door asking?" she questioned Marla, who, unlike her, had taken some advanced Spanish in high school.

Marla slowly sat up. "He asked if someone knew that they had Americans here," she translated as best she could, trying to get her breathing under control. "The other guy told him to forget it or not to worry about it."

Sara continued to work on her shackle.

"Where are we?" Marla whimpered.

"No idea." Sara squeezed the steel circle, attempting to access the locking mechanism from a slightly different angle, just as her father had shown her.

"Why would—"

"I got it!" Sara suddenly announced, releasing her foot from the silver restraint. Just that amount of movement was enough to send another jolt of pain up her spine.

"Seriously, are you okay? Marla asked her again.

"No, I'm not okay!" Sara said sharply now. "Neither of us is *okay,* Marla. But if we don't get the fuck out of this room, things are going to get a hell of a lot worse for us than just some busted knee."

Marla wiped the tear from her cheek, attempting to compose herself. "You're right."

Sara abandoned her mattress and hobbled across the room to Marla's bed, where the two girls embraced silently for a moment before Sara began working on Marla's cuff. Once free, Marla dropped her legs over the edge of her mattress onto the floor and took a moment to reestablish her compromised equilibrium.

The girls left the bed and crept their way to the open door, where they took turns peeking out into the hallway, discovering that they were on the second floor of what appeared to be a two-story house. They found no signs of movement in either direction.

"I think we should try to make our way to the stairs at the end of the hall," Sara suggested.

Marla nodded.

They each took a deep breath and stepped out of the bedroom. Sara led the way, limping and steadying herself on the wall, attempting to relieve some pressure from her knee.

Soon, they arrived at an open door on the opposite side of the hallway. Sara pressed her chest against the wall and cautiously peeked her eye around the doorframe. The inside of this bedroom looked eerily similar to the one they had just escaped from. On the mattresses were two young females, lying unconsciously beneath identical yellow bedsheets. Marla maneuvered herself behind Sara to have a look, and when she discovered the other prisoners, she gripped onto the back of Sara's arm. They stepped back from the door and met face-to-face.

"What do we do?" Marla whispered in a panic.

Sara glanced to the top of the stairs.

"I don't know, but whatever we decide, we need to find an exit first," she reasoned. As she said it, she noticed a vacancy in Marla's eyes. "Are you alright?"

Marla gave her head a shake. "Sorry. Everything just feels like it's moving in slow motion."

"Yeah, I feel it, too," Sara admitted. "Whatever they've been giving us must still be affecting our systems. We just need to keep moving."

The girls slipped past the bedroom and crept to the stairs that looked to lead down into a white-tiled kitchen on the ground floor of the mysterious house. Sara gripped onto the railing and began to limp down each step until she eventually stood on the second-to-last. From this position, she could hear what sounded like a television in a distant room off to the right. The girls pressed their backs tightly against the wall, listening intently, and discovered that the channels were actively being changed. Sara worked up the courage to lean herself out from the staircase a little. On the left side of the kitchen—opposite the noise from the television—she spotted a doorless coat closet with a full-length mirror next to it. Just then, a flash of movement in the mirror's reflection caused Sara's heart rate to skyrocket. She retracted her head back into the stairwell and held her breath. Marla sensed Sara's rapid rise in anxiety and froze with fear.

A man had entered the kitchen from a hallway to the right and was talking on his phone. Though he was oblivious to the girls' presence in the stairwell across the room, his voice began to grow louder as he closed in on their location. Sara could feel Marla's frantic heart beating through the fingertips that were clawed on her arm.

"Yes, they here now," the man reported into the phone in spotty English. "Yes. No worry."

As the stranger approached, the girls shut their eyes and pressed their backs even more forcefully into the wall. Just before the man was about to turn the corner to go up the stairs, he suddenly stopped, listening to further instructions from the caller.

"OK, no problem. I go there now," he said.

The man resumed his pace and walked past the staircase, heading for the door. Just before he arrived, Sara poked her head out again, discovering that he was the taller of the two kidnappers—the one who had remained at the bedroom door while his partner assaulted them. Sara watched him flip open the security panel next to the exit and type in a four-digit code. '*2-8-7-3 . . . 2-8-7-3 . . . 2-8-7-3. . .*' Sara began repeating the digits over and over inside her head. The man closed the cover, pulled open the door, and quickly exited the house.

Once he was gone, the girls entered the kitchen and made their way to the door silently, while the television continued to play on the other side of the house. Sara flipped open the security panel and saw a green light indicating the system was active.

"Is the alarm going to go off if we open the door?" Marla wondered.

"I saw him enter the code," Sara revealed. "2-8-7-3."

There was a mixture of elation and confusion on Marla's face. "What are we waiting for? Let's get out of here."

Sara looked Marla straight in her eyes. "If anything happens before I get back down here, I want you to enter the code and get yourself out of this house, okay?"

"What? No!" Marla's face took on a look of abject horror. "What are you talking about? Where are you going?" She grabbed Sara's arm, looking as if she might burst into tears.

"We can't just leave those other girls in this house by themselves."

"We'll go get them help!" Marla pleaded. "The cops will come back for them! Don't leave me! Please!"

"I'll be right back, Mar. I promise. Just hide yourself in the closet, and I'll be back before you know it."

"We don't even know where we are," Marla whimpered. "And your knee..."

"It's not that bad," Sara lied. "If I can't get their cuffs off quickly, I can at least tell them that we're sending back help—just like you said, okay?"

Reluctantly, Marla agreed, releasing her ironclad grip on Sara's arm. She tiptoed to the doorless coat closet and began hiding herself behind dangling clothing.

"I'll be right back," Sara assured her once more. "If anything happens, don't wait, just go get help."

Sara limped back across the kitchen and began to climb the carpeted stairs. She peeked over the landing and saw no new signs of movement in the hallway, then made her way directly to the bedroom where they had discovered the other girls.

Poking her head around the edge of the doorframe, she found the situation inside the room unchanged. Both girls had their bodies and faces covered by yellow bed sheets. Sara made her way to the bed on the left, looking around the room as she did so. Unlike the space she and Marla had just woken up in, there were random personal effects strewn about this one. When Sara arrived at the head of the mattress, she gently withdrew the sheet, revealing the face of a young girl with flowing black hair and an elegant button nose. She couldn't have been more than fifteen or sixteen years old. As the cotton sheet swept across the girl's chin, her eyes flickered open, revealing chocolate brown irises and pinpoint pupils that stared up at Sara.

"I'm here to help you," Sara whispered to her. "I'm going to get you guys out of here."

The dazed girl stared blankly at the stranger who was now moving towards the foot of her mattress, bobby pin in hand. Sara withdrew the remainder of the sheet from the girl's bare feet, and to her surprise, she found no restraints on either of her ankles. Sara looked at the pint-sized girl who now sat upright in her cotton-candy pink pajamas.

"You're not tied up?" Sara asked, confused.

"Quem e Voce," the young girl replied too loudly and in a language that Sara didn't think sounded quite like Spanish.

"English?" Sara said before placing a finger in front of her lips, requesting the girl to lower her voice.

"Quem e Voce," the girl repeated at an identical volume.

Sara decided that it might be more prudent to try her luck with the hostage on the other bed. She made her way across the room and immediately removed the bedsheets from a second pair of equally unrestrained legs.

"Cici!" the tiny girl from the first mattress called out to her roommate, who woke from her slumber and sat upright. She was much more solid-looking than the first, with dirty blonde hair, thick angular eyebrows and a round face. She appeared to be at least a decade older than the other girl.

"What you doing?" She questioned Sara in a thick, unplaceable accent.

"Don't worry, I'm not one of them. I just woke up in one of the other bedrooms with my friend," Sara whispered. "We found an exit downstairs. We can escape."

"Ascape?" The girl seemed to fumble with the word.

"Where are your cuffs?" Sara pointed at the girl's naked ankles, miming circles with her fingers.

"Ela Quer?" the girl from the first bed said loudly.

"Tell her she needs to be quiet," Sara instructed, trying to use the blonde as a translator. "I think there's still someone downstairs watching television," she pointed at the floor. "We need to leave. Right now." She grabbed the blonde girl's arm, trying to pull her up from the bed.

"Why you want to leave?" She resisted Sara's tugging. "We almost there."

"Almost where?" Sara felt frustration building inside her now. "What the fuck are you talking about? There's a door downstairs. It's unlocked. We can *escape*."

The word seemed to register this time, and the blonde girl's face suddenly became more serious. She looked at her roommate.

"ESCAPE!" she hollered loudly. "ESCAPE!"

A look of terror flashed across Sara's face as she stumbled back from the bed. Suddenly, the girl with the black hair jumped up on her mattress and began to scream as well, although it was not clear that she fully understood the word's meaning. "ES-CAPE! ES-CAPE! ES-CAPE!" she parroted as loudly as her tiny body would allow.

"What the fuck are you doing!?" Sara shouted at them, backpedaling wildly out the door. Her knee suddenly gave out, causing her to crash violently into the wall across the hall and onto the floor. She scrambled onto her hands and knees as the shouting behind her continued.

Reaching the top of the stairs, Sara heard a loud commotion in the kitchen below. A door slammed. Glass shattered. Sara stood and attempted to descend the first step, but her knee buckled, causing her to tumble down the stairs in a chaotic flailing of arms and legs. Her head smashed against the unforgiving tile floor, sending a high-pitched ringing into her ears and starbursts throughout her vision. She took hold of the wooden railing and slowly pulled herself back to her feet, attempting to steady her shell-shocked brain.

The ringing in her ears began to ease, but was quickly replaced by Marla's terror-filled screams. Sara looked across the kitchen and discovered the man with the dragon tattoo straddling Marla, pinning her arms against the floor. He was drawing a dark, oil-colored liquid into a large syringe and hollering at Marla as she struggled against the force of his body weight. He dropped the glass vial and plunged the needle deep into her thigh, using his free hand to cover her mouth, muffling her screams.

"Marla..." Sara mumbled through the taste of metallic blood in her mouth, having bitten her tongue during the fall. She hobbled toward the door to scream for help. Whatever had been in the syringe worked on Marla quickly, putting an unconscious end to her struggles. The kidnapper removed his hand from her mouth and spotted Sara limping towards the exit.

"Where do you think you're going?" The predator rose to his feet, taunting his prey. He closed the distance quickly and kicked Sara's legs out from under her, causing her to fall violently onto her back, fifteen feet short of the door. Standing over her, the man reached down for her flailing arms. Suddenly, Sara sent a powerful kick into his groin with her uninjured leg, causing him to drop backwards onto the floor. Sara flipped onto her stomach and got back to her feet as the kidnapper groaned in agony behind her.

"Get her!" she heard him shout as she neared the exit.

A pair of bare feet stomped across the kitchen floor, and suddenly, Sara felt two spindly arms wrap around her. Looking down, she discovered the dark-haired girl from the bedroom locked around her waist. Sara shoved the weightless youngster to the ground and took hold of the copper-colored doorknob. She had barely pulled the door inward an inch when something smashed into the back of her head like a freight train. She crashed into the door and dropped onto the tiles.

Sara blinked in and out of consciousness, and the room began to spin. She mustered just enough strength to roll over onto her back and discovered the blonde from the bedroom standing over her, holding a silver frying pan in her hands. The tattooed kidnapper rose to his feet, and in Sara's cerebral haze, she watched as he removed a bottle of pills from his pocket and quickly dispensed a few tablets into each of the girls' outstretched hands, commending them for their efforts.

"You're almost there..." he told them, wearing a sinister look on his face. Sara's concussed brain finally reached the limit of what it could endure and went offline.

CHAPTER sixteen

The elevator carrying Frank and Mike had completed its descent to the *Science, Engineering, and Technology* floor of the FBI Building in Manhattan, and the steel doors slid open. When they stepped out, they found the entire level to be a bustling beehive of activity.

"Good afternoon, gentlemen." Winston was there to greet them, wearing his white lab coat and holding a wooden clipboard. Just then, a flame-thrower was discharged inside a safety-glassed laboratory over his right shoulder, roasting a mannequin dressed in a silver flame-retardant hazmat suit.

"Holy shit!" exclaimed Mike, whose eyes widened at the sight of the orange and yellow fireball of dragon's breath. "What's all this?"

"Oh yes, I forgot to mention, we *do* have some inter-agency demonstrations happening this morning."

"Looks like a full-blown dork convention," Mike teased. "Where's the guy who signs your comic books?" He pretended to look around. "Or is this more like one of those Dungeons and Dragons LARPing parties?"

Winston raised an eyebrow. "Frank, please try to ensure your pet monkey doesn't get distracted by the flashing lights and shiny objects."

"Only if you promise me a banana when we're done," Mike countered.

The three men made their way across the floor, passing a workstation where an engineer removed the lid from what looked to be a run-of-the-mill silver coffee tumbler. On the inside was a collection of multi-colored wires that seemed to impress the bespectacled onlookers, who scribbled furiously onto their little notepads. At the next station were three middle-aged women dismantling a high-powered CPU and discussing the components. Eventually, the trio arrived at a door, where Winston swiped the key card that hung around his neck. Frank and Mike followed him inside a small room and made their way over to a stainless-steel table, on top of which lay two canvases, twenty-four by thirty-six inches. Between them was a black box contraption with a pair of flat metal arms protruding from its sides. The canvas on the left displayed a painting of an idyllic autumn landscape with a gurgling aquamarine brook and craggy, snow-capped mountains in the distance. The canvas on the right was blank.

"What do you have here?" Frank asked as they positioned themselves at the table's edge.

"Whoa! That looks like one of those paintings the guy on TV used to make when I was a kid," Mike commented. "You remember him, Frankie? He had the big puffy hair, ugh, what was his name?"

"Bob Ross?"

"Yeah!" Mike replied excitedly. "Man, that guy could put you into a trance with his soft talking ways..." he reminisced. "Did you guys get Bob Ross over there in England, Winny? No, no, wait, let me guess. Your guy probably had some *really* fancy British name, like Sir Robert Rossington the III, or something, right?"

Winston stared at Mike for a moment. Rather than engaging, he turned his attention to Frank.

"I've brought you down here today to show you our latest 3-D printing technologies. Traditionally, these devices have operated by fully encapsulating a solid object, taking its precise measurements, and then layering polymer to construct an identical duplicate," Winston explained, pressing a button on the console of the black box, activating the metal bars. They began to move in perfect unison, slowly duplicating the image on the left to the canvas on the right. "We've modified that technology to operate an open-air system and found it to be quite proficient in the reproduction of art."

"How long does it take to make a copy?" Frank asked, bending down to inspect the underside of the spray bar.

"It all depends on the complexity of the work: its size, the medium used, and the variability of pigmentation. But generally speaking, an average-sized painting such as this can be fully copied in thirty to forty-five minutes. Additionally, we have the ability to download a file to print a copy at a later time."

"What do you say we print ourselves off a few Mona Lisas and start living like kings?" Mike joked.

"Unfortunately, the duplications will not hold up under intense scrutiny," Winston explained. "While they may look identical to the naked eye, this technology lacks the ability to sufficiently age the medium at a microscopic level."

CHAPTER seventeen

Two long tables had been set end-to-end inside the conference room at the back of Zinex Pharmaceuticals' San Francisco branch. Each of the employees in attendance had received an identical email from Ken Collins requesting their presence on a day when the office was normally closed. Although the CEO had not divulged any specifics regarding the impromptu meeting, most in attendance believed it likely involved the branch's lackluster sales for the previous three quarters, which included the release of a highly anticipated medication that their branch had been tasked with rolling out. After six months on the market, revenue from the novel drug had fallen abysmally short of projections.

The people in the room chatted idly amongst each other, glancing from time to time at the clock on the wall. Collins was late, and the senior-most employees knew that his tardiness was no coincidence; it was a direct message to everyone in attendance: *"My time is more valuable than yours—don't you ever fucking forget it."*

Finally, through the glass wall, and on the opposite side of the fifteenth floor, the elevator doors slid open, revealing the CEO, flanked by two other high-profile Zinex executives carrying briefcases. The conversation inside the conference room simmered into a hush as the three sharply-dressed figureheads began their imperial march across the office.

On Collins' left was his second-in-command, CFO Derek Crenshaw. A math prodigy by age six, he had once managed a multi-billion-dollar portfolio at a prominent hedge fund until he was charged with stock manipulation, fraud, and a slew of other nefarious white-collar crimes. He quickly cooperated with the SEC, providing names and evidence against his co-conspirators, and by doing so, he avoided serving prison time for the unethical indiscretions he had masterminded.

On Collins' right was Jessica Blount, Zinex's COO. Once a highly sought-after, cut-throat criminal defense attorney—and former Miss Rhode Island—she had been personally headhunted by Collins three years ago. It was rumored that she had been promised complete autonomy in her progression up the corporate ladder, which had ultimately landed her in her current post.

The gang of three arrived at the glass doors of the conference room and entered one by one. Collins moved quickly to the head of the table on the far side of the room, with his posse following closely behind. Once they were in place, the two underlings set their briefcases on the table and took their seats. Collins elected to remain standing, pouring himself a glass of water from a black-and-silver carafe. He took a long, slow sip before setting the glass back down on the table.

"Barbara Nelson..." he said flatly.

A petite, thirty-year-old redhead with a high ponytail that matched her librarian-style eyeglasses turned her head. Having only been employed by Zinex for four years, she was one of the most junior employees in attendance.

"Uh, yes, Mr. Collins?" she replied.

Collins stared intently at the bookish-looking woman until the direct eye contact seemed to lift her out of her chair.

"Yes, Mr. Collins," she repeated, attempting to feign a bit of confidence.

"Miss Nelson, have you ever heard of the medication, Talproxinol?"

Barbara appeared puzzled. Of course, she had; it was the underperforming medication that the branch had been assigned to roll out.

"Umm, yes, sir. It's used for the treatmen—"

"And you *are* a resident of California?" The CEO didn't bother letting her finish.

"Uh, yes, sir..." She smiled nervously, looking around at some of her colleagues. "Born and raised right here in San Francisco."

"That surprises me," Collins said without emotion.

The grin on the redhead's face slowly disappeared, and the sound of Derek Crenshaw unclipping his briefcase filled the room. The CFO handed his boss a singular spreadsheet from within.

"Because by the looks of *these* sales numbers, I would have guessed that there isn't a single person in this entire fucking state that knows that drug exists!"

Instinctively, Barbara knew to sit back down.

"Now," Collins proceeded with the inquisition, "can anyone in this room tell me which branch was *originally* tasked with Talproxinol's release?"

No one dared to supply the answer.

"Nobody, huh? Perhaps Miss Blount here can fill us in," he said, looking at his COO.

"Houston," she produced the answer without hesitation.

"And Derek, why do you imagine I might entrust the Houston branch with such a responsibility?"

"Because Houston has a flawless track record of consistently surpassing launch estimates, year after year, regardless of the product," the CFO responded robotically.

"They certainly do, don't they..." Collins nodded, satisfied with the answer. "So then, how was it that *this* branch ended up in charge of our most anticipated launch in the last half decade?"

Nobody in the room uttered a word as the CEO scanned the crowd. Eventually, his gaze settled on the branch's general manager, Curtis Wildfell—a balding, nicotine-dependent forty-six-year-old with a graying goatee and an easy-going, down-to-earth manner that his subordinates appreciated.

"Curtis!" Collins called out to him with what felt like a sarcastic friendliness. "I almost didn't see you there!"

"Good morning, Mr. Collins," Wildfell responded somewhat sheepishly.

"Derek," the CEO turned his attention back to the human calculator sitting next to him, "can you tell me where this location ranked in sales metrics, I dunno, let's say...three years ago?"

"Nationwide?"

"Please."

"Fourth."

"Fourth!" Collins echoed the figure with emphasis. "Wow! That's pretty damn good!" After all, Zinex does have many locations, don't we?"

"Thirty-three, sir," Crenshaw quantified.

Collins focused on Curtis again. "What about now, Derek? Where does the San Francisco branch rank...now?"

"Dead last," he reported flatly.

"Last?" Collins looked mystified. "No, no, no, that can't be right. From fourth to last? In just three years? That's impossible. You've made an error."

"I don't make errors," Crenshaw replied arrogantly. "Numbers don't lie."

"Hmm," Collins scratched his chin. "Perhaps we need to slow things down and take this one step at a time. Three years ago, San Francisco was kicking ass and taking names, and then suddenly, *BOOM*, everything fell off a cliff. Can anybody hazard a guess as to what might have changed in that time?"

Silence.

"Oh, you know what it probably was?" Collins decided to field his own question. "I bet that the average American finally decided to get off his fat fucking ass and start exercising and eating properly." He nodded. "The problem is, people have become *so* healthy that they simply don't need our medications anymore. Yes, that must be it. Don't you agree, Miss Blount?"

The ex-attorney shook her head. "The average American has never been more unhealthy, and the use of pharmaceuticals in this country is at an all-time high. Our industry is booming."

"Well, then. I'm stumped..." Collins shrugged his shoulders, theatrically turning his back to the crowd. A few seconds passed by in awkward silence. "Hey, wait a minute!" The CEO suddenly turned around and moved down the right side of the table, taking a position directly across from Wildfell. He set his hands on the backs of the chairs of two frozen employees. "When did you take over operations at this branch, Curtis? It's been a while now, hasn't it?"

The manager cleared his throat. After a long, drawn-out moment, he finally spoke. "Three years ago..." he admitted, looking as dejected as a puppy caught ripping apart its owner's favorite slippers.

"You and I had a meeting about a year ago, didn't we?" Collins pressed forward, while Wildfell seemed to sink into his seat.

"One year ago, ladies and gentlemen, Curtis and I sat in his office, one floor above," he pointed at the ceiling, "and he begged me, he fucking *BEGGED* me not to fire him! I had to sit there and listen to his sob story about his divorce and the custody battle he was having for his kids and blah, blah, fucking blah..." Collins stared at the man with disgust. "He claimed that the underperformance of the branch wasn't his fault. '*If only I had a new product to launch*,' he told me. '*One I could really sink my teeth into. Then things would turn around.*'"

Curtis' cheeks flushed red with embarrassment as he relived the meeting inside his mind.

"At that time, Talproxinol had just passed stage three approval," Collins continued. "And against *my* better judgment, I agreed to give you one last chance."

The manager remained silent, his eyes dropping to the table in front of him.

"But I made a stipulation, didn't I, Curtis?"

Everyone in the room could hear the restrained anger building up in the CEO's voice now.

"Come on now, Curtis! Don't be shy! You had no problem flapping your fucking gums when we made the deal!"

Curtis' eyes lifted slowly, begging for the verbal assault to end.

"*YOU* said—and I quote— *'If things don't turn around after the first quarter of Talproxinol's release, I will tender my resignation immediately!'*" Collins recounted loudly. "Now, Derek," he pointed a finger back to the head of the table without taking his eyes off his prey. "When did those quarter reports come out?"

"Over three months ago, sir."

"Three *fucking* months ago!" Collins echoed with volume. "Well then, I guess my next question would be, WHY THE FUCK ARE YOU STILL HERE?" he hollered angrily across the table. "Do you think I'm some sort of fucking idiot? Did you think I'd just forget what you said and let you run this branch into the ground year after year after year, with no repercussions? I gave you so many fucking chances, you incompetent piece of shit!" Collins gnashed his teeth like a rabid animal. "I even gave you the chance to resign quietly and bow out with whatever pathetic semblance of dignity you might have had left!" He snarled, looking as if he might lunge across the table and strangle Wildfell with his bare hands. "But you couldn't even do that much, could you?"

Three security guards had stepped off the elevator and were quickly approaching the boardroom.

"Go upstairs, collect your shit, and get the fuck out of my building, Curtis! You're fired!"

The guards entered the conference room and positioned themselves behind the now former manager. Curtis pushed his chair away from the table, slowly stood up, and began his walk of shame towards the exit. Just before he reached the doors, he stopped and turned to face his old boss.

"The sales tactics you promote at those other branches, like Houston, are completely unethical, and you know it!" he raised his voice, which caused the largest of the three security guards to place a suggestive hand on his shoulder. Curtis shook off the man's grip and suddenly bolted around the end of the table toward Collins. He made it to within ten feet of the CEO before the security guard chased him down and wrapped an arm around his neck, stopping him dead in his tracks. "You're paying doctors to prescribe medications and mrrmguhh," was all Curtis got out before the heavily-muscled guard squeezed in the choke more forcefully, causing Curtis' eyes to bulge out of his head, halting his speech.

"Let me remind you of something." An evil smirk spread across Collins' face as he walked toward the oxygen-deprived man, being dragged backward toward the exit. "Every one of us in this room has a signed NDA. That means, if *anybody* speaks of Zinex's business practices—especially baseless fabrications like the one you've just made—I can guarantee the financial ruin not only of you, but of every member of your immediate family, as well. And that includes those snot-nosed brat kids you don't get to see anymore, Curtis," Collins heartlessly twisted the knife.

The security guard pulled his detainee out of the room, and Collins turned around to scan the faces of the remaining employees. Every one of them was sitting in silent, wide-eyed disbelief. Collins began making his way back to the head of the table.

"Mr. Crenshaw..." The CEO's voice suddenly sounded calmer and more level-headed. "How much was Zinex compensating that man?"

"Including the company car and benefits?"

"Sure. Lump sum it for me."

"Approximately $425,000."

Collins looked through the glass, watching the security guards climb inside the elevator and surround the ex-manager. "425,000 dollars...to fail." Collins shook his head. "And, Miss Blount, how many people work in this particular office?"

"San Francisco has fifty-five full-time employees."

"How many are in attendance today?"

"Twenty-one."

Collins glanced at Curtis' now-empty chair.

"Pardon me. Twenty, sir," the CFO corrected herself.

"I'm wondering if anyone in this room can hazard a guess as to why you were all invited to this meeting instead of your co-workers?"

Not a single hand rose, not a single syllable was uttered.

"Well then, let me tell you *exactly* why you are in here," he paused for effect. "It's because, according to Mr. Crenshaw's metrics, the twenty of you are the only ones in this *entire* branch who have consistently done their jobs to any respectable degree in the past three years."

The statement took a moment to sink in, but once it had, pairs of traumatized eyes began to lift from the table. A thousand scattered thoughts collectively ricocheted, as an ethereal sense of relief began to flood through the room.

"Curtis Wildfell was dead weight," Collins proclaimed. "Yet despite him, all of you somehow persevered. Well, the dead weight is gone now, people!" he began to rally the troops. "And as an apology for what you've had to endure, I'm going to divide the $425,000 Zinex would have wasted on that *loser* over the next year and put it directly onto your next paychecks! Now, how does that sound?!"

Twenty heads simultaneously turned toward the CEO, and looks of bewilderment gave way to smiles as the click-clack of mental calculators began to drown out any thoughts of the emotionally and professionally crippled former boss.

"Curtis Wildfell no longer exists to you!" Collins made it clear. "If anybody believes this is unfair, please feel free to join him. Hell, I'll even give you a nice little severance package, and you can be on your merry fucking way! But I have a sneaking suspicion that none of you want that, do you? I think that the people still inside *this* room are a bunch of fucking *winners!*" The statement elicited the nodding of heads and looks of determination. "What I see is a bunch of winners who want to make a shitload of money and *succeed* in life! Am I right!?"

A chinless, heavy-set man in a gray-flannel suit near the end of the table suddenly clapped his hands loudly, and a few others joined in by shouting affirmations.

"Miss Blount?" Collins placed his hands on her shoulders.

"Yes, sir?" She continued to stare straight ahead.

"Seems a tad bit quiet in here for a group of people who just pocketed twenty grand before lunch, doesn't it?"

"Very."

Just then, a middle-aged woman wearing cherry-red lipstick and diamond stud earrings rose from her seat and let out an excited hoot, prompting others to stand, cheer, and begin to high-five each other. Before long, the conference room was transformed into a high school pep rally for capitalists. Collins tapped Derek Crenshaw on the shoulder, and he too rose to his feet, closed his briefcase, and removed it from the table.

"Fuck it! Let's double it!" Collins shouted over the noise. "Forty thousand dollars each!" The cheers grew even more raucous when the CEO directed the room's attention towards a mule train of white-gloved servers exiting the elevators, pushing half a dozen catering carts in their direction.

"I'm leaving Miss Blount as your interim manager until I can find a suitable replacement," Collins announced, causing the employees to direct their applause towards their new boss. "She'll be implementing some new sales tactics around here that you'll all be adhering to going forward. As for the people who were not invited to this meeting today," the CEO pointed through the glass at the empty desks, "most are being let go, while a few others are being spoken to about their performances and put on probation as we speak. And if things don't change, they'll be out of their asses too," Collins threatened. "Moving forward, if you have *any* deadweight on your team, bring it to the attention of Miss Blount *immediately,* and I can personally guarantee it will be dealt with. And just remember," he arrived at the door and took hold of the handle, "what happened in this room today stays between us. Nobody needs to know anything about the termination or the bonus compensation you received. Just be sure that the next time I come back, you're all still on the right side of this glass." Collins wrapped a knuckle on the door before pulling it inward. "Now, enjoy your lunch!" The boisterous cheers continued as the two executives stepped out of the conference room, and the catering carts were wheeled inside.

Collins and Crenshaw reached the elevators and called the unit down from above. Moments later, the silver doors slid open, and inside stood Curtis Wildfell, holding a cardboard box filled with his personal effects. The same group of security guards surrounded him, readying themselves should another angry interaction occur. Just then, over Collins' shoulder, a loud cheer suddenly erupted inside the conference room when the catering staff activated a three-tier chocolate fondue fountain, and glucose-rich lava began to flow down its side. A look of confusion and heartbreak spread across Curtis's face. Collins leaned an ear back toward the commotion.

"Shit, Curtis," an evil smirk spread across the CEO's face. "Who would have thought they'd be so excited to get rid of you?"

CHAPTER eighteen

In a nightmarish fashion, Sara's eyes opened, and she once again found herself in the same bedroom that she and Marla had attempted to escape from three days earlier. Every day since then had been the same: she would wake up in a drug-induced stupor, usually around noon, be given a ration of nearly inedible food, and then administered a dose of tranquilizing opioids, restarting the same submissive cycle all over again. Sara looked across the room and saw Marla confined to the same bed, face down on a pillow. Sara hadn't seen her conscious since their failed escape attempt in the kitchen, leading her to believe that the kidnappers must have placed them on different sleep schedules to prevent any further acts of cooperation going forward. Regardless of all else, Sara just wanted to ensure that Marla hadn't given up hope.

For the past two days, Sara remembered drifting in and out of consciousness, under the paralytic effects of the drugs, and seeing the violent captor with the dragon tattoo lying next to Marla. Though Sara's brain wouldn't allow her to fully conjure up all the horrifying acts she had witnessed, what she did recall was that each time the abuser climbed onto Marla's mattress, he would place his red-cased cell phone on top of the nightstand between the two beds. It was for this reason that Sara had intentionally consumed as much of the awful-tasting food as she could yesterday in the hopes that the increased caloric intake would dampen some of the narcotic's sedative effects and allow her to wake up earlier than usual, before the man arrived for his sadistic ritual.

The plan seemed to have worked. The clock on the wall displayed the time as a few minutes before 10 AM. And from what Sara had pieced together from her fugue states, the predator usually arrived shortly after this time. But as the minutes ticked by, Sara began to doubt herself. *Maybe he's already come and gone? Maybe he's been reassigned? Maybe it was all just a dream?*

At 10:30, when all hope had nearly been lost, Sara finally heard footsteps and a jingling of keys from down the hall. She quickly repositioned herself on her side, ensuring that both Marla and the nightstand were in view. Next, she pulled the faded yellow bedsheet high up over her face, leaving just enough room for her one squinting eye.

A padlock must have been installed on the exterior of the door, because Sara could hear the stranger fumbling to open it. Moments later, the door creaked inward ominously, and she could sense the man's cold-blooded energy lurking in the hall. Before he entered the room, the kidnapper took a moment to glance back towards the stairs. Satisfied with his solitude, he stepped inside the room and closed the door quietly behind him.

The man walked over to the foot of Marla's bed, entering Sara's field of vision. He caressed the back of Marla's calf before his hand slowly crept up her body. Sara's blood boiled as the man's disgusting fingers reached Marla's lower back. Suddenly, he stopped, and his head snapped back toward Sara across the room, and her eyes slammed shut.

Oh my God! Did he see me? Sara began to panic as she listened blindly through the uncomfortable silence that filled the room, slicing at her mind like a rusty razor blade. She could feel the man's eyes examining her. After a few more torturous seconds, she heard the springs on Marla's mattress creak in compression as the captor transitioned himself to a horizontal position, facing Marla's unconscious and vulnerable body. Sara opened her eyes slowly and focused on the nightstand.

The phone wasn't there!

Sara had just begun to doubt her hazy recollections when she heard the kidnapper mumble something to himself and then flip onto his back. Sara resealed her eyes, and she soon heard the distinct *clunk* of a cell phone being dropped onto a wooden surface.

Once the man rolled over, Sara opened her eyes and discovered the phone. Slowly and silently, she began to maneuver herself to the edge of the mattress, inch by inch, balancing her weight on her elbow and never taking her eyes off the back of the kidnapper's head. She reached out cautiously, pausing each time the monster produced a guttural grunt or micro movement. Eventually, her hand hovered directly above the phone. She reached down and carefully took hold of the device, but as she lifted it off the table, a link on her ankle restraint suddenly slipped from its tensioned position on the bedframe and produced an audible *SHINK!* of scraping metal. Sara froze, her heart thumping inside her chest, as she watched the kidnapper's head lift from Marla's pillow. Time stood still as her eyes bore into the back of his skull, waiting.

After a few more agonizing seconds, he finally seemed to relax, lowering his head onto the pillow. Sara quietly transitioned herself back onto her mattress, pulled the sheets over her head, and turned to face the wall. She tapped her finger on the screen under the cover of darkness, causing the phone to flash to life and prompt her for a password. Sara searched for an *EMERGENCY 911* button in hopes of being able to dial the police without having to enter a code, but the feature did not seem to exist. Her heart sank as she swiped her fingers around the screen, hopelessly searching for some obscure way to access the locked device. A wave of nausea washed over her.

Just then, a fuzzy memory materialized in Sara's head from the foiled escape attempt. Inside her mind, she found herself standing on the staircase that led down into the kitchen, watching the taller kidnapper pass by. He had just finished his phone call in which he was instructed to leave the house, and Sara saw him place a red-cased phone into his pocket. She suddenly realized it was the same device she now held in her hands. *The phone must be connected to the house itself, being passed between whoever is on duty,* Sara reasoned. And if that is the case, then it was likely that the code to the house and the code to the phone would be the same.

Inside her memory, Sara watched as the man arrived at the door and flipped open the security alarm panel. Just as he was about to enter the code, the springs on Marla's mattress began to groan spastically across the room, breaking Sara's concentration and drawing her out of the memory. She opened her eyes under the covers. *What was it?* she asked herself. *Four digits...* of that, she was sure. *One of them was an 8,* she recalled clearly—the number she had worn playing sports her entire life. *But the others?* Sara shut her eyes and did her best to ignore the horrifying acts taking place across the room. Her brain eventually complied in re-conjuring the memory. The kidnapper in the kitchen arrived at the alarm, and Sara watched him open the panel and enter a 2. The repulsive noises from Marla's bed amplified and pulled Sara out of her memory again, but she bore down and reattached quickly enough to see the man enter a 3, close the faceplate, and exit the house. *Starts with 2, ends with 3.*

Sara opened her eyes and began entering guesses into the device. She tried 2-8-8-3 first in hopes of a repeat digit. It was denied. She tried 2-2-8-3 and 2-8-3-3 next, receiving the same result. Suddenly, the phone displayed a warning in Spanish. Instinctively, she knew it was a lockout message: one more incorrect entry and the phone would disable itself. She closed her eyes and thought about her mother and father. She thought about Marla.

When Sara entered the memory this time, it felt much more vivid than before, and she found herself able to abandon the staircase and follow the kidnapper across the kitchen. When he arrived at the alarm panel, Sara peeked over his shoulder and watched him enter the 2 and the 8. For a moment, the man seemed to hesitate, as if he could somehow sense Sara's ghostly presence behind him. Finally, he entered a 7, then the 3, closed the face plate, pulled open the door, and quickly exited the house.

Sara's eyes bolted open. *2-8-7-3!*

She entered the code, and the phone immediately unlocked, revealing a collection of Spanish apps on the home screen. Sara pulled up the keypad and dialed a 9, but suddenly the lack of English speakers inside the house gave her pause. *Is 911 even the number to call in other countries?* she asked herself. *Will I be able to properly communicate what is happening before the man across the room hears me?* Sara realized the only number she knew by heart was her father's landline at the FBI, as it had been the same since she was a child, when her mother allowed her to call him on his lunch breaks. Sara quickly entered the ten-digit number and pressed send. Suddenly, a recorded voice came blaring out of the phone. *"LONG DISTANCE CHARGES MAY APPLY. PLEASE STAY ON THE LINE."*

Panic struck when Sara realized the phone was set on speaker mode. She attempted to decrease the volume as quickly as possible, but the damage had already been done. The springs of Marla's mattress sounded across the room, and she felt the kidnapper's weight hit the floor.

"Pick up!" Sara pleaded into the phone.

The sheets were torn off Sara's body in a flash, and she instinctively tucked the phone into her chest as tightly as she could before the man jumped on top of her, slapping at her face and grabbing for the device. Sara scurried away from him as he screamed at her with a primal savagery, prying at her fingers that were death-gripped around the phone. Realizing she wouldn't be able to overpower him for long, Sara drove her elbow up into his jaw, creating enough separation to allow her to drop the phone down between the mattress and wall, hoping to buy herself time for a few more rings. The monster shook off the impact and jumped onto Sara's back, driving her face down into the mattress next to where she had released the phone.

"DADDY! HELP!" she screamed down into the dark void, unable to determine if her father had answered by this point. "THEY'VE GOT ME AND MAR—"

The man covered Sara's mouth with one hand and drove his forearm into the back of her neck. Sara twisted away from his grip momentarily and swatted his sweaty palm off her face. "DADDY! I DON'T KNOW WHERE I AM! THEY'RE ALL SPEAKING SPAN—"

The kidnapper wrapped his forearm around her throat and squeezed, increasing the pressure until Sara felt as if her spine might snap in half. She coughed and sputtered as the man ripped her body away from the wall. Her legs now dangled and thrashed off the side of the bed while darkness crept into her vision from all directions. She could see Marla lying motionless on the mattress across the room, her shirt pulled up to the bottom of her breasts and the top of her skirt undone. Sara flailed around in convulsing spasms until her visual field shrank into a terrifying tunnel. Soon, the darkness took over.

*****

Frank was crouched next to his desk at work, searching for a folder in a small gray filing cabinet, when his landline began to ring. Mike, who was sitting at Frank's computer searching the electronic database for the digital version, looked over at his partner.

"Who is it?" Frank asked, sounding uninterested in the prospect of stopping the hunt to take a call.

Mike pulled the base of the phone toward himself and checked the caller ID. "Unknown Caller," he read. "Looks like a foreign number. Country code 52."

"It's probably just another one of those spam calls we've been getting," Frank decided, just as his eyes came across the file he had been looking for. He stood from his crouch and leafed through the folder's contents as his phone continued to ring. "Just let it go to voicemail."

"I thought the I.T. guys were supposed to be cracking down on this stuff? This is the FBI, after all..." Mike pointed out the irony.

"Yeah, well, what can you do?" Frank shrugged, still focused on the report.

"Oh, you know who it probably is?"

"No. Who?"

"It's probably one of those Nigerian Princes that needs to offload his billion-dollar inheritance to someone here in America, just like in those emails."

"You're an idiot." Frank grinned, not bothering to look up.

"Come on, Frankie, I can't let you miss out on this once-in-a-lifetime opportunity. All your wildest dreams might be contained in one single phone call!"

"Don't answ—" Frank tried to stop him, but it was too late. Mike had already lifted the receiver and placed it against his ear.

"Good afternoon! This is Michael, Mr. Adler's personal assistant!" He winked at Frank. "When should my client expect the massive cash transfer? Or perhaps you'll be sending him gold bars instead?" Just then, Mike heard a strange *clunking* sound on the other end of the line, followed by some inaudible, muffled noises. The smile slowly abandoned his face. "Hello?"

"Alright, that's enough, Mike," Frank decided, tossing the file folder on top of his desk and making his way around to the other side. "Hang 'er up."

Mike continued to listen to the garbled, static-filled sounds coming through the receiver. "Hello?" he said once more. Suddenly, there was only a dial tone.

Mike looked at the base of the phone and saw Frank's finger depressing the switch hook.

"You know that's how they get you," said Frank. "Those call bots are programmed to dial every single number, and when they find someone stupid enough to pick up, you get put onto a list, and that's when the *real* telemarketing starts."

Mike slowly set the phone back on its mount. "Yeah..." he said quietly.

"Hey!" Frank snapped his fingers in front of his partner's face, helping to break him from his trance. "Don't worry. I'm sure there's another handsome Nigerian Prince out there who will come sweep you off your feet."

Mike smiled, beginning to forget the strangeness of the call. "You promise?"

"Definitely," Frank nodded. "In the meantime, we've got a meeting to get to."

CHAPTER nineteen

A long-legged, honey-blonde waitress wearing a seamless magenta skirt arrived at a corner booth of a swanky Manhattan restaurant to collect a signature from Ken Collins and Derek Crenshaw for their pricey mid-afternoon lunch. During the handoff, the CEO ensured his fingertips lingered on hers for a moment too long. She was accustomed to the constant barrage of pathetic flirtation attempts by the neighborhood's cavalier and ego-inflated corporate clientele. However, being the service-industry veteran that she was, she feigned perfect obliviousness to Collins' touch to avoid further escalation, and more importantly, any damage to her bottom line.

Just then, the CEO heard his cell phone vibrating inside his blazer, which was hanging on a hook next to him. He reached a hand blindly into his coat. When he eventually pulled out his device, he found the screen to be blank, and the buzzing persisted. Collins quickly realized that the call was coming from the phone Ernesto Diaz had provided him.

"I gotta go," Collins informed his lunch companion. "I'll see you back at the office."

Crenshaw nodded, and the CEO abandoned the booth, weaving his way through a maze of tables toward the diamond-plated front doors of the restaurant. He stepped out onto the busy New York City sidewalk, looking right and then left, and quickly selected the less trafficked of the two alternatives. He donned his jacket and pulled the phone from his pocket.

"Hello?"

"Greetings, my friend," Diaz said, always careful not to use names, even on encrypted lines like these. "How have you been?"

"No complaints. You?"

"Very well. I'm not disturbing you, am I? I know you are a very busy man."

"Not at all," Collins assured him. "I was just making my way back to the office."

"Perfect! I'm just calling to confirm that our meeting for next week is still on?"

"Absolutely. I'll be there."

"Good. Good. And everything else is going well?"

"Like clockwork."

"That is what I like to hear!" the Mexican professed in his gravelly voice. "No issues with your *family*?" Family was code for the payments that were consistently being deposited into the CEO's offshore bank account.

"The family has been growing nicely," the businessman grinned, turning a corner.

"Very good. I am certain we will have more time to discuss such matters when I see you next week, but while I have you on the line, I have a small favor to ask, if you don't mind helping me out?"

"No problem," Collins agreed out of habit, momentarily forgetting he was speaking with one of the most dangerous men on the planet.

"A painting has been purchased from a private collector close to New York, and it needs a place to be stored. Do you think you might be able to hold on to it for me?"

"Uh, sure. Is it..." Collins was searching for a tactful way to ask the question.

"No, no..." the cartel boss chuckled. "It is not stolen if that is what you are hinting at. I can assure you, it was purchased quite legally."

"Either way, it's no problem. When do you think it might arrive?"

"Tomorrow."

The brevity of the request surprised Collins, but he didn't hesitate. "How long should I expect to be in possession of it?" he wondered, getting a whiff of warm chickpeas, garlic and cilantro from a popular falafel vendor as he passed by.

"Well, that's the thing," Diaz paused. "I'm not completely sure at this time. It may be a few weeks, perhaps a few months. It all just depends on when the right time to transport it to Mexico comes along."

"No problem," Collins replied, thinking of the many benefits of currying additional favor with the drug don.

"I just need you to know something, Mr. Collins," Diaz's voice became markedly more serious, "this painting is very special to me. And because of its value, an authenticator will need to meet with you to recertify the piece once it arrives, and then again before it leaves your possession. It's all very standard procedure when these items change hands or travel internationally. But I want to be very clear, it is not the monetary value that makes this piece so important."

"Just out of curiosity, what kind of price tag are we talking about here?" Collins inquired, displaying his constant obsession with money.

"It was purchased for just over fifty."

"Oh yeah, a few years ago, my interior decorator *insisted* I get a painting like that for my Malibu beach house," Collins recalled. "It wasn't until I shelled out the fifty grand that I found out it was just a bunch of fucking triangles," he laughed.

"Million."

"Huh?"

"It was purchased for fifty *million* dollars."

"Holy fuck!" Collins exclaimed much too loudly, receiving a scornful look from a mother who was passing by in the opposite direction with her two small children. "Are you sure you wouldn't rather just store it in a safety deposit box at a bank or something?"

"Artwork is meant to be displayed, Mr. Collins!" Diaz insisted. "It has already been hidden away for far too long."

"Yes, of course," the CEO agreed immediately. "I'm sure I can find a spot for it at my penthouse here in Manhattan. The building is *extremely* exclusive," he boasted. "And the security, top-notch."

"Splendid."

"This thing must be pretty special," suggested Collins.

A silence hung on the line for long enough that it caused the CEO to remove the device from his ear, thinking perhaps the call had been dropped. *"Hello?"*

"Very special indeed..." Diaz finally said.

Collins was quickly approaching a pair of white-haired grandmothers with aluminum walkers who had stopped at the corner of a busy intersection. The *DON'T WALK* signal had already been flashing in bold red letters for some time. Impatient and unwilling to wait, Collins cut between the two seniors, bumping elbows with the woman on the right, knocking her and the walker down to the concrete, along with the brown paper bag containing the groceries she had just purchased from a bodega. Collins glanced back as he jogged across the intersection, catching a glimpse of the mule train of apples and oranges now bouncing down 2nd Avenue, and a sinful smirk appeared on his face.

"Well, I won't keep you any longer," Diaz said, his voice returning to a more relaxed tone.

"Sounds good," replied Collins, reaching the other side of the street and hailing an approaching taxi. "I'll see you Wednesday."

CHAPTER twenty

"Are we *sure* we want it there?" Donna asked Frank as he positioned a small stainless-steel refrigerator they had just transported from their house in the city inside the completed cabin. "This little kitchen area is already so cramped."

"You may be overthinking it," Frank suggested. "It's not like we're going to be hosting fancy dinner parties in here or something."

"Yeah, I suppose you're right."

"I'll tell you what you should be worried about, though," said Frank.

"What's that?"

"When Mike finds out you hijacked this beer fridge from our garage without clearing it with him first," he joked.

Donna smiled as the sounds of a car crunching its way down the long gravel driveway floated into the cabin through the open front door.

"Expecting someone?" Frank wondered.

"Oh yeah, I forgot to mention that Carol is stopping by. There's a farmer's market out this way we want to check out."

Frank and Donna went outside and saw a four-door, beige hatchback approaching. Carol pulled in next to Frank's truck.

"Morning, Carol," Frank greeted Marla's mother through the open passenger-side window.

"Hi, guys!" she replied from inside the car.

"How was the drive out?" Donna inquired.

"Great! The traffic really dies down when you get out of the city."

Frank smiled. "Yeah, that's the whole point."

"Did you want to get going to the market right away, or would you like to have a coffee first?" Donna offered.

"I'd love a cup."

"Perfect. Come on in. You can leave your car parked right there," Donna instructed.

Carol killed the engine and stepped out. "Hey, I know you guys are going to think I'm crazy, but did you hear from Sara before they left on the excursion?"

Frank deferred to his wife.

"Of course," she replied. "Why do you ask?"

"Oh, I'm sure it's probably nothing," said Carol, as the three made their way to the cabin, "but did Sara say anything strange at all?"

Frank and Donna exchanged glances.

"I don't think so?" Donna responded, shaking her head. "I mean, I guess her texts have been a bit more brief since she left, but considering they are two teenage girls on vacation, that's just kind of what I've come to expect."

"Yeah, that's what I was thinking too, but then Marla's last message was really strange, and I'm not quite sure what to make of it."

"What did she say?" Frank wondered.

"Well, we were texting our goodbyes, and I suppose I was feeling a bit lonely and sentimental, so I told her how proud I was of her and that I'm sure her father feels the same way," Carol paused. "That's just how I've always talked about Henry since he passed."

"Of course," Donna nodded understandingly.

"But listen to what she sent me back..." Carol removed her rose gold phone from her purse as the trio entered the cabin. She located Marla's last text message and read it aloud. *"Love you Mom. Tell Dad I love him too. Can't wait to see you guys when I get home."*

Donna looked at Frank with confusion on her face.

"Henry's been gone for almost ten years now," Carol reminded them. "Marla's never said anything like that before."

"Hmm, yeah, that is a bit strange," Donna agreed. "But maybe she's just being *figurative* or something? I'm sure she and Sara are both a little homesick—even if they don't want to admit it."

"Yeah, you're probably right." Carol nodded. "Maybe I'll just ask her about it when they're back on shore with service. I'm sure I'm just overthinking things."

Frank made his way over to the cupboard and removed two blue coffee mugs. He set them down on the counter next to the cheap department store coffee maker they had recently purchased and filled them with aromatic chocolate-brown liquid.

"I'd offer you milk and sugar," Frank smiled at Carol, "but we happen to have *neither* out here at the moment."

"Black is great," Carol assured him. "It sure is nice inside here." She looked around the little shack. "It's very quaint. Are you two sure you don't want to save all that money on the build and just live in here full time?"

"In a space this tight? Frank and I would strangle each other in about three weeks," Donna teased.

"More like three days." Frank smiled, handing the women their beverages. "If you guys don't mind, I have some stuff I need to get organized in the bedroom."

"No worries. Do your thing, hun," said Donna.

Frank made his way into the bedroom, removed his phone from his pocket, and typed a text to Sara.

'You two had better call your mothers as soon as you get back from the excursion, or they're bound to work themselves up into a full-blown tizzy! Then you'll be sorry! :P' he teased his daughter.

Frank set the phone down on the nightstand next to the queen-sized bed, which occupied the lion's share of the bedroom's limited floor space.

"Are you looking for anything specific at the farmer's market?" Frank could hear Carol asking Donna out in the kitchen. He removed a forest green travel-sized suitcase from on top of the four-drawer dresser and set it on the mattress. Just as he began to unzip it, he stopped and looked over at his phone across the room, while Carol's comments played inside his head. *'Marla's last message was really strange, and I'm not quite sure what to make of it. Did Sara say anything strange at all?'*

Frank abandoned the suitcase and made his way over to his phone, lifting it from the nightstand. He quickly located Sara's last text message—the one she had sent just before they left for the excursion.

'Text you when we get back Dad. Love you!"

Dad... Frank stared at the word. It was just like the text that arrived during the BBQ with Mike and Janice. He had dismissed the peculiarity both times, but now, after hearing Carol's story, it stuck out like a sore thumb.

Frank reemerged from the bedroom.

"Donna, do you mind giving Sara a quick call? I can't find one of the boxes she packed for me before she left."

"What box?" Donna looked confused. "They're on the excursion, remember?"

"Yeah, I know," Frank replied, "but just give her a call anyway. Who knows, maybe they'll hit a patch of service out there somewhere. I just had some important work stuff in that box, is all..." He attempted to gently force his request without raising suspicion in Carol.

Donna picked up on whatever Frank was trying to convey to her. "No problem," she said. "I'll give her a shout now." As she dialed Sara's number, she made sure to flash Carol a smile. "Straight to voicemail," she reported to Frank almost immediately.

"Okay, maybe leave her a message and tell her to call if she happens to get service before they're back on shore."

Frank wasted no time exiting the cabin and making his way to his truck. Once he arrived, he opened the back door and found his laptop where he had left it. He quickly shut the door and walked back towards the cabin.

Donna met him just outside the front door.

"What's going on?" she asked with a hint of concern, making sure she spoke quietly enough so that Carol wouldn't hear her inside.

"I'm not sure," Frank admitted, "but something's off." He pulled out his phone and handed it to her. "Look at Sara's last text."

Donna read the message and then looked up at Frank once she had discovered the anomaly. "*Dad?*"

"Hey Frank," Carol's voice floated out from inside the cabin, *"do you want me to try to call Marla as well? She's got a brand-new phone. Maybe it gets better reception than Sara's?"*

"Sure," Frank replied evenly.

"What are you planning on doing with *that*?" Donna asked, pointing at the laptop in Frank's hands.

"Is the Wi-Fi set up out here yet?" Frank asked.

"Not until next Thursday."

"*Shit.* I won't be able to connect to the FBI server from here, then. It won't allow a hot spot connection."

"FBI server?" Donna frowned. "You're not planning on tracking Sara's phone, are you? Remember what happened the last time you did that? She found out and didn't speak to you for a week."

"Yeah, well, maybe she shouldn't have been at a lake party instead of studying at a friend's house like she said she was," Frank justified his actions.

"Straight to voicemail, too," Carol called out.

"No problem," replied Frank. "I probably just forgot the box back at the house in the city or something."

"What can I do?" Donna asked.

"Just take Carol to the farmer's market like you were going to. Mike's house is closer to here than ours. I'll just drive over to his place, connect to the server, and make sure everything is as it seems. Like Carol said—it's probably nothing."

Carol suddenly appeared at the door behind Donna. "I left Marla a voicemail as well," she reported, then saw the truck keys in his hands. "Heading somewhere?"

Donna's eyes met Frank's, and she stepped in. "Frank just realized that we don't have internet set up out here yet, and he was supposed to get a couple of things sent off for work this morning."

"Oh, that stinks," Carol replied, scrunching up her chubby cheeks. "It seems like you're always working, Frank. Once you guys sell the house in the city and get out here full time, you're going to have to slow down and smell the roses a little, you know." She smiled. "*In fact,* with all these big, beautiful trees around, I might just have to get you a hammock for your birthday!"

"Sounds good," Frank attempted a smile, but his thoughts were already halfway to Mike's house.

* * * * *

"I have the program loaded," Mike told Frank, leading him to the office near the back of the house. "When did all this funny business begin?" he asked about the anomalies in the girls' text messages.

"I'm not exactly sure," Frank admitted. "At least since that BBQ the other night, but looking back, a lot of things aren't adding up."

Mike entered the office first and pulled back a well-worn black leather chair from the computer desk. Frank took his seat in front of the monitor while Mike remained standing, looking over his shoulder. Frank entered Sara's cell phone number into a rectangular search box below the FBI seal, then calibrated his initial parameters for a time shortly after the girls would have landed at the San Diego airport. After hitting enter, the computer immediately populated a secondary window containing a slowly rotating globe. Frank and Mike watched as the view began to descend into the Western Hemisphere, forcing South America from the bottom of the screen. As the North

American landmass expanded, a tiny red dot eventually appeared in Southern California. The zoom continued inward until the circle settled directly over the airport. A digital clock near the top of the window began moving forward at an accelerated pace.

"They would have been collecting their luggage at this point," Frank commented.

A moment later, the red dot abandoned the terminal, moved quickly through the parking lot, and began to blink its way down the highway.

"They're heading to their first hotel," Frank explained as the orb crossed a bridge into a dense urban area comprised of many commercial buildings. The dot suddenly disappeared.

"Where'd it go?" Mike wondered.

"This program is only able to pick up tower triangulations when the phone is in active use—sending texts, making calls, refreshing emails—so it can be sporadic," Frank explained. "Pinpointing exact locations to nearer than a couple of city blocks can be tricky."

The tracker reappeared near an outlet mall that the girls had visited shortly after their arrival, then disappeared again.

"How long did the girls stay at this first hotel?" Mike asked. "You said they're heading north as the trip goes on?"

"Yeah, they plan to stay in each area for about a week or so, I think," Frank nodded. "Donna has the full itinerary written down at home. Once they get back from this excursion, they're mostly staying in hostels to save money, but they wanted to ease into it with a nicer accommodation to start."

The dot arrived near the Ambassador Hotel, and the speeding clock ticked its way through the evening and night as the girls slept. Late the next morning, the orb left the area and crept north on the I-5.

"According to Sara's texts, they were heading to Trestles Beach that morning," Frank explained. Slowly, the dot diverted off course and began to make its way inland, eventually settling near Temecula.

"Temecula?" Mike stared at the screen. "What's in Temecula?"

"No idea..." Frank looked just as perplexed. He zoomed in on the subdivision where the tracker had disappeared.

"There it goes," said Mike when the dot reappeared and began to move back toward the ocean. It eventually settled off the coast of Trestles Beach as expected.

"They were there all day," Frank recalled from Sara's text.

"That far out?"

"What do you mean?"

"Well, that tracker looks pretty far offshore, doesn't it? I imagine they would have left their phones on the beach while they were in the water. I guess it could just be a locating anomaly like you mentioned." Mike paused. "Unless..."

"...they were on a boat." Frank finished his partner's thought.

"Did Sara mention anything like that?"

"Not that day."

The tracker continued to appear and disappear five or ten miles off the coast for the remainder of the day. Eventually, it began to move inland.

"They'll be heading back to their hotel now," Frank suggested.

Shortly after the dot abandoned the beach, it disappeared again. Frank's eyes continued to track a path south towards the Ambassador, but suddenly, the circle reappeared in the same neighborhood in Temecula, causing Frank and Mike to exchange glances.

Just then, Janice arrived in the doorway behind them.

"Hi, Frank," she greeted. "I saw your truck on the street when I was pulling in. I didn't know you were coming by. How are you?"

Frank's attention remained fixed on the screen.

Mike met his wife at the door. “Hey, can I talk to you out in the kitchen for just a sec, sweetie?”

“Yeah...sure,” she agreed, catching a glimpse of the GPS map on the monitor. She followed Mike down the hallway and into the kitchen.

“What’s going on?” she asked immediately.

“I’m not exactly sure. Frank called me on his way in from the acreage, asking to use our computer to track Sara’s phone.”

A look of concern appeared on Janice’s face. “Is everything okay?”

“I think so. It sounds like maybe the girls weren’t entirely truthful about where they were staying or something. I’m not too sure, Frank hasn’t told me much yet.”

“Where’s Donna? Does she know what’s going on?”

“Yeah. She was with Frank at the cabin when he started piecing things together.”

“I was just about to head back out to a hair appointment. I should cancel until this is all sorted out.”

“I don’t think that’s necessary,” Mike shook his head.

Janice exhaled. “Alright, well, please keep me posted. And in the meantime, if Donna or Frank need anything from me, just let me know.”

“Will do, babe,” Mike gave her a peck on the cheek and made his way back toward the office.

“Where are they now?” he asked Frank as soon as he entered the room.

Frank was still focused on the map. “They must have stayed in that Temecula neighborhood overnight and throughout the next day,” Frank reported. “It’s evening again now, and they just arrived at a restaurant in San Diego. I cross-referenced it with a picture Sara sent her mother that evening.”

“Did she—”

“They’re on the move again,” Frank interrupted when the dot appeared on some random highway, leaving the city.

"Where the hell are they going now?" Mike said in a whisper.

"There doesn't seem to be much out that way," Frank commented before the tracker disappeared again. He used the mouse to zoom in around the area where it had vanished.

"That looks like an industrial area to me," Mike suggested, assessing the widely-spaced, rectangular rooftops from the bird's-eye view.

"It's almost midnight," Frank pointed out. "Why would they be way out in a place like that? I can't—"

The orb suddenly reappeared and reversed course, abandoning the industrial area, moving quickly toward the highway, then disappeared again. Frank and Mike kept expecting the dot to reappear. Only this time, it didn't. Hours ticked by on the clock.

"Where'd it go?" Mike asked what they were both thinking. "Do you think maybe Sara shut off her phone for the night or something?"

"It should still ping the tower intermittently, unless the battery was removed."

Just then, the view on the screen zoomed out and shifted drastically to the southeast as the clock sped past 8 AM the following morning. The little red dot was now hovering above the small Mexican city of Puerto Peñasco, also known as Rocky Point.

Frank and Mike exchanged looks of disbelief, having both read the same stories of how this once beautiful seaside tourist town had become infested with violent drug cartels in recent years. Frank zoomed in on the sparsely developed suburb that the tracker was now suspended above.

"What the fuck..." said Mike. "That can't be right. Are you sure Sara's information was entered correctly?"

Frank toggled back to the original search window and double-checked. "Looks right to me."

"It can't be," Mike repeated. "Try Marla's number to see where her phone was at this exact moment in time."

Frank cleared Sara's information, quickly replaced it with Marla's, and pressed Enter. Once again, a secondary window was populated, displaying the same rotating globe. Frank and Mike watched as the view gradually descended into Rocky Point—a place that, unbeknownst to them, was now controlled by none other than Ernesto and Dennis Diaz.

CHAPTER twenty-one

The intercom inside Ken Collins' upscale Manhattan penthouse buzzed to life just after he had finished a phone call berating a senior manager at Zinex's Chicago office for ten straight minutes. Collins made his way over to the ten-inch touchscreen next to the silver doors of his private elevator and answered the call. A matronly concierge with almond-shaped eyes and chestnut hair appeared on the screen.

"Yeah?" Collins said brusquely.

"Good afternoon, Mr. Collins, I have a gentleman here to see you," the woman reported, referring to the middle-aged, bespectacled man wearing the off-the-rack suit standing in front of her. "He's just a *teeny* bit early. Shall I send him up now or—"

"Jesus Christ, Cindy. Yes, send him up! I don't have all day!" Collins barked. "And here's a little piece of advice for you: in this world, early is on time, and on time means you're late!" He quickly disconnected the call before she had a chance to respond, then glanced over at the large wooden crate in the middle of his sunken, white-walled living room. The package had been delivered by private courier yesterday in the late afternoon when Collins was on his way out. He had neither the time nor inclination to open it before the authenticator arrived today.

Collins stepped away from the elevator momentarily and entered his modern, marble-countered kitchen to retrieve a square bottle of overpriced water from the top shelf of his stainless-steel refrigerator. He cracked the lid and took a long sip as he strode back to the touchscreen, which now displayed a high-angled view from the camera inside the approaching elevator. On the screen was the geeky-looking man holding an oversized briefcase in his right hand.

As the elevator came to a stop, Collins watched the authenticator take a step forward, expecting the doors to separate for him at any moment. To the man's surprise, they didn't. He retracted his foot and looked around with confusion, reaching out to press a button on the panel in front of him, but nothing seemed to help.

Collins was enjoying his voyeuristic game on the other side of the door, knowing that access to the suite needed to be granted by the occupant inside. He watched the slender, bookish visitor shift uncomfortably inside the little box that was quickly transforming into a claustrophobic prison cell. The man began waving his hand at the camera until Collins finally tapped a finger on the screen. The doors slid open, and the two men locked eyes.

"Well, hello there, sir," the man greeted Collins in a squeaky underpowered voice, transferring his briefcase to his non-dominant hand and offering his host the other. "My name is Arthur, and I understand you have—"

Collins turned his back. "It's in that crate over there..." he pointed towards the living room. "There's a pry bar on the table next to it, but don't go making a fucking mess. My cleaning lady doesn't come until Tuesday."

Arthur stepped out of the elevator and glanced at the pine box. "Okay, thank y—"

"I'll be in my office. Let me know when you're done," The CEO demanded before quickly disappearing into another room and closing the door behind him.

Arthur sighed quietly. The truth was, he had grown accustomed to this level of rudeness and arrogance often displayed by the upper-class clientele he commonly dealt with. He tolerated it, he told himself, not because he was meek and mild-mannered, but because it granted him access to a world of art that most in his profession could only dream of. He had once been employed as a museum curator until word of his seemingly unmatched authentication and appraisal skills got out. Soon, hordes of auction houses, insurance companies, and the like were calling, attempting to lure away his lucrative talents. Eventually, he signed on with the secretive *Samson Corporation,* which had arranged for him to view some of their clientele's most impressive private collections. He caught on quickly by not asking too many probing questions, focusing solely on authenticity and appraisal, and never pressuring a client to reveal how they might have acquired a piece if they weren't willing.

Approaching the crate, Arthur circled it slowly, searching for the best angle of attack. Eventually, he slipped the pry bar beneath the lid and applied some downward pressure until the galvanized nails gave way. Removing the top, he leaned it against the side of the crate. Inside, he could see the top of a singular painting, approximately twenty-four inches tall and eighteen inches wide, wrapped inside a transparent blue bag and surrounded by thick protective cushioning. Arthur carefully exhumed the painting and let the plastic sheath drop to the floor. The lights above his head illuminated the painting in his outstretched hands.

On the canvas were two figures: a teenage boy and girl, both with jet-black hair and light brown skin. The girl was sitting upright on a bed with her back propped up by two white pillows, while the boy stood next to her, smiling proudly. The girl stared longingly at the viewer with prominent eyebrows that seemed to connect in the middle of her forehead, and a right leg that appeared slightly smaller than her left. When Arthur recognized that this was no artistic error, his eyes widened considerably. He turned the canvas over in his hands carefully and located a date scrawled on its backside. Setting the painting down on the table, he quickly made his way over to the door where Collins had disappeared.

"Sir!" he called to his host, gently tapping on the hardwood, excitement evident in his voice. "Excuse me, sir!"

A moment later, the door opened, and Collins emerged. He stepped past the authenticator and made his way towards the living room.

"Done already?"

"No, I've just started, sir. But is this what I think it is?" Arthur asked, following closely behind.

Collins didn't respond. Instead, he arrived at the table and looked the oil painting up and down. *"That's it?"* He sounded entirely unimpressed.

"Is this not part of your personal collection, sir?"

"I'm just holding it for someone."

"Do you not recognize her?" Arthur pointed at the girl on the bed.

Collins leaned in. "Who? Unibrow? No, why?"

"Well, I still need to verify this, of course, but at first glance, I believe that to be Frida Kahlo..."

"And what about *that* guy?" Collins pointed at the boy. "Who's he?"

"I'm not sure," the authenticator admitted. "Perhaps a relative?"

"Frida Kahlo..." Collins repeated the name aloud. "I've heard that name somewhere before."

"She was—"

"Wait, didn't some hot chick play her in a movie once? Penelope Cruz? No, no. Salma Hayek. Yeah, she even had that ugly eyebrow painted on." He smirked in remembrance. "So, who painted this thing, anyway?"

"I believe that she did, sir."

"And that's good or something? Because if I'm being honest, it doesn't look that great to me."

The authenticator ignored his host's ignorance and lifted the painting from the table again, holding it in the air, clearly mesmerized by it. "Until now, I had only heard rumors of a painting that predated all her others. I believe this may be it..."

CHAPTER twenty-two

"I'm just not sure it's a good idea," Mike said to Frank inside Frank's rental storage unit. He had been protesting his partner's insistence on flying to San Diego immediately to track down the girls himself.

"And what exactly do you think I should do, Mike?" Frank looked up from the duffel bag he was currently packing with gear. He had already contacted the Ambassador Hotel and discovered that Sara and Marla had only stayed one night.

"Well, maybe we should be coordinating this with the Bureau? For fuck's sake, we don't even know what's going on yet," Mike raised his voice a little, but quickly put his emotions back in check. "Look, I'm just saying—let's think this thing through."

Frank located a small black lockbox inside one of the blue plastic totes in the back corner of the unit. "You know as well as I do, Mike, if those girls were with their phones when they disappeared into cartel territory, coordinating logistics for an international border crossing would take way too long."

Mike rubbed the back of his neck. He knew Frank was right. "Alright, but I'm coming with you."

"I appreciate it, but I might need someone here to access our servers."

Mike hadn't thought of that.

"Do you remember me talking about a guy named Bennett from my time in the service?" Frank asked.

"I think so," Mike nodded. "He's in a couple of those photos in your garage, right?"

"Yeah," Frank nodded, placing the lockbox back inside the tote. "Five or six years ago, at our last reunion, he had mentioned that he ran a private security business down there." Frank zipped up the heavy pack and slung it over his shoulder. "If I end up having to cross the border, maybe I can give him a call to point me in the right direction."

Frank and Mike abandoned the cramped storage unit, and Frank pulled the door down onto the concrete floor and quickly secured a thick padlock in place.

"Be careful out there, Frankie," Mike said. "Keep your head on straight, and I'll be here if you need me."

"Thanks, Mike. Hopefully, this is all just some big misunderstanding."

CHAPTER twenty-three

A thick-necked henchman, missing two fingers on his left hand, led Ken Collins deep inside Ernesto Diaz's Mexican mansion. The pair eventually entered a room near the rear of the house, containing an ornate, handcrafted red brick fireplace lining its back wall. The guard instructed Collins to wait inside until his boss arrived, then promptly took his leave.

Collins began to wander around the room, taking in the many novel sights it had to offer: an antique grandfather clock, a Mayan-inspired armoire, a turn-of-the-century roll-top desk, and two tan leather couches facing each other. As with every other room in the house, a vast collection of oil paintings hung on the walls. For some reason, the familiarity of the surroundings prompted the CEO to think of Hank Phillips. Since being introduced in the eagle's nest above the pool two months ago, the pair had remained in close contact.

Directly above the fireplace's impressive mantle, Collins arrived at a painting measuring four by five feet, bordered by an intricately hand-scrawled wooden frame. The image on the canvas depicted a large fishing vessel, struggling mightily against a vicious oceanic squall. Half of the crew were clinging to life on different parts of the seemingly doomed ship as its sails were being ripped to shreds. The remainder of the seamen, however, were much calmer and more reserved, gathered around a radiant figure on the other side of the vessel. Collins reached out and began running his finger along the painting's ornamental edging until he accidentally nudged it off-center. He took a half step back, assessed the lopsidedness he had caused, and did nothing to remedy it.

Below the painting, on top of the stone mantel, lived a collection of antique silver-framed black-and-white photographs. In the first image, three Mexican teenagers were standing in front of a four-foot-tall, whitewashed fence. Each wore a dirt-stained work shirt, weather-beaten blue jeans, and had a forehead dappled with the sticky sweat of a particularly sweltering summer.

"My brothers and I..." a gravelly voice suddenly arrived from somewhere behind Collins, causing him to flinch. The American turned his head and found Ernesto Diaz staring intently at the photograph. "That's Dennis on the right," the kingpin pointed to the smallest but most menacing-looking of the bunch. Ernesto then directed the CEO's attention to the next photograph. It was even older than the first. In it was a wiry-looking Mexican in his early twenties with a thin black mustache and a crooked smile. Next to him stood a powerful chestnut-brown draft horse. Something about the young man's face felt familiar.

"Is that?"

"From my painting," Diaz confirmed with a nod.

"Who is he?"

"My father," Ernesto revealed, reaching out a gnarled finger and touching the edge of the silver frame.

"Your father knew...?"

"Miss Kahlo? Yes, of course!" the cartel boss smiled proudly. "They grew up together."

Collins nodded.

"Look *here*," Diaz directed his guest's attention further down the mantle to the second-to-last photograph, which contained seven young children—four boys and three girls. The oldest of the bunch was probably ten or twelve years old, and they were standing in front of a dilapidated shack with a large wooden cross affixed to its exterior wall.

In the front row was a younger version of Ernesto's father. Next to him, the same undersized girl from the painting, wearing a homemade, polka dot patterned dress.

"This photograph was taken after Sunday School, I believe," Diaz explained. "My father and Miss Kahlo were inseparable! Even when she contracted that awful disease and was forced to isolate from the other children, my father would sneak over to her house late at night to visit with her and keep her spirits up."

"Lucky he didn't catch it and become a cripple himself," Collins replied, completely missing the point.

"She painted the piece you have in your possession shortly after the next tragedy in her life," Diaz explained, ignoring the comment.

"That bus accident?" Collins guessed, having read through Kahlo's Wikipedia page shortly after the authenticator had left his penthouse.

"Yes, unfortunately, her boyfriend at the time abandoned her, leaving her to fend for herself," Diaz said with disdain in his voice.

"Were she and your father ever...?"

"Lovers? No, no," Diaz answered resolutely. "It was never like that between the two of them. My father said they *were of one soul*, but in the way a brother and sister are."

Somehow, the answer seemed to disappoint Collins.

"My father stayed by Miss Kahlo's side throughout her entire recovery, encouraging her to express herself in any way her spirit saw fit. He always knew she had great talent and creativity inside herself that the world needed to see. Once she had regained some of her strength, she made him the painting you have in New York. It was her first," Diaz confirmed what the authenticator had determined. "Unfortunately, Miss Kahlo's romantic tastes never did improve, and she soon found herself enamored with another man."

"That Diego guy?" Collins guessed, having read about him, too. "It sounds like they had a pretty tumultuous relationship."

"They certainly did!" Diaz nodded. "And he was extremely jealous of the relationship between my father and Miss Kahlo. It wasn't long until he gave her an ultimatum: she could continue her friendship with my father or be with him. She could not have both."

"And she chose Diego..."

"Yes." Diaz shook his head regretfully. "Miss Kahlo cut off all communication with my father immediately. He was so heartbroken that he could not bring himself to keep the painting, for it reminded him of the loss of the dearest friend he had ever known, so he gave it away."

Collins looked at the happy faces of the two young children in the photograph again.

"Even when my father began to hear stories of Miss Kahlo's success as an artist, he continued to push all thoughts of her out of his mind. It wasn't until her untimely death at the age of forty-seven—long after my father had gotten married and started a family—that something inside him changed. Suddenly, he was unable to forgive himself for not reaching out to her for all those years and convinced himself that perhaps Diego would have softened his stance with the passage of time, allowing them to reconnect and reconcile. That is when his obsession with locating the painting first began." A determined look spread across the cartel boss's face. "The first thing my father did was try to contact the man he had given the painting to all those years before, but he, too, had passed away, and his family explained that he had sold the painting not long after receiving it."

"To who?"

"They had no idea," Diaz shrugged. "My father was only able to gather bits and pieces of information regarding the painting's movements over the years. You must remember, this was long before the internet existed, and my father was just a simple farmer with very limited means. The trail soon ran cold."

"Shit."

"But even as his mind began to deteriorate in his later years, my father never stopped talking about the painting. Just the mere mention of Miss Kahlo's name would trigger him into a fond reminiscence about their childhood together. And at the very end, when things got really bad, he would ask me to bring him his painting so he might look at it," Diaz said hauntingly. "I could never bring myself to tell him the truth, but thankfully, his limited attention span would have him drift away soon enough."

"How did you finally locate it?"

"By the time my father passed, I had become an avid art collector myself, and I began to hear rumors of an early Kahlo that existed in a private collection in the United States. As you can imagine, this ignited my own desire to find out if the stories were true."

"How long ago was that?"

"I suppose it must have been," Diaz searched his memory, "fifteen years now. It took many, many years just to identify the individual who possessed it. A man up in—"

Ernesto suddenly stopped speaking. Collins looked over and found him staring at the off-centered painting hanging above the fireplace with an intensity that filled the entire room. The kingpin's head turned slowly, and he locked eyes with Collins, whose chest tightened with dread. After a few agonizing moments, Diaz reached out a hand and straightened the artwork to its former symmetry.

"A man up in Vermont," the cartel boss finally continued, allowing Collins a chance to breathe again, "able to trace his family lineage back to the Mayflower. Old money. At that time, he was already of an advanced age—a grandfather in his early eighties. Eventually, I was able to confirm that the painting he had in his private collection was indeed my father's. My people repeatedly attempted to arrange a meeting with him, but he was completely uninterested in doing so, let alone selling me anything. I was told that no amount of money I could offer would change his mind."

"I have to imagine that a man in your position might have the ability to *procure* the painting by different means..." Collins said in a suggestive tone.

"I will admit to you, Mr. Collins, that for a moment, I did consider such things. However, by that point, I had already pursued the painting so doggedly that its disappearance would surely have been connected back to me. But more importantly, I knew that my father would not have approved of obtaining his beloved artwork in such a manner, even if it did result in its return to Mexico, where it belongs. You see, Mr. Collins, my father did not approve of the life I pursued. He was a hardworking, blue-collar laborer who blamed me for involving my younger brothers in this world of mine. In fact, there were long periods in which he and I did not speak."

"So, getting this painting back is some sort of peace offering to his memory?" Collins suggested.

"Perhaps it is..." Diaz seemed to consider the idea for the first time before continuing. "Soon, my associates discovered this man had a daughter who would inherit all his assets when he died."

"Including his art collection..."

"Precisely," the cartel boss nodded. "I sent people to contact her, and they struck up a deal which allowed us to have the first opportunity to view and bid on the collection before anyone else saw it."

"How'd you manage that?"

"It was clear that she had no interest in art whatsoever, so my people told her that if they found anything to our liking, we would be willing to pay substantially more than its appraised value."

"And she didn't realize you specifically had the Kahlo in mind, did she?"

Ernesto shook his head.

"There's still one thing I don't quite understand," said Collins. "If this guy was in his eighties, fifteen years ago, how is it that you're just getting your hands on the painting now?"

A smile grew on the Mexican's face. "Because that miserable old bastard kept on living until he was ninety-eight years old!" Diaz cackled. "There was nothing I could do but wait!"

"Yeah, those stuffy old New Englanders live forever, don't they?" Collins smirked.

"Yes, but thankfully, it will be in my possession soon. And I want to thank you again for holding on to it for me. I can't imagine it will be long until you are relieved of your duties."

"Well, it's in good hands until then," Collins assured him.

Just then, a knock sounded behind the two men, and they turned around. Strangely, the open door was empty, and they looked at one another with confusion. Suddenly, Hank Phillips' head poked around the edge of the doorframe where he had hidden himself.

"Heeeeyyyyoooooo!" he shouted, entering the room and walking over to where the two men were standing at the fireplace. "Kenny, you handsome son of a bitch!" he greeted with a back-slapping hug. "And Ernie!" He shook Diaz's hand voraciously. "You look younger every time I come around! There must be something in the water down here!" He winked at Collins.

"You're too kind," replied the cartel boss with a smile.

"I wasn't sure you were going to be able to make it," Collins said, looking pleased that he had.

"You didn't think I was going to let you take all the credit, did you?" Hank replied, then turned his attention to Diaz. "Didn't I tell you this guy was going to do some big things?"

The same guard who had led Collins to the room earlier appeared at the door.

"Yes, Paco?" Diaz spotted him first.

"Dennis and the others have begun to arrive, sir," the henchman reported. "Should I bring them back here, or?"

"Bring them into our usual meeting space," the cartel boss instructed. "We will be in momentarily."

The guard nodded and then quickly disappeared.

"Well, my friends," Ernesto turned his attention back to the Americans. "Perhaps we should get going so the others can sing your praises as well."

CHAPTER twenty-four

The unrelenting Californian sun beat down on the windshield of the gray, mid-sized car that Frank had rented upon his arrival at the San Diego International Airport. During the long flight, he had called every place he thought the girls might have visited. Down the street, past the next set of traffic lights, he spotted the palatial Ambassador Hotel. As he neared the front of the building, a carob-brown Cadillac was abandoning a curbside parking spot, and Frank took its place. He got out and walked towards the revolving doors of the Art Deco high-rise.

Inside the lobby stood a Tiki-themed coffee shop, a pastel-colored gelato stand, and a magazine kiosk with a sleepy, gray-haired senior citizen wearing a threadbare tam o' shanter at its helm. Frank made his way past the shops, abandoned luggage carts, and a towering water feature that sent a cacophony of deep-throated gurgles throughout the high-ceilinged lobby.

At the check-in counter up ahead, Frank spotted a middle-aged businesswoman in uncomfortable-looking three-inch heels flanked by her two rose-patterned suitcases. She was deep in conversation with a dainty male hotel clerk sporting a gravity-defying blonde Pompadour, black nail polish, and five or six piercings in each ear. The counter extended to the left for another twenty-five feet, where a door with the word MANAGER embossed on a golden plaque could be seen. Frank headed straight for it, catching the clerk's attention in the process.

"Excuse me, sir," the young man broke his conversation to call out to Frank in an effeminate voice. "I'll be right with you once I'm done helping this nice lady." He turned back to the guest and unsubtly rolled his eyes before handing her an invoice.

"I already spoke with the manager on the phone," Frank replied, trying to indicate that the clerk's attention was not necessary. When he arrived, he reached a hand over the counter to unlock the latch and let himself behind the desk. "She told me to—"

"Nevertheless, sir!" The flamboyant young man raised his voice a couple of octaves after the woman had departed. He rushed over to Frank.

"Now that you've *waited* your turn..." he said with passive-aggressive condescension. "Welcome to The Ambassador, how may I help you?"

The young man had intentionally positioned himself in front of the gate to block Frank's access. Frank withdrew his hand and took a moment to glance over his shoulder, watching the woman exit the building. He turned his attention back to the clerk. He didn't have time for this shit.

"The first thing you can do is wipe that smug fucking look off your face, *Stephan*." Frank read from his name tag. "And when you're done with that, turn your ass around and get your boss," he demanded. "As I already told you, I spoke with—"

"Excuse me, sir?!" the uppity clerk chortled, tapping on a silver placard attached to the top of the counter. "Can you read what this says?" he questioned Frank's literacy while combing his slender fingers through his hair.

Agitation was building inside Frank.

"Here, let me help you..." the clerk continued. "It says, this establishment has a *zero-tolerance* policy for any abusive language or behavior!"

Frank found himself squeezing the edge of the counter in a last-ditch effort to remain calm. "Listen, buddy. Just go get your manager, and we won't have any problems."

"Is that a threat, sir?!" The clerk's eyes widened with excitement. "How about I call security and see what they have to say about your little attitude?" He reached for the phone.

The instant his fingers made contact, Frank's hand came crashing down on top of his, and a look of open-mouthed horror spread across the young man's face.

Frank leaned in. "I guess you'd rather we go get her together..."

Frank hopped over the counter, keeping the young man's hand pinned down against the phone. Stationery items were knocked onto the polished floor, and the now cowering clerk let out a tiny *eep* when Frank landed next to him.

* * * * *

Inside the office, Miranda Phillips was sitting at her computer when she heard the pens and papers scatter onto the floor outside her door. Seconds later, there came a knock.

"Come in?" She looked at the door curiously.

It opened slowly and revealed Frank holding the young clerk by the top of one of his pierced ears.

"You must be Agent Adler?" she guessed immediately. "And by the looks of it, you seem to have met Stephan..." The look on her face indicated to Frank that she knew exactly how their initial interaction had gone down. "You'll have to excuse him. He means well, and we love him dearly, but he can be a *little,*" she searched for an appropriate word, "*excitable* at times."

Frank released his grip, and the clerk immediately began to rub the feeling back into his ear.

Miranda came around the side of her desk and approached. "Are you okay, Stephan?" she asked the now sheepish-looking employee empathetically. "This is Special Agent Adler. He's with the

FBI and has come to gather some information on a couple of our former guests. I'm sure that you and Agent—"

"Please, call me Frank."

Miranda smiled. "Stephan, I'm sure you and *Frank* just got off on the wrong foot, now, didn't you?"

Looking like a shell-shocked soldier who had just recently emerged from a foxhole, the young man nodded slowly. "Sorry, Agent Ad, uh, I mean, Frank," he stuttered. "I didn't realize—"

"Water under the bridge, kid. Sorry about the ear." Frank reciprocated.

Just then, Miranda spotted a young Asian couple approaching the front desk behind the two men.

"Would you like to take a break to compose yourself?" Miranda asked, subtly directing his attention towards the inbound pair. "I can call Jimmy down from six to help out for a while if you'd like."

Stephan looked over his shoulder at the tourists, then back to his boss. "No, of course not," he said, straightening his bow tie and regaining a bit of pep in his voice. "It would be my pleasure to greet our guests."

"And we'll keep Frank's visit here today just between us, yes?"

He looked at Frank. "Absolutely," he agreed, with duty-bound enthusiasm.

"Thank you very much, Stephan," said Miranda, and Frank nodded appreciatively.

Miranda invited Frank in and closed the door behind him. She walked back around her desk, offering Frank the chair opposite. On her computer, Miranda pulled up the security footage that Frank had inquired about on the phone earlier. She tapped a finger on her keyboard, and a video was cast onto the forty-two-inch television that hung on the wall between them.

"Here's a view of the front desk from our Baker Street entrance at the time those two female guests checked in." She clicked her mouse, and the recording began to play.

Frank watched as patrons entered and exited the building while a heavy-set woman in her early thirties with tawny shoulder-length hair shuffled papers, handed out key cards, and interacted with guests.

"You'll see those two females arrive through the doors at the bottom of the screen in just a moment here," Miranda explained.

Right on cue, two teenage girls with suitcases in tow suddenly appeared from the bottom of the screen. Almost immediately, the one on the left turned her face back towards the camera, taking in all the lobby had to offer. Frank felt a pang in his chest. It was Sara. She spun back around and continued along, with Marla skipping next to her in her usual upbeat, animated fashion.

"As you can see," Miranda continued, "there wasn't anybody with them at check-in time, as you suggested may have been the case. I even looked to see if someone was perhaps waiting for them outside, but as you'll see from *this* view," she changed to an exterior shot of the building, "there was nobody out there either." She switched back to the lobby view, and Sara and Marla were now engaged with the female clerk at the desk. Frank watched as Sara accepted a tiny envelope with the key cards to their room, along with instructions on how to get there. The girls collected their bags and made their way toward the top of the screen, walking past a bank of elevators in the process.

"Do you have a camera inside those elevators?" Frank wondered.

"We do, but unfortunately, their room was located on the main floor of our east wing," she said, referring to a door barely visible in the top corner of the screen. "And I checked the digital records of their key cards and determined that they were not used to access any other levels of the building during their stay."

Frank nodded, keeping an eye on the security footage as Miranda continued.

"I'd be happy to escort you to the room they stayed in, if you think it might be helpful to your investigation? I upgraded the two guests who were occupying it shortly after you called. However, you should probably be aware that they were the second set of patrons to have stayed in that room since the girls."

Frank was grateful for the consideration but declined the offer, knowing that the room would be of no use to him after receiving that level of foot traffic and multiple cleanings. "Is there footage of their check-out at the front counter the following day?"

"Unfortunately, they checked out using the television inside their room," Miranda explained, locating another file on her computer. "According to our log, they did so at...10:42 AM. Shortly after that, they can be seen exiting the east wing toward Argyle Street at the top of the screen." Miranda seemed to sense Frank's next question. "Sorry, there's no camera at that location."

The time stamp in the bottom corner of the screen read 10:29 AM. Miranda began to fast forward the video, causing guests to move at an accelerated pace through the lobby, checking in, checking out, taking pictures, loading and unloading luggage carts.

"Wait..." Frank suddenly stood up from his chair and took a step towards the television. "Go back."

Miranda looked at the time stamp. It read 10:36. "The girls haven't left their room quite yet," she tried to explain.

"Rewind it slowly."

Miranda complied, and the footage began to reverse direction. She searched the television screen for clues that might indicate what had caught Frank's attention. "I don't—"

"There!" Frank pointed at two slightly out-of-focus male figures near the top of the screen. One was wearing a black baseball cap, aviator sunglasses, and a tacky gray and white polyester tracksuit. The other had shoulder-length platinum blonde surfer hair, blue board shorts, and a red t-shirt. They were walking backward in slow motion towards the Argyle Street exit, having come from the east wing. Miranda stopped the video before they disappeared off the screen.

"Do you know them?" she asked.

Frank stared intently at the young men. “Can you pull up the check-in video again?”

Miranda clicked her mouse, and the previous footage reappeared on the screen. “Here are the girls at the counter again. They receive their room keys...grab their luggage...and head past the elevators toward the east wing,” she narrated.

“Keep it rolling...” Frank instructed her once Sara and Marla had disappeared through the door.

Five seconds passed. Then ten. Just then, the same two young men entered the hotel through the Argyle entrance. Miranda’s eyes widened.

“Now, watch where they go,” Frank instructed.

Chatting idly, the pair crossed the top of the screen and disappeared into the east wing. Frank pulled his cell phone out of his pocket.

“Is it possible that they all just happened to be coming and going at the same time on both days?” Miranda wondered. “I can check our system and try to determine if they had a room rented in that wing.”

Frank was already swiping through pictures. “According to your log, you said the girls checked in on the 8th and checked out on the 9th, correct?”

Miranda looked at her screen to confirm the dates. “Yes.”

Frank turned his phone around to face her. On the screen was a photo that Donna had received from Sara. In the picture, Sara and Marla were standing back-to-back inside a trendy cosmetics shop at a San Diego outlet mall. Each was holding a hairdryer vertically next to their heads, doing their best *James Bond* impersonations. Miranda studied the image, uncertain how it connected with the two young men she had just seen in the security video.

“Look at the reflection in the mirror,” Frank advised her.

Over Marla’s left shoulder hung a large oval-shaped mirror. Near the edge, the face of the guy with the blonde hair was visible.

"That picture was taken on the 10th," Frank explained, turning his phone back toward himself. "The day *after* that footage." He swiped through a few more photos and quickly returned the screen to Miranda.

This photograph was a high-angled selfie taken by the girls near a popular beachside taco truck. Miranda scanned the background and quickly spotted the dark-haired guy with the baseball hat and aviators placing an order at the walk-up window.

"You know these men?" she asked Frank again.

"No," he admitted. "I didn't even make the connection until I saw this lobby footage."

"Did something happen to these girls?" Miranda finally had to ask. "Maybe their families will know who these two men are?"

Frank hadn't revealed to her that his investigation was personal when they spoke earlier, and he hesitated to do so now, but Miranda picked up on the delay. "The taller girl," she studied Sara's smiling face in the photograph, "she's your daughter, isn't she?"

Frank didn't need to respond.

"Yes, I can see the resemblance now."

"We've lost contact with the two of them, and I think something may have happened," he explained. "I'm here as a father, not an FBI agent, and you're the only one out here who knows any of this. I don't want to spook anyone who might be involved. I'm hoping I can trust—"

"I have a daughter of my own, Frank..." Miranda revealed. "Her name is Rachel. She just turned fourteen. If you need anything else from me going forward, just ask. And don't worry, your story is safe with me."

"I appreciate it."

"What are you going to do now?"

"Now that I know those two guys were with the girls on multiple occasions, I'll send their photos to my partner back in New York and have him run their faces through a recognition software program to see if anything pops up."

"I can forward you this security footage to your phone as well."

Frank nodded with appreciation as they made their way to the door. Miranda pulled it open and offered Frank her hand.

"Good luck, Frank."

*****

By the time Frank hit the freeway, he was already on the phone with Mike.

"What's happening?" Mike asked.

"I just sent you some images and a video of two Caucasian males in their twenties. I need you to run them through our face-rec software to see if anything comes back. And maybe ask Winston if he has any other ideas for identifying them."

"I'm on it," said Mike. "You think these guys are involved?"

"It's starting to look that way."

"You're at that hotel now?"

"I just left," Frank explained. "I'm on my way to Temecula as we speak."

"You have an address?"

"Negative, that tracking program only narrowed it down to within a couple of blocks, but it's a residential area, so maybe if I knock on a few doors, I can find someone who saw Sara, Marla, or those two guys around the neighborhood at some point.

"Alright, I'll get working on those images. If you need anything else in the meantime, let me know."

"Will do."

CHAPTER twenty-five

Frank approached a middle-class suburban neighborhood that looked the same as all the others he had seen in Temecula so far: bright, quiet and packed with tropical green foliage. He took a left onto Pembina Drive and parked his rental car under the shade of a towering palm, near the epicenter of where the tracking program had triangulated the girls' phones. Frank stepped out of the vehicle and made his way around to the passenger side, where he rifled through his black duffel bag on the back seat. Stashed inside was a loaded 9mm handgun, which he tucked into the back of his jeans, concealing it with his shirt. After pocketing a few more items, he closed the door and began to walk along a concrete footpath that divided the well-manicured front lawn of a vinyl-sided, two-story house.

Frank pressed the button of a modern-looking doorbell, producing chimes inside the residence and a ringing in the speaker. He listened for any movements on the other side of the door. Hearing nothing, he took a step back and glanced at the large picture window to his right, then up at the second story. After a couple of additional rings, Frank decided to move on to another house. Just as he stepped off the porch, a female voice suddenly arrived through the speaker.

"Hello?"

Frank turned back, attempting to sound as friendly as possible. "Yeah, hi there, I'm just in town for a surprise party for my nephew, and I seem to be a bit lost," he fabricated a story to maintain his cover in the area for the time being. "I tried calling his mother—my sister, that is—to get the address again, but she's not picking up. I know he lives in one of these houses around here. Oh, you know what..." Frank acted as if he had suddenly been struck by a thought, "I have a picture of my nephew here on my phone. Maybe if you come to the door, you might recognize him as one of your neighbors?"

"Oh, uh, sorry," apologized the voice. "I'm just at work right now. The doorbell is connected to my cell phone, but maybe if you hold your photo up to the camera, I could tell you if I've ever seen him around?" she offered. "But I should warn you, I only just moved in a couple of months ago, so I haven't gotten the chance to meet too many of my neighbors yet."

Frank pulled out his phone and swiped through photographs until he landed on a cropped image of the blonde guy from the security footage. "Here's one." Frank squared his device up to the doorbell as best he could.

"Hmm...No. Can't say I've seen him around, sorry."

"No problem, ma'am." Frank turned and took a step off the porch again.

"Oh, hey!" the voice called after Frank, stopping him in his tracks. "You know who would probably know?"

Frank turned around.

"You see that old brown brick house on the other side of the street, to your right? Maybe the fifth or sixth one down."

Frank scanned the area and spotted a house that fit the bill. "568?" he read off the green mailbox perched atop a white 4x4 post.

"Uh, yeah, I think so." She didn't sound certain. "It has a garage on the right side?"

"Correct."

"Okay, yeah, that's the one then! There's an old, retired couple who live there," the woman explained. "They've been on this block for like fifty years or something. *What were their names?*" she asked herself aloud. "Oh shoot, I can't remember, but I met them when I first moved in," she paused, whispering random names to herself. "Anyway, if your nephew lives around here, they'll know which house is his. The lady is an absolute sweetheart! He, on the other hand, well, *he's* a little more..." She seemed to be searching for an apt descriptor. "Doesn't matter, go have a talk with them."

"Thanks."

Frank arrived at 568's tightly cobblestoned footpath and walked past a faded astro blue 1965 Buick Riviera that had been dripping an oil stain on the driveway for decades. Arriving at the front door of the house, he raised his hand to knock, but before his knuckles made contact, the raspy voice of a lifelong male smoker sounded somewhere to his left.

"Ain't interested, bub!"

Unable to immediately locate the source of the voice, Frank lowered his hand and took a step back, scanning the top of the five-foot-tall wooden fence until he spotted the top of a shiny bald head, with a pair of wildly unkempt eyebrows and harshly squinting eyes. "Whatever you're selling, I already got one!" the old-timer assured Frank.

Frank decided to proceed with the same friendly demeanor as before. "No, sir, I'm not selling anything. I—"

"Ya, ya, ya! I spotted you over at Shannon's house down the street there," the half-pint cut him off. "You one of them religious nuts, huh?" The eyes squinted even more tightly. "Why you gotta come preach your nonsense at my house?"

"No, sir—"

"And just *who* exactly are you converting, anyway?" he demanded. "All my life, I never met one person who said, *'I wasn't too sure about the Jesus stuff until that big guy stopped by last Wednesday!'* So let me say this one more time, buster! I ain't interested!"

The front door of the house suddenly swung open in front of Frank, revealing a pudgy woman in her mid-seventies with a kind, cherubic face and curly, white hair.

"Why, hello there, young man. Can I help you?" She smiled sweetly at Frank.

"Oh, Christ! *Now* you've gone and done it, Agnes!" the curmudgeon hollered from behind the boards. "Close the damn door!"

Frank watched as the top of the egg-shaped head began scurrying down the fence towards a gate.

"Henry?" the woman leaned out of the door.

The gate's metal clasp began to rattle violently until a hobbit-like senior appeared and began shambling his way across the lawn as quickly as his stumpy, arthritic legs would allow. "Don't let him in the house, Agnes!" he warned his wife as he closed in. "That's how they getcha!"

"Who's your friend, Henry?" Agnes wondered, clearly accustomed to her husband's antics.

"Hi there, ma'am," Frank attempted to isolate the seemingly more level-headed of the pair before the angry gnome arrived. "I'm just in town for my nephew's surprise birthday party," he repeated his cover story. "He lives in this neighborhood somewhere, but I seem to have misplaced the addr—"

"HA!" the old man barked, finally arriving at the front door and positioning himself directly in front of Frank, next to his wife. "Oldest trick in the book! You think I never heard that one before, chum?"

"Now, Henry, you be nice," Agnes told him. "A surprise party? Oh, my word, that sounds like fun!"

"Yes, ma'am," said Frank. "I have a picture of—" Frank had just begun to lift his phone when a set of hairy knuckles grabbed onto his wrist.

"Here! Lemme see that!" Henry demanded, yanking the screen towards himself for a closer inspection. "She ain't gonna remember nothing anyhow."

"Would you like a cookie, dear?" Agnes suddenly offered Frank out of the blue.

"Uh, no thank you, ma'am," Frank declined, attempting to split his attention between the increasingly erratic pair.

"Yeah, I've seen this bozo before!" Henry reported, releasing Frank's wrist.

"You have?" Frank's eyebrows raised slightly.

"Nephew, eh?" He looked Frank up and down.

"Uh, yeah, my sister's—"

"You ever think of telling that hippie to get a haircut?"

"Well, I—"

"I'll go put some tea on..." Agnes said suddenly, heading back inside and closing the door behind her.

"Don't mind her," Henry suggested, his voice softening a little for the first time. "She ain't playing with a full deck of cards, if you catch my drift," he tapped his finger on his hairless scalp.

Frank didn't respond.

"She's got the dementia," Henry clarified. "Gettin' worse by the day."

"I'm sorry to hear that."

"Yeah, well, that's life, ain't it! Anyway, your nephew lives about ten houses down *that* way," the old man pointed in the opposite direction Frank had just arrived from. "On the other side of the street—a big, ugly, yellow bastard of a house with a cheap chain-link fence."

Frank looked in that direction.

"That nephew of yours is always having different people over," Henry complained. "In fact, I called the police on him a couple times when I heard loud music playing during one of my evening walks! But them cops don't do nothing either! Waste of my damn tax dollars, if you ask me!"

"Alright, well, thanks for the information," Frank said, attempting to extricate himself before Henry got rolling again.

"Yeah, well, try not to lose the address next time, slick!" Henry ordered, turning his back and beginning to shuffle towards the gate, muttering to himself. *"Guy goes around the whole damn neighborhood, disturbing everybody, asking silly questions. Who the hell has a surprise party in the middle of a weekday anyway? Doesn't anybody work anymore..."*

* * * * *

Frank had just spotted the yellow stucco bungalow forty yards down the road when a roofless red Jeep suddenly sped past in the same direction, quickly peeling into the house's asphalt driveway and disappearing down the other side. Not having gotten a look at the driver, Frank picked up his pace. When he reached the end of the driveway, he caught a fleeting glimpse of the blonde-haired driver wearing checkerboard shorts, a teal tank top, and a pair of black flip-flops just before he disappeared around the back corner of the house.

It was him!

Frank looked at the large picture window at the front of the house, obscured by two unpruned manzanita bushes, and decided they would provide him with enough cover from the street to survey the scene inside the residence. He snuck across the lawn, slipped between the shrubbery, and stepped up on the leading edge of an old, unused cedar planter box. Through the open slits of the cream-colored blinds, Frank spied an open-concept living room that contained an L-shaped sectional, a glass-top coffee table, a black bookcase, and a fifty-inch flat-screen television. On the far wall was an open door. A sudden flash of movement in the hallway caused Frank to drop down and press himself tightly against the stucco. He waited a few seconds, then slowly peeked back up over the base of the window and found the room empty.

Frank abandoned the bushes and made his way around to the back of the house, keeping a vigilant eye out for nosy neighbors. When he arrived at the back door, he took hold of the silver handle and found it was unlocked.

Once inside, Frank could hear a vacuum cleaner churning in a distant room and smelled the pungent aroma of a freshly lit joint. He crept through a mudroom, which seemed strangely absent of shoes or clothing items, continuing into a powder blue kitchen with white trim, stainless steel appliances and a set of red-handled pots and pans hanging above a central island. Frank moved silently across the linoleum and found a stack of unopened mail near the edge of one of the quartz countertops. He shuffled through the letters and found they were all addressed to the same man—John Hillenbrand. Frank set the stack back down on the counter, continued into the hallway, and peeked into the first room, discovering it to be the den he had spied through the window moments ago.

Continuing along, he passed two closed doors and paused to listen outside each one for any noises, but he heard nothing. The sound of the vacuum grew louder as Frank approached the last door on the left. He slipped his hand behind his back and removed his gun, letting the warm steel hang down next to his thigh. As he neared the edge of the door, he peeked inside the room and saw the blonde man's back as he extended and retracted the cordless stick vacuum cleaner vigorously across the carpet, while puffs of white smoke billowed around his head. Frank took a single step inside the room when suddenly, the vacuum stopped. Frank quickly pivoted himself out of the room and set his back against the wall on the opposite side of the door.

A shadow grew in the hallway, and Frank tightened his grip on his gun, raising it next to his head, readying himself for engagement. The vacuum cleaner emerged from the room first, quickly followed by a sandalled foot. The target turned right towards the kitchen, completely oblivious to Frank's presence on the other side of the door. Frank lunged and took hold of the back of the young man's neck, driving him down onto the floor and sending the vacuum crashing into the wall. Frank squeezed with force and pinned his face against the carpet. "Where are they, you piece of shit!" he growled.

The young man struggled against Frank's grip but quickly realized it was futile. "Owww! Owww! Owww!" he squirmed. "Whooooa maaaan! I don't got no money, bro! There's some weed out in my car, but it's all I got! Owwwwwww! It's yours, man! Take it!" he offered, in a near parody of a California surfer accent.

"The girls!" Frank shouted. "Sara and Marla! Where are they?" He cocked the hammer, flipped the man over onto his back, and stuck the barrel into a face covered by a mess of disheveled yellow hair.

"I don't know any Marla, bro! I knew a couple of Sarahs in high school, but I haven't seen them in years!"

Using the tip of his gun, Frank swiped the blonde strands off the young man's face.

"For fuck's sake," he suddenly withdrew the gun and retrieved his phone from his pocket. He held the picture from the surveillance footage next to the downed man's face for comparison. It was close, but it wasn't him. *"Fuck."*

"Am I trippin', bro?" the surfer asked aloud, hands still raised defensively in the air. "I think maybe that weed was laced with something..." He looked up at Frank, beginning to question if perhaps the big man was merely a figment of his imagination.

Frank offered him a hand. "No, you're not *tripping,"* Frank assured him. "I got the wrong guy." He motioned with his fingers to indicate that the lift assist was a limited-time offer. The young man finally grabbed hold, and Frank pulled him to his feet.

"So, you're like looking for your wife or something? Is she, like, cheatin' on you? Hey, wait a minute, you said *two* different girls' names, didn't you?" The pothead suddenly looked as if he were trying to decipher the world's most difficult riddle. "Whoa, man! Is your old lady cheatin' on you with, like, another chick? Oh man, that's messed up."

Frank stared at the kid, wondering just how many brain cells he had destroyed by smoking marijuana in his early teens. "I'm looking for my daughter and her friend," he explained. "They came out to California on vacation, and I think they may have stayed somewhere in this neighborhood. I saw you pull into the driveway, and you looked like one of the guys they were with. That's why I snuck up on you."

"Whoa, that's a bummer, dude," the kid said, bending over to recover his downed joint. "This is actually my parents' house, though. Well, one of their rentals, I mean. I just clean their properties and arrange the bookings and all that. Just until my band makes it..."

Frank didn't respond.

"The Grease Traps," the stoner revealed the name of his indie-rock band. "You ever heard of us? I'm the drummer. Brandon." A goofy smile spread across his face.

"Can't say I have," Frank responded, devoid of interest. "But good luck with all that." He stepped past Brandon and over the downed vacuum, making his way into the kitchen.

"Hey, wait a second!" Brandon suddenly called out, following him into the next room.

Frank reluctantly turned around. "What?"

"You don't, like, have any pictures of your daughter and her friend, do you?"

"Why?"

"Well, I dunno, maybe I might have, like, seen them around the neighborhood or something when I was cleaning here one day?"

In his haste to extricate himself from the botched identification, Frank had completely overlooked this possibility. It was a long shot, but perhaps the scrambled-brained hipster could be of some use after all. Frank took out his phone and showed him the picture of Sara and Marla at the food truck.

"Have you ever seen these girls around?"

The kid's bloodshot eyes examined the screen for a long time. "Hmm, no, don't think so. Sorry, bro."

Frank nodded and was about to put his phone away.

"Hey, wait a second." Brandon reached towards the device and used his fingers to zoom in on the photo. "I've seen *that* guy before, though! Yeah, that dude owes me a bunch of pot!"

Frank turned his phone around and discovered that Brandon had zoomed in on the guy with the dark hair from the security footage, who was standing next to the taco truck order window. "Wait? You know *him*?" Frank didn't understand.

"I mean, yeah, sorta. Remember how I told you that this place is a short-term rental?"

Frank nodded.

"Well, a few weeks ago, I was down at Mission Beach and after shreddin' some serious gnar with the boys, I was in the parking lot saying that I had to bail to clean this rental in Temecula. Well, these two guys in the next car over must have overheard me talking, because they said they were looking for a place to rent out this way. So, I pulled out my phone, showed them the listing, and found out that the dates they wanted were free, so I told them they could book it online. That's when they told me they didn't, like, have credit cards or nothing. I said, *'Listen dudes, that's, like, a major problem, cause you gotta have something on file, you know, for like damages and all that stuff.'*"

"Uh-huh."

"That's when they offered to pay me in pot instead. At first, I'm thinking, no way, buds, I already got a dude for that. But then the dark-haired guy from your phone there, he opened the trunk of his car and pulled out this huge duffel bag, just slammed full of weed bricks. He said he'd give me two for the rental, one right then, and one on the day they checked out." Brandon explained. "Bro, I knew just one of those bricks was worth *at least* five times more than the cost of this place—even with the damage deposit—so how could I say no, right? So, I blocked off the dates, took my first *payment*, and that was that."

"And your parents didn't question why there was a gap in the bookings?"

Brandon chuckled, "Dude, my parents own like *nine* different rental properties, and they can barely turn on a computer. Besides, I think they were in like Argentina, or South Africa at the time," he guessed cluelessly. "So, yeah, I gave that guy my phone number and sure enough, a few days before the rental dates, he texted me to make sure everything was still on. I told him, '*Yeah, bro, good to go.*'"

"Then what?"

"Uh, yeah, so once they arrived, I sent him the standard welcome text on the first night, just to make sure the house was all good, and asked if they needed anything. I remember he responded right away, saying the place was cool and that they were all set. After a few more days, I kinda wanted to arrange for my second *payment,* so I sent him another message telling him I could stop by anytime on their final day to meet up. A few hours went by with no response, so I figured maybe this dude wasn't comfortable discussing stuff like this over the phone or something," Brandon shrugged understandingly. "I knew I was going to be up this way cleaning another house that day anyway, so I figured I'd just pop by and see if we couldn't get things sorted. When I pulled in, I didn't see a car in the driveway or anything, so I went to the back door and knocked, because that doorbell is broken. Actually, now that I think of it, I still gotta call the handyman to come take a look at that thing..." he drifted off.

"You knock."

"Oh yeah, so I knocked, and when I did, I could hear, like, keys jingling or whatever, and I look down and see them hanging there. At first, I thought maybe this dude had got distracted on his way out, so I call him up again. Suddenly, his number is disconnected. So, I let myself inside, just to make sure everything in the house was okay, and found they'd already bailed. They must have only stayed a few nights and then took off. Now, I'll admit, at first, I was pretty pissed, but then, like I said before, just one of those bricks was worth *way* more than the rental, so I figured I'd let it slide, for like, good karma or whatever," he grinned stupidly.

"You still have this guy's phone number?"

"Uh, I think so?" Brandon took out his phone and scrolled through his contacts.

"What was his name?"

"I think it was Stan, maybe?" he tried to remember. "No, no, wait, here it is...*Steve*. But like I said, he disconnected his phone."

Frank didn't care. He grabbed the phone from Brandon's hand and quickly copied the number into his own before tossing the device back to him. Unsurprisingly, the kid botched the catch, and the phone fell onto the floor with a *clunk*.

"Hey, wait a second, bro," Brandon said, bending over to retrieve the downed device. "You're not going to, like, tell the cops that I got paid in weed, right?" he questioned Frank, who was already heading towards the door. "I only told you all that stuff 'cause you're, like, looking for your daughter and I wanted to help you out."

Frank pulled open the door and turned back momentarily. "I'll tell you what, Brandon. Let's both just agree that we never met, alright?"

"You got it, man. Scout's honor!" the stoner offered an awkward salute before Frank disappeared out the door.

CHAPTER twenty-six

Mike was seated at his desk at work, attempting to distract himself from Frank's dangerous solo mission with some cursory paperwork, when his cell phone rang.

"Where are you?" Mike asked immediately.

"On the freeway," Frank explained, overtaking a maroon minivan carrying a family of five singing along to something on the radio. "I'm heading out to that industrial area where the girls' phones pinged the towers before they disappeared into Mexico. Did you find out anything about the businesses in that area?"

"There's an auto parts manufacturer, a metal works place, a recycling depot, and a couple of other smaller shops. I called a few of them to ask if there's anything out there that two teenagers might be interested in. Nobody could think of anything. But I did speak with this one guy, though. Hold on a sec, I wrote it down somewhere here..." Mike sandwiched the phone between his ear and shoulder, searching for the blue Post-it note he'd scribbled information on earlier. "Lloyd."

"And what did Lloyd have to say?" Frank weaved between a red Jeep and a beige sedan, nearly clipping his mirrors in the process.

"He owns an animal feed manufacturing plant out there and mentioned that about eight months ago, when he was working late on a weekend, he saw a bunch of coaches—you know, like tour buses with the blacked-out windows—coming and going from up the road. He said he didn't think much of it at the time, thought maybe they had taken a wrong turn off the highway or that somebody was having a Christmas party."

"Did he see which address they were heading for?"

"No, but they were going north of his shop."

"What's this Lloyd guy's address?"

"1867 Dunning Road," Mike read his sloppy handwriting off the blue square. "I checked Google Maps, and there's only about half a dozen more buildings past his place in that direction before the road comes to an end."

"And no one else you spoke to noticed anything like that?"

"Negative. Lloyd told me that more than half the businesses in that area are abandoned, and anything open operates on a nine-to-five, Monday to Friday type schedule."

Frank dipped his head to get a better look at a green exit sign that was tacked to the approaching overpass.

"What did you find out in Temecula?" Mike wondered.

"It looks like Sara and Marla were staying with those two guys at a short-term rental there."

"Did you contact the booking site yet?" Mike mirrored Frank's earlier thought process. "I can get on that next."

"That's the hitch." Frank veered across two lanes of traffic to get onto the next exit, drawing angry honks from other motorists. "These guys are some sort of low-level drug dealers," he explained. "I just ran into a pothead that manages the rental for his parents and found out that they paid him with weed under the table for their stay, so there's no paper trail."

"Shit. And you believe his story?"

"Trust me, this kid was way too stupid to come up with a cover that quickly."

"Fair enough."

"I did manage to get a first name for the guy with the dark hair, though. *Steve*. It might be fake, but why don't you run it, along with his physical description, through our database against any marijuana busts in Southern California in the last few years and see what comes back."

"On it."

*****

Frank's rental car rumbled down a dusty gravel road, having abandoned the freeway fifteen minutes earlier. Just as Mike had said, most of the buildings out this way were abandoned, run down, or both. Up ahead to the right, Frank spotted a processing plant surrounded by a rusty eight-foot chain-link fence topped with drooping barbed wire. Posted on its face was a red placard with faded block letters that read *Lloyd's Premium Animal Feeds.* Frank continued past, deciding to conceal his presence in the area until he could complete some basic reconnaissance.

Eventually, the ungraded road curved itself through a swath of dense forest where green conifers towered over the drainage ditches like ancient sentries. As the car bounced around the last meandering section of the bend, a 10,000-square-foot gunmetal gray steel-sided industrial building appeared on the left side of the road.

Frank pulled his car into its lot and crept down the side of the building until he arrived at a door near the back of the structure that he had spotted from the road. He killed the engine, got out, and walked to a chain-link fence that jutted out from the back corner. Inside the enclosed back lot, he saw a rusted, mocha 1980s Dodge Ram pickup truck parked in front of a windowless twenty-foot-tall garage bay door. Frank abandoned the fence and returned to the door, where he noticed a small security camera stationed just above it. He thumped his fist heavily against the door's metal face and listened for any signs of movement inside. Hearing nothing, he pounded again, then took a few steps back and waved a hand at the camera above his head.

*****

Inside the building, Frank's image was being projected onto a small cube television that sat atop a filthy workbench cluttered with tools. The movement on the screen eventually caught the attention of a greasy-handed mechanic wearing blue dirt-stained coveralls and a black welding mask. He stopped grinding a stubborn lug nut off a piece of corrugated metal and flipped up his mask, exposing a deeply lined, weather-worn face with a patchwork of white whiskers, and set down his tool. "*Who's this now?*" he asked himself aloud in a hybrid Midwest accent, grabbing a roll of blue shop towels off the counter. He spat a mouthful of smokeless tobacco juice onto the dust-caked floor and continued to monitor the stranger on the screen.

*****

Outside, Frank had abandoned the door and was walking back to his vehicle when suddenly a voice arrived from behind him.

"Help you?"

Frank turned and saw the aging mechanic leaning out from the door.

"Uh, yeah..." Frank approached the rustic-looking man, visually assessing him as he did so. "This might sound a bit strange, but my daughter lost her phone last week, and when we activated the '*find your phone*' feature, it told us that it had been out in this general location," he fabricated.

The mechanic studied Frank, not offering an immediate response.

"After that, it seemed to have disappeared over the Mexican border," Frank added. "I know it's probably a long shot, but I figured I should at least come out here to take a quick look before she buys herself a new one."

"Your kid's phone was way out here, you're trying to say?" The tradesman cocked his head slightly. "I find that hard to believe. Where'd she lose it?"

"That's a good question," Frank shrugged. "She was at a few different locations the day she misplaced it, so I'm not entirely certain," Frank decided to offer the seedy-looking stranger as little information as possible for the moment. "The funny thing is, I don't think I've ever seen her put that phone down for more than two minutes." Frank chuckled, attempting to appear harmless until he could further his read. "Teenagers, right?"

The grimy-looking mechanic didn't partake in the humor. Instead, he only wiped his brow, spat out another mouthful of tobacco juice, and continued to stare at Frank. "You stopped by any of the other shops out here yet, inquiring about all this?" He asked, gesturing a dirty hand back down the road in the direction Frank had arrived from.

"Haven't had a chance yet," Frank replied. "Although I did speak with a guy on the phone who had mentioned seeing some buses heading out this way late one night. You ever seen anything like that out here before?"

The grease monkey hesitated. "Nah, but I'm semi-retired, so I don't spend a whole lotta time out here myself anymore. Can't imagine any buses coming out this way, though."

Frank looked past the tradesman into the building and saw a suspended metal platform that ran across to another open door, leading into the main bay. To the left, there was a set of descending stairs.

The wrench-turner peeked back over his shoulder slowly to where Frank was looking.

"Lots of space out here for a retired guy..." Frank commented, his remark falling somewhere between a question and a statement.

"Well, I used to have a pretty sizable operation," the mechanic finally bit, touching the edge of the doorframe with one of his filth-encrusted fingers, as if remembering better times. "But these companies nowadays, they get all their replacement parts from over in China for dirt cheap, so nobody bothers fixin' nothing no more." He shook his head with disdain. "Truth be told, I was considering closing this shop about a year ago, when a couple guys showed up and asked to rent out the downstairs. I had only ever used it for storage, so I figured, why not? Can't imagine why they wouldn't have just bought one of these old, abandoned shit boxes around here, but I wasn't about to talk myself out of a deal."

"Maybe I could speak with them?" Frank inquired. "About my daughter's phone, I mean."

"Ain't nobody ever down there," the mechanic reported matter-of-factly. "They just use the space for storing aircraft parts, I think they said."

"Is there a phone number I could reach them at?"

The man's eyes suddenly turned serious, as if he realized he'd said too much. He stepped out from the door, removed the blue shop towel from his pocket, and gave his hands another workover. "If that phone of yours went over the border, it's bad news, pal."

The statement piqued Frank's attention. "Why do you say that?"

"Because people are always coming here to dump shit into our trash bins when nobody's around," he explained. "And once the dump trucks come to collect it, they take it straight across the Mexican border. That's big business, ya know?"

"What is?" Frank asked as the mechanic stepped past him and began walking towards the car.

Frank followed.

"Paying other countries to take our trash!" the tradesman said resolutely. "And once those Mexis have it, they just put it on a big barge and pass it off to *some other* third-world country. And do you know what *those guys* do with it?" He spat next to Frank's tire and turned to face him.

"No. What?"

"Soon as they get out of sight, they just dump it all overboard. *Sploosh!* Right in the damn ocean!" he mimed. "So as far as your kid's phone goes, I think you're shit out of luck, pal. I wouldn't bother wasting any more of your time." With that, he wrapped his knuckles on the hood of the car, indicating that the conversation had come to an end. He made his way past Frank and headed back toward the door.

Something felt amiss. Frank decided he needed to get inside the building.

"Yeah, you're probably right..." Frank defaulted back to the same faux-friendly voice as before. "Hey, before I take off, do you mind if I use your bathroom real quick? It's kind of a long drive home."

"Feel free to take a piss anywhere you like," the tradesman gestured an open hand to indicate the solidarity of their surrounding environment as he continued to walk away.

"Well, it's, uh, you know, it's not just..."

The mechanic had just reached the door when he grasped the specificity of his visitor's request. "Yeah, alright, fine, I got a shitter in here," he said, motioning for Frank to follow him inside. "Come on."

"Thanks."

As Frank approached, he removed a pack of chewing gum from his pocket, unsheathed two sticks, and placed them inside his mouth.

"Straight ahead," the mechanic said impatiently.

Frank stepped onto the metal platform and slowly made his way across to the next door, looking to his left down the stairs as he did so. The daylight flooding in from outside was just enough to allow him to spot a door at the base of the stairs with a security camera stationed above it. The restless mechanic hurried himself past Frank. "Come on now, I ain't got all day."

Frank lingered for a moment longer before following the tradesman into the high-ceilinged bay.

"I couldn't help but notice another camera at the bottom of those stairs," Frank said.

"Yeah, so?" the mechanic replied, as the pair weaved their way through a labyrinth of workbenches and heavy-duty parts.

"Well, I was just thinking, maybe if I gave you the date and time when my daughter's phone was out this way, you could have a look at your security foot—"

"These cameras don't record nothing," the mechanic didn't bother letting Frank finish. "The only reason I got them in the first place was to lower my insurance premiums. It's all just for show. Criminals only need to see a camera to deter them."

"So, you didn't see me waving at the door earlier, when I arrived?"

Frank picked up on another split-second hesitation.

"Nah, I heard you banging."

"And you don't have any issues with people trying to break in here?" Frank decided to push the point a bit more.

"Look around you," the mechanic gestured with a hand as they walked. "You see anything in this place worth stealing? Besides, I got a gun in my safe in the office over here. If someone ever tries breaking in, they better hope I'm not around, or they'll surely regret it!" he chuckled, as they arrived in front of a four-by-six-foot plexiglass window on the far side of the bay. The room inside looked to have once functioned as an employee lunch area with a collection of old chairs and tables, but now they only acted as additional surface space for heaps of useless scrap metal, tools, and outdated mechanical devices. "Bathroom is down *that* way. Second door." He pointed to the right.

"Alright, thanks."

Frank made his way down the paint-peeled wall, eventually approaching a second window. He slowed his pace, allowing himself some time to look inside the room. In the middle was a dilapidated computer desk with an ancient-looking monitor, surrounded by a whirlwind of yellowing invoices. Just before Frank reached the office's open door, he slipped his hand inside his pocket and located a black, pill-shaped case that contained a tiny microphone recording device. He ducked through the door to his left.

"I said the second door!" Frank heard the mechanic shout out in annoyance from where he had left him.

Frank quickly removed the microphone from its case and enveloped it inside the wad of white gum from his mouth. He could now hear the mechanic's boots clomping loudly in his direction. Frank looked around, then reached his hand under the desk and stuck the rubbery glob to its underside. He quickly turned around and headed back toward the door, just as the mechanic appeared in the plexiglass window, looking irritated.

"You don't hear too good, eh?" the tradesman snapped at Frank, meeting him at the door.

"Sorry about that. I thought you said *next* door on the left," Frank suggested, stepping past him and out of the office. "I'll come get you when I'm done."

The mechanic watched Frank like a hawk until he disappeared into the bathroom, then made his way back into the room where he had been grinding earlier. Upon entering the space, he switched off the tiny television on which he had spotted Frank and threw a grease-stained towel over it to conceal its presence.

After five or six minutes of tinkering, the mechanic set down his wrench and headed back out into the bay, emerging at the same time Frank was coming out of the bathroom.

"Come on," the repairman called out, motioning for Frank to follow him to the exit.

Once Frank stepped outside, he turned and made one final attempt. "If I could just grab the phone number for your tenants downstairs before I—"

"It's time to just cut your losses," the mechanic shut him down. "It's only a phone."

"Alright," the pleasantness Frank had tacked on to his voice earlier was gone now. "Maybe I'll see you around..."

*****

"Something was definitely off," Frank explained to Mike, now sitting inside the rental car parked a mile down the road, tucked tightly against the side of one of the abandoned structures.

"You think this guy knows where the girls are?"

"No, I don't think he's involved to that extent, but whenever I mentioned the basement or the tenants, he would deflect."

"He wouldn't let you down there?"

"No," Frank shook his head. "I considered showing him the pictures of those two guys from the surveillance footage to try to gauge his reaction, but I didn't want to tip my hand too early, just in case he knows more than he's letting on."

"So, what now?"

"I planted a bug in his office, and I've been listening in since I left, but I'm not sure he even goes in that room anymore. Whatever the case, once he's gone for the night, I'm going to let myself inside and poke around."

"What do you t—"

"Hold on a sec, Mike." The portable speaker on Frank's dash had suddenly crackled to life. He brought it up to his ear. "I can hear him now. I'll call you back later."

* * * * *

Inside the shop, the mechanic had entered the office and was rifling through the rickety drawers of the desk in search of a cell phone that had been given to him by the basement tenants, along with a year's worth of rent paid in cash. "*Where is that fucking thing?*" he muttered, slamming one drawer shut before opening the next. Finally, he spotted the device in the bottom compartment, snatched it up, and scrolled to the only number that had been programmed into the phone by the renters. It was filed under X. The mechanic dialed the number and placed the phone against one of his wax-encrusted ears. After five or six rings, the call seemed to connect; however, only an eerie silence arrived.

"Hello?" the mechanic questioned the dead air.

"Yes?" replied a monotoned male voice.

"Yeah, uh, this is Clifford here. One of you people gave me this cell phone a while back. Told me if I had any issues, I should call..."

"Yes."

The mechanic squinted indignantly. "What do you mean, yes? I'm calling because there was just some big guy out here poking around, asking a bunch of questions, like a damn cop or something! I'm done with all this shit!"

"Done with *what* exactly?" the voice held its stability.

"Well, I mean, I just don't want you people using my basement no more, is all. In fact, I've been thinking about putting the shop up for sale again," he lied. "So, it's time for you people to move on."

"You were paid for the entirety of the year, were you not, Mr. Clifford?"

"Well, yeah..." the mechanic began to pace around the room. "Maybe what I can do is give you back some of that money, you know, for the remaining time."

Silence.

"Listen, this ain't the first time someone has come out here asking questions," he raised his voice a little. "And now some of the neighbors are making comments about the late-night activities going on. I don't know what the hell you're doing down there, but I just don't want nothing to do with it anymore, alright?"

"We had an understanding, Mr. Clifford. In exchange for the large cash payment, which you needed so desperately at the time, you agreed there were to be *no* inquiries into our affairs."

The mechanic's thoughts drifted back to the financial turmoil he had found himself in when he was forced to take in the mysterious entity that now occupied the basement. "Look, I still have absolutely no interest in whatever you got going on down there. I just don't want to be involved. It's nothing against *you people*."

More silence.

Clifford's patience finally evaporated. "Alright, listen, asshole, don't make me get the cops and lawyers involved now," he threatened hollowly. "It's not like we ever had a written contract or nothing."

"Now why did you have to go and say something like that..." the voice said ominously.

"Well, I'm ju—"

"Consider the arrangement dissolved, Mr. Clifford."

The statement caught the mechanic slightly off guard. "Alright, well, I'll just have to move some funds around," he said, trying to imagine how he was going to come up with money he did not possess.

"That won't be necessary."

"Pardon?"

"The arrangement is fully terminated. No future monetary transactions will occur."

"Oh, well, good then," Clifford said, his eyebrows raising slightly. "If you people got any belongings down there, do you have any idea when you might be able to remove them from the building? I don't want to rush you or nothing, but I'm leaving on a fishing trip upstate tomorrow morning for a couple weeks. Maybe it might be a good time to do it while I'm gone?"

"Everything will be vacated from the premises prior to your return," the voice said robotically. "The keys will be left in the lockbox, and we ask you to leave the cell phone inside so we can collect it."

"Well, hell..." the mechanic grinned, exposing his brown teeth. "I appreciate your understanding with all this. It was just one of those things, you know, poor timin—"

"Goodbye, Mr. Clifford." The call was suddenly disconnected.

The mechanic removed the phone from his ear and looked down at the now blank screen. *"Fucking beaners..."* he muttered derogatorily, despite having just been granted the deal of a lifetime.

* * * * *

Inside the rental car, Frank's ears perked up when he heard the slur. It wasn't the racism that surprised him—just one look at the aging mechanic might lead someone to suspect that bigotry was a mainstay of his character—but the statement was a confirmation that the girls' phones being tracked into Mexico was not likely a coincidence. Frank heard a desk drawer shut and the tradesman exit the office. After a couple more hours of power tools whining in the distance, a prolonged silence arrived through the speaker, leading Frank to believe the mechanic was done for the night. By this point, an inky blankness had crept in all around his car, completely obscuring its presence from the road. After a few minutes, a pair of headlights appeared over the ridge, and soon, the old pickup truck rumbled past and disappeared toward the freeway. Frank started his engine, pulled out from the hiding spot, and began to make his way back to the shop.

Frank parked in the same spot as before, got out, and glanced back down the desolate road from which he had come, finding it barren and quiet. He popped the trunk and removed his tactical vest, tools, and a pair of mechanic's gloves. A stiff breeze washed over the area, bullying the tips of the surrounding pines as he approached the building.

Upon arrival, Frank examined the door's deadbolt assembly and discovered that the components were relatively cheap and flimsy, and he was certain that the mounting plate could be easily manipulated to expose the internal screw set and provide him quick access to the building. Frank removed a lock-picking kit from his vest, along with a pair of black-rimmed glasses. He set the frames on his face and pressed a tiny button on the left arm next to his temple, activating tiny LEDs in the upper corners of the glasses, casting a small spotlight onto the door. Using an L-shaped tool from the kit, Frank pried off the faceplate and removed the exposed fasteners with his screwdriver. Taking hold of the silver doorknob, he twisted it forcefully. After a bit of initial resistance, the knob's twin fell onto the metal platform inside the building with a reverberating *clang*. Frank inserted his finger into the newly created cavity and forced the remainder of the assembly off to one side before removing a length of coiled black tubing with a miniature camera embedded in one end from his vest. Slowly, he fed the snake through the hole and then pressed a secondary button on the arm of the glasses, causing a projection of the pitch-black interior of the building to appear in front of his eyes in the lens. Sensing its darkened environment, the camera transitioned itself into a bright green night-vision mode.

Frank adjusted the position of the camera by twisting a control knob at the base of the tool, eventually revealing a forty-five-degree rotating thumb lock on the other side of the door. He studied the simplistic component, then retracted the tubing from the cavity and quickly affixed a steel wire attachment with a circular loop that extended four or five inches above the camera. Reinserting the tubing back into the hole, Frank quickly readjusted the camera to its former position. After a few unsuccessful attempts, he managed to capture the end of the thumb lock in his snare. He wrapped the tubing around his wrist, gave it a tug, and the deadbolt slid out of its cradle, relinquishing its hold on the door. Frank deactivated the glasses and returned them to his vest, along with his other tools.

Entering the darkened corridor, Frank crept past the metal stairs. He continued into the bay, removed a flashlight from his pocket, and activated it. He began to weave the same circuitous path between work benches as before, heading for the pigsty office space to recover his microphone and search for the cell phone the mechanic had been using.

Frank entered the office and scoured the top of the desk for documentation related to the basement tenants, but found the paperwork uselessly outdated—in some cases, two or three decades old. He reached a hand blindly under the desk, attempting to recover the listening device. Unable to locate it, Frank bent over and directed his flashlight to where he had placed the bug earlier, quickly discovering that the gum had become unstuck and fallen to the floor, along with the microphone. Fortunately, the room was in such a state of disarray that an errant item such as this had little chance of being detected.

Frank pocketed the device and began opening desk drawers one by one, searching for the phone. The first three contained only pens, pencils, spent print cartridges, batteries, a mechanical calculator, and other ancient stationery. In the bottom drawer, he finally spotted the device. Tapping a finger on the screen, the phone prompted him for a password. Frank tried 1-2-3-4, hoping that the device had been set up for maximal simplicity, but was denied access. Next, he tried 1-1-1-1, garnering the same result. Sensing the futility, Frank pocketed the phone, shut the drawer, and abandoned the office.

Once back inside the bay, Frank took a left, quickly passing by the bathroom facilities he had pretended to use earlier, and eventually arrived at the exit in the corner diagonally opposite to where he had come in. He pulled the door inward, producing an ominous groan. On the other side of the door was another platform, the reverse of the one on the opposite side of the bay. Stepping onto its metal grating, he directed his light to the left, illuminating the stairs.

Frank's footsteps echoed as he descended, and his flashlight cast jagged shadows on the surrounding walls. At the base of the stairs, he arrived at another door. Taking hold of the knob, he twisted it, attempting to determine if another breach might be possible. To his surprise, he found that it was unlocked.

Walking down a red-carpeted hallway, Frank's underpowered flashlight created a milky haze around him, matching the stagnant subterranean air. Twenty feet ahead to his left, Frank spotted three additional doors, each with a camera stationed above. To his immediate right was an open entryway. He directed his flashlight inside the room, illuminating a large space packed with tables and chairs covered with white sheets.

Frank entered the room and navigated his way through the maze of cloth-covered furnishings, lifting sheets here and there to reveal stacks of modern electronic equipment, round serving trays, and glassware. Eventually, he reached what appeared to be a bar, with huge speakers sitting on top of its polished surface. Directing his light to the left, he discovered a panel of light switches on the wall. He walked over and flipped the first switch towards the ceiling. Nothing happened. Frank activated the remaining switches until the last one finally produced a low buzzing hum above his head. Slowly, a symphony of *pings* and *tings* filled the room as fluorescent tubes sprang to life. Frank deactivated his flashlight and made his way over to a heavy-duty sliding door. Attempting to push the metal slab along its track, he discovered a pair of half-inch pins securing it to the floor and ceiling. The top bolt released easily, but the bottom was jammed inside its concrete crevice. Frank rattled the edge of the door forcefully, attempting to loosen the pin's grip, but it wouldn't budge. He stomped a heel on the bolt, and finally, it shifted loose. Frank bent over, pulled the pin from the floor, and began to slide the door down its track.

Suddenly, a guttural roar sounded behind Frank, causing him to release his grip on the door. He turned and caught only a fleeting glimpse of the incoming giant before he smashed into Frank, driving him violently into the door and onto the floor. Face down, Frank attempted to turn himself over, hoping to gain a defensive position before the next vicious onslaught arrived, but found himself being lifted off the floor by his attacker's twenty-four-inch arms. Frank was now trapped chest-to-chest with the beast in a debilitating bear hug, with his legs dangling and all the breathable air being squeezed from his lungs. Even at six-foot-two and two-hundred-and-fifty pounds, Frank looked like a child dangling from the behemoth's ogre-like grip as his ribs and intercostal muscles *popped and snapped* with each of the hulk's twists and shakes. Frank felt the gun behind his back shift before it fell to the floor with a *clunk*. His vision began to blur.

Frank tilted his head back as far as his current confinement would allow, then drove his forehead downward directly into the crown of the attacker's shaved, cinderblock head. Painful starbursts flashed in Frank's vision, feeling like he had smashed his head into a brick wall. Completely undisturbed, the nearly seven-foot monster looked up at Frank with a sadistic grin on his face and amplified his squeeze.

As unconsciousness neared, Frank reached down and grabbed onto his attacker's face, digging his thumbs into the man's eye sockets. The giant bellowed in pain as Frank reefed on his pliable sclera. Finally, the hulk let go, dropping him onto the floor at his feet and allowing him to gulp down some much-needed oxygen.

The brute stumbled backward a few steps, furiously rubbing his eyes as he blinked his vision back into existence. Just then, Frank noticed a carbon fiber knee brace poking out from the bottom of the giant's blue-and-white basketball-style gym shorts. Sensing an opportunity, Frank sprang off the floor, aiming his shoulder directly at the joint. Before he made contact, the mass monster swatted Frank across the side of his head with his frying pan-sized hand and sent him flying into one of the surrounding tables, sending boxes of stacked glassware crashing to the floor.

The hulk descended upon Frank, who had only just managed to get back up on his feet, and swung a looping hook aimed directly at his head. Frank ducked the punch and sent a pair of body shots into the man's exposed kidneys. Both blows were enough to incapacitate a normal human, but Frank found they had very little effect in penetrating the copious amounts of muscle and fat that were insulating the giant's internal organs.

With impressive athleticism, the brute spun around and grabbed onto Frank's tactical vest, catapulting him through the air like a rag doll, sending him crashing through a stack of cardboard boxes, scattering electrical equipment in all directions. Frank rolled onto his back as the hulk approached and delivered a boot to the man's braced leg, dropping him onto one knee. Frank took the opportunity to grab a long, orange extension cord that had fallen onto the floor next to him and quickly got to his feet. He looped it around his opponent's tree trunk neck, then tossed the remainder over an exposed beam in the ceiling. Wrapping the cord tightly around each of his wrists, Frank used his body weight to lean back and pull the colossus up from his genuflected position on the floor, cinching in the noose. The hulk's face began to redden.

Just when Frank thought he had finally gained the upper hand, his opponent suddenly reached up and took hold of the cord above his head with one of his massive paws. With a mighty tug, he jerked Frank forward out of his angled stance, and before Frank could reset his footing, the brute had already spun himself around to face his failed hangman. He removed the cord from around his neck and held it out in front of himself between his two meaty hands, staring menacingly at his opponent across the room. A sinister grin came upon his face before he snapped the fourteen-gauge cord in half, like a piece of dental floss.

The man planted his foot on the base of the round-topped table next to him and drove his powerful forearm down upon its leading edge. Like an oversized poker chip, the top of the table detached and tumbled across the room, crashing into the face of the bar next to Frank. The man took hold of the table's three-inch round metal bar with its circular base still attached and approached.

Frank glanced over to where his gun had fallen and quickly determined that there wouldn't be enough time to recover it before his adversary delivered a spine-busting hack. Despite nearing exhaustion, Frank knew his only choice was to ready himself for another round of combat. The giant closed in and swung the table base with enough force to remove Frank's head from his body. Frank was backpedaling, avoiding each of the decapitating blows, when he suddenly tripped over a cardboard box and landed on his back. The hulk moved in and tomahawked the weapon at his opponent on the floor, who rolled left just fast enough to avoid the impact. The giant re-raised the reverberating post high above his head and steadied himself for another hack. Just then, Frank sent a powerful kick into the man's braced knee, producing the sickening sound of dried twigs snapping.

The table base fell to the floor with a *clang,* and the giant toppled over, clutching at his destroyed joint and groaning in agony. Frank stood and recovered the heavy implement, needing two hands to lift it. He stepped forward and raised the table post high above his head, taking aim. Just then, his opponent lifted a hand, silently pleading for mercy. Spiteful rage burned inside Frank's chest as thoughts of burying the edge of the weapon deep into the man's skull flooded his mind. After a few drawn-out moments, Frank finally released his grip, and the weapon fell to the floor.

Leaving the disabled giant where he was, Frank made his way over to where his gun had settled by the sliding door. After retrieving it, he grabbed a chair and dragged it over to the injured man, placing it in front of him. The hulk looked at Frank curiously, before gripping the seat and laboriously lifting his four hundred pounds off the floor. He settled into it uncomfortably.

"Who the fuck are you?" Frank grunted at him.

"Shouldn't I be asking you that?" the man responded, his voice harboring a distinct southern drawl.

"Don't make me ask you again, fat boy," Frank warned, discovering that his opponent looked younger than he had seemed during the frenzied combat.

"Name's Angus," the human refrigerator reported through clenched teeth as he attempted to reposition his bungled leg.

"Well, *Angus*, why don't we start with what the fuck you're doing out here?"

"What am I—" the young man nearly answered another of Frank's questions with one of his own, but thought better of it. "I work security."

"Security?" Frank frowned. "For who?"

Angus hesitated.

"Listen, I don't have time for your bullshit," Frank barked. "Tell me who owns this place and why exactly you attacked me."

Angus looked genuinely bewildered.

"Are you deaf or fucking stupid?"

"I thought you were talking to the owner today? That old mechanic guy upstairs..."

"Not the building, Angus. Who rents *this* space? Down here." Frank gestured around the room.

"Ac—"

"Wait," Frank interrupted. "How did you know I was talking to the guy upstairs today? *He* told you that?"

"No," the big man shook his head. "I've never met him."

"Jesus Christ," Frank muttered under his breath, shaking his head at the Abbott and Costello routine going on.

Sensing his interrogator's growing frustration, Angus spoke up, "Listen, I got a message a couple of hours ago saying that somebody had been out here today, snooping around, asking that old guy questions. I was told to come check things out."

"Sent by who?" Before Angus could provide an answer, Frank decided to change his line of questioning. "Have you ever seen a couple of teenage girls out here?"

This inquiry appeared to perplex Angus as much as all the others. Frank had finally had enough. He stepped forward and kicked the bottom of his size eighteen shoe, sending a jolt through his injured knee.

"AARRRGGGHHHH!" Angus howled, pulling his leg towards himself, compounding the agony. "Yeah, I've seen teenage girls around here!" he hollered, cradling his knee. "Half the people who attend these parties are teenage girls!"

"*Parties?* What parties?" Frank tried to wrap his head around the statement. "What *is* this place?"

"It's, like, a venue, I guess you'd call it. A single location on an underground circuit."

Frank didn't follow.

Angus tried to think of a better way to explain it. "You ever seen the movie *Fight Club?"* he asked, slowly re-straightening his busted leg.

"They host fights down here?" Frank looked at him suspiciously.

"No," He shook his head. "I'm just saying, in that movie, they would use random locations so that nobody ever knew where or when the next one was going to happen. It's kinda like that, but for parties."

"And you work as a bouncer at these things? Is that what you mean by security?"

Angus nodded.

"So, there are other locations like this one?"

"Yeah, they use all sorts of places."

Frank paused, considering something. "If no one knows where or when these parties are going to take place, then how do *you* know when to show up for work?"

"I get a message on a pager."

"A pager?" Frank looked at him incredulously. "Like from the 80s?"

"Yeah," Angus nodded. "I dunno, he said something about them being analog? I don't know anything about technology, that's just what I was told."

Frank could see that Angus' complexion was paling, and beads of syrupy sweat were forming on his brow. "Who exactly is *he*?"

"Look, I already told you. All this stuff is really hush-hush. It's not like—AARRRGGGGHHH!"

Frank had kicked the bottom of his shoe again. "I want a fucking name!"

"Salazar!" Angus finally revealed, gripping onto the sides of the chair in anguish.

"And how do I get hold of this Salazar guy?"

"That's what I'm trying to tell you!" Angus barked back. "I don't have *any* contact with the guy. Zero. None. Except for whatever comes through my pager. And those messages only arrive a day or two before an event."

"So, let me get this straight. You want me to believe that some guy named Salazar, who apparently, you've never even met, provided you with a pager somehow, so you could work security at these underground parties? Is that *really* the best story you can come up with?"

Angus fidgeted uncomfortably.

"That's interesting..." Frank studied him more closely now. "I didn't notice it at first, probably because you had all that adrenaline pumping through your system during the fight, but I can see it now," he stared at him. "It's as clear as fucking day."

Angus wiped away a droplet of sweat that had formed on the tip of his nose, eyeing Frank sheepishly.

"Yeah. I've seen that look you've got on your face a thousand times before," Frank continued. "You're a fucking junkie. And I bet if I sit your ass here long enough, you'll chop that fucking leg off with an axe just to get a fix. Isn't that right, big boy?"

The young man's eyes dropped to the floor, and a look of shame spread across his face.

"So, what's your drug of choice?" Frank wanted to keep the pressure on him. "Pfffft, who am I kidding? Guys like you don't give a shit. You'll sniff, swallow or inject anything you can get your fucking hands on, won't you?"

Angus' eyes glazed over. "It's not like that..." he said softly.

"No, of course it's not. It never is," Frank balked. "Why don't you tell me what *it is* like then, Angus?"

The giant's eyes searched around the room before they settled back on Frank. A deflated exhalation of breath caused his double-wide shoulders to slump forward despairingly.

"I'm from Mississippi originally, from a small town you've never heard of," Angus said, running a finger beneath his snotty nose. "I grew up on a dairy farm, playing football, and luckily for me, I was decent enough on the gridiron that I had my choice of any college I wanted to lace up for."

Frank's eyebrows furrowed, but he allowed the story to continue.

"After talking to a bunch of scouts, my old man decided that USC was my best choice. I ended up getting a full ride, and with the O-line coach they had, everybody said I was a shoo-in first-round pick one day. So, I packed up and came out here to California. I worked hard, kept my head down, and sure enough, by the time I entered my senior year, I was projected to go top ten in the draft. But early that season, in a game against Stanford, I got clipped and felt a *POP* in my knee. Turned out it was my ACL." Angus shook his massive head, recalling the moment he received the news in the campus hospital.

"Luckily, Coach got me hooked up with one of the best surgeons in the state, and before I knew it, I was rehabbing with a physio. I felt like everyone was looking out for me, helping to prove to them scouts, that my injury was just a fluke.

"I got cleared to play quickly, and in my first game back against Washington, I was feeling good, settling back into my old rhythm, but in the third quarter, for some reason, they left me out on special teams for a punt. I held my block, heard the kick get off, and slowly began to make my way down the field. I had no intention of trying to make the tackle, I mean, just look at me..." he gestured at his enormity, "blazing speed wasn't exactly my game. Suddenly, out of nowhere, *BANG!* I'm on the turf again with the exact same blinding pain as before, only this time, it was my *other* knee," he referenced the joint Frank had just mangled. "And the worst part was, nobody even hit me this time. The dang thing just blew out, all on its own."

A memory from the past suddenly popped into Frank's mind. "Angus *Johnson...*" he said, putting two and two together. "I remember that game. Your injury was all over the sports highlights."

"Yeah, and it ended any chance I ever had at making it to the bigs," the super-sized young man explained, wiping the back of his hand across his now heavily perspiring forehead. "It was like, suddenly, I had the plague or something. My coaches didn't bother checking with me anymore, and my name disappeared from the athletic world. I certainly never got another call from a scout."

"That's when you started using..."

Angus nodded. "After my first surgery, the doctors gave me some pain medication, and I only took them for about three days because I hated how foggy they made me feel, so I tossed 'em out and switched over to Advil and toughed it out. But after that second injury, when I felt like everyone had abandoned me, I started to crave the brain fog," Angus admitted. "The last thing I wanted to do was think about anything—about my injury, about the fact that my playing days were over, about any of it. So, I took the pills just to zone out. When I'd run out, I'd tell the doctor that my knee still hurt, and he just kept giving me more. Pretty soon, I could barely get myself out of bed, I was failing my classes, and one day, I just stopped showing up for school altogether.

"Up until that point, I'd always worked at an off-campus nightclub to make some extra cash," Angus continued. "After my first injury, the bar was really understanding. They let me take the time off to heal up and told me they'd have a spot waiting for me whenever I returned. But after the second knee, it was a completely different story with them, too. Suddenly, the manager said they couldn't wait around for me to heal up again, and I found out through one of the bartenders that it was because the owners were afraid of the liability.

"By then, the doctor had finally cut me off from refills, but I remembered a guy who lived in my dorm during my freshman year who had supplied some people I knew with pills that helped them study all night. So, I contacted him and sure enough, he said he could get me anything I wanted." Angus shook his head again. "But because I wasn't working at the club anymore, my funds were getting tight, and I was having trouble paying for my supply. That's when my dealer mentioned that he might know someone who needed help."

"Salazar..." Frank guessed correctly.

"My dealer warned me that this wasn't going to be just some regular bouncing gig. He said that '*privacy and discretion were going to be of the utmost importance*' and that '*I'd never have a set schedule or meet Salazar*'. That's when he gave me the pager and explained that all the dates, times, and locations would show up on there. Obviously, I was skeptical at first," Angus admitted. "I figured this Salazar probably didn't even exist, or if he did, he would just wind up being some scam artist. But by that point, I was so desperate for pills, I figured I'd take my chances, so I agreed.

"I remember pulling out the little bit of money I had scrimped together to buy another dozen pills, which by that point, was only going to get me through another day or two—but my dealer wouldn't take it. Instead, he handed me this Ziplock bag crammed full of pain meds and explained they were a signing bonus from Salazar. *That's* when I knew this bouncing gig was the real deal."

Questions swirled inside Frank's head, colliding with one another. "How long until you were contacted on the pager?"

"About a week or so."

"And how did the job start?"

"I just shadowed Dallas for my first couple shifts."

"Dallas?"

"Don't get your hopes up," Angus tempered Frank's expectations. "That's not his real name. We were all given code names, you know, to keep everything discreet and separate from our personal lives."

"What were you called?"

"Memphis."

"And you shadowed this Dallas guy out here, at this location, to start?"

"Not right away, no," Angus shook his head. "The first couple times were at a smaller venue up near San Bernardino."

"And what exactly goes on at these parties?"

"Could be anything, really," Angus shrugged. "Most of them are just like massive raves, but the people who attend them aren't the regular clientele you'd see at those kinds of things. It's kind of hard to explain. But the first thing Dallas told me was not to ask any questions and to make as little contact with the patrons as possible."

"And nobody recognized an NCAA football player?"

"Never," Angus shook his head. "I guess that's the thing about playing a sport where a helmet covers your face and you're not some pretty boy quarterback. And besides, I don't think most of the people who attend these events are the sport-watching types."

"You must have had some inclination of who was behind these parties?"

"I mean, we heard rumors..."

"Like what?"

"I dunno," Angus shifted nervously in his seat, "like that maybe the Mexican cartels used these parties to move drugs or something."

Frank's face grew more serious. "Were there a lot of Mexicans at these events?"

"I guess."

"What the fuck do you mean, *you guess?* You must have heard people talking when you let them in? Were they speaking Spanish or not?"

"This is Southern California!" Angus snapped back. "Just because somebody speaks Spanish doesn't make them Mexican."

Frank could tell the big man was desperate for a fix. "Listen, just tell me what I need to know, and I'll let you get your drugs."

"I haven't used in days now," Angus suddenly revealed. "The dope sickness is still coming and going in waves, but it's getting better."

"You quit?"

Angus nodded.

"Why? Why did you suddenly decide to stop?" Frank questioned, feeling as if something was eating the giant from the inside. Something that he needed to get out.

Angus exhaled. "Obviously, I knew there was illegal stuff happening in these places," he admitted. "I would look the other way if I saw people snorting coke in the bathroom or making a hand-off under a table. Heck, with my addiction in full force, who was I to judge? But lately, things seemed to be going sideways at this location."

"What do you mean?"

"Well, for one thing, the girls they had coming here seemed to be getting younger and younger. On top of that, it was becoming normal for Dallas to take guys into the back rooms and rough 'em up. And I mean *hard,*" Angus sent a fist into his palm. "And it wasn't because they had done anything wrong, it was like they were being invited here just to get beat up. On top of all that, more of the female patrons seemed to be getting over-served, sometimes to the point of unconsciousness," Angus recalled. "And whenever that happened, Dallas would separate them from the rest of the crowd and arrange transport with the limo driver. That was completely against protocol. Everybody who attended these events was supposed to arrive and leave together on the buses."

"Who's this limo driver?"

"An older guy who used to hang out back here during the parties sometimes," Angus pointed to a sheet-covered table near the back of the room where Frank had entered. "I started to realize that whenever things would go sideways, he always seemed to be around."

"What did this guy look like?"

"He was short, with a big nose," Angus explained, picturing the man in his mind. "He had acne scars on his face and always wore the same brown hat."

"And you never spoke to him? Not even when he came through the door?"

"No. Dallas would always bring him through this side of the building after the night had already started," Angus remembered. "He told the rest of us to just leave him alone, and that he was only here in case we needed emergency transport. He made it clear—this guy was off limits."

"Did he ever cause any trouble?"

"No," Angus shook his head. "That was the thing, I'd just see him hanging around the back here, then something would go down, and once things settled, he'd be gone—like a ghost."

"And what does all this have to do with you kicking your drug habit?"

"The other night, there was a party out here, and when I arrived, Dallas told me that three people would be arriving in a cab after the buses—a blonde guy with long hair and two girls. He told me to let them in, no questions asked. Again, this was completely outside our normal protocols, but because stuff like this was happening more often, I didn't think too much of it. Sure enough, once the party had been going for a while, they showed up. I didn't say anything to them; I just let them in and brought them downstairs."

Frank nodded.

"A little while later, I was conducting a perimeter check outside when I thought I could hear voices coming from the fenced-in yard on the other side of the building."

"Was that unusual?"

"Very," Angus suggested. "Everybody is supposed to remain inside and out of sight for the entire night. So, I hoofed it across the front of the building, thinking maybe I'd catch a couple of smokers who had somehow snuck their way out. Instead, through the fence, I see Dallas standing next to that limo driver, and the old guy is hollering at this other young guy with black hair."

"You didn't know the guy he was yelling at?"

"No, I'd never seen him before," Angus shook his head. "I couldn't tell exactly what the limo driver was saying, but I could hear the young guy pleading with him, saying something like '*Mr. Lopez. Please. I'll figure something else out...*'"

"The limo driver's name is Lopez, then?"

"That's what *this* guy was calling him anyway." Angus nodded. "Suddenly, they spotted me at the gate, and they all just stopped talking and went quiet. Dallas walked over to where I was standing, and the other two slipped back inside. I asked Dallas what was going on."

"What did he say?"

"He just brushed it off," Angus recalled. "He tried to tell me that the young guy had been pestering the limo driver for a ride after the event. When he said no, it started an argument, and Dallas brought them outside to resolve things."

"And that was completely out of the ordinary?"

"Absolutely. It made no sense at all."

"What did you mean when you said the limo driver was arguing with some *other* young guy?"

"I'm getting to that," Angus assured him. "So, I go back inside to my post, and for a while, things are normal. Then, all of a sudden, Dallas came rushing over to me in a panic and said that the dark-haired guy had pulled a gun and was threatening the blonde guy and the two girls in the back stairwell. Dallas told me to head up the stairs on the other side of the building, and that he would position himself at the base of these stairs to block reentry.

"Do you carry weapons at these events?"

"Just pepper spray," Angus revealed. "I had barely even made it outside when I heard the first gunshot on the other side of the building. It stopped me dead in my tracks," Angus admitted. "After a few seconds, I mustered up enough courage to get myself to the front corner of the building. From there, I could see that the gate to the yard was now wide open, which was strange."

"How so?"

"Because when I saw that argument earlier, it was locked. So, I don't know who would have opened it if Dallas was inside the whole time? Anyway, I start making my way across the front of the building, and that's when I heard a second gunshot and a girl scream."

Frank felt his heart skip a beat.

"I must have frozen in place for like twenty or thirty seconds, just trying to decide what to do, listening for anything that might give me a clue as to what was happening. That's when I heard what sounded like a car door closing and gravel crunching beneath tires, so I made my way over to the gate. Just before I got there, the limousine rolled past me and disappeared down the road.

"And you didn't think to call the cops at this point?"

"Nobody is allowed to have cell phones at these events," Angus explained. "Not the staff, not the patrons. Nobody. I was even told they had scanners on the buses that could detect cell phone signals."

"Why?"

"They don't want any pictures or videos getting out on the internet," Angus explained. "And honestly, I think most of the people who frequent these things enjoy the privacy anyway, so it was never an issue."

"What if there was an emergency?"

"There was always a phone locked up in the safe somewhere, but only Dallas had access to that."

"Did you see who was inside the limo when it drove past you?"

"I could see that Lopez guy driving, but the back windows were all tinted black."

"What happened next?"

"The door at the top of the stairs was open, so I went over to take a look. As soon as I stepped inside, I could smell it...like a coppery metallic taste in the back of my throat."

"Blood."

"Yeah, and lots of it." Angus gave a solemn nod, paired with a blank stare. "When I looked down the stairs, I saw Dallas dragging a body up toward the platform. His head snapped around when he heard me, and he told me to lock the door and come help him. By that point, I was so out of it, it felt like a dream or something. I just did as I was told."

"Whose body was it?" Frank prepared himself for the worst.

"That dark-haired guy who had been arguing with the limo driver."

Frank's eyebrows furrowed. "I thought you said *he* was the one with the gun?"

"Yeah, but the way Dallas explained it to me was that the blonde-haired guy had lunged at him, attempting to disarm him at the base of the stairs, and it turned into a wrestling match. I guess the gun accidentally went off, and the dark-haired guy got shot.

"And the two girls?"

"He said they were put into the limo with the blonde guy to get them out of there."

Frank felt frustration and relief simultaneously. "Then what?"

"Dallas told me people were on their way. I thought he meant the cops, but I quickly realized that wasn't the case," Angus frowned. "I just remember him saying that if anyone ever found out about any of this, we were both dead—if that weren't the case already. I started freaking out, and I was trying to get more information out of him, but then a knock sounded on the door behind us. He told me to keep my mouth shut and that he'd handle it."

"Who was at the door?"

"Two guys wearing, like, butcher's outfits or something, you know, like, big aprons, gloves, goggles, and all that stuff. Neither of them said a word to either of us; they just grabbed the body from the platform and hauled it away."

"To where?"

"They threw it inside the back of a big cargo van," Angus recalled. "And that's when three other guys wearing white hazmat suits, carrying brushes and buckets, stepped inside."

"Nobody inside the party had heard the earlier gunshots and was asking questions by this point?"

"The music is so loud at these things, World War III could be happening outside, and none of them would hear a thing."

Frank nodded.

So, anyway, Dallas took me aside again and said, '*I need to be 100% certain that I have your absolute discretion regarding this incident*'."

"What did you tell him?"

"I told him that I didn't even understand what the heck had just happened," Angus explained. "That's when he tried to tell me that the two guys were some kind of rival gang members with a previous beef and that the two girls just happened to get caught in the middle of things. I knew he was lying, but considering everything I'd just witnessed, I didn't think it was a good idea to argue. I remember asking him if he thought we could trust that the limo driver wouldn't say anything."

"What did he tell you?"

"He got really serious..." Angus recalled the look on Dallas's face. "More serious than I had ever seen him before. He said, *'Don't ever mention him again, you hear me? Not to anyone!'"*

"You two must have been covered in blood from carrying the body up the stairs," Frank suspected. "Obviously, you couldn't just go back inside or home for the night looking like that."

"One of those rooms in the back hall there has a shower," Angus pointed past Frank, referencing the three doors with cameras above them. "We would always change into our uniforms once we arrived, so we had a spare set of clothes with us. I remember, Dallas radioed one of the other bouncers to make sure this door back here was locked and that the hall was clear. Then, we stripped off our clothes and handed them over to one of the hazmat guys," Angus explained. "Dallas showered first, then me. While I was in there, he went back into the party to make sure everything was still running okay and put one of the other guys in charge for the rest of the night. I think he must have grabbed the satellite phone from the lockbox, too, because when I was in the shower, I could hear him talking to someone."

"To who?"

"I'm not sure." Angus shook his head. "But I heard him mention something about a safe house over the border."

Frank's eyes widened.

"After that, I just sat with Dallas in that back room for what felt like an eternity. We didn't speak, we didn't look at each other, we just sat there, waiting for the night to end." Angus stared off blankly. "And my mind just kept replaying what had happened, over and over—the two guys, the two girls, the gunshots, and that body..." He looked as if he might be sick. "It was just lying there at the bottom of the stairs." He looked at Frank. "I knew what I had to do."

"What's that?"

"I need to get myself clean and get home."

"Home?"

"Back to Mississippi," Angus specified. "But I figured whoever I was working for would probably be watching me like a hawk now, you know, to see if I was acting strange or whatever. So, I've just been trying to act completely normal since then. Heck, I even bought more pills from my dealer, to keep up appearances, but I flushed them down the toilet. Then, yesterday, when I figured enough time had passed, I booked myself a bus ticket home. And it looked like I was in the clear, until that page came through tonight saying that somebody had been out here, snooping around, asking questions."

"Why not just ignore it?"

"At first, I did. But then I started getting paranoid, thinking maybe they were testing me to see if I could still follow simple instructions. And I knew if I didn't respond, it would be a major red flag, so I decided I'd just make my way out here, look around, and hopefully not find anything. But when I arrived, I saw your car parked on the side of the building, and then the gun tucked behind your back when I came through the door. I figured they must have found out about my bus ticket and sent someone here to take me out. I'm sorry, mister, I was just trying to get you before you got me," he explained about the attack.

Frank knew Angus was telling the truth just by observing the regret and innocence in his eyes. "My name's Frank," he offered.

"I'm sorry, Frank," Angus apologized again.

Frank pulled out his cell phone, tapped on the screen, and began swiping through photos until he found the one he was searching for. "I want you to think back to that night, Angus," he instructed the big man before turning the screen to face him. "Were these the two girls who arrived in the cab with the blonde guy?"

A picture of Sara and Marla taken at the airport just before they departed JFK was on the screen. Angus's face tightened. He stared at the image, hypnotized by it.

"Well?" Frank prodded.

"Yeah, that's them," Angus admitted quietly. "Are they okay?" He looked up at Frank as nausea filled the pit of his oversized stomach.

"I'm not sure. That's why I'm here."

"I should have stopped the limo that night. I should have stepped in front of it and let it hit me..." Angus began to ramble, as his eyes welled with regret. "I should have just called the cops as soon as I got home. I was just so messed up on all the drugs. I—"

"Yeah," Frank decided to put a stop to the self-hatred. "There are a lot of things a lot of us *should* have done differently, Angus. But my guess is, if you had, you would have wound up at the bottom of those stairs, too."

"How can I make this right, Frank?" Angus looked at him with desperation.

"If anybody reaches out to you, asking what you saw out here tonight, you tell them that you came here and saw absolutely nothing out of the ordinary. Got it?"

Angus nodded.

"When does your bus leave?"

"Tomorrow morning."

"Get your ass on that bus and get back to Mississippi, and stay off those fucking pills," Frank ordered him. "Because if you don't, soon enough, you'll be injecting that shit, and that's a real quick way to wind up dead."

"That might be the only thing that saved my life the first time. I'm deathly afraid of needles. Just the sight of them things causes me to pass out immediately," he explained. "But it doesn't matter, I'm done with all that stuff, Frank. You have my word. Never again."

Frank believed him. Angus was just a kid who had some bad luck and got caught up in some worse shit.

"I want you to lay low with your family when you get home. Don't talk to anyone about anything you saw around here until I get everything sorted out on my end. Then, I'll make sure somebody comes out to Mississippi and gets your official story for the record, alright?"

Angus nodded.

"Now, I have to get going," Frank told him. "Are you going to be able to get yourself out of here with your knee?"

"I've played through worse," Angus gave a stoic nod. "I'll manage."

* * * * *

"So, you just left him there?" Mike asked with concern, sitting in front of his computer back in New York in a pair of blue boxer shorts and a thin white tank top. He had been fast asleep when Frank's call came in. "What if this guy rats you out?"

"Not going to happen," Frank assured him. "He was already planning on leaving the city before I arrived. He's done."

"And that Dallas guy?" Mike asked as Frank pulled back onto the freeway. "You don't think Angus could lure him out for a meeting, so you could put some pressure on him? Maybe it would give you direct access to the limo driver."

"There's no avenue for contact," Frank explained of the one-way pager. "This whole operation is a spider network. If I go plucking at the wrong part of the web before I get down into Mexico, they're all going to feel it."

The computer screen loaded in front of Mike, and he read the results. "I don't see a connection between anyone named Lopez and Rocky Point, where the girls' phones were tracked."

"Yeah, I figured as much," Frank replied, speeding through the darkness. "I'm going to switch cars right away here, and once I get over the border, I'll purchase a couple of burner phones and try to get in touch with Bennett. Maybe his security company will have a local database for me to look through."

Just then, Donna appeared in the open doorway behind Mike wearing a set of borrowed pajamas beneath a mint green bathrobe.

Janice had invited her to stay the night rather than having her spend more time in a lonely, empty house waiting for updates.

"Is that Frank?" she asked Mike, unable to fall asleep, worried sick about the girls.

Mike nodded.

She walked over to the desk. "Let me speak to him."

"Hey, Frank, Donna is spending the night," he explained. "She wants to talk to you."

It bothered Frank to no end that he didn't have definitive answers regarding the girls' whereabouts yet. "Put her on."

Donna had just placed the phone against her ear when Frank sensed her presence. "How are you holding up?" he asked.

"Did you find them yet?"

"No. Not yet."

"Are you okay?"

"I'm fine," Frank said, taking the next exit. "You're spending the night?"

"Yeah, Janice and Mike were kind enough to offer. What have we learned so far?" she asked Frank in the way only the wife of a federal agent would.

Frank didn't want to keep her in the dark any longer. He knew she was strong enough to handle the truth.

"They never made it on that excursion," Frank explained. "And I don't think it was Sara who was texting us for the last while."

"Oh my God," Donna gasped.

"And from what I learned tonight, I think they were with their phones when they disappeared over the border."

"You're going down there, aren't you?" Donna exhaled. The question was rhetorical; she knew Frank wouldn't just sit back and wait for the agency's red tape and time-wasting procedures. "What should we do about Carol? She thinks Marla is on that excursion. In a couple of days, when those girls are supposed to be back on shore, if Marla doesn't call—"

"If I can't find them before then, we have no choice but to break the news and alert the authorities."

"Okay," Donna steadied herself. "Go get our girls back, Frank. I'll take care of everything here in the meantime. Just bring them back safe and sound, you hear me?"

"I will. Now, try to get some sleep, and I'll finish up with Mike. I love you."

"I love you, too."

CHAPTER twenty-seven

Frank glanced in the rearview mirror of his new rental car and watched the border patrol booths sink into the horizon. He hadn't had any trouble crossing into Mexico; in fact, the sleepy-eyed customs agent with the wrinkled uniform had barely mustered the energy to scan Frank's passport.

Frank reached into the stiff brown paper bag on the passenger seat and removed one of the two burner phones he had just purchased at the duty-free shop, along with some water, granola bars, beef jerky, and a few other items. He quickly freed the cheap device from its plastic prison, dialed the number he had for Bennett, and then connected the call to the car's speakers. He placed the phone in the cup holder next to his thigh.

"Hello?" A deeply masculine voice arrived through the speakers.

"Bennett?"

"Depends on who's asking..." Before Frank could respond. "Wait a minute, is that you, *Tank?*"

"Yeah," Frank confirmed. Tank, being a nickname someone in his squadron had tagged him with all those years ago.

"How the hell are ya, brother?" Bennett said enthusiastically. "Goddamn, it's good to hear your voice!" He paused to check the caller

ID again. "Where ya calling from? This number looks Mexican. You down here with the family on vacation or something?"

"No," Frank replied flatly.

"Boys trip then? Fuck yeah! Count me in!"

"It's not like that, Benny..."

Frank's old teammate picked up on his subdued responses, and his voice became serious. "You alright, buddy? What's up?"

"Are you still running your security contracting business down here?"

"That's affirmative. I've got a really good group of ex-military guys working for me. Why do you ask?"

"I'm wondering if you might be able to look into something for me?"

"Anything," Bennett agreed without hesitation. Frank could hear paper rustling and the *click* of a ballpoint pen.

"You'll have to bear with me, Benny, because what I have is spotty at best," Frank warned. "I'm looking for info on a guy by the name of Lopez. He's Mexican and likely in his 60s. I believe he may own a limo company with possible cartel connections," Frank explained. "And operates on both sides of the border."

"Which cartel?"

"I'm not sure," Frank admitted. "My guess would be whoever has a stronghold up in the northwest at the moment."

"You weren't kidding," Bennett replied. "That's not a lot to go on. Is the FBI looking into this guy for something?"

"No. They're not involved."

"Hmm, alright then. Okay, tell you what, leave it with me and I'll see what I can flush out for you."

"I appreciate it."

"If you haven't heard back from me by tomorrow evening, give me a shout back, alright?"

"Will do. Thanks."

* * * * *

Frank had covered the remainder of the drive down to Rocky Point in just over four hours, pushing the rental car to its limits on a few of the blacktop's most desolate straight stretches. Upon entering the lonesome, dust-stricken suburban area where Sara and Marla's phones had been tracked, he found that a vast majority of the building lots were still in the earliest stages of construction.

As Frank was cruising along, staring out his driver's side window and stealing glances at the abandoned work sites, something suddenly flashed in his periphery, causing his head to snap forward. Through the windshield, two dark-haired boys, perhaps eight or ten years of age, had darted out directly in front of the car, chasing down an errant soccer ball that had escaped from behind a broken-down yellow excavator on the side of the road. Frank stomped his foot down on the brake pedal as hard as he could, causing the vehicle's nose to dip violently and his tires to lay down black strips of superheated rubber, producing a high-pitched *SCREEEECH.* Frightened by the unexpected and ear-piercing noise, the two boys froze with fear as the car's bumper bore down on them. Mere inches from impact, the vehicle finally came to a jarring halt, sending a plume of white dust and smoke billowing around the youngsters. Moments later, when the particulate storm had settled, Frank found himself staring through the glass at the boys in an unblinking, tension-filled silence. Eventually, the taller of the two children broke free of his catatonic state and took a slow step back from the car's hot grill. He made his way over to where the soccer ball had come to rest against the opposing curb, collected the well-weathered sphere, and doubled back across the road, grabbing onto his still-stupefied playmate's sleeve, tugging him away. After the boys had disappeared behind a pile of hastily stacked building materials, Frank pressed the back of his neck into his headrest, exhaling a mixture of relief and frustration, and peeled the sole of his boot off the brake pedal.

After a few more minutes of driving, Frank eventually spotted the only fully constructed house in the entire area that the GPS tracking program had defined back in Mike's office. It was a large, white vinyl-sided, two-story structure with a Dutch gabled roof and an attached two-car garage that stood at the very end of a cul-de-sac. Frank parked his car a block away on the perpendicular street next to a rust-stained industrial garbage bin. He stepped out of the car and performed a 360-degree scan of the deserted, sun-scorched neighborhood before popping the trunk and removing the carpeting that covered the spare tire. Frank unscrewed and removed a ten-inch bolt that held the donut in place and set both items aside. In the crevice was a black nylon roadside kit. Frank removed it, and inside, where the jack and tools had once been, was a large caliber handgun, two clips of ammunition, and a few other accessory items he had stashed before crossing the border. He loaded the weapon, chambered a round, and concealed it behind his back.

The sun beat down on Frank as he approached the house, and the silence around him was only broken by the distant buzz of a table saw or the rhythmic pounding of a hammer at some far-off construction site. As Frank neared the residence, he noticed that all the windows were affixed with exterior security bars.

Frank climbed three white concrete steps that led up to the house's plum-colored front door and found no signs of surveillance equipment on the cramped porch. What he did discover, however, were two nearly imperceptible indentations in the face of the door, suggesting that a security bar was present on its other side. Frank leaned in and listened for movement inside. Hearing nothing, he turned, descended the stairs, and made his way over to the garage doors.

A rectangular box, slightly larger than a television remote control, was positioned at chest level on the flashing next to the first overhead door. Frank flipped up its face plate, revealing a standard grid of numbers. Removing his pocketknife, he slipped the blade between the box and the thin aluminum behind it. With a flick of the wrist, Frank popped the box loose, allowing it to dangle by two wires that disappeared into a golf ball-sized hole in the brown metal. Frank severed one of the wires, removed its sheathing, and twisted the two ends back together into a neat splice, restoring power to the unit. This was a trick the FBI had been using for years. By disrupting the power in such a way, security codes could often be reset, as if being set up for the first time. Frank quickly completed the reprogramming, and the overhead door lifted from the concrete.

Once inside the dimly lit garage, Frank passed by a mid-sized black SUV. As he approached the door that would lead him inside the house, he could hear the distant sound of a television coming from somewhere deep inside. He pushed the door inward slowly, inch by inch, revealing a white-tiled, open-concept kitchen and dining area. Peeking into the room cautiously, he spotted a doorless coat closet next to an exterior door. To his right was a hallway, where the sounds of the television were coming from.

Frank entered the kitchen silently, removing his gun from behind his back and carefully crossed the tiles. Once he arrived at the entrance of the hallway, he set his back against the wall. From this new vantage point, he could see two sets of stairs—one leading up from the basement and another climbing to the second level. Just then, he heard a man laughing at the Spanish-language television program behind him in one of the rooms down the hall. Just as Frank was developing a plan to isolate the individual inside the room, a sudden movement flashed across the kitchen.

A teenage girl with long, flowing black hair had suddenly emerged from the stairs leading up from the basement. Just as quickly as she had appeared, she vanished, heading up to the second floor, not noticing Frank on the other side of the room.

Frank abandoned the hallway and backtracked across the kitchen to where the young girl had been. He climbed the stairs slowly until he reached a vacant hallway with gray carpeting on the second floor. The nearest door on his left was partially open. Frank approached and quickly maneuvered himself inside the bedroom, gun in hand, but found two empty beds draped in dull yellow sheets. With nothing of interest inside the space, Frank abandoned the room.

Down the hall, two doors sat directly opposite one another. Frank placed his back against the right wall and moved silently towards the openings. As he approached, he identified the room on the left as a bathroom. A large rectangular vanity mirror inside was open to an angle that allowed him to see into the bedroom behind him. In the reflection, Frank discovered another pair of beds with yellow sheets.

Just then, Frank heard movement behind him, and suddenly, the same black-haired girl he had spotted down in the kitchen appeared in the mirror. She was making her way over to the nightstand between the two beds, wearing nothing but a black thong now. Opening the top drawer, she removed a hairbrush and began to run it through her silky hair, looking out the barred window in the direction opposite Frank. Frank concealed the gun behind his back and took a moment to glance back toward the top of the stairs. When he directed his attention back to the mirror, he found that the young girl had turned around and was now staring directly at him in the reflection. Frank prepared himself for her to scream and to cover her exposed breasts, but she did neither.

"Hola?" the girl said inquisitively, still brushing her hair.

Frank pivoted himself inside the bedroom.

"Hablas Inglés?" he asked her quietly, using one of the few phrases he remembered.

"Si," the youngster answered with the friendliest of smiles, activating a pair of adorable dimples on each of her rosy cheeks. "Yes, I getting much better at English now," she said proudly.

Frank spotted a fluffy white towel hanging over the back of the chair next to the door and offered it to her. "To cover yourself with..." he mimed while averting his gaze.

The girl looked at the linen curiously, completely unfazed by her nakedness. She shrugged, then covered herself as requested.

"Do you live here?" Frank asked.

"Live?"

"Yes, uh, is this your home? Uh, your casa?"

"Oh, no, it is, how you say, a place to stay—before my trip," she tried to explain. "I go away soon."

"Is there someone else here?" Frank asked slowly. "Someone downstairs watching television, maybe?" Frank drew a box with his fingers. "Is this *his* house?"

"Si," the girl nodded, though Frank could tell she didn't fully comprehend his inquiry. "Always someone here—Mr. Donny, Mr. Pedro... or Mr. Marcus," Frank noticed the smile disappear from her face at the mention of the final name.

"What about other girls? Girls like you. Are they also staying here before their trips?"

"Si, yes of course," she answered matter-of-factly. "Many girls have come and go since I arrive. I have no left yet, because I have been sick, but I take my medicine now and it makes me feel much better." She smiled again. "I will leave soon. Just like all the others." She nodded assuredly.

Frank recognized immediately that the *'medicine'* she was referring to was certainly illicit narcotics, and the *'sickness'* was withdrawals.

"Are you friends with Mr. Donny and Mr. Pedro?" she asked Frank.

Frank offered a half-nod, wanting to continue his line of questioning. "How many other girls are staying here right now? Can I speak with them?"

"They have all left," she explained, deciding to take a seat on the edge of the right mattress. "The last of them, maybe one or two days ago now, I think?" Her face scrunched a little as she tried her best to remember. "I cannot be sure. I have been sleeping very much. But I hear Mr. Donny talking on the telephone, saying that more girls will be coming soon."

"You mentioned a Mr. Marcus before?" Frank wanted to tap into the earlier body language. "Does Mr. Marcus give you medicine as well?"

The young girl's eyes dropped to the floor. "No," she said quickly.

"How old do you think Mr. Marcus is? What does he look like?"

The girl's tiny feet shuffled nervously on the carpet. "I not know. Maybe he is 30?" she guessed. "He has black hair and a big, scary dragon." She placed the palm of her hand on the side of her neck.

"A tattoo, you mean?"

She nodded, and her shoulders sank lower.

"What does Mr. Marcus do around here, if he doesn't give you your medicine?"

"He comes into the room when I am dreaming," she said, looking up at Frank with somber eyes. "*After* I have already taken my medicines, when I am very sleepy. When I cannot wake up. Even though I not awake, I can still feel him. Even though I cannot move... I know he is there." She stared off vacantly for a moment before looking back at Frank. "Mr. Marcus is a very bad man."

Frank felt rage and disgust in the pit of his stomach.

"But very soon I leave here and meet many new friends on my travels," the young girl went on, her eyes brightening once again. "Some of the other girls told me that we are going to far-away places and will meet very nice men." She looked at Frank hopefully, as if seeking confirmation.

"What's your name, sweetheart?"

"Sofia." The girl smiled widely.

"It's nice to meet you, Sofia. I'm Frank."

She stood up from the bed and walked over to him and extended her hand. "Mr. Frank, it is very nice to meet you, too."

Frank shook her hand. "Sofia, I need to tell you something. The medicine you are being given..." he paused, trying to think of the best way to explain it to her, "it's not what you think it is. You aren't sick. Well, you are, but it's *because* of what they are giving you."

A look of confusion slowly spread across Sofia's face as she tried to understand the statement. "But I still go away, right, Mr. Frank?"

"I think, for now, it's best that we just get you back to your family."

"I have no family."

"I'm sorry to hear that, Sofia," Frank empathized. "But the men inside this house, I believe they may be part of a cartel." He allowed a moment for this to sink in.

"Yes, of course."

The look of confusion was now on Frank's face.

"The cartels are the only ones who can help," Sofia suggested. "It is, how do you say, *impossible*, any other way."

"But they're drugging you, Sofia," Frank tried to make her understand.

"No, no. It's just my medicine. For my sickness."

"Sofia, I need you to listen to—"

"Wait..." She suddenly cut him off. "You are not a part of the cartel, then?" she asked, taking a few slow steps backward between the beds.

"I'm looking for my daughter and her friend," Frank explained. "Maybe if I show you a picture of them, you can tell me if you've seen them in this house?" He reached his hand into his pocket.

Suddenly, a look of horror spread across the young girl's face.

"It's okay, Sofia," Frank attempted to calm her. "I'm just getting my phone."

Sofia began to physically tremble with fear.

"Sofia?"

Suddenly, the hair on the back of Frank's neck stood on end, and time slowed to a crawl. Just then, the unmistakable sound of a gun's hammer being cocked back sounded just behind his head. Without hesitation, Frank threw his body to the right.

BANG!

The ear-shattering clap of a bullet casing being struck sent a high-pitched shock wave deep inside Frank's departing skull, and he saw the pillow on the bed spit out a geyser of polyester confetti. Sofia shrieked at the top of her lungs. Frank's body crashed violently into the wall, but he quickly regained his balance and spun around to face the shooter, who had made the error of closing the distance between himself and his target. Frank lunged forward and struck the side of the outstretched weapon with his palm milliseconds before the next shot rang out.

BANG!

The second bullet lodged itself in a wall somewhere over Frank's left shoulder, and Sofia let out another bloodcurdling scream. Frank locked onto his attacker's wrist and drove the barrel of the gun towards the ceiling.

BANG!

Chunks of plaster rained down on the two combatants as they wrestled for control of the weapon, eventually toppling themselves onto the bed next to Sofia, who was still frozen with fear.

Frank pushed himself off the mattress, slamming the man's wrists across its metal frame, sending the pistol sailing through the air until it landed next to the base of the nightstand. The Mexican retaliated with a hard-driving uppercut to Frank's jaw. Frank blocked his next looping hook with his forearm before delivering a devastating kick squarely into the man's unprotected abdomen, sending him reeling backward into the wall next to the door. Frank closed in quickly, but his opponent sprang forward, wrapping his arms around the top of Frank's legs, attempting to topple him over. Frank backpedaled, maintaining his balance, while sending hammer fists down on the man's spine. Frank reached a hand behind his back for his weapon, but the sudden impact with the wall caused him to lose his grip, and the gun fell to the floor and was kicked into the corner. The Mexican clung to Frank's lower body, furiously attempting to kick out his legs. Frank reached down and wrapped his powerful arms around his waist. With a bend of his knees and a burst of strength,

Frank began to lift his adversary off the floor. The Mexican's legs thrashed in the open air as his body rotated up towards the ceiling. Suddenly, Frank reversed course and sent him hurtling back down to the floor, where the back of his head impacted with such devastating force that it fractured the base of his skull, causing him to momentarily lose consciousness.

Frank took hold of the incapacitated man and dragged him across the bedroom, slamming him forcefully into the wall next to the door to rouse him. Frank recovered his weapon as the injured man spat a mouthful of blood onto the floor between his legs, leaving a long string of sticky sputum hanging from his bottom lip onto his shirt below. The kidnapper rotated his head to one side, and Frank caught a glimpse of the intricate dragon tattoo on his neck.

"What are you doing with these girls?" Frank demanded, pointing the gun at the man's head.

The kidnapper's evil, soulless eyes met Frank's. "Fuck you," he said in near-perfect English.

Frank took the butt of his weapon and smashed it into his nose, opening an oozing gash across its bridge. "Where's my daughter? I know she was here!"

A disturbed smile crept onto the man's sadistic face—the same look Frank now imagined Sara and Marla must have witnessed during their captivity. "One of these whores is your daughter?" the man replied, a small blood bubble forming at the corner of his mouth.

Frank wanted to put an end to the kidnapper's pathetic existence, but he knew, for now, he was the best chance he had to work his way up the ladder.

"Sofia says she's being sent somewhere. Where are you trafficking these girls?"

"You're not going anywhere, you stupid bitch!" the seated cartel man shouted past Frank at Sofia, who was still frozen in place between the beds.

Frank drove his fist into the man's already broken nose, flattening it further. "Watch your fucking mouth!"

The Mexican wiped the underside of what was left of his nose with his forearm, painting a streaky red line from wrist to elbow. "Everything is changing now. The whole system..." the man said cryptically, grinning ominously through the pain.

"What do you mean?"

"American girls. Girls like your daughter. There will be more soon," he said, then focused on Sofia again. "You think they're going to want a slum whore like you?!" he berated her. "You'll be back in the city turning tricks in no time!"

Frank drove his knee into the man's face, sending his head bouncing off the wall with a hollow thud. More snotty blood leaked from his nostrils as he looked up at Frank.

"You touch me again and I guarantee you'll never see your daughter again!" he threatened. "Which one was she, anyway? That tasty little blonde?"

Frank felt his hand tighten on the grip of the gun, knowing the predator was referring to Marla. "Where did you send them?" Frank demanded.

"South," the kidnapper replied vaguely.

"Listen here, you c—"

BANG!

A small hole had suddenly appeared in the drywall next to the Mexican's head. He looked past Frank with a scowl on his face. "You fucking bi—"

BANG!

The second bullet ripped through the center of his forehead and sprayed a scarlet-colored mist onto the wall behind him. His body slumped forward lifelessly.

Frank turned around and discovered Sofia standing between the two beds, holding the kidnapper's gun she had recovered from the floor next to the nightstand. Frank naturally raised his weapon in defense.

"I no go now?" Sofia questioned, as tears began to stream down her cheeks.

"FUCK!" Frank hollered in frustration. "Why would you do that!? I needed him alive!"

Frightened, Sofia took a half step back.

"No, no, no, it's okay, I'm sorry," Frank lowered his voice. "I'm sorry, Sofia. I didn't mean to yell. I'm going to get you out of here, okay? Let's just both of us put down the guns, and we'll get everything figured out. It's okay." He slowly removed one of his hands from his weapon and presented her with his open palm.

"He was a very bad man, Mr. Frank," Sofia stared at the dead man's body in a daze, gun still raised. "Very bad."

"I know he was, Sofia. I know," Frank said slowly, lowering his gun completely. "But he's gone now. He can't hurt you any—"

"But he right, you know," she continued, as if she hadn't heard Frank at all. "When I hear Mr. Donny on the phone the other day, he said no more Mexican girls, only Americans now," she reported. "I thought I'd be the last to go..."

"Sofia, you don't have to go anymore. Don't you understand? You can go home."

Sofia's vacant, empty eyes locked with Frank's. "I told you, Mr. Frank," she said quietly. "I have no family." More tears rolled down her cheeks. "I have no home."

Frank tried to think of anything that might comfort her in this moment.

"And if the cartel finds out I had a chance to kill you, and I didn't, they never let me live."

Frank's face grew serious. He looked at the weapon in her hands. "Sofia..." he said evenly, "let's both just keep calm, okay? We can figure this out. Nobody needs to know *anything* about what happened here today. I can protect you. Nobody needs—"

"I sorry, Mr. Frank..."

"Sofia," Frank said more forcefully now, "Lower your weapon."

"I can't go back. Nunca. I can't," she began to ramble incoherently in Spanish.

Frank raised his gun, though he couldn't fathom having to use it on this tortured soul. She had already been through so much. His only hope was that she would somehow miss her mark, and he could disarm her. "Sofia..."

Without warning, Sofia suddenly curled the gun up beneath her chin.

"Nooooo!" Frank shouted, reaching out for her.

It was too late.

The bullet tore through the barrel and entered her skull just below her chin, ripping through her brain and lodging itself in the ceiling above. Frank rushed across the room and slipped his arm beneath Sofia's back, catching her just before she hit the floor. He tilted her head towards himself, but it was futile. All the life force had already exited her body along with the bullet. Frank lifted her from the carpet and positioned her towel-wrapped body onto the mattress, laying her head gently on the pillow, which began to absorb the crimson blood from the exit wound. Regret and hatred washed over Frank.

Off in the distance, Frank heard the sound of sirens wail to life, and he questioned whether it was time to involve the local police and the Mexican government by exposing the nefarious acts that had gone on inside this house. He wondered how that would compromise Sara and Marla's immediate safety and just how deeply the cartels had their tentacles in those agencies. Whatever his decision was going to be, he knew he needed to make it quickly, because the sirens were a long way off but certainly heading in his direction.

The burner phone suddenly vibrated inside Frank's pocket. It could only be Bennett, as even Mike didn't have this number yet.

"Bennett?" Frank answered.

"Yeah, hey, buddy, I've got some info for you here," he explained. "Where you at?"

"I'm inside some house in Rocky Point, and some shit just went down. The cops are on their way."

"What kind of shit?" Bennett asked with obvious concern in his voice. "How bad are we talking?"

"As bad as it gets…" Frank admitted. He knew it was time for him to lay all his cards on the table. "Benny, my daughter and her friend are missing down here in Mexico, and I tracked their phones across the border to this house. It sounds like they may have been taken further south."

There was a prolonged silence.

"Bennett?" Frank prompted.

"Frank, you gotta get the fuck outta that house right now," Bennett said with the utmost urgency. "The cartel owns everything in that area. And if those are sirens I can hear in the background, they'll own those cops too. Get the fuck out of there and start driving south to my place as fast as you can."

"There's a girl here, Benny," Frank said, looking down at Sofia's lifeless body on the bed.

"*Fuck.* Is she…?"

"She's dead."

"Unfortunately, there's nothing more we can do for her then, Frank. And if you want the chance to find your daughter, I'd highly suggest you not be around when those crooked cops arrive."

As much as Frank wanted to scour the house for clues relating to Sara and Marla, he knew Bennett was right—it was time to leave.

*****

Frank scanned every inch of his rearview mirror for what felt like the hundredth time since he had abandoned the house. Finally, he felt certain that none of the inbound brigade of police cruisers had noticed him calmly pulling out onto the highway as they sped past into the housing development in the opposite direction.

"I'm clear," he told Bennett, who had just finished explaining the route to his house more precisely.

"Alright, good. Now, like I said, it's going to be another five or six hours to my place from your current location. But if they moved the girls south, they surely would have come this way anyhow."

"Copy," Frank replied. "I'll see you when I get there."

After disconnecting the call, Frank located the second burner and dialed Mike's number.

"HEY! This is Mike," the voicemail recording began after a few rings. *"I can't answer my phone right now. And the truth is, I'm probably sitting on my ass, staring at the caller ID and trying to decide if you're cool enough for me to answer. So, why don't you leave a message, with your absolute best attempt to capture my attention, and I might just consider giving you a call back." BEEP!*

"It's me," Frank said, purposefully not using any names. "This is the phone I'll be contacting you on for the foreseeable future. I can't go into any details right now, just in case this line is somehow compromised, but I wanted to let you know that I'm moving south to meet up with that contact I had mentioned previously," he said of Bennett. "It may be premature, but I need you to follow through with the plan *immediately."*

CHAPTER twenty-eight

Frank's dust-covered rental car crested the final ridge on the last dirt access road leading to Bennett's remote property. Two long rows of thirty-six-inch solar-powered light posts stretched for nearly a mile down an arrow-straight driveway towards a towering residence situated in the middle of the 240-acre tract of barren rural farmland in the heart of Mexican nowhere.

As he neared the house, the compact dirt transitioned into a paved asphalt driveway that horseshoed itself elegantly around a twelve-foot-tall, three-tier stone water fountain in front of the recently constructed estate with a three-car garage. As Frank rounded the turn, he saw the house's arch-topped front door open, and a tanned, heavily muscled American in his mid-forties, wearing beige cargo trousers, cowboy boots, and a white tank top, emerged from inside. Bennett had a short black mohawk, crystal blue eyes, and a pair of sleeve tattoos covering his powerful arms. Frank parked his car, killed the engine, and stepped out.

Bennett made his way around the rear of the vehicle. "It's good to see you," he said, as the two heavyweights embraced with a handshake and back-slapping hug. "I just wish it were under better circumstances."

"Thanks for helping me, Benny. I appreciate it."

"Anything for you, Tank."

The pair made their way to the trunk, where Frank removed his black duffel bag, and they continued toward the front of the house.

"Before we go inside, I should probably—" Frank began.

"Burn every piece of clothing you're wearing?" Bennett finished the thought, as if he could read his old friend's mind. "Way ahead of you. I've got a burning barrel going out back and a hole dug next to it for the ashes," he explained. "I'll bring you out a fresh set of threads, and then we can come back inside and get all this shit figured out."

"I brought a change of clothes with me." Frank lifted the bag.

"Of course you did," Bennett grinned at the forethought. "Alright, head around back and do your thing. The barrel is maybe three hundred yards out in the field. I left some extra gasoline and firewood if you need it, but it was rocking hot last time I checked, so I imagine it's probably still good. Once you're done, come through the back door and meet me in my office on the second floor. I've got some news you're going to want to hear."

As badly as Frank wanted to dive into whatever information Bennett had collected, he, of all people, knew that following proper protocols regarding the disposal of evidence was crucial at times like these.

*****

After completing his task, Frank approached the back of the house and stepped onto the concrete perimeter that surrounded Bennett's elegantly illuminated backyard pool, leading him to a set of French doors.

Frank stepped inside the house and entered a room that might be described as a fusion between a nineteenth-century social parlor and a modern-day study. Towering bookcases lined each wall, guarded by bronze statues, marble sculptures, and a vast collection of antique furnishings. A five-hundred-gallon saltwater aquarium with dozens of peacock-tailed fish occupied nearly an entire wall. The smell of hard-fibered wood and leather-bound books filled Frank's nostrils as he made his way across the room and walked through an open door.

The ceilings inside the main foyer were nearly forty feet at their apex, and Frank discovered a pair of curving staircases on each wall that met overhead, forming a mezzanine. Frank craned his head back and saw Bennett leaning over the ivory-colored railing.

"We all good?" Bennett called down to Frank, who was approaching the base of the left staircase.

"Yeah." Frank nodded.

"Alright, come on up. Let's get—"

Suddenly, a phone rang somewhere to Bennett's right. "Shit, I gotta get that," he apologized. "Just head into the office. I'll only be a minute."

Frank climbed the stairs and arrived to where Bennett had just been standing. He looked over the banister, across the foyer, and through four large rectangular windows. From this vantage point, he could see the back half of his rental car parked next to the fountain, and most of the illuminated driveway slicing through the darkness.

Frank abandoned the railing and made his way inside the office, which contained a sprawling wooden desk, topped with a collection of high-powered computer processors, twin twenty-four-inch monitors, a laptop, and some other technical equipment. A pair of five-wheeled office chairs faced one another on opposite sides of the desk.

Frank set his duffel bag on the ground next to his chair and had just begun to take his seat when he noticed a band of light projecting from the back corner of the room that seemed to be coming from a slightly open pocket door.

Frank walked over and peeked through the twelve-inch gap. On the back wall of the hidden room, he saw a line of black-framed photographs that eventually led to a five-foot-tall glass display case in the far corner. Frank immediately recognized the closest photo just inside the door as one he had seen many times before; in fact, an identical copy was hanging on the wall of his garage back in New York.

Frank took hold of the edge of the heavy pocket door and slid it down its track, further into the wall, then stepped inside the room.

Squaring himself to the photograph, he saw seven youthful, bright-eyed Marines posing confidently between two camouflaged military vehicles. The image had been taken during one of Frank and Bennett's first overseas deployments nearly thirty years ago. Frank leaned in, studying the faces of the soldiers who stood shoulder-to-shoulder, wearing confident, oblivious smiles. For a moment, Frank's mind wandered back to the horrific events that had unfolded the next day, but he forced them out as quickly as they had arrived.

He continued down the wall, examining each of the subsequent images, including the one of a freshly enlisted baby-faced Bennett who was standing between what Frank assumed to be his parents. A few photographs further depicted Frank and Bennett after their final mission, just before Frank had retired from the armed services to marry Donna and pursue a career with the FBI. The two men stood next to one another, faces smeared with green-and-black camouflage combat paint. With them were Jack Pattison and Harold Klimkowski, both of whom were killed by a well-hidden IED during a subsequent tour.

Lost in the memories, Frank accidentally bumped into the glass display case in the corner that he had spotted from the door. Inside, on the uppermost shelf, were Bennett's service medals. Below them were a pair of silver handguns with custom grips balanced in an elegant X. Frank recognized the weapons immediately. They were a gift he had given to four of his closest teammates the day before he had retired.

Frank turned and surveyed the rest of the room. Near the wall opposite the photographs, there was a large, sand-colored burlap tarp covering an unidentified four-foot-tall object. Next to it was the green passenger side door of an armored military vehicle with an encircled five-point star painted on its face. Hanging on the wall above were two of Bennett's issued uniforms crisply displayed in cases of their own. Next to them, an old Marine flag featuring a stoic eagle perched on an anchor piercing the globe. The remainder of the wall was filled with guns, knives, grenades, ammunition, and various other military contraband.

Frank approached the tarp and lifted a corner, revealing a powerful, army-issued heavy machine gun perched atop an overbuilt, three-foot-tall custom tripod. Frank hadn't seen a weapon like this in decades. He ran his hand along the gun's leading edge, feeling the kinetic power of the dormant death machine. His eyes followed a belt of golden ammunition that flowed gracefully to the floor, and coiled between the legs of the tripod like a hibernating python.

"Feels like a lifetime ago, doesn't it?" Bennett's voice suddenly sounded behind Frank.

Frank turned and saw his old friend leaning against the wall by the entrance. "Where the hell did you get this thing?" Frank asked of the machine gun.

"You ever see that episode of M*A*S*H* where Radar sends all those Jeep parts back home, piece by piece?"

"Come on..."

"Not shitting you, buddy," Bennett shook his head, grinning. "I sent most of this stuff back during different deployments."

"And nobody noticed?"

"Do you remember some of our ordinance guys back then?" Bennett smirked. "Most of those guys could barely spell their own names, let alone track equipment properly."

"That's true," Frank recalled. "But what if you get caught with this stuff now?" he asked, referring to the grenades and other live weaponry.

"This is Mexico, Tank..." Bennett replied. "Nobody down here gives a shit about any of this stuff. They've got enough problems of their own. Besides, this room is basically impenetrable. I had this hidden pocket door and custom security system installed. And these walls are cored with steel."

"I got in pretty easily."

"I left it open for you," Bennett revealed. "I figured the FBI probably brainwashed all the detection skills out of you by this point, so I'd better make it easy for you," he teased. "Pretty fucking cool though, right? It's like a trip down memory lane every time I come in here."

Frank took one last glance around the room. "Yeah, lots of memories, for sure..." he trailed off.

Bennett realized that Frank's mind was focused on the whereabouts of his daughter and her friend. "I'm sorry, Tank. Let's go figure out how to get your girls back, and we can reminisce about all this shit some other time."

*****

Frank had taken a seat across from Bennett in the office.

"When you originally called me, I put out some feelers on the dark web, asking about the cross-border stuff you mentioned involving the limo guy," explained Bennett.

"What did you find?"

"At first, not much," Bennett admitted. "But a few people said they would look into it and get back to me."

Frank nodded.

"A few hours later," Bennett continued, "when the preliminary information started flowing in, I gave you a call, and that's when you told me you were at that house in Rocky Point and broke the news about your daughter. Once I realized just how personal this was for you, I wanted to really dig into my resources. But before I could even start, DMs from the earlier chat rooms started pouring in."

Frank leaned forward.

"Suddenly, people were questioning *me* about who had been asking about the limo guy up north and all that stuff," Bennett raised an eyebrow that had been split by a piece of shrapnel twenty years ago.

"And what did you tell them?"

"I didn't say shit."

"Who are these people?" Frank wondered. "Others in the private security sector?"

"A few, yeah," Bennett replied. "But everything is anonymous in these forums."

The lack of specificity frustrated Frank, but he understood how it worked. After all, the FBI often gathered some of its most important intel on the dark web.

"But listen to *this*..." Bennett continued. "Suddenly, I get a call on my cell phone, I don't know, maybe an hour or two before you arrived, and it was from a blocked number. And I mean *blocked,* blocked, Tank. Because with the software I have, I can trace just about anything, but not this one."

"Who was it?"

"Whoever it was must have been to that house where you left those bodies," Bennett suggested. "Or at least spoke to someone who went there."

"What makes you say that?"

"Because the caller knew that whoever had been there was ex-military or special forces. The way it had all gone down."

Frank's thoughts drifted back to the blood-stained bedroom.

"At first," Bennett continued, "I told this guy that I didn't know what the fuck he was talking about, but somehow, he knew that I'd been asking about that Lopez guy online."

"What did he sound like? American? Mexican?"

"He was speaking English, but I could definitely detect a bit of an accent."

"What else did he say?"

"At first, he tried using some basic pressure tactics, threatening that if I didn't reveal who was poking around up north, they were going to come kill me and all that." Bennett shrugged. "To be honest, it sounded like a bunch of blowhard shit, so I decided to test the waters."

"How so?"

"I told the guy that he should be very careful, because *maybe* whoever had been to that house in Rocky Point wasn't just ex-military but employed with a very specific branch of the US government."

Admittedly, Frank wasn't thrilled with having that kind of information being floated around, but he understood that Bennett had diminished options by that point. "What did he think about that?"

"He thought I was full of shit, too, at first. But when I held the line, his tune changed pretty quickly.

"What do you mean?"

"Well, for one, the threats stopped immediately," Bennett explained. "I must have caught him off guard, and I can't be certain, but it sounded like he was muting his end of the line occasionally."

"Maybe discussing this new information with other people in the room with him?" Frank suggested.

"That's exactly what I thought." Bennett nodded. "So, I started pressing him a little harder, thinking that if I could just keep him off balance, he'd eventually slip up and reveal something he shouldn't. I told him that he and his buddies had no idea what kind of shitstorm would blow their way if they didn't get their act together. Suddenly, this guy tells me that he needs time to consider the new information that's come to light and that he will call me back. Then he hung up."

"Fuck," Frank said, sitting back in the chair with disappointment. "And he hasn't called you back yet?"

"Negative."

"And he didn't give you a—"

Suddenly, the burner phone Frank had been using to call Bennett vibrated inside his pocket. He pulled it out and looked at the screen.

"Who is it?" Bennett wondered.

Frank turned the screen to face Bennett. *NO CALLER ID* flashed on the screen. "Nobody else has this number."

"Do you think—"

Frank answered.

"Agent Adler, I presume?" came a voice just as Bennett had described.

"Who is this?"

"It is truly unfortunate that any of our paths had to cross."

"It's going to be unfortunate for one of us. That much I fucking guarantee," Frank threatened, as Bennett stared at him across the desk, unable to hear the other side of the conversation.

"I certainly hope not..." the caller said evenly.

"Who are you?"

"Who we are is not important."

"I'll be the judge of that, asshole," Frank noted the man's pluralized response.

"Well, it certainly cannot be as important as getting your daughter and her young traveling companion back to you safely, can it?"

Frank's eyes widened. "What have you done with them?"

"I've just spoken with my associates, and they informed me that the girls were taken by a rival faction."

This guy talks like a fucking lawyer, Frank thought to himself. Regardless, he could tell that he was lying. "What about Sofia and all the other girls at the house in Rocky Point?" Frank turned to the offensive. "Rival factions at work up there, too?"

Silence.

"Hey, fuck face, I'm talking to you," Frank raised his voice.

"My associates believe it would be in everyone's best interest if we stick to the issue at hand," the man suggested, sounding as if he was receiving orders in real time. "Although we have no way of knowing for certain, we assume you've made your way south to your friend's house out in the country?"

Frank's expression grew even more serious.

"What's wrong?" Bennett asked from the other side of the desk.

Frank stood up from his chair and quickly abandoned the office, making his way out to the mezzanine. He peered through the windows into the darkness of the night. Only the lines of illuminated lampposts were visible. Bennett arrived next to him.

"You can relax, Agent Adler," said the man on the phone. "I give you my word that no one is looking for you. And that includes the police. You can assure your friend, *Mr. Bennett, is it?,* that he too is safe for now."

Frank could tell the caller was being truthful, insofar as he seemed to want a hand-off of the girls to occur. The last thing these people needed was for Frank and Bennett to be roaming the countryside looking for more trouble.

"It is 10 PM now, Agent Adler. Make your way south on Highway 15," he instructed. "In approximately three hours, I will call you back at this number and give you more specifics."

"Just give me all the info now," Frank demanded.

"Patience, Agent Adler. This will allow my associates the time needed to ensure that all the pieces are in place."

Frank was unsure how to interpret the statement. *Do these guys need more time to locate the girls, or just to transport them from wherever they are? Or maybe they were simply buying time to set up an ambush?*

"How do I know that you have the girls?" Frank questioned. "I want proof."

"I can assure you, you will have all the proof you need very soon. But my associates have one caveat that I have not yet mentioned."

"Yeah, what's that?" Frank was disgusted at the thought of taking orders from these low-life scum, but currently, he didn't have a choice.

"To ensure that you come alone, someone will be phoning Mr. Bennett on his landline every hour, on the hour, from now until the hand-off occurs. If at any point your friend fails to answer his phone, the meeting is off. Do you understand?"

"I'm on my way," Frank said, then quickly disconnected the call.

"What the hell is going on?" Bennett needed to be filled in.

"I'm heading south for a handoff. Whoever this guy is, he's going to call me back in a few hours with specifics, but I have to leave right now." Frank abandoned the railing and headed back inside the office.

"Alright, let's suit up," Bennett replied, following closely behind Frank.

"No can do. They told me I need to come alone."

"Fuck that," Bennett dismissed the notion. "I know this country like the back of my hand."

"I don't doubt you do, Benny," Frank said, picking up his duffel bag off the floor and slinging it over his shoulder. "But they're going to be calling you on your landline here every hour, and if you don't pick up, even once, it's all over."

"I'll transfer my landline to my cell phone," Bennett countered. "These guys won't even know the difference."

"I can't risk it," Frank replied. He stepped around Bennett and abandoned the office, quickly descending the curved stairs.

Bennett followed. "Well, at least let me send a couple of guys from one of my crews to tail you. You won't even know they're there."

Frank reached the foyer and turned back to face his old friend. "Listen, I appreciate it, Benny, I do, but I need to do this part alone. They seem to have a bead on everything that's gone on so far."

"Alright, Tank," Bennett relented, "but if *anything* gets fishy out there, you call me, and I'll be on my way."

Frank nodded.

"And once you get your girls back, if you need a place to bring them, you know my door is always open, brother."

"Thanks again."

Frank left the house, crossed the horseshoe driveway to where his rental car was parked. He opened the door, tossed the duffel bag onto the passenger seat, and started the engine. As he pulled away, he and Bennett nodded to one another, then Frank stepped on the accelerator and tore down the driveway.

*****

Once Frank reached the highway, he dialed Mike's number on the second phone.

"Where you headed?" Mike asked immediately.

"I just left Bennett's. Whoever has the girls just made contact. I'm heading south for a meet in a few hours."

"You think it's a hand-off?"

"Sounds like it. Whoever these guys are, they were smart enough to separate me and Bennett."

"What if they go to his house?"

"Don't worry about Benny," replied Frank. "He can handle himself just fine."

"Did you tell him about—"

"Not yet," Frank already knew what Mike was going to ask. "I think it's best we continue to keep everything compartmentalized for now."

"Fair enough. Okay, keep your phone on, and I'll continue to track you using the GPS program."

"Will do."

*****

Frank had not slept in nearly forty-eight hours, but the copious amount of adrenaline coursing through his body was more than enough to keep him vigilant as the miles ticked on. He had left the house well over two hours ago, and Bennett had called twice to confirm that he had received both check-ins.

The phone in the cup holder next to Frank's thigh rang.

"Yeah," Frank answered.

"Agent Adler, I imagine you have been moving south as instructed?"

"Just give me the directions, asshole."

"When you have traveled a ways into Sinaloa, you will come across a small town on the left side of the road with a series of old stone buildings—you can't miss them," the caller suggested. "Continue fifteen miles past the last structure, and you will be presented with the option to head east or west. Go *east*. You will travel for an additional forty-two miles toward the foothills, where the road will eventually come to an end. Take another left and travel seven miles. You will arrive at a lone two-story warehouse on the right side of the road with a car parked out front. A man will be waiting for you inside."

Frank recorded every detail in his mind.

"If you can provide me with your current location, I can estimate your time of arrival."

Frank realized the caller was fishing for information regarding his current whereabouts. Obviously, he had not been able to track his progress up to this point. A few seconds of silence passed.

"Agent Adler? Are you still there?"

"I'm looking for a mile marker, dipshit," Frank said. When he eventually sped past one, he subtracted thirty and announced the number.

"I thought you might be a little further by this point..."

"Yeah, well, I've been sticking to the speed limit," Frank lied. "I'm not looking to get pulled over."

"Fair enough," the caller seemed satisfied with the explanation, and with that, Frank had bought himself some reconnaissance time when he got closer to the location.

"Now, let me talk to the girls," Frank pressed him again.

"Patience, Agent Adler. Once—"

Frank hung up, not caring to listen to another bullshit excuse. He dialed Mike on the other phone.

Mike answered on the first ring. "What's up?"

"I've got a location," Frank reported, providing him with the details he had just received. "I'm going to need topographic maps of that area. Also, find out if any back roads access that site."

"On it."

"I bought an extra half hour of recon time."

"Hey, what about your rental car?" Mike wondered. "Can it be traced back to you?"

"No, when I swapped them, I did it *properly*," Frank said, meaning that he had used a fake name and identification on the rental company's automated online booking site, never having approached a service counter.

"Perfect."

"An extraction point needs to be set up soon as well."

"Already in the works," Mike reported.

CHAPTER twenty-nine

Only the soul-stirring howl of a lone coyote, hiding in the surrounding foothills, broke the silence outside Frank's car as he slowly approached a gray warehouse in the middle of the arid Mexican landscape. The solitary reprieve from the darkness was a limited amount of light being cast from the three large vertical windows on the building's north face, which illuminated a mid-sized black sedan near the front corner of the building.

Frank parked fifty yards back and killed the engine. He got out and walked cautiously toward the towering warehouse, his head on a swivel, listening intently through the stillness of the night air. Reaching the structure's singular door, he pulled it open and stepped inside a poorly lit corridor.

"In here, Agent Adler," a man's voice sounded from somewhere deeper inside the building. "I am unarmed."

Frank walked down the hallway slowly, approaching a door that led into an open bay to his right. As he entered, he saw a Mexican man in his early thirties with a thin build, olive-colored skin, and dense black stubble covering his face sitting on a wooden chair. He was dressed in a well-tailored navy-blue suit, white dress shirt, and brown leather shoes, giving him the appearance of a banker rather than a gangster.

Frank looked to his right.

Sara.

She was seated on a metal folding chair, leaning heavily on a large, solidly built wooden table. Her clothes—the same jeans and white blouse she had been wearing for days—were filthy and tattered. Her hair was unkempt and disheveled. A pyramid of tightly banded US currency sat on the table next to her.

Sensing her father's presence, Sara attempted to lift her bowed head, exposing cloudy, tear-filled eyes. *"Daddy?"* escaped her dehydrated lips in a broken whisper. She reached out a hand, but the powerful tranquilizing narcotics in her system caused her arm to drop back down onto the table, and her head soon followed.

Frank focused on the man across the room as he walked over to Sara. "Where's Marla?" he demanded.

"My name is Carlos, Agent Adler," the man introduced himself in an accent more pronounced than whoever Frank had been speaking with on the phone. "I have been sent here as a repres—"

"I don't give a fuck what your name is," Frank cut him off, knowing any information the man offered would be fully fabricated. "Where's Marla?"

"Unfortunately, Agent Adler, someone was operating outside the accepted code of conduct," the man in the chair said cryptically. "The people I've been asked to represent tonight want you to know that your daughter and her friend were never supposed to be involved in any of this."

As Frank neared Sara, he suddenly spotted a black body bag against the far wall of the bay, almost stopping him in his tracks. Next to it was a large double-strapped brown leather satchel.

"I regret to inform you that when they found your daughter, her traveling companion was discovered to be unresponsive. I was told they did everything in their power to revive her, but unfortunately, it was just too late."

The statement triggered Sara into a fit of heart-wrenching sobs, her face still buried in her forearms. Frank placed his hand on her shoulder, feeling the raw emotion coursing through her exhausted body.

"It's going to be okay, sweetheart," Frank told his daughter, kissing her on the back of her head, as salty puddles formed on the table beneath her face. "I'm here now."

Frank made his way over to the body bag and took hold of its heavy-duty zipper and slowly pulled it down the track as Sara continued to whimper at the table behind him. The widening slit eventually exposed Marla's face, half-covered by strands of her long blonde hair. She lay motionless, eyes closed, lips swollen in a hypoxic shade of blue. Frank unzipped the bag further and caught a glimpse of the track marks on her forearm. He exhaled a single remorseful breath and resealed the bag.

"What's this?" Frank asked, referring to the leather satchel.

"The men I represent want you to know that they take transgressions like these very seriously," Carlos said, attempting to stand from his chair.

"SIT DOWN!" Frank roared from across the room, causing the Mexican's eyes to widen. He quickly complied.

Frank lifted the satchel off the floor by one of its straps, causing the top to spread open. Inside, he could see the twisted, duct-taped top of a heavy-gauge translucent plastic bag. He took hold of it with both hands and allowed the surrounding satchel to drop to the floor, then lifted the heavy bag to eye level. Inside, he saw three decapitated heads. The two on top belonged to the young men Frank had been searching for from the hotel surveillance footage. Each of their skulls contained a bullet hole. The head on the bottom was facing in the opposite direction. Frank rotated the sack and discovered an older Mexican man, whose face was frozen with a look of horror from the final, violent moments of his life.

"These are the three men responsible for what happened to your daughter and her friend," the man across the room suggested. "I was told that the two Americans—to which my associates have *absolutely* no connection—were heavily indebted to Mr. Lopez."

"What was he planning on doing with the girls?"

"Nobody knows, Agent Adler."

Frank knew he was lying.

"As I said, these three men took it upon themselves to operate outside the traditional boundaries—"

"Boundaries?!" Frank raised his voice, dropping the heads to the floor with a sickening thud. He made his way across the room toward the seated man.

"I know it may be difficult for you to understand, Agent Adler, but things down here operate much differently than they once di—"

"Give me your phone," Frank demanded.

A curious look came upon the man's face, but he complied, removing his device from his pocket. "I can assure you this phone contains no information that would be of value to you."

Frank didn't care. He snatched the device from his hands and quickly patted him down for weapons.

"As I said earlier, I am unarmed," Carlos insisted, but allowed the search. "I am merely a messenger."

Frank slipped the phone into his pocket and made his way back to where Sara was sitting, looking up through the three large rectangular windows at the crescent moon stationed just above the nearby foothills. "What's *this*?" Frank motioned a hand toward the pyramid of cash on the table next to Sara.

"Two million dollars," the Mexican explained, as if it were the most natural thing in the world. "My associates want you to take it back to America along with your daughter. You can split it with the blonde girl's grieving family or keep it all for yourself. The choice is ultimately yours," Carlos shrugged. "But understand something, Agent Adler, the three men who triggered these unfortunate events have been brought to justice, and this money is in no way an admission of guilt. It is merely to ensure that everybody goes their separate ways and moves on," he said, like a lawyer presenting closing arguments in a court case. "Do you understand?"

Frank looked at his watch as he made his way around the back of the table and stood directly behind the pyramid of money. He stared at it intently. Suddenly, he reached a hand behind his back and withdrew his gun.

"What are you doing?" Carlos demanded. "I am only a messenger!"

Rage boiled inside Frank as he stared daggers at the man across the room. He felt his finger slide inside the trigger guard. Carlos straightened in his chair, and a look of nervousness spread across his face.

Just then, Frank felt something touch his wrist, and it was enough to break his vengeful, hate-filled trance. He looked down to discover Sara's hand on his forearm. Her head was raised. Her eyes were glassy and desperate.

"Daddy..." she whispered up at him.

Frank stared into his daughter's pain-ridden eyes.

"I just want to go home," she said, attempting to stand. Immediately, she collapsed into her father's arms.

Frank cradled Sara's fragile body against his own and kissed the top of her head. "Okay, sweetheart," he relented, shifting her weight so that he could return his weapon to its former position behind his back.

"I don't want your money," Frank said to the man across the room. "Once I get my daughter out to the car, I'll be coming back for Marla. She needs a proper burial. Don't move."

The color slowly crept back into Carlos' face.

*****

Exiting the building, Sara was limping badly due to her injured knee, but with her father's assistance, she was able to keep pace. However, once they reached the passenger side door of the rental car, the intensifying effects of the opioids took over, and Frank felt her legs buckle. He caught her and placed her unconscious body inside the vehicle.

"Just rest now," Frank said softly, buckling her in place. "I'll be right back."

Frank shut the door and popped the trunk. Soon, the sounds of zippers and Velcro opening and closing filled the night air. He shut the trunk and made his way back to the warehouse.

Entering the bay, Frank walked directly to where the body bag lay against the far wall.

"I know that emotions can run high in these types of situations," Carlos suggested, as if forgiving Frank for pulling his weapon earlier.

Frank ignored him, lifting the empty brown satchel from the floor. He carried it over to the table, placed it next to the stacks of cash, and began filling the bag.

The man across the room looked at him inquisitively.

"I couldn't do this in front of my daughter..." Frank said quietly.

"I understand," replied Carlos, a tiny grin forming on his face.

Once Frank had transferred the last of the bills into the bag, he removed four sets of handcuffs that he had collected from the trunk of the car and tossed them across the bay, where they landed noisily in a puff of dust in front of the Mexican's expensive-looking leather dress shoes.

"What are these for?"

"Secure your arms and legs to the chair," Frank ordered.

"I can assure you, Agent Adler, I have no intention of trying to follow you once you leave this building."

Frank stared at him, unflinching in his demands.

"As you wish," Carlos exhaled a breath of annoyance. "Someone will surely be sent out here in an hour or two if I don't check in."

Frank watched as Carlos collected the four cuffs from the floorboards and encircled each of his ankles and wrists, securing three of them to his chair. The fourth, dangling from his left wrist, he shook in the air, indicating his inability to complete the task himself. "Perhaps you could assist me with the last?"

Frank lifted the fifty-pound satchel off the table and walked over to Carlos, dropping the heavy leather bag onto his lap. He proceeded to secure the final cuff in place and tightened the other three to a much more uncomfortable tension, causing the seated man to wince with each squeeze of the steel.

Satisfied with the level of restraint, Frank lifted the bag off the man's lap, looking him in the eyes as he did so. Slowly, Frank slipped one of the straps over the Mexican's head so that the heavy sack hung open around his neck, suspended in front of his chest, six inches above his lap.

"What are you doing?" Carlos twisted his head, attempting to alleviate some of the pressure from the back of his neck. This only caused the leather strap to dig more deeply into his bony spine.

Without saying a word, Frank reached into his pocket and pulled out a translucent plastic bottle he had retrieved from the trunk along with the cuffs. Carlos forced his head back against the weight of the satchel and stared at the container. Frank flicked off the lid with his thumb, sending it bouncing across the floor and out of sight. He stepped forward and squeezed the sides of the container, releasing a stream of urine-colored liquid into the open bag. The fluid quickly soaked into the bills and seeped through the bottom of the bag, dripping down onto the Mexican's lap.

"What the fuck are you doing?!" Carlos shouted at Frank as the pungent fumes stung his nostrils. He began to struggle against his restraints.

Frank aimed the bottle higher and doused the man's head, face, and chest with the remaining liquid, causing his eyes to burn with irritation.

"You had your chance!" Carlos suddenly shouted. "I gave you your chance!" Just then, he tilted his chin down toward his chest. "Take him out! Now!"

Frank looked down and noticed that two of the buttons on the Mexican's dress shirt had come undone during his struggles, exposing a thin black wire taped to his chest. Frank immediately dropped the empty container onto the floor and spun around, staring up through the large rectangular windows.

Carlos spat out more of the acrid accelerant, hollering even more loudly into the microphone. "Shoot him!" he ordered his snipers in the foothills, expecting the bullets to break through the glass at any moment. "NOW!"

Only silence followed.

Frank turned around slowly and faced the seated man. "They've been taken care of..." he said flatly.

Four hundred yards away from the warehouse, on a rocky outcropping, lay the lifeless bodies of two cartel men. Each had a bullet in their still-warm skulls, and a pair of unused high-powered rifles lay in front of them.

Frank walked across the bay to Marla's body bag, as Carlos struggled against his restraints.

"Agent Adler," he attempted to restore some of the former calmness in his voice. "I am only a messenger. I had nothing to do with any of this."

Ignoring him, Frank squatted down next to the vinyl cocoon and lifted it off the floorboards, placing it gently over his shoulder. It felt so light. So wrong.

Frank turned around and approached the bound man.

"You claim to *only* be a messenger, Carlos," he said, his voice bathed in hatred. "*Maybe* you're right. *Maybe* you aren't the one who injects these young girls with drugs. *Maybe* you aren't the one who steals them from their families. The one who rapes them. The one who transports them around like fucking cattle!" Frank shouted, suddenly producing a silver lighter from his pocket.

"No, no, no, no!" Carlos pleaded.

"But someone took *my* daughter! And they murdered her friend! And now they have the fucking balls to try to buy my silence?!"

Frank growled. "Well, I guess it's lucky for me that I came across a simple, blind-eyed, no-responsibility messenger like yourself, Carlos, because I want to be sure my message gets back to those people loud and clear!"

Frank snapped the lighter into action, producing an ominous yellow flame that caused Carlos' eyes to double in size. Frank stepped forward and tossed the lighter inside the satchel, instantly igniting the accelerant-soaked cash into a raging fireball that consumed the man's lap, chest, and face, and set off a series of blood-curdling screams. Black and green smoke quickly choked out all the breathable air from the bound man's lungs, and his arms and legs spasmed uncontrollably as his skin melted and his hair singed down to its roots. Carlos threw himself backward onto the floor, continuing to scream as the flames raged on.

*****

Sara was still unconscious inside the rental car when Frank emerged from the warehouse with the black body bag balanced over his shoulder, and the last of Carlos' terror-filled screams followed him out the door. Just then, Frank spotted a pair of headlights rapidly approaching from down the dirt road to the south. The inbound vehicle was less than three hundred yards out and closing fast. By the time Frank reached the rental car, an SUV had ripped into the lot, and its headlights spotlighted him holding the body bag. Frank held up a hand to block the blinding lights from his eyes and heard a door open. The driver jumped out.

A moment later, Mike emerged from the light.

Once Frank had left the cryptic voicemail for him, after leaving the house in Rocky Point the morning before, Mike had immediately followed through on their prearranged plan to catch a covert flight to Mexico. The final leg of Mike's journey had landed him at a private airstrip not far from Bennett's, where he was able to discreetly obtain the SUV. Frank had intentionally withheld Mike's involvement from Bennett so they would both have plausible deniability if things went sideways. Once Frank left Bennett's house, Mike was able to follow him using his open cell phone signal, and they eventually met up and performed the reconnaissance with the extra time Frank had bought, where they discovered the snipers in the foothills.

"You alright?" Mike asked Frank as they walked to the back of the SUV with the body bag. Mike glanced forlornly at the vinyl coffin, having heard the entire exchange between Frank and Carlos inside the building on Frank's open cell phone.

"Yeah."

Mike opened the back hatch, revealing a black .308 sniper rifle with scope, still warm. He pushed it to one side.

Frank looked at the weapon, then at Mike. "You good?"

Mike nodded.

Frank laid the black body bag next to the gun, and the two men took a step back. After a moment, Mike closed the hatch, and he and Frank made their way to the rental car. Opening the passenger side door, Frank wrapped his arms around Sara and unclipped her seatbelt. Her eyes flickered open momentarily.

"Everything's going to be alright, honey," Frank said reassuringly as he carefully removed her from the vehicle in a fireman's carry. "You're safe now."

"Did you find a good spot to ditch this car on our way out?" Mike inquired, following Frank back to the SUV.

"Yeah, follow me with the girls," Frank instructed. "There's a spot four or five miles down the road. I'll light it up there and jump in with you."

Mike nodded.

"Is the extraction site set?" Frank asked as he buckled Sara inside the backseat of the SUV.

Mike pulled the satellite phone from his pocket and quickly dialed a number.

"Winston, is the chopper inbound? Frank and I are approximately twenty minutes out from the extraction site." He listened for a response and then disconnected the call. "We're all set."

CHAPTER thirty

Ken Collins and an armed Mexican guard were walking along a leaf-littered path cut through a dense swath of Mexican jungle on one of the Diaz brothers' thousand-hectare properties near the outskirts of Guadalajara. This place was much different from Ernesto's compound. There were no pools, no partygoers, no loud music out here, only a raw and wild ecosystem harmonized by exotic birds perched in the foliage overhead.

The CEO had been in town, visiting Zinex's labs, when one of Diaz's associates summoned him to the property before his departure. Because Collins had a couple of hours to kill before his flight home, the impromptu meeting posed no inconvenience whatsoever. During the chauffeured drive to the property, he had texted Hank Phillips to inquire if he, too, would be in attendance today, but had not yet received a reply.

A flock of noisy green parakeets took flight from the sun-speckled canopy overhead, causing Collins to momentarily stop and observe the sudden migration. The guard continued, and the CEO could now hear someone approaching from behind. He turned and saw it was Dennis.

"Morning, Dennis," Collins attempted to greet him.

The cartel boss didn't even consider returning the pleasantry; instead, he only pointed to where the guard had carried on.

Collins looked and discovered that Ernesto had appeared on the path up ahead and was engaged in conversation with the guard.

"Move," Dennis grunted.

This level of indifference was nothing new to Collins. In fact, he was certain that Dennis Diaz didn't care for him at all, and the feeling was mutual.

The conversation between the guard and Ernesto concluded, and the guard turned around and marched past Collins and Dennis, eyes straight ahead.

"Take a walk with me, Mr. Collins," Ernesto called out to the American, turning himself around and continuing back in the direction he had arrived from. "There is something we need to discuss."

Collins picked up his pace and eventually caught up, leaving Dennis to follow at a distance.

For nearly ten seconds, the two men walked in silence.

"The labs are running smoothly..." Collins finally attempted to alleviate the awkwardness, stepping over a gnarled branch that had fallen during a windstorm the night before. He slapped a bloodthirsty mosquito on the back of his neck. "Everything is ticking along just fine."

Ernesto offered only a nod, making Collins wish that the old man would hurry up and get to whatever reason he had been called here for.

"Have you eaten yet?" Ernesto finally spoke.

"Uh, yeah, I had breakfast at the hotel. It was shit, but what do you expect?"

Through a gap in the trees up ahead, Collins could see a large clearing in the jungle. In the center of the half-acre void stood a single, towering hardwood with dense, neuronal branches and drooping yellow bell-shaped leaves. It was the largest and most imposing specimen on the entire plantation.

"You won't mind if I have something to eat while we speak," Ernesto said, more of a statement than a question.

"Not at all," Collins shrugged, taking a moment to look back at Dennis, who was about thirty yards behind. "What is it you want to discuss?" he asked Ernesto.

Not receiving a response, the two men entered the clearing.

Next to the base of the tree, the CEO could now see a cast-iron breakfast table topped with a multitude of food and drinks and surrounded by chairs. Something suddenly caught Collins' eye in the tree's canopy. He looked up and discovered two men standing on one of the tree's robust limbs, forty feet above the table. The sight stopped Collins dead in his tracks. He looked at Ernesto, who continued to walk straight ahead, then back up again.

The man on the left was dressed entirely in black, including the bandana that covered the lower half of his face, obscuring his identity. He appeared to be stabilizing the other man, who had a brown burlap sack pulled over his head and whose hands were tied behind his back. It was then that Collins discovered the noose around his neck, tied to the branch between his feet.

A sudden gust of wind swept across the clearing, and Collins watched the bound man's knees quiver as he struggled to maintain his balance. Collins' stomach dropped when he saw the man in black remove his hand from his shoulder, causing his knees to buckle. Without the additional assistance, the hooded man pitched forward and plummeted down toward the table below. After twenty feet, the rope reached its limit, resulting in a vicious spine-snapping *CRACK!* that echoed through the surrounding foliage, causing hundreds of tiny starlings to take flight.

The corpse now dangled in the air like a broken marionette.

Ernesto turned back to Collins, completely undisturbed by the event. "Come along," he ordered the American.

Collins' legs were like stone. He looked back at Dennis, who was now leaning casually against the bark of a towering palm at the edge of the clearing. He grinned at him ominously and lit a fresh cigar.

"Mr. Collins," Ernesto said more forcefully. "Join me. Now."

Collins' mind raced. Everything had seemed amicable during his last visit. *Who was the man in the tree? Why did they kill him?* He knew one thing for sure: making Ernesto ask him a third time to join him was definitely not the answer. Collins finally convinced his legs to ambulate as his stomach did its best not to regurgitate his breakfast.

Ernesto arrived at the table and took his seat. Collins approached cautiously, looking up at the dangling body above his head. The burlap sack had fallen off during the descent, and the body rotated slowly, revealing the victim's bloated, purple face. Collins' heart jackhammered when he discovered the slain man's identity.

It was Hank.

The Texan's usual goofy smile was replaced with eye-bulging, fear-stricken terror. Collins looked at Ernesto, who had just finished pouring himself a glass of freshly squeezed orange juice and was now scooping a spoonful of purple caviar onto an oyster cracker. The kingpin placed the appetizer into his mouth and chewed as Collins scanned the table's loaves of bread, pats of softened butter, circular deli meats, blocky cheeses, and crystal bowls filled with exotic fruits.

"You are certain I cannot offer you something to eat?" Ernesto asked again.

Collins seemed to be having trouble formulating a response with Hank's boots hanging ten feet above his head. *"Why?"* he finally managed to get out.

Ernesto selected another cracker and held it in front of himself, studying it as if there was a message from the far reaches of the universe embossed on its backside. Finally, he scooped up a thick glob of caviar and placed it into his mouth. He leaned back and looked up at the dangling corpse.

"I find it interesting that you Americans use baseball phrases for the events in your lives," he mused. "The one I find particularly confusing, however, is *three strikes and you're out...*"

Collins finally took his seat on the other side of the table.

"Perhaps, in a game of sport, this might be reasonable, but when it comes to business, I think that *one* strike is more than enough. Wouldn't you agree, Mr. Collins?"

The CEO didn't have the faintest idea of how to respond.

"It turns out your friend Hank was selling information to the Chinese," the cartel boss finally revealed.

"The Chinese?" Collins didn't understand. "I don't know anything about that."

Ernesto leaned forward and studied the American across the table. After a few agonizing moments, he finally spoke. "Fortunately for you, Mr. Collins, I believe that to be the truth." Ernesto raised his hand and summoned his brother across the clearing. Dennis extinguished his cigar on the bark of the palm and made his way toward the table. "Mr. Collins," Ernesto continued, "you need to assure me that this turn of events will not impact anything we have started. After all, we have only just begun."

The CEO nodded his head robotically, now understanding that Hank's murder was Ernesto's way of making a statement. He and Dennis wanted to give him an up-close and personal experience of just how brutal they could be, should they ever be crossed.

"How long?" asked Collins.

Ernesto raised an eyebrow.

"How long was Hank working with the Chinese?" The CEO specified.

"I've had my suspicions for a couple of months now," Dennis announced, arriving at the table. He pulled out the chair next to his brother and took his seat facing Collins. "I confirmed it last week."

"Do you know if he told them anything about—"

"We don't believe so," Ernesto predicted the American's inquiry.

Collins looked up at the scratched soles of Hank's cowboy boots, then back at Ernesto across the table.

"Too many strikes, my friend," Ernesto said ominously. "Too many strikes."

CHAPTER thirty-one

Frank exited the elevator on the seventh floor of the FBI building and turned right, heading towards Jack Morrison's office. Clutched in his right hand was an internal report, still warm from the printer. As Frank approached the AD's door, Kristen, his redheaded assistant—who had recently graduated from the University of Syracuse—stood up from her seat.

"Good morning, Agent Adler," she smiled cautiously, trying to assess Frank's current mood after overhearing the intense interactions he and her boss had been having in recent weeks. "Mr. Morrison is currently on a phone call," she tried to explain. "I can have him call you at your desk once he's finished. Or perhaps you'd prefer to schedule a meet—"

Frank ignored her and continued straight ahead.

"Wait! You can't go in there!"

Frank threw open Jack's door, causing it to bounce violently off the rubber baseboard stopper.

"I'm sorry, Mr. Morrison," Kristen rushed past Frank, attempting to get ahead of the incoming freight train.

Jack looked up from his phone call. "I'm going to have to call you back later, Charlie," he said, then quickly hung up. "Good morning, Frank," he attempted to welcome his old friend with geniality, though he knew Frank had no intention of returning the pleasantry. He turned his attention to his assistant momentarily. "It's no problem, Kristen," he smiled at her empathetically. "Frank is always welcome in here."

"Okay, yes, of course, sorry, Mr. Morrison," the nervous young lady rambled. "Can I get you two a coffee?" she offered, backing toward the door to the safety of her desk.

Frank didn't respond. His eyes were still locked on the AD.

"No, we're fine," Morrison answered. "Thank you."

Kristen offered an awkward half-bow and then quickly exited the room, closing the door gently behind her.

"Now Frank..." Jack already knew what was coming.

"What the fuck is *this*?" Frank tossed the stack of unstapled papers across the desk, knocking a mug of ball-point pens onto the floor.

"You know how things work around here, Frank. Those reports are not the *be-all, end-all."*

"It says that our people found no evidence of a human trafficking ring between Southern California and Mexico."

"I can't imagine the stress you've been under, Frank, but you've been coming in here for nearly a month now demanding further investigations, and let's face it, I doubt you've even provided our guys with *all* the information I imagine you might have."

"We both know *exactly* how this is going to play out now!" Frank raised his voice. "The second that bullshit report got filed, it killed any chance we have of moving forward! Tell me I'm wrong, Jack! Tell me I'm fucking wrong!"

"I'm going to make sure it's not like that for this one, Frank. I'll keep—"

"It says our contacts staked out the locations where the trafficked girls were *rumored* to have been abducted and held," Frank said of the mechanic's shop in San Diego and that Mexican stash house in Rocky Point. "I was there, Jack! I saw that nightclub setup! I watched Sofia blow her fucking brains out with my own two eyes! Did they even bother to look?!"

"Jesus Christ, Frank! Keep your voice down!" the AD demanded, lowering his own into a stern whisper. "If anybody *ever* finds out that you went across the border—doing whatever type of shit I can only imagine you did—me, and anyone else who knows you were down there, will lose our jobs immediately. And *you*? They'll send your ass straight to prison! For fuck's sake, Frank, of course, they looked! But you told me yourself the cartel knew you were an agent. Do you honestly think they'd be stupid enough not to scrub and abandon both those places, two minutes after you left? Hell, I'm surprised they didn't just burn them to the ground!"

"Why is there nothing in that report about Angus?" Frank asked of the bouncer. "You assured me that agents would be sent to Mississippi last week to talk to him. I gave you my word that I wouldn't contact him until after proper protocols were followed, but now that I've read *that* bullshit report, I'll be flying out there myself!"

Jack raised an eyebrow. "Wait... Nobody told you?"

"Told me what?" Frank responded indignantly.

"We *did* send an agent out there last week."

"Then why the fuck isn't it in the report?" Frank demanded. "They—"

"He's dead, Frank..." Jack said softly.

The revelation caught Frank by surprise. *"What?"*

"When they arrived at his house, his father explained that he had died of an overdose in a bathroom stall at a gas station on the bus ride home. It must have been the day after you spoke with him in San Diego. I'm sorry, Frank, I thought you knew."

"That's not possible..." Frank said with disbelief. "He was done with drugs. I could see it in his eyes."

"You said it yourself, Frank—Angus was an addict. It's not easy to just stop cold turkey like that. And I'm sure the pressure of what he had witnessed and having to return to his family after dropping out of school. It was probably just too much for him."

"I don't buy it," Frank said defiantly.

"Frank, they found him dead on the bathroom floor with the fucking needle sticking out of his arm!"

Frank's thoughts suddenly flashed back to his conversation with Angus in the basement. *"That might be the only thing that saved my life the first time."* Angus had told him. *"I'm deathly afraid of needles. Just the sight of them things causes me to pass out immediately."*

"Bullshit!" Frank charged. "They must have gotten to him! Just like the mechanic! You think the fatal heart attack that guy had during his fishing trip was just a coincidence? It's all connected!"

"Jesus, Frank, listen to yourself."

"They must have found out that Angus was skipping town, caught up with him at a rest stop, and injected him with drugs. We need to open a full investigation into his death."

Morrison stared across his desk.

"And I need an assignment that will get me back down into Mexico," Frank demanded. "I don't give a shit what it's for. Just make it happen."

"Have you completely lost your fucking mind?" Jack wore a look of concern on his face now. "Those cartels already know you were poking around down there," he reminded Frank. "Every mole they have at the border will have your picture. They're just praying you're stupid enough to come back!"

"I don't give a fuck."

Morrison lowered his head in frustration and let out an audible sigh. "Frank, you're starting to spiral. And your behavior lately has been erratic, at best. You're just too damn close to this thing. Don't you remember those guys overseas?" Morrison was speaking about his own time in the military. "Somebody would watch one of his buddies get picked off by a sniper, or blown up by a roadside bomb, and they'd lose their fucking minds, seeking vengeance, forgetting every basic protocol we had! They'd start making up reasons to engage. We both know what happened to those guys, Frank."

Frank knew exactly what happened to *those* guys, but they weren't him. This situation was different.

"They'd end up fucking dead, Frank!" Jack raised his voice. "And in the process, they'd put everybody else in danger!"

Frank stared across the desk with contempt. "Pick up that fucking phone and get me down to Mexico," Frank demanded. "I'm not going to ask you again."

Morrison exhaled slowly. "I'm sorry to have to do this to you, Frank, but it's for your own good," he transitioned to a more official tone. "Special Agent Adler, I am hereby placing you on a paid leave of absence, commencing immediately. You are to relinquish your firearm, along with your identification. If you—"

"Are you fucking kidding me?" Frank cut him off in a low grumble, glaring with venomous hatred.

"If the situation were reversed, I know you'd have my best interest in mind and do the same for me."

"If the situation were reversed, I'd have your fucking back," Frank countered, pulling the holster off his hip and tossing it across the top of the desk, knocking more stationery onto the floor.

"I know you can't see it right now, but trust me, *this is* having your back," Morrison reasoned. "Nobody will know you've been placed on leave. It will be coded in the system as vacation time. Whenever you're ready—"

"Fuck you," Frank said evenly and without remorse. "And if you want my ID so badly, you can go get it from my locker downstairs."

"Come on, Frank, I'm just—"

"You remember where the agent lockers are, don't you? You used to have one down there with us before you came up here and became just another pencil-pushing yes man."

With that, Frank turned around, exited the office, and slammed the door behind him.

CHAPTER thirty-two

Nearly a month had passed since Frank's suspension began, and he was slumped forward on the table inside the tiny cabin, bathed in the dim yellow glow of an underpowered desktop lamp. Three weeks of beard covered his face, and his arms were splayed wide, steadying him after another evening of consistent drinking. The search for answers regarding the girls' abduction and its connection to the elusive human trafficking ring continued. During that time, he had only spoken to Mike sporadically and was unwilling to accept any visitors.

On the table in front of Frank lay the same mess of over-handled documents that he had collected and been obsessing over. Included in the chaos were photographs of James and Steve, their online communications with Sara and Marla, Angus' death certificate, pictures of the limo driver, mug shots of the man Frank had set ablaze inside the warehouse, satellite images of each of the properties he had visited, old business records from the dead mechanic's shop, and aerial maps of the suburban neighborhood in Rocky Point where the girls had been held. Next to all that lay a 9MM handgun and a bottle of Jack Daniels that had been relieved of half its contents. Inside, Frank felt even more pathetic than he looked. He dropped the same report he had scoured for the hundredth time onto the table and laid his face into his palms.

Suddenly, a flash of bright white light sparked from the blackened recesses of his mind, transporting him back inside the Mexican warehouse. Frank found himself standing above the body bag that contained Marla's corpse. *Flash!* The memory dial began to spin. Frank was now at Marla's funeral, where Carol was bawling uncontrollably, clinging to her daughter's casket as an empathetic funeral director did her best to comfort a mother who would soon bury her child in the same cemetery plot where she had laid her husband to rest ten years earlier. *Flash!* Frank was back inside the warehouse. Sara was leaning heavily on the table. Her head lifted slowly. She reached out for him. *Flash!* Frank found himself watching the last bitter argument he had had with Donna just outside the cabin's door. She was in tears, pleading for him to return home, pleading for him to find a way to move on after he had exiled himself to the acreage due to the pressure he was placing on Sara, fishing for additional information regarding her abduction and confinement. Deep down, Frank knew she had to start piecing her life back together. The last thing she needed was to continuously relive her trauma through his inquiries. Unfortunately, Frank couldn't walk that path himself yet. In his heart, he knew there were more girls chained to beds out there—trapped inside whatever *new system* the rapist with the dragon tattoo had hinted at before he had been killed by Sofia. *Flash!* The memories began to blend into each other—spinning, stretching and blurring the confines of his mind. They raced out of control. Sara. Marla. Sofia. Donna. Angus. Frank finally forced his eyes open and jolted himself back to reality inside the cabin. He looked down and found the gun gripped tightly in his hand. He stared at it, transfixed.

Just then, Frank heard what sounded to be a vehicle approaching the cabin, breaking his trance. He looked at his watch. It was long after midnight, and nobody had come to the acreage in weeks. *Have the Mexicans finally had enough of my inquiries?* Frank wondered. *Maybe they feel enough time has passed and they can send someone to tie up another loose end, just as they had with Angus and the mechanic.*

Frank shut off the lamp and stood from the table, gun in hand. He made his way over to the small window near the front door. By the spread and height of the approaching headlights, Frank could rule out both Donna's and Mike's larger vehicles. However, it was much too dark outside to determine anything more than that.

Frank abandoned the window and crouched next to the door, cracking it open just wide enough to see through the slit. He watched the vehicle come to a stop next to his truck fifty feet away. The driver killed the engine, but the headlights remained activated, shining directly into Frank's eyes through the gap. Frank slipped the barrel of his weapon between the door and its frame, aiming it just above the right headlight, as a dark silhouette appeared and began to slowly make his way toward the front of the cabin. Frank tightened his grip on the gun and took hold of the doorknob.

"Frank?" said a man in an English accent.

Frank felt the tension in his body ease. He relaxed his grip on his weapon, stood from his crouch, and pulled open the door. "I almost shot you, Winston," Frank admitted. "What are you doing out here?"

"Apologies for my late-night intrusion, but I was hoping that you might invite me inside so we can speak?"

Frank looked at his visitor with whiskey-glassed eyes. "Yeah, alright," he agreed, somewhat reluctantly.

Winston stepped past Frank and entered the cabin.

"You want a drink or something?" Frank offered as they made their way over to the evidence-filled table.

"No, I'm quite alright, thank you," Winston declined, taking a seat.

Before he sat down, Frank removed the bottle of booze from the table and placed it inside a cupboard above the sink, along with his gun.

"Winston, I know why you're here," he said, walking back to the table and taking the chair across from his visitor. "I'm not coming back to work until I get all this figured out."

Winston inhaled deeply. "Frank, what I'm about to tell you is something I've kept a secret for nearly my entire life."

Frank's eyebrows furrowed, and his inebriated gaze focused.

"I'm curious what you may have heard of my past?" Winston wondered.

"Not much, I guess. I assume that you must have worked for an intelligence agency in the UK before coming to America. Or maybe something in the military-industrial complex?"

"Truth be told, Frank, I was actually born in a small town a few hours from Amsterdam to Jewish parents, just before the outbreak of the Second World War," Winston revealed. "When the war began, the Nazis imposed a velvet glove approach in my country, leading my parents—and many of the other villagers—to believe that if they simply waited out the conflict, things would eventually go back to the way they once were.

"My father was a highly skilled carpenter. My mother, a homemaker. I, their only child. As the war raged on, the situation in my country deteriorated quickly, and the German war machine demanded more and more from my people, both in terms of food production and military manpower. My parents did their best to shield me from the escalating tensions, but some of my earliest memories involve overhearing their terrified conversations after they put me to bed. Raids became common, and soon, members of our community began to disappear at alarming rates.

"One day, my mother and I were in the kitchen—I at the table, she at the sink—when my father burst through the front door in a frenzy. I remember the frantic look on his face as if it were yesterday," Winston recalled. "'*They're coming!*' he shouted in Dutch, grabbing hold of my arm and rushing me past my mother up into the loft.

"By that point, my parents had heard tales of Jews hiding in their attics and crawl spaces attempting to evade detection. Unfortunately, the Nazis had heard them as well, and my father knew if these men ever arrived at *our* house, they would certainly search these spaces immediately."

"'*You and Hendrik hide where I showed you!*' my father instructed my mother, who was now climbing the stairs to the loft with me. '*I'll go back downstairs and deal with the soldiers.*'"

"Who's Hendrik?" Frank wondered.

"Hendrik was my birth name," Winston revealed, before continuing. "You see, my father had constructed a hiding space under the floor of the loft, using scraps of wood from an old barn that had once stood on our property. We had practiced removing and replacing the floorboards countless times in the months leading up, should an event like this ever occur."

Frank imagined Winston as a small child crawling into the dusty hiding space and felt the young boy's helplessness in the pit of his stomach.

"I remember lying on my back, looking up at my mother as she placed her foot next to me. Suddenly, a fist began pounding heavily on the front door of the house, and she froze in place, struck with terror. Next came the angry shouting—demands for the door to be opened immediately. The men were hollering in German, and I could hear my father attempting to buy us more time. '*Just a minute!*' he responded in Dutch. '*One moment! I'm coming!*'

"Suddenly, the sounds of splintering wood filled the house, and my mother quickly withdrew her foot. I remember grabbing at the bottom of her dress, attempting to pull her back down into the hole, but it was no use.

"'*Where are the others!?*' the Nazi officer demanded of my father downstairs, stepping through the broken door and looking around the empty house. '*You have a wife and son. It says so right here!*' he referenced the census book in his hand. '*Bring them to me! Now!*'

"My mother dropped quietly onto her knees and leaned down into the crawl space," Winston explained. "At first, I believed she had reconsidered and was joining me inside, but when I felt a single tear fall onto my cheek, and she gently kissed my forehead, I knew what was coming next. She quickly pressed herself out of the cavity, placing a single finger in front of her lips, urging me to remain silent.

"I struggled against her attempts to replace the floorboards, but found my efforts were in vain. Once she had secured the last of the planks, I was fully concealed in darkness, wanting so badly to burst forth from the claustrophobic space to be with my parents, but my weakness and fear barred me from doing so.

"Eventually, my eyes adjusted to the blackness, allowing me to discover a small band of light coming from just behind my head. I turned myself over silently and lay face down, now able to see through the spaces between the ceiling boards and observe the scene below.

"My father was seated at the kitchen table as two German soldiers searched our house. Adjusting my position slightly, I could see the officer standing at the head of the table, spewing racial venom at my father as he continued to demand the whereabouts of his family members. My father acted as though he did not understand German, when in actuality, he spoke it quite fluently.

"Just then, much to my father's dismay, my mother descended the stairs from the loft, and the soldiers halted their frenzied search and set their weapons on her.

"'*You have news of my son!?'* she suddenly questioned the officer in our native tongue.

"'*Your son?'* the officer tilted his head suspiciously, apparently understanding our language. He motioned for his underlings to resume their search.

"'*Yes, my son, Hendrick! He has been missing for nearly two weeks now,'* my mother lied. '*My husband and I spoke with one of your men in town about it last week. You have found him, yes?'* She feigned a bit of excitement.

"'*To which of my men did you speak?'* his black eyes squinted.

"My mother looked over to my father, not missing a single beat in her charade. *'I am not sure what his name was. Can you remember, dear?'*

"My father shook his head morosely, going along with the ruse.

"'*He was a younger gentleman...*' my mother continued, '*perhaps eighteen or twenty. Oh, my Lord, we were in such a panic that day! I cannot seem to recall his name.*' Suddenly, my mother employed a more serious tone. '*Wait, have you not found my Hendrick, then?*' she questioned the unspeaking officer, prepared to ramp up her hysteria.

"The Nazi did not reply; instead, he motioned for his soldiers to go upstairs and search the loft, and my heart began to pound when I heard their boots clambering up the steps. Every muscle in my body tensed as my darkened chamber reverberated while the men above me searched. After a few moments, the soldiers stopped, and one of them shouted something in German down the stairs.

"'*It seems my men have found your little hiding spot,*' the officer announced to my parents, staring up at the ceiling. '*Call out your boy,*' he ordered them sternly. '*I've had enough of these games.*'

"'*I told you. Our Hendrick is missing,*' my mother responded defiantly.

"The Nazi stared at her, and I could see the rage percolating beneath the surface. He slowly reached his hand down, unclipped his holster, and removed his pistol, aiming it directly at my father's chest.

"'*Let me be perfectly clear with you,*' he threatened my mother now. '*When my two men remove those floorboards and find your...*' he set his census book on the table and flipped through his ledger, '*five-year-old son—or any others you may be hiding up there, for that matter—I am going to shoot your husband right where he sits. Do you understand me, you vile rat?*'

"My mother stood her ground," Winston recalled. "The officer shouted up his orders, resulting in the resumption of his soldier's frenzied activities above me. I closed my eyes and pressed my forehead into the board in front of my face, redoubling my breath-holding efforts, knowing that, at any moment, two pairs of war-torn hands would reach down and snatch me up from my hiding spot. Nails began to screech, and wood began to splinter as the soldiers ripped up the floor. I remember squeezing my eyelids together so tightly that my face ached.

"All at once, the commotion suddenly stopped, and it was replaced by a confused and hushed conversation. I heard one of the men shout something in German down to his officer, and when I finally mustered the courage to unseal my eyes, I found myself still surrounded by darkness."

"'*It seems as though you were telling the truth,*' the officer said to my mother, looking up at the ceiling with a crooked grin on his face. He lowered his pistol and ordered his men down from the loft. Eventually, they marched past him and out the front door of the house, shutting it behind them."

Frank leaned forward, fully engrossed in the tale. "They left you in your hiding space?" He didn't understand.

"No," Winston replied with a shake of the head. "My father, being the skilled carpenter that he was, had constructed a decoy chamber just next to where I was hiding," he revealed. "He had built it to be obvious and easy to find, playing directly into the Nazi ego."

The ingenuity impressed Frank, causing him to nod.

"I continued to observe the scene unfolding below," Winston continued. "'*We came today to relocate the remainder of your village to our labor camps,*' the officer explained to my parents, '*so that you can be of greater service to the Fuhrer's great war effort. However,*' the German seemed to be considering something in his mind, '*now that I've learned of your missing child, I certainly cannot ask you to abandon your house in such a trying time, can I?*' he suggested. '*Although it does make me wonder what kind of parents you are. Having a missing child, yet here you are at home in the middle of the day while your little boy is out there all alone? For two weeks, was it?*' he said in a mocking tone.

"I watched my mother's face tighten.

"'*I know if it was my son who was missing, I would be searching for him every waking minute of the day until he was found safe and sound,"* the Nazi passive-aggressively berated them. *'Perhaps it is possible that you people are even more pathetic than I imagined.'*

"My father attempted to explain their presence in the house by suggesting that there were many children in the community who were missing, and concerned parents were searching in shifts. He said that he and my mother had been out all night looking and had just returned home moments ago.

"The Nazi had heard enough, and he raised his gun, aiming at my mother.

"*'No! Please, let her go,'* my father said quickly. *'This is all my fault—you are right. I should be out there looking for my son. In fact, my wife begged me to do so; she begged me not to rest, but I came home instead. I've failed them both,'* my father lied, attempting to condemn himself and save my mother's life. *'Please, just let her go.'*

"I wanted to call out from the ceiling and reveal my presence, but I was paralyzed by fear," Winston said, his body tensing as he relived the moment in his mind. "Suddenly, he turned the gun on my father and two shots rang out in rapid succession, and I heard my mother scream. She leapt from her chair to where my father had fallen to the floor and frantically attempted to stop the bleeding from his chest. The Nazi approached her as she cradled my father on the floor, begging for him to wake up. That is when I saw the officer raise his pistol, and a third shot rang out. The crying stopped."

Frank winced, picturing the horrific scene in his mind.

"The bullet had entered through my mother's temple and blown out the opposite side of her skull, leaving her face fully intact. I watched her collapse to the floor with a hollow thud, and her lifeless green eyes stared up at me in the ceiling above," Winston remembered.

"Panic gripped me, and suddenly I felt as though I had no breath left to hold. My vision blurred as I watched the monster who had slaughtered my parents step over their lifeless bodies, and flick a speck of my mother's flesh off his lapel, as if it were no more significant than a biscuit crumb. He placed his weapon back into its holster and made his way to the door, whistling an ominous tune.

"Once he arrived, the man took hold of the doorknob, and suddenly, the whistling stopped. He turned around and took in all the destruction he had just caused, then slowly tilted his head up toward the ceiling, staring precisely at the spot where I was lying, and a malicious smile spread across his face. After a few agonizing moments, he resumed his whistling, turned around, and exited the house."

Frank sat wide-eyed. "How did you finally escape?"

"I remained in the ceiling for two more days, trying my best to avoid looking down at my parents' bodies, which were now being visited by hungry mice and rats. I continued to hear gunfire in the distance and decided that the men who killed my parents were doing the same to our neighbors.

"Eventually, my thirst grew so fierce that if I remained in place any longer, I feared I would die. So, I made my way downstairs to the sink and frantically consumed as much water as my belly would allow before making my way over to my parents to have a closer look. The putrid smell of their rotting corpses, combined with my lack of sustenance, caused me to become dizzy, and the room began to spin violently around me. I dropped to my knees next to my mother, and everything went black. The next thing I remember was waking up in the back of a military vehicle, surrounded by British soldiers."

"They had liberated your village?"

"Yes," Winston nodded. "And they explained to me that the story the Nazi had told my parents about the relocation of families to the labor camps was a fabrication. Instead, the Germans had been retreating and were simply attempting to exterminate as many of my people as they could before they left."

Frank felt at a loss for words. *What could anyone possibly say to a man who had endured such a horrifying ordeal as a child?*

"After that, I spent the remainder of my childhood transitioning from one Dutch orphanage to another," Winston continued. "Perhaps unsurprisingly, I became disruptive and argumentative, and as I reached my early teens, my attitude only worsened. You see, I harbored a deep hatred and resentment, not just toward the man who killed my parents, but also towards myself, for not being able to save them, for cowardly hiding in the ceiling as they died. I hated myself for doing nothing," shame plagued Winston's voice.

"You were just a little boy."

"Nevertheless," he replied, clearly still unwilling to fully accept the logical justification, "by the time I was fifteen, I had attempted suicide twice," he confessed, "and I had begun a long stretch in a juvenile detention center, continuing down my destructive path. However, one day, I was informed that I had visitors," Winston recalled. "When I walked into the room, I found two men waiting for me. They were both dressed in matching black suits and ties, and I didn't recognize either of them. I assumed they were just another pair of psychologists attempting to analyze me, like all the rest. But when the man on the left suddenly lit a cigarette, it triggered my memory and took me back to the day inside the military vehicle when I had woken up."

Frank thought for a moment. "He was one of the British soldiers who had found you in the house?"

Winston nodded.

"'*Do you remember me, Hendrick?*' the man with the cigarette asked me in broken Dutch as I slowly took my seat across the table. I nodded, unsure of what to make of the reunion. I looked to his partner, who sat stoically beside him, analyzing my every movement and mannerism.

"'*I have been informed by the staff that you speak English quite fluently,*' the man I recognized said in his native tongue. '*I hope you do not mind if we continue in that way, because as you can tell, my Dutch is not so good.*' He winked and grinned, tapping his cigarette on the edge of the table, sending ashes onto the floor below.

"*'Please allow me to introduce myself, my name is Malcolm Connelly, and this is my associate, Charles.'* He gestured towards his partner, who offered a quick nod. *'Do you think you might like to take a walk with us outside, Hendrick?'*

"*'I'm not exactly allowed to just leave—'* I tried to explain to him, but Malcolm stood up and cut me off with a wave of his cigarette. *'It's already been taken care of,'* he assured me. *'Come along now.'*

"I followed the pair to the rear of the detention center as guards seemed to appear out of nowhere to unlock doors for us that I hadn't even known existed. Eventually, we exited the building, made our way through the staff parking lot, and beyond the towering fence until we reached an area of secluded woods. Once inside the privacy of the snow-topped evergreens, Malcolm revealed that after the war, he had returned to his job with MI6, where he and Charles had been put in charge of forming a unit to take part in what he described as a *'highly confidential assignment.'*

"He began to probe my knowledge of events that followed the war, and in my typical defensive fashion, I told him that I had as much interest in remembering the war as I did in performing a ballet for him and Charles out there in the woods, certain my poor attitude would discourage any further inquiries into matters I wanted so fiercely to forget. To my surprise, my snide comment didn't seem to deter him at all. He pushed forward, asking if I had heard of the Nuremberg Trials. Sensing that his tenacity could not be easily foiled, I explained that I knew only what they had taught us in school—they were international trials involving Nazi leaders, with investigations into the war crimes they had perpetrated. Malcolm nodded, as if satisfied with my rudimentary explanation, and went on to tell me that the lawyers had discovered that many of the highest-ranking Nazi officers—some of the true architects of the Holocaust—had successfully escaped Europe before the war had ended, and that many of the men in the news—the ones the world believed to be the top brass—had had bosses of their own, who unfortunately were not able to be identified before the trials commenced. It was decided that a clandestine force would need to be created to locate all of those who had escaped justice."

Frank tried to comprehend the magnitude of the statement he had just heard. "Winston, are you suggesting that there were Nazis higher up the totem pole than Hitler?"

"No, no, of course not," Winston dismissed the notion. "Adolf Hitler was undoubtedly the man in charge; however, there was evidence to suggest that there were many more Eichmanns, Himmlers, and Gorings than the general population realized."

Frank nodded.

"Malcolm explained that back then, he and Charles were tasked with selecting the team responsible for tracking down these rogue entities. They were allowed to use whatever methods they deemed fit to bring these men to justice, but no arrests were to be made, no extraditions requested, and public trials were off the table."

"Search and destroy..." Frank said quietly.

"Naturally, I had to ask Malcolm why he had bothered coming to find me and tell me all of this. Was it out of pity for the child who had witnessed his parents' murder all those years ago? Did he believe that, because someone had tracked those men down, it would put my mind at ease? Perhaps he thought it would help me to straighten out my life?"

"What did he say?"

"As it turned out, these were not his intentions at all," Winston replied. "Rather, he explained that, since the inception of his program, the list of targets had hardly a dent in it. He and Charles believed this was due to the constant rigors of international travel and the need for his operatives to reside in foreign countries alone for weeks or months at a time, stalking targets and gathering intel. The men they had selected for their unit had families and commitments. They had already sacrificed so much during the war, and Malcolm began to feel it was unfair to ask them to continue to give up more of their lives. Additionally, all the participants had lengthy military service records, which hindered their ability to create successful aliases and remain undetected for long."

"But you didn't have any of that..." Frank realized.

Winston nodded. "I was young, foreign, and the only documentation of my existence since the war had been my confinement to the Dutch orphanages and detention houses. I had no friends, no family, no ties to society as a whole. Malcolm revealed that he had secretly been checking in on the little Jewish boy he had rescued all those years ago, and when he discovered that I had attempted to take my own life, he began to develop the idea of making me an asset for his government."

"And his superiors agreed?"

"Not at all," Winston admitted. "As you can imagine, tales of my mental instability and hatred toward authority were of immediate concern. Nothing about me appealed to any of them, but Malcolm saw something in me. He accepted full responsibility should anything go wrong."

"And what did *you* think about all this?"

"I know it sounds mad, Frank, but for the first time since my parents were taken from me, I suddenly felt as if I was being given a purpose in life again."

Frank nodded.

"I'm not exactly sure what Malcolm and Charles had done to get me released from that detention center that day, but the moment I agreed to their offer, a car suddenly appeared in those woods, and we were taken to a private air strip, where we all boarded a small plane.

"Once we were in the air, my training commenced immediately," Winston remembered. "Malcolm had me recite my new name over and over and over again, explaining that, once we set foot on English soil, Hendrick would no longer exist. The records at the detention center would show that *that* boy had indeed been successful in taking his life. From now on, I would be known as...James."

Frank's eyebrows sank.

"I'll get to that," Winston assured him. "Over the next three years, I spent every waking moment training to acquire the skills I would need for my new life. I was given extremely limited contact with the outside world as Malcolm sculpted me into a finely tuned machine. Eventually, when my handlers believed I was ready for field work, they placed me with a surveillance unit. Once I proved myself competent with them, I was assigned my first solo mark."

"Where?"

"Most of the escaped Nazis had scattered themselves throughout Central and South America," Winston revealed. "My first target lived in Nicaragua. Of course, I was slow at first, but as my mark count began to increase, so did my proficiency. Soon, I could cross borders like a ghost, slipping in and out of communities without being noticed. Months turned into years, years into decades, all fueled by flashbacks of my parents' murder. Hatred drove me to eradicate every person responsible for the atrocities that happened to my people, and eventually I even tracked down the man who had killed my mother and father."

"He had escaped as well?"

"Yes. He had fled Europe a few weeks before the war ended," Winston nodded. "By the time I found him, he was in his seventies, living in a small fishing village in Ecuador. I watched him for some time. Stalking him like a predator, feeling as if my entire existence had culminated in this one point in time. When I was ready, I silently extracted him from his home and brought him deep into the jungle. I explained to him who I was and recounted every detail of what I had witnessed from my hiding spot in the ceiling all those years ago."

"What did he say?"

Winston paused.

"Perhaps *that* part of the story might be best saved for another time..." he suggested. "I think what is important is that I tell you exactly what I felt after I took that man's life."

Frank leaned in.

"Nothing."

"What do you mean, *nothing?*"

"Killing that man didn't bring my parents back," Winston explained. "And it certainly didn't fill the void that their absence had created inside of me." He leaned back in his chair. "You see, Frank, in all that time between their murders and my missions, I had never taken a single solitary moment to consider how I would feel once it was done."

"Do you regret killing him?"

"No," Winston replied honestly and without hesitation. "That man needed to die for what he had done all those years ago. There was no doubt about that. But I came to realize something that day. I realized that I had allowed this man to not only take the lives of both my parents, but mine as well. I was nearly forty years old by that point and had never taken the opportunity to become close to anyone. I never pursued a relationship. Never had a child. None of it.

"Naturally, I did my best to bury these intrusive thoughts and move on to my next mark. But with my mind not fully engaged, I became sloppy and careless. Before I knew it, I botched a job, and my face was captured on surveillance video and broadcast globally, resulting in an international warrant. And because I was working outside any official agency, I had no protection if apprehended. Luckily, I was able to get myself back to London.

"After lying low in the city for a few days, I eventually met with Malcolm in secret. He was nearing the end of his career by that time and explained that he had pulled some strings to get me into a top-secret government program that had been established decades earlier between a few of the allied nations. In this program, compromised operatives could undergo facial reconstruction surgery and minor body-altering procedures to change their appearance. Following the operation, they were hired by one of the participating nations' government agencies, where they would be trained for a position to live out the remainder of their lives in anonymity. Of course, it was fully understood that if any of us broke the secrecy and sanctity of the program, we would be eliminated immediately."

"That's how you ended up with the FBI," Frank reasoned.

Winston nodded. "And that is when my name changed for a second time."

A look of seriousness washed over Frank's face as he pieced together the connection between Winston's story of vengeance and his own.

"Listen," Frank said flatly, "I understand what you are trying to say, Winston, but I can't just move on from what happened to those girls. Especially because I know it's still going on. I understand that killing that man didn't give you the closure you hoped it might, but at least—"

"I'm not suggesting you simply move on," Winston stopped him. "What I *am* suggesting is that you figure out your endgame. Decide what needs to be done, and once you've accomplished it, stop there. Because if you can't do that, you *will* lose your family, Frank. And trust me, nothing is worth that. Do you understand?"

"I do, but let's be honest here." Frank felt agitation rising inside himself again. "I've covered every single angle of this thing. Investigated every lead. And I've completely stalled." He slapped his palm on the top of the table, sending a couple of the photographs helicoptering off the edge. "Sara was drugged. Marla was raped and murdered. And Sofia blew her fucking brains out because she *knew* that American girls were coming to take her place in that house!" Frank raised his voice. "There's more of them chained to beds down there right now! I just know it! My *endgame* is to eliminate whoever is at the very top of this trafficking ring. Once that's done, I'm out. But, as you can tell, I can't even seem to figure out where to fucking start anymore!"

Winston looked over to the window into the darkness of the night and exhaled. "Frank, although it violated every condition of my program, I reached out to some of my former contacts from my tracking days. As you can imagine, most of them have passed away by now, but I was successful in reaching an individual with whom I used to share information regularly. This man sent me something tonight, and I believe it may be of value to you."

"Go on."

"I received an audio recording," Winston explained. "It's from a few years back, but it features a man from here in New York attempting to traffic females to an unknown source down in Mexico."

"And you have this recording on you?"

"I do."

"What the fuck are we waiting for?" Frank raised an eyebrow.

"I have one caveat, Frank. If I grant you access to this intel, you must sober up and get a proper night's rest before you act on it. Because this impulsive, reckless, cowboy rubbish you've been engaging in since you returned from Mexico is beneath you."

"Fine," Frank agreed quickly.

Winston removed a small black recording device from his pocket, set it on the table and pressed play. A scratchy recording was projected from the speaker.

'How much we scorin' for Americans across the pond now?' a man on the recording asked.

'I don't know anything about that,' came a response in a muffled baritone, distorted by some sort of voice-modulating equipment.

'Oh, come on now, don't play with me, homie,' the first man countered. *'Someone told me you was the man to call. I want in! I got good connections up here in New York, man. I can send you whatever you need—blondes, brunettes, short, tall, skinny, fat, you name it! Shit! I'll even split the money wit you.'*

"Turn it up," Frank requested.

Winston complied, and the recording continued.

'I have no idea,' the second man stonewalled again.

'Yeah, yeah, ok, fine. Maybe you don't, but you gotta at least know who I could talk to.'

'*Listen,*' said the distorted voice bluntly, '*even if I did know—which I don't—why would I ever discuss it with someone I don't even know? Besides, now is not—*'

'*That's right you don't know me, G! If you did, you'd know this ain't my first rodeo, bro. I been helpin' sell bitches to these motherfuckers for years! Shippin' that prime-ass pussy all over the world! You can trust me, bro, you don't have to w—*'

The recording ended abruptly.

Frank picked up the device, looking as though he wanted to shake more information out of it. "Is that it?" he asked, setting it back down on the table. "Who the fuck are these guys?"

"Obviously, voice analysis could not be used on the man using the distortion device, but I was able to get a hit on the man from New York."

"Who is he?"

"His name is Adrian Jackson."

Frank ran the name through his memory bank. It sounded familiar.

"You've heard of him?"

"Wait a minute..." Frank said quietly, standing and quickly disappearing into the bedroom. Moments later, he reemerged with a laptop and set it down on the table. Winston made his way around to the other side to view the screen. Frank logged in to the FBI database using Mike's credentials. "They revoked my access during my suspension," he explained to Winston, as the program loaded. "What did you say that guy's name was again?"

"Adrian Jackson."

Frank entered the name into the search box, which quickly populated a digital file including mugshots, a rap sheet, and other personal information.

"That piece of shit," Frank said the moment he laid eyes on the gangster.

"You know this man?"

"Yeah, Mike and I dealt with him years ago. He's a wholesale drug dealer with ties to one of the Mexican cartels, but I haven't heard his name in years. I don't think we ever had enough on him to put him away for selling narcotics, but I think he did a short stint for a couple of vicious assaults." Frank confirmed this with the information on the screen next to the African American's mug shot.

"Do you think he might have connections to human trafficking?"

Frank didn't respond; instead, he jotted down Jackson's last known address onto a scrap of paper.

"Frank..." Winston said wearily after Frank had stuffed the note into his pocket. "You said you'd wait until morning and do this thing properly, remember?"

Frank walked over to the kitchen counter and retrieved his truck keys and gun from the cupboard. "I'm sorry, Winston," he apologized, moving toward the door.

Winston stepped directly in his path. "You're in no condition to take on something like this tonight, Frank. You need clarity of mind."

Frank stopped short of Winston. The gun hung down next to his thigh.

"Winston, I appreciate what you've brought me tonight, but I'm walking out that door, so please, just step aside." Frank placed his hand on Winston's upper arm to gently guide him aside. In a flash, Winston grabbed Frank's wrist and tugged him forward, off-balancing him. He then brought his right leg behind Frank's left, curling his heel into the back of Frank's leg, dropping him onto one knee. Caught off guard by the surprise take-down, Frank attempted to wrap an arm around Winston's waist, but Winston countered with a perfectly aimed chop to Frank's throat. While Frank hacked and coughed, Winston effortlessly extracted the gun from his grip, removed the clip, expertly cleared the chamber, and set the toothless weapon onto the table. He then recovered Frank's truck keys from where they had fallen onto the floor.

"I'm sorry I had to do that, Frank," Winston apologized, taking a step back. "Hopefully, that is enough of a wake-up call for you to realize that you are in no condition to leave this cabin tonight. I'll return your keys in the morning," he said, before turning around and disappearing through the door into the darkness of the night.

Frank slowly rose to his feet and made his way into the bedroom. He pulled open the top drawer of his dresser and pushed aside a mess of crudely folded t-shirts to reveal a black .38 caliber handgun. Removing it from its resting place, he tucked it behind his back. Next, he retrieved a metal clothes hanger from the closet and abandoned the bedroom. As he passed the table, he pocketed the recording device.

Once outside, Frank approached his truck and jammed the straightened coat hanger into the driver's side window, quickly unlocking the mechanism inside. After opening the door, he reached a hand beneath the steering wheel and tore open the console, revealing a tangle of colorful wires. Frank located, cut, and exposed two, and then touched them together. Like a startled stallion, the truck's engine suddenly roared to life. Frank jumped inside, pulled the door closed, and left a spray of crushed gravel in his wake as he peeled away from the cabin.

CHAPTER thirty-three

The front tire of Frank's truck clipped the curb as he attempted to park a half block back from Adrian Jackson's last known address. Leaning forward, Frank peered through the windshield to gain a better view of the gloomy, low-income, high-rise building down the street. The decrepit structure towered over its neighbors, and Frank felt his palms tighten on the steering wheel as he focused his attention on the twelfth floor.

After gathering a few items from the back seat, he climbed out of the vehicle, checked his watch, and discovered it was nearly two in the morning. The surrounding streets were deserted and filthy, strewn with abandoned sleeping bags and ragged make-shift tents of the drug-addicted homeless population, most of whom were out wandering back alleys, looking to score their next fix. Frank had his gun concealed behind his back and kept his head on a swivel as he walked down the deteriorating sidewalk toward the concrete building. Upon arrival, he found the front doors unlocked. This was unsurprising, as there was likely very little of value inside to steal, and most of the neighborhood's worst criminals were tenants anyhow. Frank pulled open the rust-hinged door and stepped inside.

The interior of the building was just as dank and grimy as the outside. Frank climbed six embrittled rubber-topped steps and entered a vacant foyer, where every wall was tagged with brightly colored graffiti. To his left stood an elevator that looked like it hadn't been serviced in decades. Straight ahead was a tempered glass door featuring a bulls-eye crack that was created by a resident who had tested its durability during a drug-induced psychosis. Frank made his way past the lift and looked through the damaged door, discovering a staircase littered with trash and recently used drug paraphernalia.

Frank backtracked to the elevator and called the car from a few floors above, setting off a cacophony of jarring mechanical reverberations inside the shaft. He took one final look around the lobby as he waited. A few seconds later, the doors spasmed open, and Frank stepped inside. The panel displayed a total of fifteen floors. Frank selected the twelfth. After a short delay, the doors shuddered closed, and the elevator began its vertical climb.

Just as the lift had finally picked up a bit of speed, it began to slow, eventually settling on the seventh floor. On the other side of the doors, Frank could now hear a muffled conversation taking place. After a moment, the doors opened in front of Frank, revealing two thuggish-looking males in their early twenties. The man on the left was white, his companion Latino, and both were wearing bandanas, tank tops, low-riding sweatpants, and colorful sneakers. Frank stood silently inside the elevator as their animated conversation continued. Suddenly, the banger on the right noticed Frank and directed his partner's attention to the stranger inside the lift. He, too, stopped talking, and all three men stared at each other for a long, awkward moment.

"Goin' down, homes?" the brown-skinned gangster spoke up.

"No. Up," Frank replied evenly.

The elevator doors began to close, and Frank felt a sense of relief. The last thing he needed was to have any unnecessary interactions with other residents tonight—people who could identify him if things got messy inside Jackson's apartment. The doors had nearly sealed themselves when a bony, tattooed hand appeared through the crack, halting their progress and sending them back open.

"Yo, don't we need to go upstairs to see Joey?" the white guy questioned his friend, flashing him a subtle look.

A conspicuous grin formed on his partner's face. "For sure," he replied.

The two young men stepped inside the elevator and took up positions on either side of Frank, who maintained his muted expression and stared straight ahead. He reached a hand toward the panel. "What floor?" he asked.

Receiving no response, Frank withdrew his hand, and the doors closed slowly. Moments later, the elevator resumed its ascent.

8... 9... 10...

The gangster to Frank's right suddenly reached out and activated the *EMERGENCY STOP* button, triggering a loud buzzing sound and bringing the elevator to an abrupt halt, suspended somewhere between the tenth and eleventh floors.

A frustrated exhalation escaped Frank's lungs.

"Listen, homes," said the hoodlum to Frank's right, turning towards him and pulling out a switchblade. He sprung the hardened steel into action. "Cough up your wallet, your phone, and whatever else you got on you," he ordered the big man, holding the weapon out just far enough that it was visible in Frank's periphery.

Frank tilted his chin up toward the ceiling to ensure there were no security cameras present.

"What? You don't hear good, *bitch*!?" the other guy suddenly chimed in, turning aggressively and barking directly into Frank's ear.

Frank, who had six inches and well over a hundred pounds on him, slowly turned his head to face him.

"Oh, you got something to say motherfucker?!" the rail-thin hooligan continued. "You're about to get cut the fuc—"

Without warning, Frank cocked his head back and drove his forehead directly into the bridge of the gangster's nose, pulverizing it into a stew of blood and cartilage. Caught off guard, his knife-wielding partner hesitated, allowing Frank time to spin around and face him. The armed man sprang into action and lunged the blade towards

Frank's stomach. Frank encircled his wrist and redirected the shank, plunging it into his partner's bony thigh, causing broken nose groans to transition into a high-pitched squeal as the blade twisted between the man's spindly quadriceps.

Frank delivered a vicious elbow across the armed man's wrist, fracturing bones and sending him down to his knees. Frank pulled the blade from the other man's thigh, causing bright red blood to spurt across his cheek and shoulder. Next, he sent a well-placed kick into the side of the man's knee, dropping him to the floor next to his partner.

Frank reached out calmly and deactivated the *EMERGENCY STOP* button on the panel, allowing the elevator to resume its ascent while the two thugs writhed in pain on the floor.

The elevator opened onto the twelfth floor, and before Frank stepped out, he selected the *LOBBY* button and deactivated the switchblade.

"Shouldn't play with knives, boys..." Frank advised the two punks, tossing the weapon on the floor between them. The doors slid shut.

Frank made his way down the gloomy hallway, fishing the crumpled scrap of paper out of his pocket to reconfirm Adrian Jackson's apartment number. *"1216,"* he read to himself as the numbers on each passing door increased in value—odds on the left, evens on the right. Eventually, he arrived at the second-to-last apartment and placed his ear against the door's peeling white paint, listening for sounds inside. Hearing only the low hum of a fan, he withdrew his cheek, leaving a smear of fresh blood on its surface.

Frank retrieved the lock-picking kit he had procured from his truck and began to operate. After a few unsuccessful attempts, he rubbed his face with the palm of his hand, trying to sober his mind for the intricate procedure. His next attempt was successful, and the deadbolt finally gave way. He replaced his tools and slowly opened the door into the darkness.

Stepping inside, Frank made his way past a small kitchenette on his left and a coat closet on his right. Peering around a corner, he discovered a small living room illuminated by the moonlight streaming through a sliding glass door that led to a rusted fire escape. Surveying the space, he saw only a worn-out brown vinyl recliner, an outdated television set with a gaming console, and a glass coffee table cluttered with magazines, cardboard take-out containers, vape pens, and dirty dishes. Glancing to his right, Frank saw a dark hallway with two closed doors that he imagined to be bedrooms. At the end of the hall was a three-piece bathroom.

Frank abandoned the living room and crept down the hall, shifting his focus from one door to the other. *Left is always right,* he thought to himself—a motto his Marine unit had come up with overseas when they were forced to make a coin-flip decision. Arriving at the door, he pushed it inward, creating just enough space for himself to step inside. The room was completely bathed in blackness, and Frank could only make out the silhouette of a bed and a nightstand on the far wall. As he approached, he saw what looked to be a lumpy, disheveled comforter, which made it impossible to tell if someone was sleeping underneath. Frank listened for any signs of life—a snore, a sneeze, a breath—but heard nothing. He slowly reached out and gripped the comforter, placing his other hand on his gun behind his back. Frank tore the blankets off the mattress and sent them sailing onto the ground behind him.

The bed was empty.

Suddenly, a blinding deluge of bright white light filled the room. Frank spun around to face the door, his eyes blinking furiously, attempting to restore his compromised vision. Just then, he heard pounding footsteps coming towards him. Frank attempted to pull his gun but was struck on the arm with a wooden implement, causing him to lose his grip, and the weapon fell to the floor. Frank crashed onto the bed, and his eyes adjusted enough for him to see Adrian Jackson standing above him, holding a baseball bat in his hands.

"You broke into the wrong crib, motherfucker!" Jackson hollered at the unidentified nighttime intruder. He tightened his grip and took another swing. Frank managed to painfully deflect the blow with his forearm, off-balancing Jackson, who was forced to readjust his footing before taking another swing. Frank grabbed an ugly purple lamp from the nightstand and hurled it at his attacker's face, shattering into a thousand pieces and opening a small cut just below his left eye. The bat fell to the floor with a *rattle*.

Shaking off the blow, Adrian charged at Frank, who had only just managed to push himself off the mattress. Jackson wrapped his arms around Frank's waist but was quickly overpowered by the larger man, who threw him into the nightstand, which crashed to the floor, sending a blizzard of knick-knacks into the air. The two combatants locked up in a bear hug and began to spin in pirouettes, exchanging body blows and crashing into the walls.

The pair flew out into the dimly lit hallway. In a moment of separation, Adrian shoved Frank in the chest, sending him reeling backward into the bathroom. Adrian charged forward like an angry bull, and Frank hooked his foot around the edge of the door, booting it directly into Adrian's incoming face, but the flimsy wood did little to impede his forward progress. He drove his shoulder into Frank's ribcage, and they crashed into the bathtub, pulling the shower curtain on top of themselves in the process.

Frank now found himself lying on top of Jackson with his legs dangling over the edge of the tub. He attempted to extricate himself, but before he made it out, Adrian wrapped the mildewed shower curtain around his neck with both hands, cutting off his oxygen supply. He pulled Frank back into the basin, while Frank clawed at the plastic noose, searching for an opening to slip a finger through, but found none.

"Sweet dreams, motherfucker!" Adrian said, tightening his grip.

Suddenly, Frank felt a surge of adrenaline, and his hands abandoned the shower curtain and gripped onto the edge of the tub.

He began to force his neck deeper into the vinyl choke, slowly pulling himself upward, hauling Adrian out of the basin. Jackson struggled ferociously, squeezing, twisting, turning, but nothing seemed to help. Frank eventually reached a standing position on the linoleum, and Adrian planted his feet onto the tub's edge. Just then, Jackson locked eyes with the red-eyed beast in the mirror across the room. He attempted to reposition his failing grip, which only succeeded in giving the big man an opportunity to slip his hands under the shower curtain. Frank filled his lungs with air.

"Sweet dreams, motherfucker..." Frank parroted back to Adrian ominously in the reflection.

Frank dove forward and catapulted Adrian over his shoulders, causing him to soar through the air until his forehead smashed through the leading edge of the cream-colored sink across the room, shattering it into pieces.

Frank rose to his feet and looked down at the now-unconscious gangster in front of him.

* * * * *

Adrian's eyes opened slowly and adjusted to the now brightly lit bathroom. His back was propped against the side of the bathtub as he touched the blood-engorged goose egg protruding from his forehead gingerly with his fingertips.

"How long have you been involved in sex trafficking with the Mexicans?" came a voice.

Jackson's head snapped to the left, and he discovered Frank standing next to the toilet, gun in hand.

"*Adler?*" Adrian finally recognized the identity of his nighttime intruder in the newfound light. "The fuck you doin' here?"

Frank stepped forward and pressed the tip of the gun directly into the swollen wound.

"Fuuuuuck! Jesus Christ! Okay! Okay!" Adrian hollered in submission, recoiling from the pain. "I don't got nothin' to do with any shit like that!"

"Oh, is that a fact?" Frank said, unbelieving.

"Yeah, *actually,* it is, motherfucker!" Adrian snapped back.

Frank removed Winston's audio device from his pocket. "Then explain this..."

Adrian squinted curiously at the black recorder in Frank's hand, wiping away the dried blood from the small cut on his cheek from the lamp. The recording began to play.

'I got good connections up here in New York, man.' Jackson's eyes widened when he recognized the voice on the tape as his own. *'I can send you whatever you need—blondes, brunettes, short, tall, skinny, fat, you name it! Shit! I'll even split the money wit you.'*

Frank fast-forwarded the recording a little.

'That's right, you don't know me, G!' The audio continued. *'If you did, you'd know this ain't my first rodeo, bro. I been helpin' sell bitches to these motherfuckers for years! Shippin' that prime-ass pussy all over the world!'*

Frank stopped the tape.

"Where the fuck you get that?" Adrian demanded immediately, concern in his voice.

"Start talking," Frank demanded. "Or else I'm going to the kitchen for a steak knife, and when I get back, I'll start removing fingers, one by one."

"Listen, bro. It's not what you think."

"Bullshit!" Frank charged. "It's exactly what I think!"

"Nah, man." Adrian shook his head, looking down at the grungy floor mat between his legs. "*I'm* the one who made that recordin'," he explained. "Years ago..."

A look of bewilderment spread across Frank's face. *Why would Adrian have made such an incriminating recording?* It made no sense.

"Listen, man, I never set out for this fuckin' life," Adrian exhaled. "I wasn't tryin' to get involved with no gangs, and fuckin' Mexican cartels, and all this bullshit. But ten years back, when I was like thirteen or whatever, some crackhead broke into my parents' crib, plannin' to rob our asses. Hell, we was poor as fuck. We didn't have nothin' to steal," Adrian explained. "Once that tweaker figured it out, he freaked out and got violent with my pops, started smackin' him around, and before I knew it, them two was in a wrestlin' match, and my mom was screamin', tryin' to break them up. That's when the gun went off..." Adrian slapped a hand on the top of his knee, mimicking the sound.

"Once that crackhead saw what he had done, he musta figured it was best to just kill the rest of us, you know, to make sure he didn't leave no witnesses or whatever. So, he shot up my pops next, and I remember runnin' toward my bedroom. That's when he got me in the back." Adrian moved one of the straps on his tank top, revealing an ugly, circular scar on his chest. "Bullet went straight through me. Dropped my ass to the floor, and I remember flippin' over onto my back and just strugglin' for breath. Well, that crack head walked over, stood above me, and just started pullin' the trigger, again and again. But he didn't have no more bullets left." Jackson shook his head. "So, he bailed out the door. After that, it was just me and my lil sister, Tish. She was like ten at the time."

Frank stared, his eyes still full of hatred, but he needed to ask. "Where was she during all this?"

"Sleepin' over at a friend's house," Adrian recalled. "Not long after the murders, the two of us got sent to live with my aunt. Hell, she did the best she could, but right away, I started hangin' out with the wrong crowd, stealin' bikes, doing whatever petty shit I could to provide for me and Tish. Before I knew it, The Wraith was recruitin' my ass," Adrian said, referring to a well-known local gang. "I just started as a lookout, tryin' to get myself some protection 'round the hood, but I was young and stupid, and before I knew it, they owned my ass," Adrian admitted. "But even at that age, I knew one thing for sure: make sure my little sis didn't know *nothin'* bout what I was doin'.

"So, five or six years went by, and I started makin' a bit a coin, you know, just enough for me and Tish to rent a little place of our own. Of course, I kept on shieldin' her from my world, makin' sure I was home in the mornin' to make her breakfast, and back in the evenin' to help her with her homework. Then, I'd slip out when she was in school, or at night, after she went to bed, to do what I had to. I guess I figured, so long as *she* had a shot at makin' something of her life, then it was all worth it, y'know?"

Frank didn't respond, but he understood.

"So, anyway, it was about that time when all the crews around here started gettin', uh," Adrian paused, as if searching for a word, "what do you call it, like when they put a whole bunch of things together?"

"An amalgamation?"

"Yeah, yeah, exactly," Adrian nodded. "Anyway, the Mexican cartel started snatchin' up everythin' they could around here—blacks, whites, whatever. They didn't give a fuck. And anybody who didn't get on board wound up dead. They even killed a bunch of the Wraith generals above me at that time, and suddenly, all my duties changed. Now, I'm bein' sent all over the country. Atlanta. Houston. Miami. Wherever. Doin' pick-ups. Drop-offs. You name it, bro."

Frank knew these locations were some of the most important narcotics distribution points for the cartels.

"So, I'd be gone for two or three days at a time, sometimes a week. And with my ass away, Tish started hangin' with some of my boys behind my back. I'm talkin' about *motherfuckers* on my own damn crew, man," Adrian said angrily. "These guys got her ass into all kinds of shit, partyin', drugs, all the things I had protected her from for all those years. By the time I finally clued in to what was goin' on, she was so deep into her addiction that I couldn't pull her out." Jackson shook his head. "One night, I just snapped, and I found a couple of the guys that were dealin' her, and I put one dude into a coma. The other, I broke his legs."

"That's when you did your stretch in prison," Frank recalled from his rap sheet on the laptop.

"Yeah, man..." Adrian confirmed with a nod. "But like any addict, Tish got pissed off at me, 'cause I had fucked up her source. So, while I was in the can, she packed up all her shit and took off."

"To where?"

"The first time I found her, she was passed out on some couch in a crack house six blocks down. The next time, it was a back alley. She was always strung out to shit when I'd find her, and things were only getting worse. I begged her to stop, bro. I begged her to get clean."

Frank could see the pain in Adrian's eyes.

"I told her that if she just went to rehab, I would ditch all the gangster shit, and we could disappear together. It would be just like old times again," Adrian remembered. "But she didn't stop. And one day—when I hadn't seen her for a week or two—I got a call from the hospital saying she had OD'd real bad and was brought in. When I went to see her, she *finally* agreed to get help. Fuck, bro, I thought we was in the clear. I told her I just needed to head out of town for two days, and when I got back, we'd bail. I remember bringin' her home from the hospital and tellin' her I'd see her Sunday. She smiled at me and said she'd be there when I got back. So, I left to do my thing. But, when I got back to town, she was gone, 'cept all her shit was still here—purse, clothes, cash, everything. And there was no note or nothin'," Adrian explained. "So, I went out searchin' for her again, checkin' all her usual spots, askin' around, but nobody had seen her anywhere this time. It was like she just straight up vanished off the face of the earth.

"So, almost six months goes by, and I suddenly get a call from the police, and honestly, I'd been expectin' it for a long time by that point," Adrian admitted. "I figured it was only a matter of time until someone found her body in a ditch somewhere. But the cops on the phone told me they had gotten a call from Albania."

"Albania?"

"Yeah, bro, one of them big metal sea container things, you know, like the ones you see down at the docks, I guess it had washed up on the shore on a beach somewhere over there, and once they cracked it open, they found it was full of dead bodies, all bloated and shit. They figured everybody inside must have been in there for a while."

Frank recalled reading something similar that had come across the wire years before at work. The authorities had never figured out who that shipping container belonged to or where it was headed.

"Because all the bodies were young girls between the ages of like fifteen and thirty, the Albanians figured it was probably part of a sex traffickin' operation or somethin'," Adrian continued. "Most were unidentifiable because they'd been floatin' around in the ocean for a while, but my sister had this big memorial tattoo for our parents on her back, with their names and the date they were killed and all that, so the Albanians looked on the internet and found an old news article about the murders back in the day, and they contacted the police over here."

"Why would your sister have been in that container?"

"At the time, I had no idea."

"And how does any of this explain why *you're* on a recording, saying you want to sell girls overseas?"

"I'm getting to that," Jackson assured him. "So, after I hear all this shit from the cops, I start checkin' round again. Tryin' to find anybody who might have connections with that sort of shit, but nobody seemed to know nothin', except this one cat who said the cartel we worked for had recently put out a standin' order that nobody was allowed to be involved with human traffickin' up here in the States no more."

"Because of the ongoing international investigation looking into that container..." Frank pieced it together.

"That's exactly what I thought," Adrian nodded. "So, I kept diggin', and some guy named Tony G kept comin' up and I found out he had just started a long stretch up at Rikers."

"What was he in for?"

"Got pinched for a murder two, I think."

"And how was he connected to all this?"

"Apparently, he had been the point man for all that type of shit comin' out of New York at one point."

"Human trafficking, you mean?"

Adrian nodded.

"And you went to see him?"

"Yeah, man."

"And?"

"When I met up with him in prison, I made up a story just like what you hear on that recordin'. I told him I had connections for girls in the city here, and I wanted to know how to move them. Shit, I knew it was weak, but it was the only thing I could come up with at the time to try to get answers about Tish."

"And what did this Tony guy tell you?"

"At first, the problem was, I didn't know this motherfucker from a hole in the ground—other than we happened to work under the same cartel. But once I got him talkin', I realized he was the kinda cat that just loved hearin' himself jaw. Soon enough, he admitted that big dogs down south had shut everything down up here and put a zero-tolerance policy on any traffickin' going forward. Right before I left, he told me about a guy in Mexico called *Scorpio*, who had been his contact before he went inside. He said I could give him a call, but he was pretty sure this guy would just tell me the same shit. Soon as I got home, I grabbed a tape recorder and called him, figurin' if this Scorpio guy told me somethin' different, at least I'd have it on tape. I dunno how the fuck *you* ended up with the recordin', though, because I deleted that shit the second he shut me down."

Frank had no intention of shedding any light on that mystery.

"A couple nights after I made the phone call, I got jumped by a couple motherfuckers in a back alley, just over there." Adrian pointed at the eastern wall of the bathroom. "They knocked me out cold and musta drugged me, 'cause the next thing I knew, I woke up in fuckin' Mexico, bro."

"How did they get you across the border?"

Adrian's eyebrows sank. "Are you kiddin' me, Adler? *You,* of all people, should know, if these people want somethin' across the border, it's fuckin' happenin'."

Frank knew it was true.

"Anyway, I woke up in some dark-ass motel room, with my head throbbin', and some big-ass Mexican dude is guardin' the door. As my vision starts to clear, and I see these two guys sittin' at the table behind me, smoking cigars," Adrian remembered. "One of them gets up and walks over, and I realize it's *Dennis fuckin' Diaz,* bro," he said menacingly, as if talking about the devil himself. "He starts threatenin' me, calling me a rat piece of shit, a spy, all this and that, and sticks a gun right in my grill. I figured that was it, bro. That's when the other guy, the one still sittin' at the table, tells him to put it down."

"Ernesto..."

"In the fucking flesh!" Adrian confirmed. "Now, you gotta understand somethin', Adler—these two motherfuckers are like myths to guys like me. Yeah, we all know they exist, sure, but it would be like wakin' up in the same room as the fuckin' President or some shit, knowadda mean? That kinda thing just doesn't happen."

"What did the Diaz brothers want with *you?*"

"Ernesto started askin' me about my duties up here in New York and bout some of the cats on my crew," Adrian explained. "I figured he was tryin' to find out exactly who I had talked to about the traffickin' shit."

"It probably got back to him that you were at Rikers asking questions," Frank suggested.

"My guess is that Scorpio guy probably ratted me out the second I hung up the phone."

"Did Diaz ever admit he was involved in human trafficking?"

"Nah, man," Adrian shook his head. "He ain't fucking stupid, bro. I think, at first, he thought I was workin' with you Feds or somethin', so they brought me down to Mexico to find out exactly what I had told y'all before makin' me disappear."

"How did you convince him otherwise?"

"I told him the truth..." Adrian looked Frank straight in the eyes. "I told him exactly what happened to my sister—that some of my boys had gotten her all fucked up on drugs behind my back, and when I tried to get her clean, she ended up in that shippin' container halfway around the damn world. I said I was just tryin' to figure out what had happened to her."

"And what did he have to say about that?"

"At first, he didn't say nothing for a really long time. He just stood there, starin' at me," Adrian recalled. "Then, suddenly, he told Dennis and the other guy to leave the room."

"You were alone with Ernesto Diaz?"

"Yeah, man, and after his boys had bounced, he had me come sit down with him at the table," Adrian explained. "He told me that family was the most important thing in the world and that what had happened to my sister was unacceptable. He said that what I had heard about the cartels forbiddin' that kinda shit up in the States was true and told me that he would have his people look into who was responsible for Tish windin' up in that container. He promised that whoever was involved would be dealt with."

"And you believed him?"

"At the time, I didn't know what to believe, but by the time I got home, two of the guys I had questioned earlier were dead. And I was told they was the ones responsible."

"So, then what?"

Adrian exhaled regretfully. "That's basically where it all ended."

Frank stared at him with contempt. "So, you just gave up? You think those two guys were the only ones involved in what happened to your sister?"

Adrian's face tensed. "Hey, fuck you, Adler! You think I just wanted to stop lookin' for answers and let it go?" He raised his voice. "I knew, if I kept pushin', I'd be right there in the ground next to her. And what fuckin' good would that have done? It sure as hell wasn't going to bring her back! So yeah, I figured at least they had gotten two of the guys responsible, and if there were no more shippin' containers in the future—"

Frank shook his head.

"Okay! Yeah, fine, I fuckin' sold out!" Adrian shouted. "Is that what you want to hear from me? You think that shit doesn't eat me up every fuckin' day?"

Suddenly, the squawk of a police radio came from the hallway outside the apartment. *"Car 29, do you need another unit assigned to your location?"* asked a police dispatcher.

Frank's head snapped to attention, and he stared down the hallway.

Adrian studied his face. "Yo, wait a minute. They ain't wit you, are they, Adler?"

"Quiet," Frank ordered.

Adrian pulled himself up onto the edge of the tub. "What kinda trouble you got yourself in?"

"Enough!" Frank pointed the gun at his head.

"Oh, you gunna shoot my ass?" He challenged Frank. "With the police outside? Nah, I don't think so," he called his bluff.

"Looks like there's some blood on this door over here, Rick," the cop in the hall said to his partner.

"I don't know what the fuck is going on here, Adler." Adrian stood fully now. "But I'm startin' to think you didn't come here tonight as no Fed, stinkin' like some drunken sailor."

BANG! BANG! BANG! BANG! A fist suddenly pounded on Adrian's door.

Frank's thoughts drifted back to the fire escape. *Would I be able to make it down twelve stories before backup arrives, after Adrian opens the door and rats me out?* One thing Frank knew for sure was that he couldn't easily explain the break-in or the assault on Jackson, even if it was in self-defense. The gangster had him dead to rights.

"How bout we go see exactly who these boys are lookin' for?" Adrian suggested, making his way out of the bathroom and down the hallway.

CHAPTER thirty-four

Bennett entered a passcode into the electronic keypad on the front door of his secluded Mexican residence. Before going inside, he activated the locks on his silver Porsche Cayenne parked in the horseshoe driveway, causing the headlights to flash twice before fading away. Only the two long rows of solar-powered light posts flanking the mile-long driveway and a tiny sliver of moon were left to provide any sort of reprieve against the blackness of the night.

Once inside, Bennett tossed his keys into a glass bowl that sat atop a four-foot-tall wooden hutch next to the entryway. He made his way over to the base of the curving staircase on the right side of the foyer, leaving the room unlit. After climbing the steps to the mezzanine, he passed by the open door of his office, heading toward the master bedroom located at the end of the hall.

Five or six feet past the office, Bennett suddenly stopped and rotated his head back toward the room, listening intently through the darkness. Hearing nothing, he turned around and approached cautiously. He reached his hand inside the room and attempted to activate the lights by flicking the switch up and down twice. Nothing happened. Peeking an eye around the door's frame, the only thing he could see was the tiny blinking lights on the backside of the sleeping computer monitors. He listened for a few more seconds, then finally seemed to relax and made his way inside the office, deciding to double-check his schedule for the following day before retiring for the night. The malfunctioning light switch could be dealt with in the morning.

Arriving at the far side of the desk, he took his seat and activated a silver reading lamp, illuminating a large figure sitting on the chair across from him.

It was Frank.

"Jesus, Tank!" Bennett's surprise quickly transitioned into a smile. "That's some stealthy entry!" he chuckled, praising his old friend, who remained stoic across the desk. "You even disabled the light in here! Nice touch. But I gotta break it to you, I did notice that the door was a *little* more open from where I had left it earlier." He tapped a finger on the keyboard in front of him, and the twenty-four-inch dual monitors sprang to life, illuminating his face a bit more. "What are you doing down here?" he wondered, tapping on a few more keys. "Didn't want to give me a heads up you were coming?"

"Haven't quite been myself lately..." Frank admitted flatly.

"I'm sorry to hear that," Bennett replied, adjusting himself in his chair slightly so he was closer to the desk. "I know protocol dictated that we not have any communication after you left Mexico the last time, but I did hear a rumor online that you successfully extracted your daughter. I was happy to hear that, but did I also read that maybe her friend wasn't so lucky?" Bennett asked somberly.

Frank confirmed this with a nod.

"Shit..." Bennett whispered with remorse. "That's terrible."

"Yeah."

"So, how come you're back now?"

"I've been digging for answers since I left," Frank began to explain. "Trying to figure out exactly what happened to those girls. How they fit into a trafficking ring? Who the major players are? How is the system set up? It felt like I was running in circles, completely unable to unravel the mess," he admitted. "I fucked up a lot of things trying to get these answers. My family, my job..."

Bennett exhaled slowly through his nose. "Yeah, and if the cartel finds out you came back down here again, they might think that things aren't over."

Frank raised an eyebrow. "Things aren't over," he stated emphatically. "And I don't give a shit what the cartel thinks."

"I know you don't, Frank," Bennett replied. "Trust me, of all the people in the world, I might be the most aware that *you* don't care," he shook his head. "But unfortunately, your presence down here again is starting to put other people's livelihoods at stake. And for what purpose, exactly?"

Frank didn't offer an immediate response, causing Bennett to look up at the ceiling, obviously frustrated.

"Why the fuck couldn't you just have taken the money, Frank?"

Frank's eyebrows sank. *"What money?"*

"I made it so fucking easy for you..." Bennett said with exasperation in his voice. "For Christ's sake. I got you your daughter back, and you were in the clear. Even if you had some bullshit ethical reason to not take the payoff, why not just be smart and walk the fuck away?"

Frank sat frozen in his chair. *"You knew?"*

"Knew?" Bennett echoed incredulously. "You have got to be fucking kidding me!" He raised his voice. "They were going to kill both those girls, Frank! And I had standing orders to kill you when you arrived at my house that night! The only reason *any* of you lived is because I talked them out of it!"

Frank's hands gripped his armrests.

"Oh, *what?* You thought you just happened to make it all the way to my house without being run down by the cartel after killing one of their guys, just by dumb fucking luck?" Bennett scoffed at the ignorance. "The Mexicans offered me more money than you can imagine to get rid of you, but instead, like a fucking idiot, I convinced them that if you just got your daughter back, you'd be smart enough to walk the fuck away! I told them if anybody could understand how shit goes down in dark places like this, it would be you!"

"You work for them?"

"Come on, Frank!" Disappointment peppered Bennett's voice. "Don't be so fucking naive! Everybody who's allowed to operate in any real capacity down here *works for them* one way or another," he admitted. "Some of us, just a little more closely than others." He grinned, silently removing a gun from its hiding spot next to his right leg beneath the desk.

Frank reached a hand toward his duffel bag on the floor next to him.

"Whoa, whoa, whoa," Bennett pulled his weapon just as Frank's hand had encircled one of the straps. "Toss it." Bennett motioned with the barrel of the gun.

Frank glared across the desk but complied, pitching the bag backward toward the darkened doorway.

"Was it worth it?" Bennett wondered, disdain taking over his voice. "Coming back here and poking your fucking nose around again? I wonder if Sara is going to think so when you don't come home? For fuck sakes, we were *brothers,* Tank! And now, it has to end like this..."

Frank remained stone-faced and silent.

"And just so you know, the reason you couldn't *unravel the mess* is because your daughter's kidnapping wasn't part of the official trafficking ring," Bennett explained. "Those two surfer douchebags were just low-level drug dealers that happened to owe that limo driver a bunch of money, and he forced them to clear their debt by handing over the girls. That underground party circuit in California was never set up to abduct girls; the cartels only used them to make money and move product, but that Lopez guy had recently started trying to sneak a few American girls into the Panamanian Pipeline under Ernesto's nose," Bennett revealed. *"That's* why you kept hitting dead ends. You were starting in the wrong place."

"But before that guy with the dragon tattoo was killed, he said they were expecting nothing but American girls soon." Frank finally spoke again.

"That's the irony in all of this." Bennett smirked. "An entirely different system *was* just being implemented around the same time."

"What do you mean?"

"Somebody finally figured out how to get girls out of the States without any of the issues they ran into in the past."

"Bullshit."

"Yeah, that's what I thought, too—at first," Bennett grinned. "But then I did some digging of my own." He reached out, took hold of the mouse and pulled up a file on his computer. "Do you know what one of my first tasks was when I started working for Ernesto?" he asked rhetorically. "He had me set up a brand new, state-of-the-art security system out at his compound there. And before I put it in, he asked that I check to make sure there were no bugs in the walls or furniture. And do you know what I found when I did my sweep? Not a goddamn thing," Bennett chuckled. "But I'm not stupid, Tank," he shook his head. "I know exactly how these Mexicans operate. I knew I might need an insurance policy one day, so when I was poking around, I slipped in a few bugs of my own and got myself tied into the system," he smiled at his ingenuity. "When I started hearing rumors flying around about a new trafficking system coming out of the States again, after the Albanians fucked everything up and got us shut down years back, I started listening in. It took me a while, sure," Bennett admitted, "but eventually I kept seeing the same two Americans dropping by Ernesto's house every month or so, and I knew I had my lead. Once I had sifted through all the bullshit, I came to learn that the rumors weren't rumors at all..." He tapped a finger on his keyboard, opening an audio file, and it began to play through the speakers.

"Let's just get into it, shall we?" said a Mexican man on the recording.

"That's Ernesto," Bennett explained, gun still trained on Frank's chest across the desk. "He called this meeting so that Dennis and one of the underbosses could be brought up to speed on the new system."

"No problem," said an unidentified American on the tape. *"Ernesto and I have had previous discussions regarding the flood of opioids into the United States in recent years and how it has significantly decreased the monopoly you once held in the illicit narcotics market,"* he explained. *"Marijuana, for example, has almost completely lost its stigma and is now legal—or on the path to becoming legal—in almost every state. Additionally, the use of cocaine has been on a slow and steady decline, and it is my belief that the mass manufacturing of substances such as fentanyl, as well as the production of designer drugs coming directly out of China, has had a direct correlation to the decline of your market share. And because the Chinese were able to corner these markets from the beginning, it has left you to play middleman for these substances."*

"A position we are not fond of," responded a different Mexican.

"Dennis Diaz," Bennett identified the voice.

"During one of my visits," the American continued, *"I gained some insight into your past ventures of selling, uh, providing females for..."* he seemed to struggle in trying to select the correct vernacular.

"Sex slaves," Dennis interjected. *"Dios Mio! Just speak plainly without all the fancy bullshit business jargon,"* he demanded of the American. *"This room is secure."*

Bennett smirked at the irony.

"Yes, please continue," Ernesto agreed, much more calmly than his brother.

"No problem," replied the American. *"Once I began to fully understand the ins and outs of your previous operation—and some of the pitfalls you ran into—I began to develop a plan for how you might avoid them moving forward."*

Frank leaned forward, listening intently.

"Years ago, my company was forced to establish a series of non-profit organizations which included safe injection sites,

rehabilitation centers, and outreach programs for the addicted on the West Coast of the United States."

"What could that possibly mean to us?" Dennis questioned, not understanding how *helping* the drug-addicted population in America could benefit anyone in attendance.

"The beauty is, the recovery rate from opioid addiction is like, I don't know, one in a thousand," the American explained. *"And those statistics involve having access to the best recovery programs that money can buy. But the organizations we created, well, I can assure you, they don't hire the best and brightest...if you catch my drift."*

Frank could almost hear the gears starting to turn in the heads of the other men in the room.

"Since the inception of these programs, data has been diligently collected on everyone who has participated in a service. Using that information, we were able to begin targeting young women who were early in their addiction, new to the streets, with little to no family or social connections. Next, we began to systematically extract these females from the streets and found that it resulted in very few inquiries regarding their whereabouts once they had disappeared."

"Extracted?" Dennis sounded much less skeptical and abrasive now.

"Without getting into a whole lot of detail, the target subject was lured away from the rest of the homeless population, placed into a holding facility, where they were kept drugged and docile, while we monitored our community connections to determine if any missing person reports had been filed. Because these particular women had very limited social networks and no opportunity to establish themselves on the streets by this point, very often it went unnoticed when they suddenly vanished."

"Explain to them what happens when a missing person report is filed," Ernesto instructed.

"In those types of situations, the subject was administered a fatal dose of an opioid and then discreetly returned to the streets, within a reasonable proximity of the original location from which they were taken. Eventually, someone came across their body, and the authorities assumed the overdose was self-administered and accidental."

Frank felt his heart sink.

"These types of deaths already occur so frequently in America that nobody even bats an eye, and the media just reports it as another 'bad batch of street drugs.'"

"*And the others?*" Dennis inquired. "*The girls who could be taken without inquiry?*"

"*That part, I'll leave up to y—*"

Bennett stopped the recording.

"Who's this American?" Frank demanded immediately.

Bennett looked at his screen and located another file, then rotated the monitor to face Frank across the desk. On the screen, a tanned man with slicked black hair wearing an expensive designer suit with gold cufflinks was standing confidently behind a lectern, speaking at a swanky gala event.

"His name is Ken Collins," Bennett explained. "Ever heard of him?"

Frank's thoughts transported him back to the evening at Mike's house when he had watched the CEO's brazen testimony at the congressional hearing. "That son of a bitch..."

"Oh yeah," Bennett smirked. "And he's in *deep,* too. Ernesto is always bringing him down here, introducing him to all his buddies. I think I even heard the old man asking him to hold on to a painting for him up in New York on one of the recordings. This idiot hasn't got a clue who he's in bed with. Pretty fucking ballsy if you ask me."

Frank shook his head in disgust.

"Well," Bennett transitioned back to the matter at hand, "as much as it pains me to do this, this is the end for you, Tank."

"How can you let them get away with this?"

"It's not my fight. I'm just a simple security consultant," he smiled sarcastically. "A very well-paid one, mind you."

Frank lowered his head. "You know what the problem is with guys like you, Bennett? Once all the money starts piling up, you pay everybody else to do your dirty work. And do you know what happens then?"

Bennett rolled his eyes. "No, what?"

"You start getting sloppy..." Frank lifted his head and stared across the desk. "You lose your *edge*."

"Oh, that's fucking rich," Bennett chuckled. "This coming from a G-man. From where I'm sitting, it looks like I have all the *edge* I need," he waggled the gun in the air.

"Now that you're done telling *your* story, maybe I can tell you one of my own?" Frank suggested.

Bennett shrugged, figuring it was the least he could do before he brought Frank out back and shot him.

"Someone stopped by my place unexpectedly the other night," Frank said of Winston's late-night visit to the cabin. "And he had an audio recording of his own. Except, on this one, there was a guy from New York talking to an American down here in Mexico by the name of *Scorpio*. Problem was, this Scorpio character used a voice modulator. That's some pretty advanced tech, don't you think?"

Bennett's eyes squinted ever-so-slightly.

"Well, I went and paid the guy in New York a visit, but unfortunately, he didn't have a clue who the hell this Scorpio guy was either. But something about that name just felt so familiar..."

Bennett stood from his chair and slowly made his way around to the front of the desk, keeping the gun fixed on Frank the entire time.

"It finally dawned on me," said Frank. "That was the same stupid nickname you used on the women in the bars overseas," he recalled. "Once I paired that with the high-tech voice distortion device and the well-timed phone calls during my last visit, it all started coming together."

"So let me get this straight," Bennett decided to stop him there, leaning against the front edge of the desk. "The entire time you're sitting in this room, you knew that I was involved, and yet you still let me get the drop on you? And you have the balls to say I've lost *my* edge?"

"I knew it was the only way I could get the last few pieces of the puzzle out of you."

"Yeah, and what fucking good is that information to you now?" Bennett raised his voice. "You planning on telling them what I did when you arrive at the pearly fucking gates?" he mocked.

A confident grin spread across Frank's face. "In your prime, Benny, a guy like you would have been able to tell that the gun he was holding had its firing pin removed... just by the weight of it."

The smile fell off Bennett's face as he looked at the impotent weapon in his hand. "Very clever," he conceded. "I guess that just means I'll have to kill you the old-fashioned way." Without warning, he dropped the gun onto the desk and lunged at Frank.

Frank didn't hesitate. He launched himself out of his chair, wrapped his arms around Bennett, and drove him back into the desk, causing one of the computer monitors to crash onto the floor, further darkening the room. Bennett responded by sending a sharp elbow across Frank's chin, followed by a looping right hook. Frank ducked the punch, locked on to his opponent, and the two began to spin around the room chaotically, each attempting to gain the upper hand.

Frank drove Bennett's back into the wall, causing a jagged crack to shoot up towards the ceiling and a chunk of gypsum to fall to the floor in a puff of dust. Bennett kneed Frank in the ribcage, cracking cartilage and knocking the breath out of him. Bennett lowered his leg to the floor and drove it back up again like a piston in a powerful engine. Frank absorbed the second shot more favorably and locked his hands beneath Bennett's raised knee, plowing him back into the wall. Frank caught Bennett with a hook to the chin but missed his mark enough that Bennett was able to spring off the wall and drive Frank backward over the toppled office chair. The two combatants crashed to the floor in a whirlwind of tangled limbs.

Bennett now found himself behind Frank and quickly attempted to wrap his tattooed forearm around his neck. Frank tucked his chin and sent an elbow back into Bennett's face, knocking out one of his incisors and forcing him to abandon the failed submission attempt. The two men got back to their feet, and Bennett wore a hedonic, gap-toothed smile. He spat out a mouthful of blood.

"It didn't have to come to this, Tank," he said, rolling his shoulders back like an ancient gladiator in the midst of single combat. "But, let's be honest, everybody in the unit always wondered, if push came to shove, who truly was the *alpha* of the pack."

"If I were you, I'd be more concerned with what those men would think of what you've become. You're not a Marine. You're a coward."

Bennett reached down and hiked up his pant leg, exposing an 8-inch Bowie knife strapped to the outside of his calf. He unsheathed the blade, and the two men began to circle each other in anticipation of re-engagement.

"Just like I thought..." Frank shook his head. "A coward to the end."

The sadistic smile grew on Bennett's face as he began to carve serpentine patterns in the air, and both men reacted to each other's micro-movements. Suddenly, Bennett lunged forward and slashed at Frank's chest with the razor-sharp steel. Frank backpedaled, avoiding the first three swipes, but the fourth sliced through his raised forearm, and crimson-colored blood quickly filled the wound.

Bennett took a moment to admire his handiwork. "Isn't hand-to-hand combat part of the FBI's training program?" he taunted. "Maybe if I swapped the knife for a pencil, you'd feel a little more at home?"

"Enough talk," Frank growled, ignoring the superficial wound. "Let's end this thing."

"With pleasure." Bennett's eyes lit up with wildness, and he sprang forward in another intensified burst of energy, swiping chaotically. Frank backpedaled, narrowly avoiding harm, and timing his opponent's cadence. Suddenly, Frank planted his back foot and rocketed himself forward, sending a devastating kick directly into Bennett's exposed abdomen, sending him reeling backward. Frank closed the distance and grabbed hold of his wrist, driving him onto the top of the desk.

As they struggled for control of the knife, Bennett delivered a vicious head butt into the bridge of Frank's nose. The impact set off a mosaic of brilliant starbursts in Frank's vision, allowing Bennett the opportunity to flip him onto his back on top of the desk. Frank felt his grip momentarily loosen on Bennett's wrist, and the blade plunged downward toward Frank's chest. Just inches before penetration, Frank managed to regain control, adding a second hand for assistance. Bennett did the same, placing his palm on top of the knife's handle. Bennett's face now hovered just inches above Frank's, his hot breath rained down on him.

"Just give it up," Bennett said with strain in his voice as the blade began gaining millimeters of downward progress. "I'll make this quick."

The tip of the blade pierced the skin of Frank's chest. He closed his eyes and turned his head as his aching muscles fought against impending death.

Suddenly, from the darkest recesses of his mind, a brilliant flash of white light appeared, revealing a vision of Marla running through the airport. *"Hellllllllllooooooo Adlers!"* she exclaimed with youthful exuberance. *FLASH!* She was now lying lifelessly inside the black body bag on the floor of the Mexican warehouse. *FLASH!* Frank saw Sofia inside the bedroom wearing an innocent smile. *"Mr. Frank, it is very nice to meet you, too,"* she said, extending her tiny hand. *FLASH!* Suddenly, her body lay motionless on the mattress, her head on a blood-soaked pillow. *FLASH!* Frank saw Sara joking and laughing with the ticket agent at the airport. *FLASH!* She was leaning heavily on the table inside the warehouse. Her cheeks were red, eyes glassy. She reached out for him. "*Daddy...*"

Frank began to feel the rhythmic pounding of his heart just below the blade and felt rage circulating through every vein and artery. Suddenly, his head turned back to center, his eyes opened, and the knife began to reverse course.

Spit began to form in the corners of Bennett's mouth as he struggled furiously to maintain his gravitational advantage, but the blade continued to retreat. With Herculean force, Frank drove himself off the desk, sending Bennett backpedaling across the room where his heel caught on the arm of the downed office chair. He tumbled to the floor, expecting to feel Frank's weight come crashing down on him at any moment, but that didn't happen.

Bennett picked himself up and discovered Frank standing in front of the desk, now holding the gun he had discarded earlier.

An arrogant smirk appeared on Bennett's face.

"That head-butt must have scrambled your brains," he suggested. "You removed the firing pin, remember?"

"That's the *other* thing about guys like you..." Frank replied. "You get so used to hearing your own bullshit lies, you don't even realize when one is coming back at you."

The smile fell from Bennett's face when he realized the missing firing pin had been a ruse.

"Guess you should have pulled the trigger when you had the chance, *alpha dog...*"

"*ARRGGHHH!*" Bennett barreled back across the office toward Frank, knife leading the charge.

BANG!

The first round penetrated Bennett's chest four inches above his heart. He continued forward, seemingly unfazed. Frank aimed lower and squeezed off a second round.

BANG!

This bullet shattered Bennett's left kneecap, dropping him onto the floor awkwardly, eight feet short of Frank. Defiant of his injuries, he began to crawl forward, blade still raised in the air. Frank took a step forward and pinched off a third round from close range.

BANG!

Bennett's hand exploded like a piñata stuffed with flesh and bone, and the knife skittered across the room into a dark corner. Bennett groaned loudly and retracted his mangled hand.

Frank took hold of Bennett's shirt collar and dragged him across the office floor, leaning him up against the front of the desk in a seated position. Frank then righted the toppled chair and set it a half-dozen feet back from his downed opponent and took a seat. Even in the darkness, Frank could see the copious amount of blood pooling beneath Bennett as he coughed and tried to adjust himself into a more comfortable position. He turned his head and spat out another mouthful of syrupy blood.

"That's it for me." Bennett seemed to concede his fate.

"Looks that way."

"And for you, too..."

Frank dismissed the comment. He had watched the life drain out of many men, and each one seemed to fade out in a slightly different manner. Some begged, some repented, some even smiled.

Bennett looked up at Frank. "When I first saw you across the desk, I figured there was a possibility you might have known," he explained. "And even though I had the drop on you, I knew there was a chance you might somehow gain the upper hand. So, I sent out a distress signal to my crew on the computer, just in case." Bennett pointed his chin toward the front of the house. "And these guys you got coming, they aren't just some random cartel men. They're the best American ex-special forces soldiers money can buy down here. These boys sold their souls long ago."

Frank stood up from his chair and walked to the door, looking over the balcony and through the windows into the darkness of the night. In the distance, he spotted four sets of headlights traveling in a tight formation at a high rate of speed, less than four or five minutes away. Frank turned back to Bennett. He was slumped over, dead.

Frank quickly realized that the road leading to the property was the only access point, so commandeering Bennett's speedy Porsche in an attempt to flee wasn't going to be a viable option. Next, Frank considered disappearing out the back of the house to find a spot to hunker down for the night, but he decided that once the inbound crew discovered Bennett's still-warm body, they would immediately call for reinforcements, who would cast a net around the surrounding area and close in on him in no time.

While he thought, Frank recovered his duffel bag and brought it over to the desk. He began to rifle through its compartments, locating a flashlight first. He activated it and placed it between his teeth. Next, he found a black handgun with ten rounds of ammunition. He set it down on the desk next to the weapon he had used to kill Bennett. Frank knew that the inbound vehicles could carry up to twenty hitmen, and his current ammo count was severely insufficient, especially if they were wearing body armor.

Glancing back at the door, Frank continued to fish around the bottom of the duffel bag until his fingers came in contact with the telescopic device that Winston had demonstrated in the mock-up motel back in New York. He took a moment to mentally map the floor plan of the house, noting the entry and exit points at the front and rear, leading him to believe that the incoming crew would likely split up on arrival and attempt to breach from both locations.

Just then, Frank remembered the hidden pocket door in the back corner of the office and the room full of Bennett's old military memorabilia. He removed the flashlight from his mouth and aimed it in that direction, finding the room was now fully sealed and invisible. If he could somehow gain entry and set up the device inside the space, he might be able to gain visual access to the surrounding rooms before the inbound death squad arrived. It was risky, but Frank knew he had no other choice.

He quickly stashed the guns and the device back inside his bag, slung it over his shoulder, and headed for the pocket door. Once he arrived, he began searching the walls with his hands for an access panel. Soon, an integrated backlit screen, slightly larger than a deck of playing cards, was illuminated on the wall. In its center was a square space bordered in green. Frank pressed a finger in the middle, turning it red. *THUMBPRINT NOT RECOGNIZED*! flashed three times before the box transitioned back to green. Frank thought for a moment, looking over at the desk, where he spotted one of Bennett's boots peeking out from its edge.

Frank abandoned the door and made his way past the body to where he had blown Bennett's hand to pieces. He began to search the floor with his flashlight, illuminating a mangled finger still encircled by a black tungsten carbide ring. Next, he came across the downed knife. Finally, resting against the baseboard, Frank spotted Bennett's meaty thumb. He scooped it up, and on his way back to the corner, he took a moment to check on the progress of the inbound armada. They were only a few hundred yards from the end of the driveway now. Frank deactivated the lamp on the desk, then continued to the corner and pressed the stiffened thumb inside the green square. *THUMBPRINT NOT RECOGNIZED!* flashed again. Frank tried once more, receiving the same result. *Maybe Bennett used his other thumb?* Frank questioned as he turned the digit over to study the print more closely. It was caked with blood. Frank rubbed the thumb vigorously against his pant leg just as the inbound vehicles reached the end of the driveway. They deactivated their headlights in an obvious attempt to camouflage their approach. Frank did the same with his flashlight, then reapplied the severed digit to the wall.

This time, the entire panel flashed green and then quickly disappeared. Frank heard what sounded to be ultra-strong magnets releasing inside the wall, and the door suddenly slid open twelve inches. Frank took hold of the edge of the heavy pocket door and forced it further down its track into the wall. He stepped inside the hidden room, closed the door as far as it would allow, and activated a light switch, illuminating the room around him. Once his eyes adjusted, he found everything to be the same as before—the framed photographs, the glass display case, the flags, the weaponry, the army-green Humvee door, and the sandy beige tarp.

Next to the light switch, Frank saw an identical thumbprint keypad. He pressed Bennett's thumb into its center, causing the door to close and its magnets to reactivate, sealing himself securely inside the room. Frank moved down the wall quickly, arriving at the glass display case in the corner, which contained the two chrome-plated guns. He dropped his duffel bag onto the floor and drove an elbow into the glass, sending crystalized shards raining down around his boots and creating a hole large enough to extract the weapons. After removing the hardware, he chambered a round in each gun.

* * * * *

The lead SUV arrived at the precipice of the horseshoe driveway. The four occupants opened their doors and quickly exited the vehicle, moving purposefully in strict militaristic fashion toward the front of the house. Each of the men was wearing a black balaclava and a full set of military-green tactical gear. The second and third SUVs pulled in tightly behind the first and emptied in the same manner. These eight gunmen split into two groups, each making their way down opposite sides of the house toward the back corners. They had been given orders to remain in place until the team at the front radioed with further instructions. The fourth and final SUV was positioned two hundred yards back from the others. Its four occupants remained inside, tasked with keeping an eye on the scene from a distance.

* * * * *

Frank had already suspended the telescopic device from the ceiling, and at the request of the remote control in his hand, it began analyzing the surrounding rooms. Oscillating grids of blue and white spun on the walls as it performed its calculations in a solemn silence. Once finished, the remote vibrated. *E1, E2, E3, and E4* flashed on the screen first, indicating errors on all four walls. C5 flashed next.

Frank quickly realized that the reinforced steel Bennett had added to the walls was too dense for penetration, and the device would only allow him to see into the room below. Frank backed himself toward a wall and pressed the *ACTIVATE* button on the remote. The floor immediately disappeared beneath his boots and was replaced by a bird's-eye view of the couches, bookcases, and other furnishings. Everything looked still and quiet inside the room, but Frank knew that could change at any moment.

*****

Four ski-masked hitmen flanked the front door of the house, with the leader communicating silently through militaristic hand signals. Radio transmissions began to arrive through their earpieces, confirming that the other two crews were now in position.

The gunman on the left side of the entryway looked through the rectangular glass panel next to the door and saw no movement inside the dark foyer. Using a glass-cutting tool from his tactical vest, he removed a softball-sized round from the pane, reached inside, and unlocked the door.

All four men stepped inside and crept silently into the high-ceilinged foyer, carrying automatic assault rifles and scanning their surroundings in smooth serpentine patterns. With no immediate threat detected, the group made their way to the base of a curving staircase and moved in a perfectly synchronized fashion as they climbed the steps.

The foursome crossed the mezzanine in a modified crouch, with three of the gunmen continuing past the open office door and down the hallway to where the other rooms were located. The leader set his chest against the wall next to the office door and cautiously peeked around the frame. By this point, the remaining monitor on the desk had already entered sleep mode, and the room was completely dark. He stepped inside and listened for any signs of movement. Hearing nothing, he activated the scope light mounted on his weapon, instantly spotlighting Bennett's lifeless body slumped over in front of the desk. Showing limited reaction to the grisly discovery, the hitman scanned the rest of the room, discovering the toppled monitor, the downed Bowie knife, and the damage to the sheet rock—all evidence of a scuffle. The three other hitmen began to file into the office; each having found their room empty and free of concern. The leader radioed down to the two teams outside at the back corners of the house to indicate that they had come across Bennett's body. He ordered them to continue holding their positions for the time being.

"Target couldn't have gotten far..." one of the gunmen reasoned, tapping the toe of his boot near Bennett's corpse. "Blood's still fresh."

"He wouldn't have stuck around for long," another suggested.

"Looks like he disabled this light switch," the hitman standing closest to the door indicated, flipping it up and down to no effect.

"He must have been waiting in here for Bennett wh—"

Suddenly, a high-pitched sound of shattering glass arrived through the wall, and all four gunmen rotated their weapons in unison, bathing the surface in scope light.

*****

Inside the magnetically sealed room, Frank had been watching as what remained of the structurally compromised glass display case in the corner began to crack further. He had been listening to Bennett's crew talking on the other side of the wall when the first few nuggets had tinkled onto the invisible floor. Frank mentally willed the remaining glass to hold steady, at least until the goon squad had exited the office, but luck was not on his side. Gravity finally took over, and the compromised case dropped to the floor, resulting in a tidal wave of crystallized shards scattering in all directions. When everything had finally settled, the voices on the other side of the wall had fallen silent.

*****

The four mercenaries moved in a single-file row down the wall toward the back corner of the office. The leader took a moment to inspect the damage to the sheetrock, touching the exposed metal with his finger. On the other side of the wall, Frank could feel their collective footsteps as he moved along with them in undetected unison towards the hidden pocket door.

The leader arrived at the corner first and placed his hand against the wall, leaning his face in to listen. As he did this, Frank lifted one of the silver guns to less than eight inches from the man's temple. Suddenly, the integrated keypad flashed to life in front of the hitman's face, having been activated by his touch. He took a step back and stared at the illuminated rectangle.

"Hidden room," he mouthed silently to his team. He examined the backlit configuration more closely, pressing his thumb inside the little green box. *THUMBPRINT NOT RECOGNIZED!* flashed in red, just as it had for Frank. He glanced over to Bennett's corpse. After a moment of contemplation, he made his way to the body.

"I need his thumb," he whispered to his crew as he passed them, removing a hunting knife from his tactical belt.

Arriving at the corpse, he grabbed one of Bennett's tattooed arms by the wrist and lifted it in the air, discovering the mutilated hand. He paused for a moment, staring at the mangled appendage, then looked back to the corner. Suddenly, he dropped Bennett's arm to the floor and pulled off his balaclava, exposing a shaved head, dark-brown goatee, and wide-set, cesium blue eyes.

"I know you're in there!" he called out in a deep voice at full volume now. "Come on out!" he ordered. Receiving no reply, he took hold of Bennett's other arm. "Cooperate, and we'll make this quick and painless!"

Silence.

"Alright! We'll do it the hard way!"

The gunman took hold of the tip of Bennett's thumb and set his blade against it. Just before he made his first stroke, the sound of magnetic locks being released arrived from the corner, and the door slid open twelve inches. The interior of the hidden room was pitch-black now. The leader dropped Bennett's arm and returned his blade to his belt. The three hitmen against the wall readied their weapons.

"Smart choice!" the leader assured the man in the room. "Now, throw your weapon out, and come out with your hands up!"

After a few moments of eerie silence, the gun Frank had used to kill Bennett slid out from the void across the back wall, coming to rest halfway across the room. The leader nodded to the gunman at the front of the line, indicating for him to retrieve the forfeited weapon.

"Good!" the leader called out.

The other hitman slowly made his way over to the gun.

"Can you see him?" one of his teammates asked in a hushed tone.

The hitman picked up the discarded weapon while focusing his scope light through the gap, illuminating the pile of shattered glass in the far corner. He turned to his compatriots and shook his head.

Just then, two nearly imperceptible *clinks* sounded from inside the hidden room, and the four hitmen looked at each other curiously. A moment later, two objects came bouncing out. The first ricocheted off the toe of the gunman's boot and headed towards the desk. The second came to rest directly between his feet. Three beams of scope light converged on the little green object, spotlighting the man on the back wall like a Broadway actor.

"GRENADES!" the leader shouted, immediately dropping himself behind the desk next to Bennett. The two men against the wall turned and attempted to flee toward the exit. The fourth, still holding Frank's discarded gun on the back wall, stood frozen in place—he knew it was too late.

BOOOOOOOOOOM!

The high explosive between his boots detonated, shredding him into pieces.

BOOOOOOOOOOM!

The other grenade detonated half a second later, sending supersonic fragments of serrated iron into the two fleeing gunmen, killing them instantly.

A high-pitched buzz filled the leader's head, but the desk had done enough to shield him from the lethality of the dual blasts. He began to hear muffled voices, and soon realized they were coming through his earpiece. He gave his head a shake, attempting to expel some of the ringing inside his skull.

"What the fuck is going on in there?" a gunman stationed outside the house demanded. *"We are going to be making entry on the Charlie side of the structure. I repeat, we will be making entry through the back door."*

The leader reached up and took hold of the edge of the still-warm desk, slowly pulling himself to a standing position. He activated his radio.

"Bennett is dead," he explained to the outside crews between labored breaths, blood trickling down from his left ear. "I have the target contained to some sort of panic room attached to the second-floor office at the top of the stairs. Three of my men are down," he said, looking at the lifeless bodies against the wall. "I don't think the target has any means of escape from his current location." He gave his head another shake, finally feeling as if he was starting to regain some of his senses. "I'll hold him in place unt—"

Two bullets suddenly tore through his skull, cutting the transmission short.

Frank was now standing in the fully open pocket door, staring down the barrels of the two powerful silver handguns. He took a moment to scan the remainder of the carnage inside the office, then stepped back inside the room. The door quickly resealed itself, and the hitman's lifeless body dropped to the floor next to Bennett.

Aside from the framed photographs that had been blown off the wall by the shockwave, the room's fortifications had easily weathered the explosions, leaving the suspended telescopic device unharmed. Frank reactivated it and, through the invisible floor, discovered a balaclava-wearing gunman silently entering the room below. He was followed closely by another. Frank began to back himself towards the wall, watching the two hitmen navigate their way around the furnishings with automatic weapons in hand. Suddenly, he felt his lower back contact something behind him.

Frank turned and discovered the sandy-colored tarp next to the Humvee door. After a moment of contemplation, he took hold of the heavy armored door, dragged it to the center of the room, and dropped it flat on the floor, sending a rumble through the entire house. The two gunmen below stopped and pointed their weapons at the ceiling above their heads momentarily, as more hitmen began to slowly filter into the room from outside.

Frank returned to the wall and uncovered the powerful machine gun, quickly balancing its pyramidal tripod base over his shoulder. He carried it to the middle of the room and set it squarely on top of the armored door. He opened the weapon's stop cover and inspected the ammo feed. Satisfied, he snapped the lid back into place, retracted the slide handle, aimed the barrel at the men below, and opened fire. *KSSHT-KSSHT-KSSHT-KSSHT-KSSHT-KSSHT!* Ammunition began to rip out of the death machine's massive barrel, causing splintered wood to suddenly appear as it geysered up from the invisible floor. A brown leather couch in the room below was quickly obliterated into a pile of kindling and cotton as the surrounding gunmen began to dive for cover. Frank pivoted the gun to his right and took direct aim at a hitman who had tried to hide behind one of Bennett's marble statues. *KSSHT-KSSHT-KSSHT-KSSHT-KSSHT!* The gunman and the sculpture exploded into a cocktail of blood, guts, and jagged rock. Frank spun left, tracking the pair of hitmen who were attempting to flee past the massive five-hundred-gallon saltwater aquarium. Bullets ripped through both men and into the face of the tank, releasing a tidal wave of briny blue water flooding across the room and knocking another gunman off his feet.

Just then, Frank felt destabilized air rushing past his head as bullets whizzed up from the room below. He released the trigger and spun himself around 180 degrees, locating one of the culprits. Taking aim, he opened fire and nearly cut the man in half at the waist.

Suddenly, the floor sprang back into full view, causing Frank to release the trigger and look over to where the telescopic device had been hanging. It was lying on the floor now, having taken a direct hit from one of the inbound rounds from the floor below. *"Fuck,"* Frank cursed to himself. Blind to his targets, he tucked himself against the tripod as the barrage of incoming bullets intensified and could feel the armor-plated door beneath him absorbing dozens of rounds.

A foundation-shaking explosion suddenly went off just outside the magnetized door. Some of the gunmen must have escaped from the room below and were now trying to gain forceful entry. Frank knew it would only be a matter of time until they figured out a way to gain access. Sensing a small reprieve in the onslaught below, Frank stood up, took hold of the machine gun's handles, and began to blindly fire through the floor, pivoting himself in a near-perfect circle. Suddenly, something stabbed him in his right calf, causing him to drop to one knee with his thumb still locked on the trigger. The powerful weapon was pulled to parallel, sending a serpentine train of fifty-caliber bullets through the wall into the office, instantly killing two of the gunmen who were trying to disable the door. A third, who had been nearer to the desk, dove for cover as rounds sprayed above his head.

Frank released the trigger and pulled himself back to his feet, testing his compromised leg's ability to bear weight. Finding it sufficient, he aimed the barrel back down toward the floor and opened fire again, continuing his 360-degree assault. The final golden-cased bullet on the once-long mule train of ammunition began to creep vertically from the floor until it disappeared inside the weapon. *DING!* The casing ejected itself from the weapon. Just then, Frank felt the floor shift beneath his feet and heard a loud *pop* and a whining *creak*. Frank's hands abandoned the spent weapon, and he looked for a non-compromised area of the floor to jump to. It was too late. Frank felt himself go weightless.

The massive circle he had cut into the floor disconnected from the rest of the room, sending thousands of pounds of man, weaponry, and building materials hurtling down into the parlor below, crushing one of the remaining hitmen on impact. Frank hit the floor and flew backward, striking his head on the plinth of a bronze statue depicting a seven-foot-tall African tribesman holding a shield. The sculpture began to teeter back and forth until it came crashing down on the floor, barely missing Frank's unconscious head with a reverberating *CLANG!*

Frank opened his eyes, and his vision began to adjust to the poorly lit room. He found himself lying flat on his back, staring up at the demolished ceiling as the last pieces of debris dropped into the room around him. Slowly, he sat up and rubbed the back of his neck, as the final death twitches of the crushed hitmen's legs finally stopped. Frank scanned the room and suddenly discovered another gunman, who was seated just like him, twenty-five feet away. The hitman seemed oblivious to Frank's presence, having been rocked by the jarring impact as well. Frank watched the gunman pull off his balaclava, revealing sharp facial features and a spotty collection of blonde whiskers on his cheeks and chin. He couldn't have been more than twenty-five years old, Frank thought. Just then, the downed gunman's head turned slowly, and he locked eyes with Frank. Almost imperceptibly, the young man's eyes crept over to where his assault rifle had come to rest near the wall, then back to Frank. Frank shook his head in warning.

Suddenly, the hitman made a break for his downed weapon, and Frank looked behind himself, spotting one of the chrome-plated guns within the debris. With his opponent nearing his weapon, Frank knew he didn't have time to stand to recover his own, so he dropped onto his back and reached a hand blindly above his head. As the other man arrived at his rifle, Frank felt his fingers contact the grip of his gun, and he drew it into his palm. The hitman lifted his weapon off the floor and squared himself to his target across the room.

BANG! BANG! BANG! BANG! BANG!

The hitman's shoulders rocked back and forth as Frank's rounds overpowered his flak jacket. He dropped backward onto the floor with his finger caught inside the trigger guard, spraying a short burst of ammunition into what was left of the ceiling above.

Frank slowly rose to his feet and walked through the debris to where the hitman had fallen, counting the bodies as he went. Upon reaching the man, Frank discovered his eyes were wide open, darting around the ceiling above him. Frank looked down and saw that one of the rounds had entered through the front of the gunman's neck and likely severed his spinal cord, paralyzing him.

"How many?" Frank asked, looking down on the young man from above.

The hitman gulped at the room's dusty air like a goldfish out of water. "Sixteen," he managed to say in a raspy voice, full of strain.

Frank quickly did the math in his head. "More outside?"

"Four."

Frank glanced at the door that led him into the high-ceilinged foyer earlier and then back at the downed gunman, who nodded slowly. Frank dropped his clip into his palm and checked the remaining count before snapping it back into place.

BANG!

Frank discarded the spent handgun and traded it for the dead man's assault rifle, radio and earpiece. He exited the parlor and entered the dark foyer, moving the barrel of the weapon smoothly and silently between the front door and the mezzanine above his head. Making his way to the door, he peeked out through a panel of glass with the missing round and saw three empty SUVs, doors open, parked by the fountain. Beyond them, he spotted the fourth vehicle a couple of hundred yards back. It was too dark to see inside, but the doors were closed, leading Frank to believe that the men were still inside, holding their position.

Frank abandoned the front door and climbed the stairs silently, feeling the pain from the splintered wood still embedded in his right calf intensify with every step. When he reached the mezzanine, his earpiece suddenly crackled to life.

"This is Delta lead," a deep and serious-sounding voice came over the radio. *"We need a status report out here. Have you eliminated the target? Over."* It was obvious to Frank that this was one of the hitmen inside the SUV. If a reply didn't arrive soon, they would storm the house or, worse yet, call for additional backup. *"Did you copy my transmission? I repeat, has the target been neutralized?"* demanded the man impatiently.

Frank had only just set his back against the wall outside the office door, looking out at the SUV, when the radio crackled again.

"Paul. It's Jake," another man suddenly replied, surprising Frank. *"I'm inside the panic room that Sid mentioned earlier."* He paused. *"Sid's dead. Everybody's dead. And this room is full of Bennett's old military shit, including the weapons the target used to kill our guys."* It sounded to Frank as though the speaker was peering over the edge of the hole, looking down into the dark parlor below. *"I can see a pair of tactical boots sticking out from under the debris down there. They're next to a silver handgun I don't recognize. I think the target must have fallen through the floor and was killed on impact,"* the hitman reported. *"Yeah, I think he's dead, Paul. Just hold your position, I'll head back downstairs to confirm."*

"Copy," replied the hitman in the SUV.

The gunman inside the hidden room took one last glance down through the hole and called out to any of his comrades who might still be alive. Receiving no response, he turned around.

Schink!

The eyes inside the hitman's balaclava widened when he found himself standing face-to-face with Frank. Hypnotized, the gunman touched the tip of his gloved fingers to the razor-thin red line that had formed on the front of his neck. Suddenly, a deluge of crimson-colored blood gushed forth from the wound, and he dropped to his knees. Frank drove the sole of his boot into the man's chest, sending him down into the room below, where he landed on his back with a hollow thud.

* * * * *

"It's been like five minutes," commented the black-haired hitman with the missing right earlobe in the back of the parked SUV. "We should go inside and see what the fuck is going on."

"Who was this target, anyway?" asked the African American with a shaved head in the driver's seat, staring at the distant house through the windshield.

"Fuck it, let's get ready to make entry," the gunman in the passenger seat agreed. He looked to be the oldest of the four, with salt and pepper hair and a square jaw. "John and I will take the—"

"Wait a second..." the driver interrupted, suddenly spotting one of his balaclava-wearing comrades exiting the front of the house. "There's Jake now."

"Jake, did you confirm the kill?" he questioned the inbound man on the radio, trying to see between the SUVs that were now obscuring his view of his teammate. Receiving no response, he tried again. *"Jake, I repeat, has the target been eliminated?"*

"Maybe his comms are down..." suggested the fourth man in the backseat.

"Can't be. He just radioed us five minutes ago."

Soon, their man reemerged from the darkness between two of the SUVs. He brought his radio up to his face. *"All targets have been eliminated,"* he reported flatly.

The hitmen inside the SUV looked at each other with confusion.

"What is that?" The blonde gunman in the backseat said, squinting and pointing a finger through the windshield. "Turn on your headlights, Brian," he tapped the driver on his shoulder, who complied, illuminating the man with the balaclava who was pulling something over his shoulder.

"Jake...?"

The dark figure set a cylindrical tube on his shoulder.

"RPG!" hollered the hitman in the passenger seat.

*****

Frank had the crosshairs of the anti-tank device set on the front grill of the vehicle, while the men inside frantically scrambled for their door handles. He squeezed the trigger, and a *WHOOOOOOSH* of pressurized air ripped out from the weapon's breech, propelling a green-tipped projectile through the warm Mexican air at 450 feet per second. Before any of the gunmen had a chance to clear the vehicle, the grenade detonated on impact, sending the SUV airborne. The vehicle's fuel tank quickly ruptured, and the fire-engulfed heap of metal backflipped, landing on its roof before a thundering clap echoed in the distance.

Frank dropped the spent weapon onto the ground and pulled the stolen balaclava off his head. He hopped inside one of the open-door SUVs, where he found the keys dangling from the ignition. He started the engine and fishtailed the vehicle around the horseshoe driveway, eventually driving past the upended SUV with the four flaming corpses inside. He removed a phone from his pocket and quickly dialed a number.

"It's done," he explained once the call had connected. "There may be more men inbound on my position. I'm in need of rapid extraction."

CHAPTER thirty-five

Ken Collins was standing in front of two brushed copper sinks inside the bathroom of his penthouse when the cell phone provided by Ernesto began to ring. He glanced down at the screen momentarily before returning his gaze to his reflection in the mirror. Running his fingers through his slicked-back obsidian hair, he adjusted the half-Windsor knot in his eight-hundred-dollar paisley-patterned tie, and then finally scooped up the device into his palm. He and the cartel boss had been working even more closely since the *incident* involving Hank in the jungle, and neither man had mentioned his name since.

"Hello," Collins answered, his eyes still fixated on his reflection.

"Good morning," said Diaz. "How are you?"

"Outstanding." The businessman flashed himself an obnoxious smile before breaking the visual love affair. "And you?"

"Very well."

Collins abandoned the bathroom and made his way down the hall.

"I'm calling regarding the item you've been holding for me," Diaz said, referring to his painting.

Collins walked over to where the Kahlo was hanging on the wall. "If you can believe it, I was just admiring it when you called," he lied, for no particular reason.

The old man laughed. "You see! Didn't I say I'd make an art lover out of you after all?!"

"Sure did," Collins played along.

"Hopefully, you have not grown too attached to it, though, because you will soon be relieved of your babysitting duties."

"Is that right?"

"Yes. She will finally come home to Mexico after all these years, where she belongs."

"That's great."

"I'm told the authenticator on your side will need to visit you once more before the international shipment, as I mentioned before. It may not be for a week or two, but I just thought I'd give you a heads up."

"Sounds good," Collins said, stepping away from the painting and heading toward the kitchen.

"Well, I won't take up any more of your time," said the kingpin. "And once again, thank you for helping me with this matter. You know just how much this means to me."

CHAPTER thirty-six

Frank approached the front of Mike's house and rang the doorbell. Nearly a week had passed since he had successfully escaped from Mexico. Since then, he had continued to stay at the cabin, rather than return to his house in the city and had yet to return to work. After recovering from his injuries and monitoring the international news feed for any reports of the carnage he had left in Mexico, it was time to see Mike.

Frank cycled through the conversation he wanted to have with his partner, with whom he hadn't spoken since before he had left for Mexico. There was bound to be tension; in fact, Frank hadn't even told him that he had been over the border again.

The sound of approaching footsteps arrived from inside the house, and a moment later, Janice pulled open the door. Her eyes widened at the sight of Frank, and the look on her face was a mixture of surprise and relief.

"Frank..." escaped her lips in a whisper.

Before Frank had the chance to speak, Janice stepped forward and wrapped her arms around him in a loving hug. "I'm so glad to see you're okay," she said, then stepped back inside.

"Thanks, yeah, I just came by to—"

"Who is it, babe?" Mike's voice suddenly came from somewhere behind her. "Is it Publishers' Clearing House coming to give us our millions?!" he joked.

"Actually, it's—"

Mike appeared behind Janice and saw it was Frank. "Oh...it's you."

Janice looked between the two men. "I'll give you two a minute."

Frank nodded appreciatively and then focused his attention back on his partner after Janice had disappeared inside the house.

An awkward silence hung in the air as Mike studied Frank, who, admittedly, looked much less disheveled than the last time they had seen each other.

"I heard you're coming back to work on Monday?" Mike finally broke the ice. "Does that mean you're done with all the Mexico stuff?"

Frank turned his head and looked off into the distance.

"Maybe it's for the best, Frankie..."

"I need you to know something, Mike," Frank faced his partner again. "The reason I was so distant after we got the girls back from Mexico is because I realized just how unfair it was for me to ask you to come down there," he shook his head. "I could have really fucked up your life. All for a fight that wasn't yours."

"We're family, Frank," Mike stated emphatically. "And that includes Sara and Donna. Janice and I would do anything for you guys. I'm just sorry you weren't able to get the closure you were looking for."

"Yeah..." Frank said quietly before changing subjects. "So, anything happening around work lately?"

"Not really," Mike shrugged. "Just the usual bullshit."

"Did I hear that they're looking to put a team together for a warehouse bust over on Hamilton soon?"

"Yeah, I think so."

Frank thought for a moment. "I'm going to have a ton of paperwork to do when I get back on Monday. Maybe you could try to convince Jack that we take the lead on that? At least it will get me off the desk for a bit."

"Sure. That sounds good. I'll run it by him," Mike nodded. "Hey, you want to come in for a beer or something?"

"Wish I could, but I have to be somewhere."

"Fair enough. Alright, well, we'll talk more about Hamilton on Monday, then." Mike gave Frank a clap on his shoulder. "I'm glad to have you back, buddy."

CHAPTER thirty-seven

The intercom next to the elevator inside Ken Collins' Manhattan penthouse buzzed. He was already waiting in front of it and tapped an impatient finger on the screen, connecting with the female concierge in the lobby.

"Good morning, Mr. Collins," she greeted him cheerily. "Your visitor has ar—"

"Send him up," Collins cut her off, immediately disconnecting the call.

The image on the screen transitioned to a view inside the elevator. In walked the briefcase-wielding appraiser, wearing a gray trilby and a similar suit from his last visit. Collins leaned in towards the camera and spied on the man as the lift crept up from the lobby. Once the authenticator had arrived on the other side of the doors, Collins held off entering the access-granting code, just as he had before, and waited for the nervousness to take over. Only this time, the man in the elevator remained steadfast, staring directly ahead of himself unflinching. Collins squinted at the tiny figure on the screen, silently demanding that he move, look up, or call out. Pressed for time, Collins finally gave up on his asinine game and entered the code.

The doors slid open, and the CEO discovered an unfamiliar face beneath the brim of the hat.

"Good morning, Mr. Collins," greeted the elderly, clean-shaven authenticator.

"Hey, you're not the same guy as last time," Collins pointed out the obvious. "Where's, uh, Arthur?" he questioned, never forgetting a name, no matter how little the human being attached to it mattered to him.

"Arthur is currently on vacation," the man explained. "May I come in?"

Collins took a step back and allowed the man to get off the elevator. "Is this going to take long?" he questioned, crossing his arms.

"If all goes according to plan, I imagine I can be in and out of here in less than an hour."

"An hour!" Collins balked. "It only took that Arthur guy like twenty-five minutes last time!"

The white-haired visitor removed his hat respectfully and flattened his hair with one hand. "Mr. Hoffman certainly is impressive, isn't he?" he sang his co-worker's praises. "Quite skilled indeed. I'll be the first to tell you that," he chuckled. "Of course, my employer would have sent him back again for this authentication, as he's viewed the artwork before, but whoever set the appointment was quite adamant that an authentication occur quickly, as I was told it is being shipped rather soon?"

Collins' thoughts drifted to Ernesto's dogged desire to get his painting down to Mexico and into his hands. "Yeah, fine, whatever," he finally relented.

"Is there perhaps a room with closable blinds or curtains that I may use?" the visitor wondered. "I need to conduct a black light screening and magnify the surface, each of which requires a different level of ambient lighting."

The CEO thought for a moment. "Use that room in the corner, over there," he said, pointing to the den near the end of the hall. "There's a desk in there and controls to tint the windows as dark as you want."

"Excellent."

"I'll be in my office making some calls in the meantime," Collins informed him. "The painting is hanging in the hallway. Come get me when you're done."

"Will do, Mr. Collins."

*****

Forty minutes had passed when the CEO finished the last of his phone calls. Glancing at the fifty-thousand-dollar Rolex on his wrist, he realized it was nearly ten o'clock. Abandoning the office, he strode over to the closed den, where he discovered flashes of white light coming from beneath the door. He leaned in and listened. It was eerily quiet inside.

Collins slowly pushed the door inward and found the room's windows were fully tinted. The authenticator was hunched over the desk with his back to the door, while a contraption emitting a bluish-green light operated above the painting. The CEO crossed the room quietly, stopping himself five or six feet behind the other man.

"Are you interested in observing the process, Mr. Collins?" The authenticator seemed to sense his presence without ever taking his eyes off the artwork.

"No, I just came in to see how much longer you're going to be. I need to be somewhere, and I had no idea you would take so long," he whined.

"Nearly finished," the authenticator assured him. "Everything looks great. No surprises here."

"No shit," Collins said obnoxiously, as he removed his phone from his pocket. On the screen was a text message from a vapid twenty-one-year-old bleach blonde named Monica, indicating that she would soon be arriving at the restaurant where they were meeting for brunch. Collins had recently met the aspiring actress at an upscale event, where she had been serving drinks, and he suggested that he could somehow *help* her career. For once, Collins didn't want to be late.

The light being cast from the machine suddenly stopped.

"Perfect timing," the authenticator announced. He began to disassemble his tools and return the components to his briefcase. "If you'd like, I can hang the painting back in the hallway for you."

"Don't bother. It's getting shipped out early Thursday morning, anyway. It can stay on the desk until they come to get it."

"As you wish, Mr. Collins. I'll just pack up and be on my way then."

CHAPTER thirty-eight

Mike closed the door of his SUV after backing it into an empty parking stall in a McDonald's parking lot. Frank was already waiting for him, dressed in plain clothing and leaning against the grill of his truck.

"Looks like we have about," Mike glanced at his phone as he approached, "twenty-five minutes to kill before the backup team arrives. They're going to set up two blocks east of the warehouse. You want to grab a coffee in the meantime?"

Frank looked past Mike in the direction of the warehouse. "I was just thinking, maybe we head down and have a quick look before everyone else arrives?"

"Yeah, alright," Mike agreed, trying to be supportive of Frank's first bust since returning to work.

They retrieved their unmarked tactical packs from their vehicles and headed down the street.

*****

"Looks pretty quiet over there," Mike commented after he and Frank had walked the five minutes and laid eyes on the three-story building two hundred yards further down the road on the other side of the mostly desolate street. "Backup is going to be stationed on Washington over *there,"* he pointed.

"Yeah, maybe a little *too* quiet," replied Frank. "Hopefully, we didn't miss it."

"You think the intel might have been shit?"

"I dunno, these guys are known to change their plans last minute," Frank continued in the direction of the warehouse.

"Maybe this is close enough for now, Frankie? We don't want to get made before everybody is in position."

Frank's eyes remained fixated on the warehouse. "I'd hate for everyone to show up and we find the place empty."

"Whatever," Mike shrugged. "If it turns out to be a scrub, we'll get these donkey fuckers some other day."

"Let's just do a quick flyby."

Mike set his eyes on the structure again. It did seem oddly quiet. "Alright, but let's just make sure we're back on point before backup arrives."

"Definitely." Frank nodded.

The two agents crossed the street and approached the warehouse. A heavy-duty chain-link fence with an automated gate jutted out from the front corner of the building, connecting with the adjacent business next door. Beyond the gate was a paved asphalt yard that appeared to wrap around the back. Frank and Mike casually approached the windowless front doors, where Frank tested each of them with a tug, finding both locked.

"Let's head down the left side," Frank suggested. "It's got a bit of cover from the street, and maybe we can see into the back lot."

Mike nodded.

They had barely rounded the corner when suddenly, they heard the mechanical gate on the other side of the building begin to rumble open. Returning to the corner, they looked across the face of the building and saw a white panel van leaving the yard. It drove across the parking lot and quickly disappeared down the street in the opposite direction.

"Shit," Frank muttered under his breath.

"Did you catch the plate?" Mike wondered. "We can call it in."

"Negative. You?"

Mike shook his head.

Frank thought for a moment, then took off his pack and dropped it to the pavement. He quickly removed his gun and radio.

"What are you doing?" Mike looked puzzled.

"Head to that door," Frank pointed down the side of the building where they had been heading. "I'm going to try to get inside the yard to disable that gate. If it's the only exit, maybe I can prevent any more vehicles from escaping."

"Whoa, hold on now, Frankie," Mike sounded concerned. "This was just supposed to be a flyby. Our backup isn't going to arrive for at least another ten or fifteen minutes. We can't make entry yet."

"Just get yourself to that door and make sure nobody comes out," Frank disregarded the warning. "You and I can communicate on Channel 8 until the others arrive. At that time, we'll switch over to the designated tac channel. They're probably already rolling by now." Frank heard the gate begin to close. Without another word, he took off in a sprint across the front of the building.

"Shit." Mike dropped his pack onto the ground and quickly donned his navy-blue FBI windbreaker, bulletproof vest, gun, and radio. He inserted his earpiece, set the base unit to the correct channel, and brought the radio up to his mouth.

"Tango Backup, this is Agent Torres, at 487 Hamilton Ave., requesting your status?" Mike broadcast over the encrypted radio waves. Four or five seconds went by before a response arrived.

"Agent Torres, this is Tango Backup," replied Catherine Heslop, the lead agent on today's backup team. She was a highly decorated field agent who had jumped ship from the CIA six years earlier and was now sitting in the back of a heavily armored FBI vehicle with seven tactically dressed agents surrounding her. *"We are inbound,"* she explained, surprised to hear from Mike already. *"Light traffic. Approximately 12 minutes out. What is your status?"*

"Cath, I just wanted to give you a heads up, Frank and I were conducting preliminary surveillance of the building and

witnessed a vehicle fleeing the premises. We were forced to converge on the structure earlier than anticipated."

"Do you have a direction of travel and a plate number for the van?"

"Negative on the plate," Mike told her. *"But it was heading east. Basic white panel van."*

"Copy. Tango Backup will now be responding Code 3 directly to your location. Sit tight."

"Copy—lights and sirens," Mike parroted back. *"And just so you know, Frank and I are currently separated on opposite sides of the building. He may or may not have his ears on yet."*

"Roger."

Mike flipped his radio over to Channel 8. *"Hey Frank, did you catch any of those transmissions on the designated tac-channel?*

No response.

Mike took both backpacks and stashed them behind a rusty green dumpster on the side of the neighboring building, then began jogging toward the door. He switched channels on his radio again.

"Tango is approximately ten minutes out," Agent Heslop announced.

*****

Frank had narrowly beaten the rumbling silver gate in a footrace and managed to get inside the yard. Instead of attempting to disable the gate, as he had told Mike, he went down the right side of the building and turned on his radio, slipping in his earpiece. The two channels were already preset in his unit. He began to monitor them simultaneously.

"Copy—lights and sirens," he heard Mike say. *"And just so you know, Frank and I are currently separated on opposite sides of the building. He may or may not have his ears on yet."* A couple of seconds passed. *"Hey Frank, did you catch any of those transmissions on the designated tac channel?"*

Frank didn't respond; instead, he made his way to the back corner of the building. After taking one last look around the yard, he pulled open the unlocked door and stepped inside.

Making his way past a staircase, Frank entered a brightly lit hallway that ran the entire length of the building. He had only taken about five or six steps when suddenly an obese Mexican with a bushy goatee, flat-brimmed purple baseball hat, and baggy gray sweatpants appeared through a door at the far end of the hall. Fortunately for Frank, the corpulent gangster was fully engrossed with his phone and failed to detect his presence at the other end of the building. A few seconds later, the man disappeared through a door to his right.

Frank quickened his pace and headed to where the gangster had vanished, discovering two bathrooms on the left side of the hall. He had just crept past the women's room when a forearm suddenly wrapped around his neck, dragging him backward into the lavatory.

*****

Mike had been stationed at the door on the other side of the building for a couple of minutes when he left his post to walk over to the barbed-wire-topped fence to gain a better view into the back lot, but found the vantage point proved useless.

"*Come on, Frank,*" he said to himself, beginning to grow frustrated by the lack of radio communication. Just then, he heard the muffled voices of at least three men coming from the back of the building, causing him to get on his radio.

"Frank, I've got chatter coming from the rear of the building. Do you copy?"

Receiving no response, he changed channels.

"Tango Backup, be advised, I will be relocating myself to the mechanized gate at the southwest corner of the building, as it was Agent Adler's last known location. I have still not been able to contact him via radio, and I have now heard multiple voices coming from the rear of the warehouse—break—Frank, let me know if you are copying these transmissions on Channel 14?"

"Agent Torres, this is Tango Backup," Heslop responded immediately. *"We are less than four minutes out. That's a negative on repositioning. Hold at your current location. We will assist upon arrival."*

Fuck that, Mike thought to himself, already on the move toward the front of the building. He heard sirens wail to life in the distance as he removed his gun from its holster.

*****

The well-worn brown carpet of the hallway transitioned into frictionless white tile beneath Frank's boots as he was dragged backward into the women's bathroom. Frank took hold of his attacker's right wrist and spun himself out of the poorly executed chokehold. He removed his gun from behind his back and forced his assailant against a vertical post separating two of the toilet stalls.

"Easy, Adler!" said a wide-eyed Adrian Jackson, now pinned up against the post.

"Adrian. What the fuck!" Frank lowered his weapon and released him from his grip.

"Yo, you gotta be quiet, man!" Adrian warned in a whisper. "We still got a crew up in here."

"This was supposed to look like a botched raid," Frank reminded him. "A stash and bail, *before* I arrived."

"Bro, I know! But the last van just left like five minutes ago. Your people didn't get eyes on it, did they?" He looked worried.

"Only my partner and I."

"Is your partner in on this shit wit you?"

"No," Frank shook his head, then quickly changed the subject. "What the fuck happened?"

"Word came down this mornin' that we needed to wait for a second drop from the stash house before that last van could leave."

"And you couldn't convince them otherwise?" Frank shook his head, annoyed.

"Yo, I was tryin' to tell them that hangin' round was a bad idea, but I knew if I pushed too hard, actin' all nervous and shit, they'd start watchin' me like a hawk," he explained. "And I needed to get away from them to stash your shit in here."

The sirens outside were growing louder.

"And I woulda given you the heads up on that phone you gave me," Adrian continued, "but you said to destroy that motherfucker if things was on track this mornin'. And they were, bro—until those last-minute orders came down!"

"Alright, I get it," Frank relented.

"Yo, you need to take your shit," Adrian told him, making his way over to the sinks. He reached his hands under the countertop, where he had hidden Frank's stash, and pulled it out. He walked back over and shoved a brick wrapped in brown paper and cellophane into Frank's chest.

Suddenly, Mike's voice came through Frank's earpiece. "*Frank, if you can hear me, I'm going to attempt to scale the gate. I can see a door down at the far corner of the building,*" he said, referring to the entrance that Adrian had left unlocked for Frank to enter through.

"Fuck," Frank muttered aloud.

"What?"

The sirens were only a couple of blocks away now.

"My partner is going to try to hop that gate and enter the building where I came in," Frank explained.

"ADRIAN! THE PIGS ARE ROLLING IN! WE GOTTA GET THE FUCK OUTTA HERE!" an unidentified gangster suddenly hollered into the empty hallway from the bay.

"Goddamnit, Adler," Adrian looked fully panicked. "There ain't no way I'm gettin' out of here in time now. If they arrest me, you better come get me out. Don't make me sit in the can for more than a couple weeks!"

The sounds of screeching tires hitting the parking lot flooded in from outside.

"Tango Backup has arrived. What is your location, Agent Torres? Have you located your partner?" Frank heard through his earpiece.

"Adler!" Adrian hollered at Frank, breaking his trance.

"Yeah, I'll take care of it," Frank told him. "But there's no way I can carry this out of here with me," he said of the stash.

Mike's voice came over the radio. *"I've gained access to the yard, and I'm heading to the door at the northwest corner of the building. I have not yet reached Agent Adler at this time."*

An idea suddenly formed inside Frank's head, and he quickly removed the outer packaging of the brick, attempting to flatten its inner contents as thinly as he could. He handed Adrian the cellophane and brown paper waste.

"Stuff that up under the sink where it was before," Frank instructed him. "Don't just throw it in the garbage. They might search in here."

Adrian turned around and complied with the orders, jamming the trash between a couple of pipes underneath the counter. Once he was certain it would remain in place, he turned back. Frank stepped forward and stuffed the flattened stash into the inside pocket of his denim jacket.

"Yo, what the fuck?" said Adrian.

"I've got nowhere to hide this on me. I left my bag on the other side of the building."

Adrian stepped back from Frank, and his hand moved toward where Frank had stuffed the stash.

"Don't touch it!" Frank shouted at him with a deadly seriousness in his voice.

Adrian's eyes widened, and his hand slowly dropped back down to his side. A look of desperation came across his face. "Yo, you know what happens to me if I get caught with this shit, right?" He stared at Frank.

"Just leave it *exactly* where it is," Frank replied. "It's flat and soft. When they arrest you, they'll only pat you down for weapons at first and then throw you in the back of a cruiser so they can secure the scene. A more thorough search won't be conducted until later."

"Fuck. Alright, fine," Jackson gave in.

"Agent Torres, what is your location?" Heslop sounded through Frank's earpiece.

"How am I going to get it back from you, though?" Frank asked himself aloud. "I'm going to get tied to this scene for hours." After a moment of contemplation, an idea suddenly struck Frank. "You need to do one more thing, Adrian."

"I ain't doing *enough* for yo ass as it is already?"

Frank pulled his gun, causing Adrian's eyebrows to rise. "Yo, what the fuck?"

"I'm in position at the rear corner of the building," Mike reported to the backup team. *"I'm ready to make a coordinated entry with your members at the front whenever they're ready."*

"It's not meant for you," Frank explained of the gun. "It's for me..."

The look on Adrian's face suggested that he still didn't understand.

"I need you to shoot me," Frank instructed the gangster, flipping the gun around and offering him the grip.

"Are you outta your motherfuckin' mind?" Jackson shook his head. "No fuckin' way!"

"We don't have time to argue!" Frank barked. "Just clip my shoulder with a round and get your ass back inside the bay with your crew. Agents are about to make entry any second now, and if we get caught together, we're both fucked! This way, I'll receive medical attention and won't be tied to the scene," Frank reasoned. "It's the only way."

"Entry Team is in position. Ready to breach."

"You better not fuckin' punk out on me, Adler," Adrian warned. "Shootin' a cop is some serious time." He reluctantly took the weapon from Frank's hand.

"Just do exactly as I said, and I'll take care of the rest. And listen, when I see you out in the parking lot after—just play along." Frank said, readying himself for impact. "Now pull the trigger!"

The bullet pierced Frank's left shoulder, traveling through a faded tattoo that some forgotten artist had inked twenty-three years ago. He hadn't felt the searing heat of a foreign projectile since his days in the Marines as a much younger man. A cascade of syrupy blood coated his muscular arm, penetrated the fabric of his sleeve, and began to drip miniature Rorschachs onto the ivory-colored tiles next to his tactical boots. By the time Frank collapsed to the floor, the shooter had already disappeared out the door of the warehouse bathroom.

"Shots fired! Shots fired!" Mike's voice suddenly reverberated inside Frank's earpiece, which had dislodged itself and come to rest in the pool of slowly expanding blood. Frank felt his vision begin to tunnel, and darkness crept inside his headspace as he heard Mike's footsteps pounding heavily on the carpeted hallway, closing in on his location.

Upon arrival, Mike kicked open the door and found his partner splayed out on the floor. He maneuvered himself inside the ferrous-scented room, confirmed the space was free from additional threats, then knelt next to him.

"I'm here, Frankie," he said, attempting to assess the seriousness of the wound. *"Agent down!"* Mike shouted into his radio. *"I repeat—Agent Adler has been hit!"*

* * * * *

Sara shifted slightly under her father's arm on the couch in the cabin, causing the memories inside Frank's head to fade away.

"Hey, sweetie," Frank whispered, placing the tip of his chin on the top of her head.

Her eyes slowly opened following her post-breakfast nap. She looked up at him. "Yes, Daddy?"

"Feel free to stick around here as long as you like," Frank offered. "But I promised Mike I'd help him set up a few things at Janice's new restaurant today. The grand opening is next week."

Sara smiled and sat up on the old, faded couch. "That's okay, I have a bunch of schoolwork I need to get started on anyway."

"That's my girl," Frank winked at her.

CHAPTER thirty-nine

"So, what do you think?" Mike asked Frank from his position behind the molasses-colored bar near the back of the new restaurant. "I figured I could put the kegs under *here*, out of the way, but close enough to be accessible for changing."

"Makes sense to me," Frank nodded, balancing on a five-rung step ladder, changing the last of the old incandescent lightbulbs to energy-efficient LEDs. "So, where's the boss lady today anyway?"

"I think she had a meeting with her seafood supplier," Mike replied uncertainly. "Honestly, it's all been such a blur. I've just been trying to keep my head down and do what I'm told," he smiled.

Frank descended the ladder. "You guys should be really proud of what you're doing here, Mike."

"Thanks. I'm just happy that all her years of hard work in the industry have finally paid off," Mike said, lifting a cardboard box full of colorful booze bottles off the floor and making his way over to the mirrored display case at the back of the bar.

Frank folded up the step ladder and set it against the wall.

"Mike, there's something I've been meaning to tell you." He looked at his partner in the mirror's reflection.

"I'm listening..." Mike assured Frank as he began to remove bottles and set them in a neat line across the back wall.

"The day of the bust, when I got shot. It wasn't supposed to happen like that."

"No shit." Mike grinned, placing a bottle of Bombay Sapphire onto the mantle.

"No, what I'm trying to say is..." Frank closed his eyes and pinched the bridge of his nose. "I had another purpose for going to that warehouse that day. Something that I was forced to keep from you, just in case things went wrong."

Mike's eyes lifted from the liquor. His face grew serious.

"The truth is, Mike, I went into the building to collect something that was supposed to be stashed inside for me. There wasn't supposed to be anybody else there when we arrived."

Confusion, anger, and contempt spread across Mike's face in the reflection. He turned around. "You son of a bitch."

"Mike, let me explain."

"You fucking snake." Mike abandoned his place behind the bar and moved quickly in Frank's direction.

"Just listen for a minute."

Suddenly, a voice arrived from behind Frank. "Yo, you better slow your boy down, Adler. He's lookin' crazy."

Frank turned around and saw Adrian Jackson leaning up against a wall behind him.

"Shit," Frank said, realizing that it was Adrian that Mike had spotted in the reflection, and he was now making a beeline for him.

Frank intercepted his partner just before he got to Jackson. "Whoa, Mike, whoa!" Frank tried to calm him. "He's with me."

Mike fought against Frank's grip, deaf to his words. "What the fuck are you doing here, you piece of shit!?" he hollered at Adrian.

"MIKE!" Frank raised his voice. "He's with me!"

Mike gave up his struggle, and he took a step back from Frank. "What did you just say? His eyebrows furrowed. "What the fuck are you talking about? This piece of shit is probably the guy that shot you."

"No," Frank shook his head. "Well, *actually,* yeah, but it's not like that."

This statement only seemed to compound Mike's confusion.

"Just let me explain," said Frank.

Mike looked at Adrian with contempt. "Yeah, you better."

Frank exhaled. "During my suspension, while I was trying to piece together the kidnapping, a source provided me with the information I needed to crack this whole thing wide open," Frank explained, referring to Winston's late-night visit to his cabin. "And it led me to Adrian's apartment late one night."

Frank's mind drifted back to the aftermath of the fight inside the bathroom of Jackson's apartment when he had learned of his sister's death inside the shipping container.

* * * * *

Suddenly, the squawk of a police radio came from the hallway outside the apartment. *"Car 29, do you need another unit assigned to your location?"* asked a police dispatcher.

Frank's head snapped to attention, and he stared down the hallway.

Adrian studied his face. "Yo, wait a minute. They ain't wit you, are they, Adler?"

"Quiet," Frank ordered.

Adrian pulled himself up onto the edge of the tub. "What kinda trouble you got yourself in?"

"Enough!" Frank pointed the gun at his head.

"Oh, you gunna shoot my ass?" He challenged Frank. "With the police outside? Nah, I don't think so," he called his bluff.

"Looks like there's some blood on this door over here, Rick," the cop in the hall said to his partner.

"I don't know what the fuck is going on here, Adler." Adrian stood fully now. "But I'm startin' to think you didn't come here tonight as no Fed, stinkin' like some drunken sailor."

BANG! BANG! BANG! BANG! A fist suddenly pounded on Adrian's door.

Frank's thoughts drifted back to the fire escape. *Would I be able to make it down twelve stories before backup arrives, after Adrian opens the door and rats me out?* One thing Frank knew for sure was that he couldn't easily explain the break-in or the assault on Jackson, even if it was in self-defense. The gangster had him dead to rights.

"How bout we go see exactly who these boys are lookin' for?" Adrian suggested, making his way out of the bathroom and down the hallway.

"They're doing it again," Frank called out to him, stopping him in his tracks. Adrian turned around slowly.

"Doin' *what*?"

"They're abducting girls."

Adrian looked down the adjacent hallway at the front door of the apartment, then back at Frank in the bathroom. "Bullshit." He shook his head, figuring Frank was just trying to buy himself time until the cops left. He disappeared around the corner.

"They took my daughter..."

After a few long seconds, Adrian reappeared. "You serious, Adler?"

Frank nodded. "And they killed her friend."

Adrian's face tightened. "They still got your kid?"

"No," Frank shook his head. "I got her back."

BANG! BANG! BANG! BANG! "This is the police! Open the door!"

Adrian ignored the commotion, continuing to observe the big man in his bathroom.

"It's only going to get worse," Frank said with certainty.

BANG! BANG! BANG! BANG! "Police! Open up!"

Adrian disappeared around the corner again. A moment later, Frank heard him open the door.

"Sorry to disturb you," said one of the uniformed NYPD officers outside the door, whose eyes widened at the sight of the goose egg on Adrian's forehead and the cut on his cheek from the lamp. "We received a call to this building regarding two men fleeing the premises with blood-soaked clothes. My partner and I were completing a sweep of the hallways, and we noticed some fresh blood on your door here," he pointed to the stain where Frank had placed his cheek before he broke in. "Are you alright, sir?"

Frank stood in silence inside the bathroom, waiting.

"Is there someone else inside the apartment with you?" the other police officer asked Adrian, trying to get a look over his shoulder into the apartment behind him. "I thought I heard another voice."

After a long pause, Adrian finally replied, "Nah, man. Ain't nobody here but me. I was just listening to some music. Maybe that's what you heard."

"How'd you get those injuries?" the cop closest to the door inquired.

"Oh, *these?* Yeah, I'm a boxer..." Adrian lied. "I had a rough sparrin' session at the gym today. I'm gettin' ready for a match next week."

"I see..." The officer didn't sound fully convinced. "You wouldn't mind if we came inside and took a quick look around, would you?"

Frank tensed.

"Yeah, actually, I do mind," Adrian denied the request outright. "You know what damn time it is?" he turned the tables. "It seems like every couple days, one of you guys comes poundin' on my door, asking me questions 'bout crackheads overdosin' and stabbin' each other up! It's just too damn much, man!"

"But there's blood on *your* door, sir," the cop in the back pointed out again.

"I'm surprised there ain't shit and piss on it, too!" Adrian replied candidly. "Look around this motherfuckin' place! This buildin' is stank as fuck. Some junkie was probably just out here shootin' up, nicked a vein, and leaned up against my door two minutes before you arrived. Stuff like that happens around here all the damn time."

Frank heard a short pause in the conversation.

"I don't have time for this shit, Rick..." one cop finally said to the other. "It's almost shift change."

The officer closest to Adrian took hold of his radio while continuing to study the man inside the apartment. He slowly tilted his chin toward the unit.

"Dispatch, this is Car 29. We've completed a search of the interior of this building and found nothing suspicious. You can release us from this call." He removed his thumb from the microphone. "Alright, sir, if you wake up in the morning and remember anything out of the ordinary, call 9-1-1, and we'll send someone over, alright?"

"Will do, officer," Adrian responded more congenially now. "You two have yourselves a good night."

After the cops had abandoned the door, Adrian appeared from around the corner again.

"Alright, Adler, it's time I do right by Tish," he said, looking Frank in the eyes. "You got a plan?"

*****

Back inside the restaurant, Frank explained to Mike how some of Adrian's information had led to the discovery of Bennett's involvement, which, in turn, led him to Ken Collins' connections with the Diaz brothers and their new human trafficking system.

"What are you getting out of all this?" Mike questioned Adrian directly.

"I just want out of the game, man." Adrian shook his head. "I shoulda stopped all this gangster shit when they murdered my sister. At least this way, if Tish and my parents are up in heaven or whatever, maybe they're lookin' down and thinkin' I finally did right by them."

Frank saw Mike's expression soften slightly. "So, you're going on the run now? I have to imagine the cartel will put a hit out on you the minute they discover you've been released from jail with no reasonable excuse."

"I took care of that..." Frank said, having accessed someone who could assist with such disappearances.

"Yeah," Adrian nodded, looking at his phone. "I'm actually on my way outta town now. I just wanted to drop by and say good luck with everythin' movin' forward, Frank."

"Keep your nose clean out there, Adrian." Frank offered him his hand. "Wherever you end up."

"I will," Adrian gripped it tightly and gave him a nod. "I'm even going to get my GED—just like Tish always wanted."

"Make her proud."

*****

Frank and Mike had slipped inside a booth and were going over further details.

"Were you able to make copies of those audio recordings between Collins and Diaz from Bennett's computer before you left Mexico?" Mike wondered.

"No, his servers would have been a fortress," Frank shook his head. "And by the time I got back home, the Mexican news outlets had already reported that there was a natural gas explosion at his house," he revealed. "They said he was sleeping inside when it happened, and the entire place was burned down to the foundation."

"Another cartel cover-up." Mike shook his head, then appeared to be contemplating something else. "There's still one thing I don't quite understand, though."

"What's that?"

"After you got shot, you still attacked Adrian in the back of the police cruiser that day," Mike remembered. "I had to pull you off him."

"Yeah, about that..."

*****

"Well, look who it is!" Frank hollered at him across the back of the cruiser. The nearer detainee's eyes grew large when he caught sight of the six-foot-two, two-hundred-and-fifty-pound federal agent now leaning inside the back of the vehicle. The shouting caught the attention of the police officer leaning against the hood of his cruiser, chatting idly with a heavyset colleague.

"Easy, Frankie!" Mike called out, closing the gap. Once he arrived, he placed a hand on Frank's uninjured shoulder and attempted to coax him back out of the vehicle. Frank shook off his grip with ease and climbed further inside.

"Which one of you pricks shot me?!" Frank demanded, driving his elbow into the nearer gangster's face, nearly knocking him unconscious. Frank continued across the backseat and grabbed a fistful of Jackson's shirt in a violent rage. As they jostled with each other, Frank slipped a hand inside Adrian's coat pocket, where he had hidden the stash, and transferred it into his sling.

"Fuck you, Adler!" Adrian shouted, struggling fervently against the tight metal cuffs restraining his wrists behind his back.

"Enjoy another stretch in prison, you piece of shit!" Frank taunted the hoodlum, finally releasing his grip and allowing himself to be removed from the back of the vehicle. Mike turned Frank away quickly and offered the NYPD officer an apologetic shrug for the sudden outburst.

"You still doing alright, Frankie?" Mike inquired with a hint of concern in his voice. "Still back on track?"

"What, *that?*" he downplayed the outburst. "Sometimes you just gotta put on a bit of a show..."

*****

A look of curiosity spread across Mike's face in the booth at the back of the restaurant. "What did you take from his coat?"

Frank reached inside his pocket, removed the item in question, and placed it on the table between them.

Mike glanced down at the object, then back up at Frank. "What is it?"

"Open it up," Frank instructed.

CHAPTER forty

Ken Collins yawned in the backseat of the town car as it drove through the fortified front gates of Ernesto Diaz's compound in Mexico. The CEO had been here so many times that the drive from the private airfield had almost become routine.

He stepped out of the air-conditioned vehicle into the sweltering Mexican sun and nodded at the same two guards who always seemed to be stationed near the front of the house. The pair remained stone-faced, staring straight ahead. Collins' usual bald-headed escort led him inside.

"Which room are we meeting in today?" The American questioned his armed escort. "The pool house? The library? The study? It's like playing a game of Clue every time I arrive," he chuckled at his own joke.

"Basement," the gangster responded morosely.

"Never been down there," the CEO remarked as the pair made their way through an arched-topped door and began descending a set of narrow stone steps.

When they arrived at the landing, the serious-looking cartel man pointed a finger down a long, curving hallway, instructing Collins to continue ahead. The basement smelled musty and dank, looking like a cross between a medieval dungeon and a survivalist's root cellar.

"That way," grunted the guard.

"You're not coming?"

The Mexican shook his head, then quickly turned around and disappeared up the steps.

Collins shrugged and began to walk down the narrow corridor. His eyes searched the empty stone walls as his leather-soled shoes echoed around him. Eventually, he spotted an open door at the very end of the hall. "Ernesto? You down here?"

"In here," the kingpin's gravelly voice sounded inside.

Collins entered the room and discovered a stern-looking, heavy-set henchman dressed in black next to the entrance. He had a tribal tattoo inked on the right side of his face and gold earrings in each of his lobes. The CEO poked his head around the man's girth and discovered Ernesto sitting at a large rectangular wooden table in the middle of the room with his back turned. Dennis was seated opposite, facing him.

"You guys rent out all the nice rooms for a conference or something?" Collins joked, making his way over to the table. Upon arrival, he discovered the Kahlo painting laid out on the table between the brothers. "Hey, look at that! It made it!" he said with a bit of excitement.

Dennis stood up from his chair and signaled for the American to take his place.

"How's everything going?" Collins asked Ernesto as he made his way around the table.

"Have a seat," the old man replied coldly.

"Sure," Collins said slowly now, taking his place on the chair that faced the kingpin. "What's up?"

"We have a problem, Mr. Collins," Ernesto said, his eyes looking distant and devoid of some essential humanistic element.

"Problem?" The CEO looked at Dennis, now standing behind him, and then over to the guard at the entrance. "What kind of problem?"

"Do you take me for a fool?" the cartel boss asked.

"*Pardon?* Of course not." Collins turned his attention back to the man across the table. "I don't understand."

"THIS!" Ernesto suddenly slammed his fist down next to the artwork. It was the first time Collins had ever heard him raise his voice. "This is *not* my painting!"

With eyes as large as dinner plates, Collins looked down at the Kahlo, even going so far as to turn it toward himself to get a better look. "What do you mean?"

Ernesto stared at the American with venom in his eyes. Time seemed to stand still.

"Wait a minute..." A little grin suddenly formed on Collins' face. "You guys are fucking with me!" he laughed nervously, determining it to be the only plausible explanation. "Was this your idea, Dennis?" he looked back. "That's a good one! I'll admit it! You got me!"

"SILENCE!" Ernesto shouted from across the table, causing Collins' head to spin back around. All signs of amusement abandoned the CEO's face.

"Mr. Diaz, I honestly have no idea what you're talk—"

"Did you think I would not notice?!" Ernesto cut him off, still shouting. "I have been waiting for *decades* to get my hands on this painting, and you thought *I WOULDN'T NOTICE*?!"

"Listen," Collins tried to get hold of the spiraling situation. "*This* is the painting that showed up at my penthouse, and it's the same one that left."

"THIS PAINTING," Ernesto rose from his seat, *"IS A FORGERY!"*

"What?" Collins looked down at the young girl seated on the bed next to the boy, his eyes darting around the canvas with incomprehension. "What do you mean?"

"My authenticator down here informed me that the paint on this canvas is no more than a month old! It is a damn forgery!"

"That's impossible!" Collins denied the claim. "He's wrong!"

"Did you think that I would not find out that you canceled the meeting with the American authenticator before the painting left your possession?"

"Canceled?" Collins looked baffled. "What are you talking about? I met with the authenticator both times."

Diaz removed a piece of paper from his pocket and set it next to the painting in front of Collins. It was an email that someone had printed out for him.

"It says that a man named Arthur was scheduled to meet with you for a second time, but you canceled the meeting the day before."

"Arthur?" Collins remembered the appraiser from the first meeting at his penthouse. "No, no," he shook his head. "Arthur was on vacation the second time. They sent a different guy," he explained. *"What the fuck was his name?"* Collins asked himself aloud, feeling himself beginning to sweat in the muggy basement. He searched his memory for a name but came up blank. "Fuck, I can't remember," he admitted with frustration. "But he was an old guy, with white hair."

Ernesto glared at him unbelievingly.

"Wait a second! He wrote his number on a business card before he left! I still have it in my wallet!" Collins suddenly remembered.

Still seated, Collins pulled the leather square from his back pocket and began jamming his fingers into the slots, searching furiously for where he had stashed the card. After dropping his driver's license and a few credit cards onto the table, he finally produced the ivory-white business card with only a phone number inked across the front. "A-ha! See! I told you!" Collins announced, looking back at Dennis momentarily, holding the small rectangle in the air triumphantly. "I'll call this guy right now, and we'll get to the bottom of this," he assured Ernesto. "This is all just some big misunderstanding." He dialed the number as quickly as he could.

Ernesto sat back down in his chair. "Put him on speaker," he instructed.

Collins complied. "It's all just a big misunderstanding..." he repeated quietly, his mind screaming for the authenticator to answer as the rings piled up.

Finally, the call connected.

"Mr. Collins, I've told you multiple times now," a man's voice arrived through the phone, sounding annoyed. "Only when I've found a buyer for your Kahlo painting will I be in contact with you! Selling a stolen painting takes time, after all!" He abruptly disconnected the call.

Collins' face turned as white as a ghost, and his eyes darted up from the phone to Ernesto across the table. "*What?* No! That's not—"

A transparent plastic bag suddenly descended over Collins' head, muffling his words. Dennis tightened his grip on the bottom of the sack as the powerhouse guard hurried across the room and took hold of Collins' flailing body. The CEO's eyes remained locked on Ernesto's as he bit at the thick plastic in front of his mouth.

BANG!

A bullet from Dennis' silenced gun felt like a slap to the back of Collins' head, causing his entire body to tighten and then immediately release. The plastic in front of his eyes turned bright red, and soon, he found himself hovering over his lifeless body as it dropped from the chair onto the cold stone floor. Then came the blackness.

*****

Back in New York, Winston had just disconnected the call with Collins and proceeded to remove the battery from the cheap burner phone. He broke the flimsy device in half, removed the SIM card, and continued down the city sidewalk. Just then, a garbage truck lumbered past, stopping to collect its next load. As Winston walked by, he tossed the disassembled parts into the rear compactor. The truck released its airbrakes and lurched forward, quickly disappearing around the corner.

*****

"So, I guess that takes care of Ken Collins," Mike said from the other side of the booth once Frank had finished revealing Winston's involvement.

Frank nodded. "But here's the thing, Mike. Even though we have enough evidence to expose Collins' involvement in extracting the drug-addicted women using Zinex's data, that doesn't guarantee the Diaz brothers will be brought to justice in their legal system."

"They're just going to revert to feeding girls like Sofia into the Panamanian Pipeline," Mike said with certainty.

Frank nodded. "So, before all this information gets brought to light, I need to cut the head off the snake," Frank tapped his finger on the object on the table between them. "And that's where this comes into play..."

CHAPTER forty-one

The guard in the basement dragged Ken Collins' lifeless body across the stone floor, leaving a streak of wet, coagulating blood in its wake. Dennis Diaz had removed all the items from the CEO's pockets and placed them with his wallet and cell phone on the table after ordering the guard to burn his body in one of their discreet locations—never to be found again.

Ernesto was still staring at the forgery on the table. "We need to locate the original," he told his brother.

"Forget that fucking painting!" Dennis hollered at him, enraged by all the time, money, and headache it had already caused them. "Bunch of sentimental bullshit!"

RRRRIIIIIINNNNGGG!

Collins' cell phone rang loudly next to the painting, but the kingpin's eyes never left the canvas.

"It's over, Ernie!" Dennis demanded of his brother. "You've—"

RRRRIIIIIINNNNGGG! The phone's squeal cut him off mid-sentence.

"You've been staring at that fucking thing since it arrived!" he continued, scolding his brother. "It's cost us our new trafficking sys—"

RRRRIIIIIINNNNGGG!

Dennis glared at the phone. "That's not even to speak of the investigation that will certainly take place into the whereabouts of Collins when he doesn't show up for work on Monday! And who knows what that fucking FBI agent found at Bennett's house before we burnt—"

RRRRIIIIIINNNNGGG!

The ear-piercing noise, combined with the disappointment from the painting, was too much for Ernesto to handle. He scooped the screaming phone off the table, ready to smash it against the wall, when something on the screen suddenly caught his eye. He looked at his brother across the table and then back down at the phone in his palm.

"What?" Dennis demanded gruffly.

Ernesto turned the screen to face his brother. The caller ID on the screen read *FRIDA KAHLO.*

Believing it to be the Englishman calling back with news of a sale, Ernesto realized this was his chance to apply some pressure and get his prized painting back. Before Dennis could stop him, he connected the call and lifted the phone to his ear.

"Hello?"

"I thought I might be able to reach you on this line," Frank's voice came through the device.

"Who is this?" Diaz demanded, barely able to contain his frustration.

"I think you can figure it out."

After a moment, Ernesto spoke again. "Agent Adler."

"I'm hoping you might be interested in meeting up with me."

"Why on earth would I ever want to do a thing like that?" the kingpin scoffed.

"Because I have something you might be interested in..."

"What of mine could you possibly—" Ernesto's face suddenly dropped, and he looked down at the forgery on the table. "My painting..." he whispered.

*****

Inside the restaurant, on the table between Frank and Mike, lay the unfolded Kahlo original.

Frank had been the one who had canceled Collins' meeting with the original authenticator and arranged for Winston to take his place. Once Winston had gained access to the CEO's penthouse, he used the duplication device inside the den to create a digital file of the painting and printed the forgery later. After Frank had the copy in hand, Adrian informed him of the date and time the cross-border shipment would be leaving the warehouse and got himself assigned. Frank did the same. On that day, Adrian slipped away from his crew and removed the original artwork from its frame, swapping the duplicate in its place. He then carefully folded the original and wrapped it inside drug packaging, intending to stash it away in the bathroom for Frank to recover minutes before the failed bust. However, due to Adrian's crew being made to stick around longer than anticipated, Frank had been forced to call an audible in the warehouse bathroom to get the painting out of the building undetected, resulting in him being shot and the staged scuffle in the back of the police cruiser to retrieve it.

"What do you want for it?" Diaz demanded. "I'll give you anything you want, just name your price."

"There's only one thing I want from you, Diaz," Frank replied coldly. "Your fucking head on a platter. And I'm coming to get it..."

ACKNOWLEDGEMENTS

I am incredibly grateful to everyone who provided their support, time, and encouragement throughout the journey of bringing this book to life.

First and foremost, to my wife—thank you for your generosity in allowing me the time I needed to shape this story into what it is today.

To my family, who graciously combed through the final drafts, your discerning eye and feedback were invaluable in sharpening the final product.

To Emma at Scott Editorial—thank you for your insightful early edits and thoughtful suggestions.

To Cherie Foxley, whose artistic talent and dedication brought my vision for the cover to life. Your professionalism is second to none.

And to my readers, thank you for your support.

For more information about my next project, check out my website at www.thomasmarkmckinnon.com and follow me on social media @tmmckinnonauthor

Manufactured by Amazon.ca
Bolton, ON

50627277R00219